In Green's
Jungles

In Green's Jungles

VOLUME TWO OF THE
BOOK OF THE SHORT SUN

Gene Wolfe

TOR®

A Tom Doherty Associates Book
NEW YORK

IN GREEN'S JUNGLES

Copyright © 2000 by Gene Wolfe

Edited by David G. Hartwell

A Tor Book
Published by Tom Doherty Associates, LLC
175 Fifth Avenue
New York, NY 10010

www.tor.com

Tor® is a registered trademark of Tom Doherty Associates, LLC.

Library of Congress Cataloging-in-Publication Data
Wolfe, Gene.
    In Green's jungles / Gene Wolfe.—1st ed.
        p. cm. — (The book of the short sun ; v. 2)
    "A Tom Doherty Associates book."
    ISBN 0-312-87315-8 (acid-free paper)
    I. Title.
  PS3573.O52 I5 2000
  813'.54—dc21
                                        00-023323

First Edition: August 2000

Printed in the United States of America

0 9 8 7 6 5 4 3 2 1

Respectfully dedicated to
Maddie and Becca

Proper Names in the Text

Many of the persons and places mentioned in this book first appeared in The Book of the Long Sun, to which the reader is referred. In the following list, the most significant names are given in CAPITALS, less significant names in italics.

Colonel *Abanja,* Generalissimo *Siyuf's* chief intelligence officer.

Captain *Adatta,* INCANTO'S chief female subordinate at the Battle of BLANKO.

Affito, INCLITO'S coachman.

Atteno, INCANTO'S host in BLANKO, a stationer.

Auk, the thief who led a party of colonists from VIRON to GREEN.

Babbie, a hus given to HORN by *Mucor.*

Badour, the guard who leaves his post to take INCANTO, HIDE, JAHLEE, MORA, and others to his officer.

Bala, SINEW'S wife.

Colonel *Bello,* an officer in the horde of BLANKO.

BLANKO, a town on BLUE founded by colonists from *Grandecitta.*

BLUE, the better of the two habitable planets of the SHORT SUN System.

Bricco, a small child cared for by FAVA.

Bruna, a docile mule belonging to INCLITO.

Cantoro, a merchant of BLANKO.

Casco, a jealous suitor, long ago.

Chaku, a mercenary from *Gaon.*

Chenille, the wife who accompanied *Auk* to GREEN.

Chrasmologic Writings, the sacred book revered in VIRON.

Comus, a minor god, Pas's jester.

Cugino, the woodcutter who makes a staff for INCANTO.

Cuoio, the name by which HIDE is known in BLANKO.

Decina, the cook at INCLITO'S farm.

Dentro, a young man who fell in love with a strega long ago.

Eco, one of the messengers chosen by INCLITO.

Evensong, the concubine who stowed away on INCANTO'S
   boat.

FAVA, a houseguest at INCLITO'S, MORA'S playmate.

Gagliardo, an astronomer of SOLDO.

Gaon, a large and prosperous town southeast of BLANKO.

Gioioso, one of *Salica's* unlucky husbands.

Gorak, a mercenary sergeant.

Grandecitta, a skyland city of the LONG SUN WHORL.

GREEN, the worse of the habitable planets of the SHORT SUN
   System.

Corporal *Hammerstone,* a soldier in the army of VIRON.

HIDE, one of HORN'S twin sons.

Hierax, the god of death in the LONG SUN WHORL.

Hoof, HIDE'S brother, one of HORN'S twin sons.

HORN, a paper-maker of NEW VIRON, appointed to bring
   SILK to BLUE.

Hyacinth, a beautiful woman of VIRON, SILK'S wife.

INCANTO, the name by which the former *Rajan* of *Gaon* is
   known in BLANKO. (Also the name of INCLITO'S older
   brother, who died in infancy.)

INCLITO, the leading citizen of BLANKO.

JAHLEE, the first of the inhumi rescued by INCANTO and
   Evensong.

Lieutenant *Karabin,* a mercenary officer.

Karn, a two-year-old boy, SINEW'S son.

Krait, the inhumu who rescued HORN from a pit.

Captain *Kupus,* the leader of the mercenaries.

Legaro, the ambassador sent by *Novella Citta.*

LIZARD, an island north of NEW VIRON, the site of HORN'S
   mill.

LONG SUN WHORL, the interior of the *WHORL.*

Maliki, the title of the ruler of SINEW'S village, used here as a proper name.

Mamelta, a sleeper wakened by *Mucor* and rescued by SILK.

Mano, a popular young trooper in the horde of BLANKO.

Maytera *Marble,* the former sibyl who accompanied the colonists BLUE and resumed her vocation there, a chem.

Marrow, a magnate of NEW VIRON.

Maytera *Mint,* the heroine of VIRON'S revolution, also known as General *Mint.*

MORA, a girl in her early teens, INCLITO'S daughter.

General *Morello,* the commander of the horde of SOLDO.

The *Mother,* a sea-goddess of Blue akin to *Scylla.*

Mucor, a woman possessing paranormal powers, *Marble's* grand-daughter.

Nadar, a madman in SINEW'S village.

Nadi, a river flowing past *Gaon.*

Neighbors, the name by which the sentient native race is known on BLUE'S western continent; the *Vanished People.*

Nettle, HORN'S wife, the mother of SINEW, *Hoof,* and HIDE.

NEW VIRON, the town on BLUE founded by colonists from VIRON.

Novella Citta, a smaller town near SOLDO.

Olivine, a young chem of VIRON, the handicapped daughter of *Marble* and *Hammerstone.*

Olmo, a smaller town near SOLDO.

Onorifica, the kitchen maid at INCLITO'S.

OREB, a night chough, INCANTO'S pet bird.

The OUTSIDER, the god of gods.

Pajarocu, a phantom town on BLUE'S western continent.

Pas, the father of the gods of the LONG SUN WHORL.

Perito, a hired hand on INCLITO'S farm.

Pig, a friend of INCANTO'S in the LONG SUN WHORL.

Patera *Pike,* an elderly augur of Viron, long dead.

Poliso, a foreign town near BLANKO.

Councilor *Potto,* VIRON'S spymaster.

Qarya, SINEW'S village on GREEN.

Quadrifons, an aspect of the OUTSIDER in the LONG SUN
    WHORL.

Patera *Quetzal,* the inhumu who became Prolocutor of VIRON,
    long dead.

RAJAN, the title of the ruler of *Gaon,* used here as a proper
    name.

Red Sun Whorl, the distant planet on which *Rigoglio* was born.

Patera *Remora,* the head of the Vironese Faith on BLUE.

Duko *Rigoglio,* the ruler of SOLDO.

Rimando, one of the messengers chosen by INCLITO.

Private *Rimo,* a trooper in the horde of BLANKO.

Salica, INCLITO'S elderly mother.

Sborso, a hired hand on INCLITO'S farm.

Schiamazza, an elderly servant in *Salica's* girlhood home.

Scleroderma, one of the colonists from VIRON, now dead.

Scylla, a goddess of the LONG SUN WHORL, the patroness of
    VIRON and a frequent visitor to INCANTO'S dreams (also
    a sea-monster of the *Red Sun Whorl).*

SEAWRACK, the one-armed woman HORN left behind in
    Pajarocu.

Captain *Sfido,* an officer of SOLDO.

Shauk, a three-year-old boy, SINEW'S son.

SHORT SUN, the star whose rising begins each new day on
    BLUE and GREEN; the *WHORL* is in orbit around it.

Patera SILK, the caldé of Viron at the time the colonists left for
    BLUE, also called Caldé SILK.

SINEW, the oldest of HORN'S sons, who followed him to
    Pajarocu.

Generalissimo *Siyuf,* the commander of the horde of *Trivi-
    gaunte.*

SOLDO, the largest of the towns established by colonists from
    Grandecitta.

Solenno, one of *Salica's* unlucky husbands.

Spider, a spycatcher of VIRON.

Sun Street Quarter, the district served by SILK'S manteion.

Colonel *Terzo,* an officer of SOLDO.

Thelxiepeia, a goddess of the LONG SUN WHORL.

Torda, INCLITO'S chambermaid.

Trivigaunte, the city that intervened in VIRON'S revolution.

Turco, a favored suitor, long ago.

Ugolo, a magnate of BLANKO.

Urbanita, a neighbor of *Volanta's.*

Ushujaa, a passenger on the lander that brought HORN to GREEN.

Sergeant *Valico,* a trooper in the horde of BLANKO.

Vanished People, BLUE'S sentient native race; the *Neighbors.*

VIRON, the city of the LONG SUN WHORL in which SILK, HORN, and *Nettle* were born.

Colonel *Vivo,* an officer in the horde of BLANKO.

Volanta, INCANTO'S hostess in BLANKO, *Atteno's* wife.

Volto, an unpopular trooper in the horde of BLANKO.

Lieutenant *Warren,* a mercenary officer.

Water Street, an avenue in BLANKO bordering the river.

WHORL, the generation ship from which the colonists came.

Lieutenant *Wight,* a mercenary officer.

Master *Xiphias,* an elderly fencing master of VIRON.

Lieutenant *Zepter,* a mercenary officer.

Zitta, INCLITO'S wife and MORA'S mother, long dead.

27th day of the Mobilization

To my Dear Friend and Councilor Incanto—

Olmo has fallen. There can be no doubt of it. Our
scouts have seen the Duko's pennant at the base camp. I
myself saw a dead trooper in purple and maroon not two
hours ago. Dragoons of the Bodyguard are here, and the
rest close behind. We bear ourselves like men, but you must
be braced for the blow.

I clawed you like a devil for supplies, I know. No more.
Take Rimando's mules and muledrivers. Rimando too.
They are the only help I can give you.

Advice: You know I tried to save the northern farms.
We shared meat and salt, Incanto. Listen to me. They are
finished. Take what you can and leave them to their fate.
These graybeards, these women and boys you found arms
for, they may fight or make a show of it from the walls. If
you march north with them, the Duko's cavalry will cut
them to pieces in half an hour. *Whatever happens, do not
allow them out of the gates.* Show the guns on the walls, call
a truce, and take the terms Rigoglio offers.

Write at once if you have word of Mora.

If I fall, do what you can for my mother. Also, Torda
and Onorifica. Shed no tears for your discourteous friend—

Inclito

Especially Torda and my mother. I.

1

A New Beginning

I have paper again, and there is still a lot of ink in the little bottle. Besides, the man who owns the shop would give me more ink if I asked for it, I feel certain. Strange how much a quire of writing paper can mean to a man who has made such quantities of it.

This town is walled. I have never seen a whole town with a wall before. It is not a big wall; I have seen others much higher; but it goes all the way around, except where the river comes in and goes out.

I do not think this is the same river we had in the south. This one flows fast but silently. Or perhaps it is simply that the noises of the town keep me from hearing the river. Its water is dark. It seems angry.

Our lazy southern river always smiled, and sometimes laughed aloud, showing a froth of white lace underskirt where it tumbled over rocks. There were crocodiles in it, or at least what we called crocodiles, sleek and shining emerald lizards with eight legs and jaws like traps. They seemed indolent as Nadi herself when they basked on the banks in the sunlight, but their doubly forked blue tongues flicked in and out like flames. I do not think they are really the same as the crocodiles on the *Whorl*, although it may be that every animal of the kind is entitled to the name, like "bird."

Which reminds me that I ought to write that Oreb is with me still, perching on my shoulder or the head of my staff, which he likes even better.

I washed my clothes in this river before we reached the town. I saw a few fish, but no crocodiles of either sort.

A woodcutter cut my staff for me. I still remember his name, which was Cugino. I don't believe I ever met a better-intentioned man, or found a stranger more friendly. He was the first human being I had seen in days, so I was very glad to see him. I helped him load his donkey, and asked to borrow his axe long enough to cut myself a staff. (I had already tried using the azoth, although I did not tell him so; it shattered the wood to kindling.)

He would not hear of it. He, Cugino, was the ultimate authority when it came to staffs, and to sticks of every kind. Everybody in the village came to him—and to him alone—whenever they wanted a staff. He would cut me a staff himself. He, personally, would select the wood and trim it in the right way.

"Everything for you! The wood, how high, where you hold it. Everything! You stand up straight for me."

He measured me with his eyes, with his hands, and at last with his axe, so that I know now that I am twice the height of Cugino's axe, and an axe-head over.

"Tall! Tall!" (Although I am not, or at least I am not unusually tall.) He stood with his head to the left, the tip of one big, callused forefinger at the corner of his mouth. I feel certain that my friend in the south never looked a tenth so impressive when he was planning a battle.

"I got it!" He clapped his hands, the sound of a plank slapped against another.

We tied his donkey (still loaded, poor beast) and walked some distance into the forest, to a huge tree embraced by a vine thicker than my wrist. Two mighty blows from the axe severed its stem twice, and a third a thick branch at the top of the severed portion.

"Big vine," Cugino told me with as much pride as if he had planted it. "Strong like me." He displayed the muscle in his arm, which was indeed impressive. "Not stiff."

He tore the section that he had cut off the tree (which must have been thanking him with all its heartwood) and tried to snap it over his knee, muscles bulging. "He's a bender, see? He's a unbreakable."

I ventured that it looked awfully big.

"I'm not through." His powerful fingers ripped away the corky bark, and in something less than half a minute I had a staff whose right-angled top came to my chin, a staff that was nearly straight and as smooth as glass.

I still have it. The staff itself belongs to me, but its angled top is Oreb's, who chides me now. "Fish heads? Fish heads?"

Pointing to the river, I tell him to fish for himself, as I know he can. I would not object to eating, but I can eat after shadelow, assuming that I can find food. This sunlight is nicely slanted for writing, which is to say that the sun is halfway down the sky. Here beside the river, the air is cool and moves not quite enough to be called a breeze. Not enough to stir a sail, in other words, but enough to dry my ink. What could be better?

Before I forget, I ought to say that what my very good friend Cugino called a vine was what we called a liana on Green. Green is a whorl made for trees, and Green's trees have solved every problem but that one.

One might almost call it a whorl made by trees, which cover every part of it except the bare rock of its mountaintops and cliffs, and its poles (or whatever the regions of ice should be called). And the trees are working on them.

In the *Whorl,* we had the East Pole and the West Pole, pylons with the Long Sun stretched between them. Thus we speak here (and on Green too) of a fictional West Pole to which the Short Sun travels, and an equally fictitious East Pole where it is imagined to originate. From a lander, one sees that none of this is true. There are no such places. Instead of being cylindrical, as we like to think of them, the colored whorls are spherical; and each might be said to have an equally imaginary "pole" at the top and bottom. That is to say that if some scholar were to build models to illustrate them, he would find it necessary to run little axles up through them so that they would turn properly, and if these axles were permitted to protrude at the top as well as at the bottom they would have the appearance of poles to the people whose whorls they held up.

A man named Inclito sat down next to me while I was writing that last. We fell to talking, as two men will who have nothing better to do than sun themselves like crocodiles of a sunny autumn afternoon, our tongues flicking in our mouths fast enough, if not quite so spectacularly.

He began our conversation, naturally enough, by asking what I was writing; and I confessed that it was foolishness, which this certainly is.

"Wisdom," he corrected me. "You are a wise man. Everyone sees it. Such a wise man would not write foolishness."

"Would a wise man write at all?" I asked him. To tell the truth, I simply wanted to ask him an inoffensive question to keep him talking, and hit upon that one.

Without batting an eye, he returned it to me. "Would one, Master?"

I had not expected to be addressed in such a fashion, but it seems to be the custom here. At home it usually meant a teacher such as Master Xiphias, the owner of a dog, or the leader of a band of musicians. I said, "A wise man might write, but he wouldn't write as I do. That is to say, he wouldn't record the events of his life. He would consider that they might be read by some innocent person who would laugh himself into fits. A wise man never harms another unless he intends to harm."

"That is well said." Inclito drew himself up. "I am an old trooper myself."

I told him respectfully that it was a most honorable occupation, but had never been mine.

"You have a wound."

I glanced down, afraid that the wound in my side was bleeding again and staining my robe.

"There too? I meant your eye." (I must get a rag to wear over that, as Pig did.) Seeing my expression, Inclito continued, "I'm sorry. It's not good to be reminded."

His own wide, square face is disfigured too, but by some skin disorder. It is not the sort of face that appeals to women; but courage, honesty, strength, and intelligence show in it very plainly. As I sit here waiting for him to take me to dinner, I know very little about him; but from what I saw and heard I think it likely that he is a man who has borne heavy responsibilities for a long time, and has driven himself harder than he drives others.

We talked for an hour or more, each of us trying to draw the other out. I doubt that there is any point in giving all of that here. I said as little as possible about myself because I did not want him to know what a hash I have made of my task. Inclito was at least as reticent, I would guess because he has a horror of boasting.

"As long as you're here," he told me smiling, "you got to think about me when you pass water. Our sewers? They're mine."

"You designed them?"

"I made some sketches. We built them, but they didn't work." He chuckled. "So we tore up my sketches and did them over."

He seems to have been a military officer as well.

"You walked here." (I had told him that I had.) "Where you going to have dinner tonight?"

"I doubt that I will—Oreb, be quiet!—I certainly hadn't planned on eating anywhere."

"You think I want you to eat in my sewers." He chuckled again. "In my house. All right? Seven. You can come at seven?"

I said that I would come at seven gladly, if he would tell me where it was.

"It's a long way. I bring you myself. Where you staying?"

Staying was vague enough for me to stretch its meaning a trifle, and I told him that I was "staying" at the shop where I was given this paper, and supplied the name of the little street.

"I know the place. Atteno, he's putting you up?"

"I hope, at least, that he won't drive me away."

Inclito laughed; he has a good, loud, booming laugh. "I show you my sewers if he does. One I got never gets wet. Would make a good place to sleep. I pick you up at six, all right? Where you're staying."

So here I am. It is not six yet; but I have nothing better to do, and the shopkeeper, who is very obliging, lets me sit in his window and scribble away. I suppose I am a sort of living advertisement. I have swept his floors again, as I did for my quire of paper, dusted off everything, and rearranged a few little items on his shelves that were in some disorder—the tasks of my boyhood. I would like to tie his bundles of quills for him, as I did for my father; but he has already tied them all himself.

I wish I could charge as much for our paper as he charges for his. Nettle and I would be rich.

What Inclito said about his sewers here reminded me most unpleasantly of the great sewer on Green, underneath the City of the Inhumi. If I am going to chronicle my misadventures (which is what I seem to have been doing) I ought to include that one, the most horrible.

Sinew and the rest were asleep. I was sitting up and thinking over Krait's brief visit when the Neighbor came. He opened the door and left it standing open behind him, and I was so busy wondering whether I should wake the others and urge them to escape while they could that I found it hard to answer him sensibly.

"You are a friend of ours?" He smiled and pointed to Seawrack's ring. His voice was thrilling in a way I cannot describe: no matter what he said, it was as though he were telling me that all the bad things that had ever befallen me had been tricks.

"Yes," I said. "I mean, I would like to be."

He smiled again. Although his face was shadowed by the brim of his hat, I could see his teeth flash. "Then will you open a sewer for us? We ask your help."

With every fiber of my being I wanted to say that I would, that I would gladly toil in his sewer for the remainder of my life if that was what he wanted. What I said instead was "I can't. We're prisoners here." Since I could see the open door beyond (and to some extent, through) him, it was an extraordinarily stupid remark.

He glanced at it. "It is true that your captors may be angry with you."

"I hope . . . Well, it really doesn't matter, but I don't like leaving my friends here. Can we take them with us?"

He shook his head.

"I didn't think so. My son?"

"No."

By that time we were out the door, which he slammed noisily behind us. "That will wake them up," I muttered. Privately, I was afraid that it would bring an inhumu.

He said, "We want to wake all of you up."

"To our danger, you mean? It's much too late for that. We know it now." I explained to him how we had taken the lander, and how the inhumi had recaptured us when we landed.

"To your safety," he said when I had finished. Now that I understand Krait's secret, I understand his remark as well; but at the time I had no notion of what he meant.

We went out a narrow door into an empty courtyard, and from the courtyard into the street. There were two luminous bodies in the night sky that were too large for stars; they seemed to engender shadows (vague and diffuse for the most part but occasionally deep) without actually giving light. I mean, of course, that they conveyed that impression.

"Are you afraid of enclosed places, or of underground places? Many of you are."

"I don't know. I haven't been in one for a long time." As soon as I spoke I recalled the pit from which Krait had saved me; and I said, "Except for one, and I was afraid of that one because I couldn't get out of it."

He looked at me thoughtfully. Written down as I have just now written it, it sounds silly; I could not see his face well enough to read its expression. I should say only that he turned his face toward me, and appeared to study me for several seconds. "You can get out of this sewer," he told me, "provided you do not drown."

"That's good."

"If you are frightened, there will be nothing to prevent you from leaving before the sewer is open again. Will you do that?"

"I suppose I might. I'll try not to. Aren't you coming with me?"

"No," he told me.

After that we walked in silence for a long time, a time in which we passed several streets—four or five at least. This was in the City of the Inhumi, and although it was late at night, it is at night that they are most active, on Green as here. It seemed strange to me then that we did not see more of them, and that they did not see us; but I know now that those who were active were seeking blood, and expected to find none in their city.

"I could go with you," the Neighbor told me. "I could open the sewer myself, without your help. It is only fair that I tell you that."

I said, "In that case, I'm doubly grateful to you for freeing me."

"If I were to help you, it would become clogged again."

He was waiting for me to speak, so I nodded.

"So it seems to me, though I may be mistaken. It will almost certainly become clogged again, even if you do as we ask. That is the most probable outcome, unfortunately."

"But not for years, perhaps," I suggested.

"That is correct, and does not matter. What does matter is that it may never be clogged again if you open it."

I believe I smiled, and I am afraid I smiled bitterly. "Do you think I've got miraculous powers?"

"If you do not know," he told me solemnly, "I do not know."

We turned in to a building even less whole than most of the buildings in that ruinous city, a roofless shell whose floors were littered everywhere with broken stones, and I asked whether we could get into the sewer from there.

"No. We could have entered the sewer from the underground room in which you were confined, and the point at which you will enter it is a long way from here. Would you object if I were to touch your face? I consider it advisable." I consented, and he anointed both sides of it with a sweet-smelling oil whose perfume seemed to me to come from a whorl more distant than the three I knew of. It suggested strange thoughts, thoughts so overpowering at the time as to be waking dreams. That may have been its purpose.

I have been talking with the stationer. His name is Atteno, as Inclito said. I asked whether it would be all right for me to sleep here in his shop tonight, and promised I would take nothing without his permission. He says he will make up a little bed for me, by which I assume he means he will loan me blankets. Quite a change! Still, I am not sorry that I left our blankets with the girl from Han, although I have been sleeping in my robe ever since. I tore it in two places going through the forest, but that good woman mended it for me.

Atteno says that Inclito is a very important man. He was terribly impressed when I told him that Inclito was coming for me. He asked whether I could "do things." I was not sure what he meant by it, and told him I could do a few, at which he looked wise and went away. "Good man!" says Oreb.

Here I feel the way that the Neighbors must feel around us. We are ready to believe that they are practically minor gods—that they know everything and possess all manner of mysterious powers; but they must seem perfectly ordinary to themselves. The one I have been writing about (he never told me his name) said to me at one point, "You think that I know everything about you and your son."

I denied it. "I thought the Neighbors I spoke with on Blue might have told you about me, that's all."

"You seemed the most likely," he said, and did not say what it was I was most likely to do or to be.

When the bronze tablet opened and I saw the swords, I hesitated to touch them.

"Will you choose," he asked me, "or should I choose for you?"

I said that it would better for him to choose, since I did not know who or what I was going to fight.

"I hope you won't have to fight at all. I don't think that you will. Do you want me to choose for you anyway?"

"I'm sure you must know more about these than I do."

He nodded and selected one. It would be easy to sketch, but I do not believe it will prove easy to describe. Let me try.

The blade was black, I suppose with age. I do not think the designs on it were writing, but I cannot guess what they were. It was widest toward the point, and sharply pointed. It narrowed toward the hilt in a concave curve, which gave it something of the appearance of a sickle in spite of its straight back.

But I have described it as I saw it when I drew it. I ought to have written first that it was in a black sheath of some hard, warm material I did not recognize, to which was attached a sword belt of many thin straps.

"Do you like it?"

I had unsheathed it before he spoke and was looking at the blade. I said, "It feels like a piece of my arm."

★

★   ★

The sun is up, and I should look for another place to sleep. I slept very little last night, Inclito having brought me back here very late, and I having eaten too much of his good dinner. It was the first meal I have eaten since the soup in Cugino's village, I believe, and so I told myself that I would have to be careful, and found that I had not been careful enough when it was too late to do anything about it. Silk told us once that experience is a wonderful teacher, but one whose lessons come too late. I have found that true all my life.

Inclito drove up in a carriage, as I should say, and I got into it with him as soon as I had written *arm*, still waving the sheet to dry the ink. "You have the bird," Inclito said. He sounded pleased.

I said something about not being able to escape him, to which Oreb himself contributed, "Bird stay!"

"When I saw you at the river you had the bird, but it flew away. I thought I was wrong. It was not your bird."

"I'm his, if anything," I told Inclito, which is the simple truth.

"The people here," he laughed self-consciously, "they think you're a witch. It's because of your bird. They believe these things."

I said that they had been very kind to me, and that although I had been among them only two days I was already very fond of them. "People here enjoy their lives," I explained to Inclito, not particularly clearly, "and people who do are always good people, even when they're bad people."

"They like you too, but your clothes frighten them. The black color."

"This?" I was about to tell him it was an augur's robe, but there seemed little point in saying so.

"They think it means you hurt people if you want to. Your bird's black, too. Red like blood."

"Good bird!"

Inclito smiled. "That's what they hope. A good bird. Witches got pet animals. Cats mostly only not all the time. *Familiares.* You know?"

He looked at me inquiringly, and I shook my head.

"It means the animal's in the witch's family. Sometimes it's really his father or his mother. Something like that. You think it's funny. So do I. I got a pet too. A horse. Not one of those. He's not my father, just my horse."

I repeated that Oreb wasn't mine.

"You got that white hair, so they think sometimes you hurt people maybe, but bad people." He laughed. "Even if they're good."

I told him that I was too weak and sick to hurt anyone, and that I had no weapons in any case; it was a lie, of course, but the truth was and is that I have no intention of using Hyacinth's azoth.

By that time we had reached the town gate, I believe. It was closed and barred, as he tells me it always is after shadelow, but the guards saluted him and opened it as soon as he reined up.

As we clattered through, he said very positively, "I asked you to dinner because I like you."

Oreb muttered, "Good man?"

I nodded, having no doubts about that.

"You're here. You want to eat? I want to feed you. But there's more."

I said, "I was afraid of that."

"You got no reason. I want our people to see you with me. Then they think you're on our side. So they don't hurt you. What's wrong with that?"

"Nothing," I told him. "In fact, it's very kind of you. I understand the open carriage now, and your driving so that both of us are seated up here."

He laughed again, such a loud and booming laugh that I half expected it to be echoed by the dark fields around us. "I always drive myself. I got a coachman to do the work, but I drive. I like it. I like the open air. I like the sun, the wind."

"So do I, in fine weather like this. May I ask who's on the other side?"

"Soldo and a couple others." Inclito waved them away as beneath his contempt. "We fight like brothers. You know how that is?"

"I've had some experience of it."

"Most towns, they're the only one from wherever they came from up there." He pointed with the whip. "Where the sun goes clear across the sky."

"The Long Sun Whorl."

"That's right. Where you come from, they got any other towns down here?"

"Not on Blue."

"That's right," he repeated. "With us it's different, a lot come. Different landers. The leaders, they're different too. All of us from Grandecitta, though. It's a real big place."

"I suppose it must be."

"Too many for one town anyway. So four. Ours is Blanko. You say you like it. So do I. What I like most, the people run it. No duko. We get together, talk things over, and we decide. There's some people nobody listens to, though. Know how that is?"

"And some who are heard with respect."

"You're a wise man. I know that already. In Saldo they got a duko, Duko Rigoglio. He wants to tell us what to do. We don't like it. He's got a lot of troopers and he's trying to get more. Give them land, huh? Silver. Horses. Whatever they want. He's got a lot. Trouble is, there's not too many for him to hire. You know Silk?" This last was said with an intonation I did not entirely understand.

"I knew him once."

"I see." Neglecting his horses for a moment he turned his head to look at me. "I'm not going to ask you your name."

Thinking of Pig, I asked him to suggest a good one.

"You want me to?"

"Why not?" I said. "You must know a great many."

"Incanto. You like it? Make people like you."

I nodded. "Then my name is Incanto. Did you hear that, Oreb? Pay attention."

"Smart bird!"

"I hope so."

Inclito said, "You want to fight me?"

"No," I told him. "Of course not."

"I don't want to fight you either." He dropped his whip into its mounting, took the reins in his left hand, and offered me his right, which I accepted.

"Then I tell you," he said. "I had a brother with that name. He's dead. He's just a little baby when he dies. My mother, she remembers and maybe she likes you for it. I don't remember. I'm not born then. Only his stone."

"In Grandecitta."

"That's right. We come. The dead, they stay. Maybe not always, though. We read about Silk here, there's a book."

I nodded.

"We think probably he's dead. Then bang!" He cracked his whip over the horses' backs. "This Silk, he's in some town way down south. Mountain town they call Gaon. He's hiring men to fight for him. Troopers. So there's nobody for Duko Rigoglio."

Inclito laughed again, this time softly. "I tell my family, I say, Silk's here, he's come to help us. I don't know how he knows about us, Incanto."

"I doubt that he does."

"You're hurt. Not your eye, newer, under your clothes. Maybe a dog bite, huh?"

I told him it was not.

"Could be a needler."

I shook my head.

"Or a slug, maybe." When I said nothing, Inclito added, "You're a lucky man. Man that's hit by a slug, usually he dies. Silk's like you. That's what his book says. He's not a trooper, but he fights too. He's got a needler, sometimes. Or with his stick." He tapped mine with the shaft of his whip.

"I'm not Silk, whatever you may think. I don't want to lie to you."

"I don't make you, Incanto. You're my brother, but we don't fight." He launched into an account of his military career, which had been extensive.

When we had driven half a league or more, he said, "I want your advice here, Incanto. Your help. Maybe you don't know why I do that."

"I could offer several guesses."

"You don't have to. I'll tell you. I give everybody in Blanko advice. How to train. How to fight. We have the meetings, I told you. It's called the Corpo, when we all come together. They want to know. I reach into my head and I tell them." He gestured, pretending to pull something from his ear. "Now I got no more. It's empty up there. So I ask you."

"Wise man," Oreb muttered, and took wing, soaring over pasture and wood.

I said, "Then my first piece of advice is that you resist the temptation to ask the advice of those less familiar with the situation than yourself."

"Good advice." Inclito clucked to his horses and made a little show of looking thoughtful. "I can't ask your advice about the war in the south? You don't know nothing about that?"

"Much less than you do, I'm sure." Nearly a week had passed since I had heard any news.

"If I was to tell you what worries me . . ." He paused as the carriage jolted along a particularly bad stretch. "If I was to tell you, maybe I could think better. It's this Silk. Not in the book, a real man."

I agreed.

"He's been hiring troopers to help fight. I said that? He has."

"Mercenaries."

"I knew there was a word. You know something about them, I can see that. He'll win, this real man they call Silk. His town'll win. These mercenaries he hires will have to look for somebody new to collect from. Will he let them keep the slug guns he gives them? He does this in the book, Incanto. You think maybe he'll do it again?"

I said, "I would imagine that most of them have slug guns already. As for those who don't and may be given them, I simply have no idea." It would be Hari Mau's decision.

"They're risky either way, these mercenaries," Inclito mused, "whether they got slug guns or not. You'll say hire them yourself, but they're risky to the one that hires them, too, and we can't. We're not rich."

"Is Duko Rigoglio?"

"Pretty rich." Inclito cracked his whip. "He gets it from his people."

I recalled Councilor Loris's scheme, although I said nothing about it then. "If you can't hire the mercenaries yourself, I doubt that it will prove possible to prevent the Duko's hiring them."

Inclito nodded gloomily.

"You may, however, be able to postpone the fighting until he is no longer able to pay them." With more optimism than I felt, I continued, "As soon as they're in his service, time will be on your side. You said he had enlisted the help of other towns against yours?"

"Novella Citta and Olmo. They're farther than Soldo, and they got dukos or something too. That's one reason."

I nodded to show I understood. "What do they stand to gain if Duko Rigoglio wins?"

"He leaves them alone, maybe. I think they're afraid of him." Inclito pointed with the whip. "You see that hill?"

The night was clear and Green shown bright overhead; there is always something ghostly about an open, rolling landscape by Greenlight, and I believe I have never been more conscious of it than I was last night.

"We can see my place from there. We're going to pull up there awhile and you can look at it."

"Is that the only purpose? To look at your house?"

"I guess I got to tell you." He cracked his whip again, urging the horses to a faster trot, then dropped it across his lap and slapped his forehead. "I'm a fool."

I said, "I have manifold reasons to doubt it."

"A fool thinking I got to tell what you already know. I'm afraid I got a spy in my house. Yes, I am."

"Your coachman?"

Inclito shook his head. "He's a stupid one, so I don't think so." He shrugged and cracked his whip again over the sweating horses. "Maybe he's stupid enough to take the Duko's cards, huh?"

"Maybe he is. Since I'm going to have dinner with you and your family—thank you again for your invitation—it might be well for you to tell me who's in your house and whom you suspect."

"All right." We had reached the top of the hill, and Inclito reined up. "In a minute I'm going to let them walk. It's better for them to walk a little when they're hot like this, not just stand around."

I nodded.

"I got no wife. It's better I tell you that first, so you understand. When we leave Grandecitta, she came with me. The lander you come on, some women died?"

"Yes. Quite a few women, and some men as well. And more children than all of the men and women combined. Please accept my very sincere condolences, however belated, upon the death of your wife."

Inclito was silent for a moment; then he inquired, "Where's your bird?"

"I have no idea. Scouting out the countryside, I imagine. He'll return when and if it suits him."

"It's better, maybe, that he's gone. That way my mother won't think you're a strego. That's a witch, it's what she calls them." Inclito smiled as he spoke, teeth flashing in his dark face; but I sensed that what he said was to be taken seriously.

"Your mother lives with you?"

He nodded. "I was going to tell who's in the house and who I can trust. So right off, my mother and my daughter. Maybe there's a spy, huh? But if there is, he's not them. You see my house?"

"If I'm looking at the correct one." It was not a single house, but a clutter of low, whitewashed buildings, half screened by a colonnade of graceful trees.

"I got good land when we come." Inclito's broad shoulders rose and fell. "They feel sorry for me because my Zitta dies. Then I help out everybody whenever I can. I help the town in a war, and after a while the corpo votes me some more. I can't use it, it's too far, so I trade with my neighbor. Two for one. He gets twice as much as he gives me." Inclito grinned for a moment. "Not a good bargain I make, huh? Always I'm a easy one when I do these things."

Feeling that I understood, I said, "Was it good land that you got from him?"

"Sure. Just like mine. Over there." He pointed. "What I give, it's not so good. A long way from Blanko, too, so I don't like it."

I said nothing, listening to the stillness of the night and waiting for him to continue.

"Back in Grandecitta we got a wise saying. You must know a lot of them."

"A few, perhaps."

"Maybe this is one. We say, if work's a good thing, why don't the rich take it? But I'm a rich man now, and I do. As much as I can, huh?" Inclito rattled the reins and the horses ambled forward. "You still want to know who's in my house? Who do I trust?"

"Yes, if you'll tell me."

"The family is me, my mother, and my daughter. I said that."

"You didn't say that was everyone."

"It is. Everybody that's related to me. There's a friend of Mora's that's staying with us for now. Her father's away."

"Mora is your daughter?"

"That's right. Her friend is Fava. She'll be at the table with us. Seems like a nice girl."

"Yet you suspect her?"

Inclito raised both hands, still grasping the reins. "I got to suspect somebody. But maybe there's nobody. You want the rest? All the names?"

"Just tell me who they are, for the present. I'll learn their names later as I require them."

"All right. I got three men to help. One's the coachman we been talking about. He's the oldest. Affito. He's only a coachman when I want him to drive this for me. It's for my mother, mostly. She wants to go, or Mora, he gets cleaned up and takes her. He's not a smart man, but he's good with the horses. Like now. You see these horses, how wet?"

I nodded.

"I drive too hard, too fast. Affito goes a little slower, he's got more left at the end. The other two is his nephews, Affito's brother's sprats. They're born out here, not like you and me."

I nodded again.

"Like I got the three men, my mother's got three women that help her, only she's really got five, because Mora and Fava help sometimes."

I asked what the three women servants did.

"A woman to cook and two girls to help around the house.

One helps in the kitchen, mostly. That's Onorifica. The other one washes floors and make up the beds, huh?"

"I believe I understand. Where do the three men sleep?"

"Where do they sleep?"

"Yes. It's no great secret is it? Do they sleep in the house?"

Inclito shook his head, more in wonder, it seemed to me, than in denial. "In back, in the big barn. They got a place like a little house in there that's just for them. I'll show you if you want to look."

"After dinner, perhaps. We'll see. What about the three women? Where do they sleep?"

"Not in there. That what you're thinking?"

"I'm not thinking at all," I told him. "I simply want to know."

"The cook in the kitchen. That's her bedroom, too, so I got to knock on the door if I want something late at night. Sometimes one of the girls sleeps in there with her. Or sometimes one will sleep with my mother. If she's afraid she'll maybe be sick or need something, one will sleep in her room on a little bed we got in there. Or my daughter will, or even Fava."

I said, "Suppose that your daughter is to sleep with your mother, and that the cook doesn't require company in the kitchen. Where would the other three sleep then?"

Laying aside his whip, Inclito wiped the sweat from his big, smoothly curved head with one large hand; he is almost totally bald, as I should have said much earlier. "You want to stay with us tonight? There's two empty rooms. Torda can fix up a bed for you."

"I'm not hinting, merely trying to find out how well placed each of these three women is to overhear your talk, to read your letters, and so forth," I explained. "Your coachman might overhear you talk with some friend, while he drove you, for example. But—"

"Hardly ever."

"Exactly. Though he might conceivably hear your mother tell a friend of hers something you had told her, so we can't rule him out altogether. The other two men seem even less likely thus far. You believe that I may be Patera Silk. May I tell you something the real Silk once said?"

Inclito nodded. "That's a big thing, huh? I'd like to hear it."

"It's in the book you mentioned. Since you've read it, you presumably read this in it. Councilor Potto said that he loved mysteries, and Patera Silk said that he did not, that he tried to put an end to them whenever he could. I've tried to be like him all my life. Also, you say you want my advice concerning the war you fear is about to start."

Inclito nodded silently.

"I'll give you some right now. Find out who the spy is, if there is one. Do that as fast as you possibly can. Then turn that spy, if it's feasible to do so. Use that spy to get false information to the Duko."

"All right, we'll try, Incanto. You and me. You got questions? Ask me anything?"

"You indicated that there would be five of us at dinner, if I heard you right—you, your mother, your daughter, your daughter's friend Fava, and me. Who will serve it? Bring out our food?"

"The girls."

"Onorifica and Torda?"

"Uh huh. Sometimes Decina will bring out the roast, if it's a special one. Sometimes my mother will come help her if she's feeling good."

Decina was the cook. But by that time we were almost at his door, and I really must sleep.

2

———◆◆◆◆———

STORIES BEFORE DINNER

I t is about the middle of the afternoon, I should judge, and I
have had an unexpected visitor here at my barrel. I tried to
make her as comfortable as I could; she did not complain, and in
fact left me a little medallion she says is pure gold. I can still smell
her perfume.

But I should not rush ahead of events like this.

I remember the Caldé's Palace in Old Viron very vividly, and
so I found Inclito's house less impressive than many people must.
To set down the truth here (as I must be careful to do in every
instance whatsoever) it was less impressive than my own palace in
Gaon as well, a palace and a manner of living that I am doing my
utmost to forget. The core of the house is the ruin of a building of
the Vanished People, and is of stone. The remainder is of brick, of
which Inclito is extremely proud. Outside, both stone and brick
have been covered with stucco and whitewashed; inside one sees
the ancient gray stones and the new red bricks. To give the house
its due, all the rooms I saw are large and possess a multitude of big
windows; the outer walls are curved, for the most part; the interior
walls are generally straight. I got the impression that many had
been exterior walls in their time, and that new and bigger rooms
had been added as the whim seized the owner, or as funds became
available.

Despite hair as white as mine, his mother looked younger than I expected, although she is clearly unwell. None of her son's heavy, coarse features can have come from her. Her face is still smooth, and I would call it almond-shaped if it were not for her hollow cheeks; her nose and mouth are small and delicate, the cheekbones delicate too, high and well defined. It is dominated by her large, dark eyes, which might almost be still-living organs in the face of a corpse.

Her granddaughter, Mora, is clearly her father's daughter, too large and too heavy-limbed and thick-waisted to be called attractive. To be fair, she carries herself well, and seems quiet and intelligent. About fifteen.

Her friend Fava is about half her size, looks blond next to Mora, and is quite pretty. Fava is—or at least appears to be—several years younger. At first I thought her nervous and self-effacing.

Inclito's mother welcomed me graciously, apologized for not rising, warned me that we had an hour or so to wait before dinner, and offered me a glass of wine, which I accepted gratefully, and which her son provided.

"Our own, from my own vines. What do you think?"

I tasted it and pronounced it excellent; and in all honesty it was by no means bad.

The daughter's friend Fava ventured, "You're a dervis? That's what Mora's father told us."

"Then it must be true," I assured her. "But first of all I'm a stranger here, and unfamiliar with many of your local terms."

The daughter, Mora, offered, "A wandering holy man."

"Wandering, certainly. And a man. Hardly holy."

"But you can tell us thrilling tales of far-off places," Inclito's mother suggested.

"I could tell your granddaughter and her young friend about the *Whorl,* which is the only distant place I've ever been to that is genuinely worth knowing about, madam; but you and your son will already have done that, and much better than I ever could."

Mora asked, "Where were you before you came here?" at which her father gave her a severe look.

"In a little village a day's travel south of your town, where a woodcutter and his wife took me in."

"This isn't a law court," Inclito rumbled.

His mother smiled. "No more questions, we promise. I shall offer a remark, however, if I may. It is not intended to be offensive."

I assured her that I was remarkably difficult to offend before dinner.

"Well, if my Inclito, my famous one, had not told me about you first, I would have thought that you were a male witch when I caught sight of you. A strego, we would have said when I was a girl. That would have made me very happy, because I would have asked you for a charm for health when the moment was ripe. If you were a strego, you'd be a good one, I'm certain, with that face."

"Then I wish I were, madam. I would be very happy to restore you to health, if I could."

"You could pray for her," Mora suggested.

"I will. I do."

Fava smiled; it was a smile, it seemed to me, at once appealing and malicious—or at least mischievous. "I want to play the game, and I'm company, too. You're older than I am, though, Incanto. Will you play the game if I beg very prettily?"

I smiled in return; I could not help myself, although like Inclito I suspect her. "If it involves running or wrestling, I beg to be excused. Otherwise I will play any game you wish, for as long as you wish it."

"Oh, I can't run!"

Inclito's mother said, "It's a silly game, really. But we do it because we used to at home. Fava likes it because she always wins."

"I don't! You won yourself last night."

"All of you voted for me out of kindness," the older woman said.

"They tell stories," Fava explained to me. "And at the end everybody votes, only you can't vote for your own. The person who wanted to play has to go last."

"Then I invite all of you to play with me," I said. "I'll need to hear your stories so that I'll know what sort of story I ought to tell."

Fava began to argue, but Inclito's mother silenced her with a trembling finger. "You must go first. I think it's by going last that you win so much."

To me she added, "We mustn't interrupt. That's the chief rule we have in this. If you interrupt, you'll have to pay her a forfeit."

Fava's Adventure:
The Washed Child

This happened two years ago, when a little group of us went to Soldo to visit our relatives there. They had a large farm. It wasn't as large as this one or as rich as this one either, but it was bigger and richer than most of the farms in that part of the whorl. Bigger and richer than most of the farms here, for all of that.

Now the farthest field of that farm was the last plowed land to the east. It was at the foot of a mountain, and beyond it the slope was too steep for plowing. They grazed sheep and goats up there, and the young men went there sometimes to hunt. They wouldn't take me with them, so one fine day I decided I'd go by myself. I didn't have a slug gun or a bow or anything of that sort, because I didn't really want to kill an animal, no matter how fine it was. I have a horror of blood, as most of you know. I can't bear to watch a pig slaughtered or even see ducks killed.

Everybody got up early there just as we do here, but I got up earlier than anybody. I was up and dressed and crossing the fields before shadeup, and as the old people say. I remember that I was afraid it wouldn't be daylight when I went under the trees, but I needn't have worried. It had started getting light before I reached them, and by the time I was in the high forest there was real daylight so that things had shadows. It was a perfectly lovely forest, too. The sheep and goats had cleared out most of the underbrush and left the big trees, so that it seemed to me that I was walking in a huge building like the cappellas of the gods back in the old whorl. Of course I've never seen those, but Salica has told me a lot about them since I got here, and that forest was like the buildings she was describing. Mora will be wondering if I wasn't afraid of getting lost, because she always is in a strange place. But I wasn't. I was climbing all the time, and I knew that all I would have to do to get back to the farm where I was staying was to follow the slope back down. I was very confident, you see, and so I went on for quite a long way.

After climbing like that half the morning, I came upon a little stream. It was icy cold, as I learned by drinking from it, snowmelt from the mountaintop. The way in which it had carved a path for itself through the rock looked interesting, and I decided to follow it awhile before I went back.

I hadn't gone very far before I heard a child crying. My first thought was that it was lost, naturally, and I hurried on up the stream to rescue it, scrambling over the rocks. But after a minute or two of that, I decided that it was probably very frightened, and if I burst in on it I might frighten it more, and it would run away. So I slowed down, and sort of crept along, though I was still going pretty fast. By good luck, the stream was making enough noise to cover up the sounds I made when I kicked a stone by accident or had to walk across gravel.

Pretty soon I came upon a very dirty woman holding a very dirty and very naked little boy so that the water came up to his knees while she scrubbed him with a very dirty rag. I dashed over to her and asked her what in the whorl she thought she was doing. The poor child was already red as beet and trembling in a way that made my heart ache for him, freezing and terrified.

The woman looked up at me quite calmly and said that he was her son and not mine, and that if she chose to wash him there that was her affair.

Well, I'm not as strong as Mora and I doubt that I'm as strong as that woman was, but I didn't think about any of that then. I shook my fist under her nose and told her that when a child is being mistreated it's the business of anyone who happens along to stop it. I said that I would never dream of interfering with a mother who was spanking her child for misbehaving or bathing him in the ordinary way, but that water was like ice and would be the death of him, and if I had to stop her by throwing stones at her or beating her with a stick, that was what I would do. I picked up a stone, finally, and she lifted him out and hugged him.

"You say this water will kill him," she said to me, "and that is truer than you can have guessed. I brought him here to drown him, and I am going to do it as soon as you go."

Bit by bit I got her story out of her. Her husband had died, leaving her with six children. For the past few years she had been living with a man whom she hoped would eventually marry her. He was the father of the child she had been washing. He had left her now, and she could not provide for so many. She had determined to lighten her responsibilities by one at least, and had settled upon this little boy, her seventh child and her youngest son, because he was the least able to resist. When they reached the water, however, she had been seized by a twisted sort of pride, and had decided to make him as presentable as she could so that his body would not disgrace the family when it was found.

When she finished, I asked whether she had changed her mind while she had been speaking. She said she had not, that the boy was clean enough now, and she firmly intended to drown him as soon as I was out of sight, adding that he looked more like his father every day. When I heard that, I knew there was only one thing to do. I got her to give me the child, and promised her that if she would come to the house where I was staying that evening, I'd see to it that she got food for herself and her other children.

It was embarrassing to go back to the house in which I was a guest, and to tell the truth something of a poor relation, with a ragged boy of about three in tow. But I did it, and they were good kind people there and fed him and contrived a little bed for him in the room they had me use. I talked it over with the lady of the house that evening before his mother came, and we agreed that the best thing would be for me to bring him home with me, and try to find a good family here that would take him in. You mustn't think, because there's some trouble between our town and theirs, that they're all bad people around Soldo. So that was what we decided, and when the boy's mother came around she gave her two nice fat geese.

Everyone agreed that he was a very nice little boy, even though he wasn't terribly bright and became rather sickly from the terrible washing he'd had, or because he had been so badly frightened when he thought his mother was going to drown him. He didn't know his name, or if he did he wouldn't tell it; we called him Bricco, because he'd been so black when I brought him there.

His mother was the problem. She came to the back door on the first night, as I said, and got the two geese. The next night she was back wanting something else, and got it, and the next night the same, and the night after that, and the night after that. On the next-to-last night they gave her two turnips, I believe, and on the last night nothing at all.

Then she went to the law and said I'd stolen her child, and the judge sent a couple of troopers to get him back. This judge wasn't the Duko, you understand, just somebody he had appointed to try minor cases.

It ended up, as I ought to have known it would, with the boy and his mother and me in court, and the relatives I was traveling with there too to back me up, and the relatives we'd been staying with on hand as well. I told the judge what had happened, just as I've told you tonight, and the mother said it was all a lie: she and her son had gone out berry picking, and I'd stolen her son the moment she took her eyes off him.

That's what she said at first, anyway. A few sharp questions from the judge showed how matters actually stood, and the woman we'd been staying with testified that she'd never once asked for Bricco back, just for food to take home to her other children.

Then the judge did a very intelligent thing. He put Bricco himself on the little platform next to him, and talked to him for a bit, and asked whether he wanted to go back home with his mother or stay with me. Bricco said he wanted to stay with me, and that ended it.

After that we set off for home right away. We'd had to stay

almost a month more than we had meant to because of the trial, and everyone was mad to go. On the first night we slept on the road, as the saying is, but on the second night we put up at an inn, having found a good one that wouldn't charge us too much. Well, you never know. When I woke up the next morning, no Bricco.

I wanted to go back to look for him, I really did, but the others wouldn't hear of it, and I didn't want to go back alone. You know how dangerous the roads are for somebody like me traveling alone. It was obvious what had happened, or anyway we thought it was. He'd gotten homesick and flown. We speculated a little on whether he'd get back there all right, and a couple of the men rode back for an hour or two looking for him. But they didn't find him, and the rest of us decided that he'd probably get home eventually, or stop off if he found someplace better.

"Right here," Fava said, "I want to stop and ask all of you what you think of my story so far. I know the rule is that nobody can interrupt, so we'll call that the end. But there's a little bit more I'll add to it when we've talked about it."

Inclito said, "It shows what a bad time poor people have in Soldo. In sixteen years, this family's lost whatever land it got. It's almost starving. We try not to let that happen here." He looked around at us, challenging us to dispute with him, but no one did.

His mother asked, "This was two years ago? You can't have been more than a child yourself, Fava."

Fava nodded and looked at Mora, inviting her comment; I could not help contrasting the two then, Mora larger already than most men, almost freakish in her blue gown and paint, and Fava half her size, and if not actually beautiful, attractive at least with her piercing eyes and blooming cheeks.

In her heavy, slow voice, Mora said, "I think you acted well throughout it all, Fava. The others won't, I know, but I do."

Smiling, Fava invited me to speak, too. "You're probably the oldest person here, Incanto, and my present host says you're very wise. May we have your opinion now?"

"If I were wise," I told her, "I wouldn't offer any opinion

until I'd heard the whole story. Because I am not, I will admit that it interested me. The bit about the trial particularly. It reminded me of a similar case I once heard of, in which a certain woman claimed that a servant girl was her daughter, although the girl herself denied it. Now let us hear the rest."

"As you wish. All this was two years ago, when I was, just as Salica says, much younger. Last year I had a chance to go back to Soldo. I jumped at it as you can imagine, and as soon as I got there I set out to find what had become of Bricco.

"It took me two days to locate the hovel in which the family lived, and as you can imagine I wasn't in the least anxious to be confronted by his mother. I talked to some of the neighborhood children instead and described Bricco to them, saying that he had been the youngest child in the house. Would any of you care to guess what they told me?"

I shook my head; so did Inclito.

"They said that the Vanished People had taken him. That a highborn woman of the Vanished People had taken a fancy to him and stolen him away. That once in a rare while they would see him still, thin and pale and looking as though he was very unhappy. But he would soon vanish like a ghost."

Inclito's mother sighed. "Honestly now, Fava. Is that a true story? You didn't make it up?"

"I don't say that he really appeared to those children," Fava protested. "I said that was what they said. And it was."

Inclito himself grunted, "Sprats tell all sorts of wild tales. Your turn, Mora. Let's hear what you can do."

Mora's History:
The Giant's Daughter

This will be the shortest story told tonight, and the simplest. It will also be the best, though I don't hope to win, or even wish to. Fava will win, as she usually does, and as she should. I wouldn't have it otherwise.

Once when the whorl was young, which was not very long ago at all, there was a certain snug and quiet town that was different from the others around it only in that it belonged to the best of giants. This giant lived in a big white castle outside the town he owned, and seldom troubled the townsfolk. The truth is that though he was very large and very strong, and rather homely, he was so kind and generous and wise and good and brave that the townsfolk could not have asked for a better owner. Nor could they have governed themselves half so well as he governed them.

You would have thought that they would be happy with this arrangement, and to give them their due most of them were. But many others were not.

"What right has he got to be bigger than we are?" they asked each other.

"What right has he got to make us look like fools by his wisdom?"

"What right has he got to be richer?" they said.

And, "He's so cheerful he makes me sick. What right has he got to smile and whistle when things are at their worst?"

"If I were as rich as he is, I'd be cheerful, too, and brave," they told each other when he couldn't hear them, and never considered that the giant had been wise and cheerful and brave when he had nothing but his daughter.

This daughter was large and strong just as he was, which meant that she was much too big to be pretty. She was also, I'm sorry to say, much too young to be wise. She went to the academy in the town with the town girls, but she stood out among them like a cow in a hen-yard. The town girls made fun of her, until one day she knocked down half her class. After that there were two parties at the academy, just as you often see in the corpo. In one was the giant's daughter. In the other was everyone else in the academy, even the teachers.

That went on for a year, until a new girl came, a new girl who was prettier than the prettiest girl in the whole academy and smarter than the smartest. Everyone in the whole place wanted to be her best friend. How surprised they were when she chose the giant's daughter! And how angry!

After that there were still two parties in the academy, and the second was still much, much bigger than the first. But the first had the girl who won every game and contest that had to do with running or jumping, and also the girl who shone the brightest in arithmetic and composition and every other subject. Then many of the other girls tried to join it. Some were let in halfway, but after a few days it was made clear to them that they were not really members at all.

Some of you may not think that was a happy ending, but if you don't you've never been in a place like that academy, where everybody who looked at the giant's daughter wore a frown.

"That was a very good story," Fava told Mora. "I'll vote for it, and I think you might win."

Mora shook her head.

"The giant won't say anything," Inclito told his daughter. "He's got troubles of his own, and maybe he hasn't paid enough attention to the troubles others have. Just the same, I'd like to hear what our guest has to say. Incanto?"

Thinking of my own account of Patera Silk's career in Viron, I said, "I believe that the best stories are those that are true, and those that the teller feels most deeply. Thus yours was one of the best I have heard, Mora."

Nodding sagely, Inclito turned to his mother. "You want to go next? Or me?"

"You," she told him.

Inclito's Witness:
The Sentry and His Brother

This was ten years ago, when we fought Heleno. I had a hundred men in that, and in my hundred were two brothers. The names were Volto and Mano, and they hated each other. When I found out how much I tried to keep them apart, but with only a hundred you can only separate two men so much.

Volto was tall and skinny, with a ugly, sour face. Not ugly like me, this is the face Pas gave me. Ugly because he's got ugly thoughts. He was one of them that it's more work to get them to work than the work that they do is, but he was a good fighter.

The young one, Mano, he's like day instead of night. Always happy, works hard, everybody likes him, and he's brave, too. A brave young man. Just the same it makes no difference. He hates Volto as much as Volto hates him. Once he tells me that when he was a little sprat Volto would beat him every time the mother and father got busy someplace else, and three, four times Volto about kills him.

We beat Heleno and for a while we stayed in their town trying to take back all they stole. There's a curfew, none of the people can go outside after dark, and I got troopers all over to keep them in, on every corner, almost, one man. Then it is like with my daughter, I think too much about my own troubles. Mano is on a corner and somebody is sick, so my sergeant has Volto take his place. He's got to take Mano's corner at the end of Mano's watch.

There's a shot and everybody comes running to see what the trouble is, and Volto's dead, too far gone to talk when I got to him. Everybody thinks Mano waits until he comes to take his place, and then he shoots him. Everybody but me thinks that. They don't blame Mano much, but it's murder just the same.

They bring in a new officer that doesn't know either of them to be the judge, a major. Now I would say it's fair, but then I thought the other way. I go to see Mano where we got him locked up, and I say, "Why did you do this thing? They're going to hang you. What can I tell them?"

It takes a long time to get the story out.

"He wanted to kill me," Mano says, "and he told me he was going to do it so our whole family would pretend afterward that I'd never been alive. 'No stone for your grave' is what he said. I'll never forget that. I thought it was just more lying, more bluff. Lying was something you had to expect if you were going to talk to Volto, just like you got to know that a horse doesn't ever forget a thing that hurt it if you're going to train horses. With Volto it was that he'd rather lie than tell the truth. If he didn't have to, he'd lie anyway. It made him feel like he was smarter than you."

"He was going to shoot you?" I said. "You had to shoot first?"

He wouldn't answer, just shook his head.

"I'll tell this major that's going to be the judge," I say. "Everybody likes you, everybody knows you're a good trooper. They're talking to him already. He's heard about you and your brother, too. He says he hasn't, but he's bound to have heard something. This town we got down here, it's too small for that. Everybody hears something."

"No," Mano says.

"Sure," I tell him. "You're tired, you just want to get back to your cantonment and go to sleep. The new man comes, and it's him. You see his face, his eyes. He's raising his slug gun to shoot you, so you shoot him."

"No," Mano says. "It would be a lie. The gods would know, Captain, and the judge would, too."

I go away, and my sergeant comes to me. He's looked at their guns, Volto's has been fired, there's still a empty in the chamber, and he can smell the powder smoke. Mano's wasn't fired. He says, "Do I tell the major?" and I tell him he's got to, because what if it comes out later?

Then I go back to Mano like before and I say, "Why did you change the guns? It looks so bad."

"I didn't," he says, and that's when he tells me. His brother gets close enough that he can see him, and points his slug gun up against his own chest. "He's got those long arms," Mano says. "I didn't think he could do it, I didn't think he could reach the trigger. I started to laugh. I'll never forgive myself. I laughed at him, and that gave him the nerve to push on the trigger."

We hadn't buried Volto yet, and he's been dead long enough that he wasn't stiff anymore. I got his slug gun and held it to his chest and stretched out his dead arm. It was short-barreled gun, and he was a tall man with long arms. Holding his hand out real straight—look here. Like this he could have done it.

Mano told the judge at his trial, and I spoke for him. Against us, a dozen said the brothers had been enemies. Many times, each had threatened to kill the other one. They liked him and didn't like saying it, but it was the truth and they'd taken the oath. The major thought it was a simple case and told me to hang Mano.

The next day was the one when we learned that war wasn't over. Poliso hit us soon as the shade's up. I put off the hanging, not because I was hoping to save Mano but because I couldn't spare the men. For two days they got us surrounded. It was the worst time for me since my Zitta died. We thought we'd all get killed, but we're going to fight to the end. But it's better if you fight to somebody else's end. We needed to send a message back to Blanko and ask for help, but they were strangling us, shoulder-to-shoulder around our position. Nobody could see how it could be done.

I went to the major. "That man that shot his brother I still got locked up," I told him. It never does to argue with people like that once they have made up their minds. "Let me turn him loose and send him back with a letter. If they kill him, they'll have done a dirty job for us. If he gets through, he'll deserve a pardon."

The major makes all kinds of objections the way I'd expected. "All right," I say, "if you won't send him, let me turn him loose and give back his slug gun. I need every man, and he's a good one."

That did it like I knew it would. We sent him and he got through, but he took a slug in the guts. By the time I got home he was dying. I went to see him, and if I'd been a day later that would've been too late. I told him he was a hero, he saved us all, and his family's going to brag about him till Molpe married. "Till Molpe gets married and a year past that." Those were my words exactly. I still remember them. And I tell him, "Twenty years, and I'll be bragging to my Mora's children that I was your officer."

The pardon came while I sat beside his bed, a big white envelope from the corpo with a white silk ribbon and a big, thick red seal that Mano was too weak to break. I opened it for him and read it to him, and he smiled. Already his face was yellow like butter in a churn, but that smile, it was a knife in my heart.

"Anybody could've got through, sir," he whispers to me. "It wasn't anything."

It was not nothing. It was as brave as I'd ever seen, and I told him.

"But to shoot a brother," he whispers, "and get let off for it afterward . . . How many have done that?"

"That's a terrible story, my son," Inclito's mother told him. "Incanto will think we're beasts here."

"Some are." He sipped his wine. "There's beasts in every town."

"So there are. So there are." The old woman nodded, her face somber, and patted her hair with a hand so white and thin that I felt I could almost see through it. "I'm glad that you mentioned it, Inclito my son. I've been racking my brain for a story that you and Mora haven't heard over and over, and it reminded me of one."

She spoke to me. "This will be a story of the old time in Grandecitta. These young people think we lie when we talk about those days, but you, Incanto, you will know better. I was a year older than Mora and Fava are now, I think. Perhaps two, but no more than that. This you will disbelieve, too, just as they do. But I was quite good-looking then."

"You are good-looking now," I told her truthfully. "At your granddaughter's age you must have been ravishing."

3

THE MOTHER'S REMINISCENCE: FROM THE GRAVE

My son has told a story of a war we all remember. This is from an older one, a war under the Long Sun. I myself was scarcely more than a child when it happened.

I was scarcely more than a child, and yet I was courted in those days by two fine young men, Turco and Casco were their names. Turco was my favorite, and to this day I can't forget how we sat under the orange trees and spoke of love and the family we would make together. When I think back on it now, it seems to me that we must have sat and talked like that often. But it cannot be, because the trees I remember are always in bloom. The years were so much longer then!

War came. Casco was rich enough to ride a fine horse, so he became a cavalryman. He rode out to see me one last time before he went away to fight. It was about noon, I think, and I had been lying down in my room. I can hear his knock, even now, and our old servant grumbling to herself as she goes to answer it. I knew who it was without looking and got up and went out to speak to him. "I will come back to you," he told me, "and I tell you now that if your sneaking, lying Turco is with you, I will lay his body at your feet. You have been warned."

Casco was a strong, brave man, but he was wounded almost at

once. He had only just ridden away to fight, that was how it seemed to me, when I got his first letter from the hospital. I do not remember now exactly all that first letter said, but all of his letters were very much alike. He worshipped me, he adored me, and if I so much as looked at any other man he would cut my nose off. And worse. I hope that neither of you girls ever receives letters like those. They are not pleasant, believe me.

As you would expect, he begged me again and again to come to see him in the hospital, and on my wedding day I did. He was unconscious and did not see me, however. You cannot imagine what a relief it was. I sought out the nurse who cared for him and asked if he would recover, and she said that he would not. What joy I felt!

Yet he did. The black wreath was still hanging on our door when he came stamping down the road in his big boots, with the end of his saber trailing in the dust. His cavalry uniform hung on him like the clothes of a scarecrow, yet he was polite when he saw the wreath and my black gown. "Your father?" he asked me.

"My husband," I told him, and he stared at me, dumbfounded.

I asked him, "Did you think yourself the only trooper to suffer, Casco? The patre united us not twenty beds from the one in which you lay, and after the ceremony they let me bring him here and nurse him myself."

How he glared! I thought he was about to fly at my throat.

"They needed the bed, you see, and they knew that my husband was going to die in spite of all that they or I could do. So they let us bring him here, and when the end came we buried him in our family plot, next to the orchard in which he and I used to sit, and not a day has passed on which I have not knelt weeping on his grave."

"Show me."

I shook my head. "If you want to see it and say a prayer for him, you may. But I won't go there with you."

Casco nodded and went through the house, and I returned to my room and locked the door. It was not until later that I learned what he had done.

He had been raging when he left me, but he was quiet when he returned, quiet and polite. I was watching from my window, and he seemed so weak and sick then that my heart went out to him. He loved me, after all, and that I did not wish to have the only kind of love he had to give was neither my fault nor his. Furthermore, he had gone out bravely to defend Grandecitta, and had suffered a terrible wound.

I went downstairs again and invited him to sit down, and offered to bring him a glass of wine and some fruit so that he might refresh himself before he returned to the city.

He thanked me and sat, and told me that he was feeling unwell, which I had seen for myself already. "A glass of wine, please." (I will never forget how pale he was under his beard, or the skull that grinned behind his face.) "A glass of any wine you have," he said, "and when I have drunk it I will trouble you no longer."

I did not believe him. I felt sure that as soon as he felt better he would pay court to me as before, and I steeled myself to refuse him. But I hurried away just the same, and filled the little glass that I had used until I was old enough to eat my dinner with Mama and Papa, and brought it back to him.

How long was I gone? I have wondered often. Half a minute, perhaps. Or a minute. Or two. No longer than that, I am sure. And yet it was long enough. He had fallen from his chair and lay dead on the floor. I dropped his wine and screamed, but it seemed a very long time before anyone came. I had gotten over the worst of my fear by then, and was on my knees picking up the pieces of broken glass and wiping up the spilled wine. It was while I was doing it that I noticed that his saber was missing. He was still wearing his sword belt and the empty scabbard.

Now I will tell you what our old servant, Schiamazza, revealed to me the next day. She had been afraid that Casco would dishonor my husband's grave, you see, and had followed him at a distance.

He had gone to the grave and stood staring down at it for a minute or two. The stone had not been erected then, and Schiamazza said he had not been certain then that it was in fact my husband's grave, in spite of the mountain of flowers I had left on it. He had looked all around him, searching everywhere with his eyes, and she was afraid he would see her, though she had hidden herself behind a tree some distance away. She thought that he was looking for another fresh grave. I myself think that he was making certain he was unobserved.

He drew his saber and knelt, and from the way he gripped the hilt she knew what he was about to do, but she did not dare cry out. Kneeling on the grave itself, on my poor Turco's chest as it were, he clasped the hilt in both hands and raised it over his head.

Schiamazza called it miracle, and perhaps it was. Perhaps it was not. You must be the judge of that.

Miracle or not, a tall man with a bird upon his shoulder stood beside Casco. Schiamazza had not seen where he came from. Nor did she see where he went when he left. Casco had raised his saber. Like a knife! And she had closed her eyes in horror. When she opened them again, the tall man was there. He was a witch, a strego, that seems certain. He spoke to Casco, and loudly enough that old Schiamazza overheard him. He said, "Only cowards strike at the dead—the dead cannot defend themselves."

Casco had lowered his saber and replied, too softly for her to hear.

"As you wish," said the strego. "Only remember that the dead can avenge themselves."

The strego's familiare spoke too. I have heard a good many talking birds, but all they say is nonsense. Schiamazza swore that this one spoke to Casco as one man to another, saying, "Beware! Beware!" It fluttered its wings, and it and the strego vanished together.

Casco raised his saber as before, held it up for a moment when he prayed or cursed, and plunged it to the hilt into the newly dug soil of my husband's grave. After that he rose and stamped and kicked poor Turco's flowers, she said, and seemed almost to dance upon his grave in his fury. It had frightened her so much that she fled.

Let me stop here for a moment or two. I see the questions in your eyes, Incanto. I will try to answer them. There was a wall around our orchard and burial plot, a stone wall about as high as that door, with two gates in it. The gate farther from the house was kept locked when it was not in use. Boys climbed the wall to steal fruit sometimes, however, so it may be that the strego climbed it, too. It is also possible that he had been in our house, and had followed Casco outside just as Schiamazza did. My father, my mother, or my brother may have been consulting him in secret. Who can say? For my own part, I think it likely that he flew into our orchard as the birds did, in a bird's shape or his own. In the *Whorl*, where we knew nothing of the inhumi, it was known that stregos can fly when they wish. You young people may mock me for saying it, but you have heard many such stories from me, and there is a grain of truth in every one of them. More than a grain, in many.

At first we thought that Casco's family would bury him, but his father and both his brothers had been killed in the same battle in which he had been wounded, and no one remained except a grandmother, an old woman such as I am now, much too foolish and confused for any business more serious than baking a pie. She gave my father money, I believe, and he made all the funeral arrangements. Casco's uniform no longer fit him, as I said, and so he was buried in a good velvet tunic that my brother had outgrown. For months afterward, I did not even know what had become of his clothes and the long saber that my brother had pulled from my husband's grave.

My first husband. That is what I meant to say. I have been married five times, Fava, though you would not think that anyone would have me to look at me now. It is still terribly hard for me to talk about these things, which would only bore you and Mora anyway. I will pass over them as quickly as I can tonight.

I married again the next summer. He was a wonderful man, handsome and kind. Autumn came, and he went hunting with two friends. It was the first time that we had been separated. He fell from his horse, they said, and when they picked him up he was dead.

For months I could not credit it. I used to awaken when the servant knocked and leave my bed, feeling quite certain that he would come back to me in a day or two. As I washed and dressed, his death would close in on me like a fist. It was horrible. Horrible!

Three years passed before I married again, a good man, quiet, hardworking, and studious. For me, he said, he was willing to dare the curse. By that time many were saying that there was a curse on me, you see. I was not yet twenty, and I had buried two husbands. The worst hinted that I had murdered them.

For seventeen months we lived together very happily. Then my father fell ill. He had workmen ditching a field he owned, a low swampy one that he thought might do to pasture cattle if it could be drained. Because he could not leave his bed and my brother was living in the city, he asked my husband to look at it for him and let him know how the work was going. His name was Solenno. My husband's name, I mean. My third husband. Gioioso had been my second husband.

Solenno was a trifle taller than Gioiosio, as well as I can remember. Or perhaps it is only that time has made him seem so. His body was still covered with mud when they brought it into the house. I have hated the sight of mud ever since, as my son will tell you. Old Schiamazza had to help my mother wash him. I could not do it. The embalmers washed him again, or so they assured me, but his body smelled of mud until the coffin was closed, even though it had been embalmed and dressed in clean, new clothes.

I talked to my mother one night. I cannot say now how long after Solenno's death it was. A week or two, or a month. Something like that. I was in despair. I did not know what to do. I told her over and over how much I had loved Turco, and I said that for me it was as though Turco had died three times.

She nodded and hugged me and heard me out, and when I had talked and wept until I could weep no more she said, "You have been trying to find him again. I thought so all along, and now I know it. Solenno looked somewhat like him, everybody saw it. And Gioioso always made me think of Turco. Their voices and gestures were just the same."

I sighed, perhaps, and wiped my eyes. I could weep no more, as I have told you.

"Listen to me, my daughter. Turco is dead. You must find someone you can love for himself, not because he reminds you of Turco."

And I did. I found Inclito's father. Do you want to know what he looked like? Look at my son. Big and strong and rough, but good. Such a good man, and he loved me as a deer the plain. He laid his heart at my feet, and we were wed. A month passed. Then two. Then three. A year! I bore a son and lost him, but next year I bore my Inclito. Together we saw him weaned, and watched him learn to walk.

One day my husband showed me a pair of dirty old boots, caked with mud. "Whose are these?" he asked me.

I looked at them. They seemed familiar, but that was all I could tell him.

"These were a trooper's riding boots. Was your brother in the cavalry? Or your father?"

They were Casco's, of course. I don't think that I had so much as mentioned Casco to my husband before that day, but I told him the whole story, exactly as I have told it to you tonight.

"Ah," he said, and he put the boots on the floor and stood beside them. "Too small for me. I could never get my feet in them, and a good thing, too, because there's something in them already."

He picked up the right boot and showed it to me, a sharp white splinter pushed through the leather at the ankle that looked almost like a sliver of bone. "That is a death adder's fang," he explained, "or anyway that's what I think it is. If the man these boots belonged to had kept his sword, he wouldn't have had to kill the thing with his feet, and he might be alive today."

From that you already understand what came before it, I feel certain. Gioioso had found the boots and worn them when he went hunting. The dried poison from the fang had entered his foot slowly until there was enough to stop his heart. Poor Solenno had found them too, in the back of the closet that had become his, and had worn them when he went to look at my father's muddy field.

It is all simple and reasonable, you will say. I am older than any of you, and it seems to me that there is more to be said. Turco had avenged himself, as the strego had warned Casco he would. Have you ever seen another person who reminded you of yourself?

No one? What about you, Fava? Incanto?

You shake your heads. We never do, you see. I have been told many times that such-and-such a woman looks exactly like me. And I have visited her and spoken to her, and come away feeling that no one could resemble me less. So it was with Turco. To my mother and me, Gioioso and Solenno seemed very like Turco. But to Turco himself they resembled Casco. Like Casco, they were rivals for my hand. And they wore boots of the same size, after all.

"That was a fine story," I told her, "one of the best that I've ever heard."

"I had to live it," she replied, "and it is far better to hear such stories than to live them, I promise you, though it ended so happily. Let us hope that neither of these girls has to endure such things."

A cheerful, round-faced young woman in a dirty apron came in to tell us that dinner was ready, and Inclito jumped from his chair. "Wonderful! I'm starving, Onie. Have you cooked up something special for me?"

She winked at him and said, "We think you'll like it," and all five of us followed him into a good-sized dining room with a fire blazing in the fireplace at one end and all four quarters of a yearling steer turning on a spit. Inclito complained of the heat at once and opened two windows, and to tell the truth I would not have been sorry if he had opened two more, though Fava exchanged her seat with Mora in order to sit nearer the fire.

Inclito's mother drew her shawl more tightly about her shoulders. "It's your turn, Incanto. We'll try to pass the food around quietly so you can talk."

Inclito handed me the wine bottle as she spoke. I thanked him and refilled my glass. "I'm very glad that our host's mother's story preceded mine," I began, "because up until then I had been trying to think of one that might win. After hearing it, I realize that I have no chance, and can tell whatever foolish tale I want. That's what I'm going to do, but I have a question for all of you first. I'm not telling my story now, so you can answer me out loud and say anything that you like. Have you ever known anyone who returned alive from Green?"

Mora said, "Nobody can go there. You'd have to have a lander of your own, one that you could make obey you."

Inclito's mother added, "Isn't that where the inhumi come from? That's what everybody says, and the people who went there from the *Whorl* are all dead."

I looked at Fava, who shook her head.

Inclito rumbled, "How could anybody know where everybody's been?"

"To the best of your knowledge," I told him.

"I think maybe . . . No." He shook his head. "Not that I know about."

"This story is about a man on Green," I told them. "I'm not asking you to accept it. If you enjoy hearing it tonight, that's more than enough for me."

Here I ought to set down my own story, but I have written myself out already. I will leave it for next time—with Oreb's return, which was actually quite funny. But before I shut up this old pen case that my father must surely have left for me to find, I would like to record a very strange dream I had last night in the shop. I would love to know what it means, and If I don't write about it soon, it seems likely I will forget it.

I was back in the pit, sitting in the middle of it as I actually did for so many hours. A copy of the Chrasmologic Writings lay next to me, a student's copy, thick and small, on very thin paper. Thinking that I might as well prepare my mind for Scylsday, I picked it up and opened it. Opposite the printed page was a picture of Scylla in red, and while I studied the facing page she struggled to escape from hers. I thought, "Oh, yes. What seems like a picture to me seems like a membrane to her, a greased skin stretched tight over the Sacred Window." In my dream this peculiar idea struck me as perfectly true and perfectly ordinary, something that I had known all my life but had rather lost sight of.

At the end of each verse I read, I watched her straining against the page with all ten arms. Very faintly I could hear her cry, "Help! Help!" And then, "Beware! Beware!," like the bird in Inclito's mother's story. I woke up—or thought that I did—but the printed Scylla was still with me, calling out, *"Help me! Help me!"*

I sat up and stared around at the little stationery shop as though I had never seen paper or ledgers before; and in the precisely the same voice Oreb exclaimed (as he so often does), "Watch out!"

4

─◆─

My Own Story: The Man with the Black Sword

I know nothing about Grandecitta, nor do I know what other cities you and your mother may have seen before you left the *Whorl*, Inclito. But I doubt that you have ever seen a city like the City of the Inhumi on Green. Before I describe it, let me say that it is very hot there and rains a great deal. You must bear both those in mind as you hear this.

The buildings of that city were not built by the inhumi themselves, for the inhumi do not like tools or use them skillfully. Its builders were the Vanished People, the same master builders who began this gracious house of yours. It was a beautiful city in their time, I feel certain, a city of wide streets, welcoming courtyards, and noble towers. A certain woman once said that my old city in the *Whorl* seemed ugly to her, because most of its buildings had only a story or two, although there were some with five and even six, and we were proud of the towers of our Juzgado. I never got to see her own city, which was said to have so many fine buildings, soaring pinnacles that rose above its palm trees like columns of white smoke some god had turned to stone.

That woman would have loved the City of the Inhumi when it was young, I feel sure; but at the time I am speaking of it was no longer beautiful. Think of a lovely woman, proud and wise. Picture to yourself the luminosity of her glance and the grace of her movements. Let yourself hear the music of her voice.

Can you see and hear her, all of you? Now imagine that she has been dead for half a year, and that we are to open her casket. The City of the Inhumi was like that. Its wide streets were littered with rubble and twisted metal, its buildings gray with lichen where they were not green with moss. Great lianas, vines thicker than a strong man's arm, stretched from one tower to another, some so high up that they seemed no more than cobwebs.

The towers of the City of the Inhumi are not of twelve stories, or fifteen, or eighteen, like the towers of the city in which I was born, but of stories beyond counting. Those towers seem to touch the sky even when you are so far from them that they can scarcely be seen. As from the cliffs, trees sprout from their sheer walls and every ledge, and the questing roots of those trees pry out huge blocks of masonry that scar the lower parts of their parent buildings as they crash into the streets. And every insect that spawns in stagnant pools is there, buzzing and stinging.

The man had been given a sword by a man of the Vanished People, a sword that was neither long nor heavy, but very sharp, its blade of a black steel (if it was steel) better than any we know. He ought to have borne it proudly, for it was a much finer sword than the finest he had ever seen, a better sword even than the sword of honor worn by the woman who had disparaged his city. He was too frightened to wear it like that, however; and noble though it was, it did nothing to defend him from the insects. Putting it into its sheath, he contrived to make the sword belt fit him, although it had never been intended for such a body as his, and with the black sword at his side he walked a very long way through the City of the Inhumi in the company of the man of Vanished People who had given him the sword, and the sheath, and the sword belt.

In his company, I said. Yet it often seemed to the man who bore the black sword that he was alone, and sometimes it seemed to him that there was not a single man of the Vanished People beside him but several. There are things that cannot be counted

because they are too numerous—the waves of the sea and the
leaves in Green's jungles, for example. But there are others that
cannot be counted because they cannot be counted, like the ripples in a pond when it rains. The Vanished People are like that at
times, a single individual counting as many, and many coalescing
into two or three. Or one. At such times it seemed to the man
with the black sword that they stood between mirrors that they
carried with them.

Or rather, that they had stood so once but had stepped away
long ago, and that the doubled and redoubled images they had
left behind had taken on lives of their own.

Cruel saw grass and twisted bushes sprouted from every crack
in the pavements of the streets they traversed, and these became
thicker and thicker, and taller and taller, too, until it seemed
almost that the City of the Inhumi had never been, or that it was
mere illusion; for its distant towers streaked the cloudy sky with
green and gray, but near to hand only the cruel leaves of the saw
grass and the contorted limbs met the eye.

They came to a steep stairway after long walking, and the man
with the black sword, who had supposed that he trod level
ground, was amazed to behold a lower city beneath the City of the
Inhumi, a place of slimes and dank caverns dotted with orange and
purple fungi, through which a broad river wandered, its black
waters as smooth as oil but softly flowing.

"This is the time for wariness," the man of the Vanished People told him.

And another said, "You would be safe from the inhumi, I
assured you, and you were safe. There are things worse than
inhumi here."

Yet another told him, "You have been safe, but you are safe no
longer."

Even as he stood at his side, he saw the one who had given
him his sword descending the stairway before him; and he followed him. There was a walkway beside the river, narrow in places
and narrower yet in others. And in some wholly crumbled away,

leaving only small stones that rolled beneath the feet of the man with the black sword, threatening to carry him into the water.

"How we deceived ourselves!" the man of the Vanished People who had been his guide said. "We thought we were building here for the ages. Another thousand years, and everything you see will be gone."

"How many of us are there?" the man with the black sword asked. He looked about him as he spoke, and saw no one.

"There are two of you," the man of the Vanished People said; and as he did, the man with the black sword saw a corpse face down in the water. He halted then, drew the sword, squatted on the crumbling walkway, and tried to pull the corpse to him with the hooked end of the sword; but he succeeded only in laying open its back, a gaping wound without blood and without pain.

At last, by leaning over the water farther than he dared, he was able to catch the hand of the corpse and move it toward him, but a maggot as thick as his thumb emerged from the cut that he had made, and lifting its blind white head struck at him like a serpent. He jerked backward, nearly falling, then slashed at the maggot and contrived to push away the floating corpse, although the point of his sword sank into it to a depth of four fingers.

"What did you want with your brother?" the man of the Vanished People asked him.

And he said that he had hoped to bury the corpse and pray for the dead man's spirit.

"So I feared. I will not go with you into the sewer you are to clear for us. You must go alone, save for such men as he. Come."

They went on, and saw more corpses floating in the quiet water; and as they walked the city closed itself above the river until the strip of daylight that shone upon the dark water was no wider than the man's hand. "This must be a terrible place at night," he said.

"This is always a terrible place now," the man of the Vanished People told him, "and you are going into a place where it is always night."

As if the voice of the man of the Vanished People had somehow revealed them, the man with the black sword saw eyes, green
eyes and yellow, that studied him unblinking from the shadows
and from the water.

At the point at which the strip of daylight vanished altogether,
there was an altar of bronze and stone. The image behind it was so
worn and battered that the man with the black sword could not
tell whether it had originally taken the form of a man or a woman,
of a beast, a star, or some other thing.

"This was our goddess of purity," the man of the Vanished
People told him.

"Would it help me to pray to her?"

The man of the Vanished People shook his head.

"I will pray to her just the same," the man with the black
sword decided. He knelt and said many things, most of them very
foolish, talking to the Vanished Goddess of purity about his task,
his sons, his wife, and his home across the abyss.

When he rose again, the man of the Vanished People had vanished, but a light gleamed on the Vanished Goddess's cold altar.
The man with the black sword reached out to touch it; he could
not feel it, yet the pressure of his fingers moved it as if it were a
pebble or a stick. He closed his hand around it, and all was dark;
but when he opened his hand the light shone as before. When he
turned toward the water, the green and yellow eyes that had
gleamed from it sank beneath it, and when he turned toward the
land, the green and yellow eyes that had watched him so hungrily
winked out.

How much farther he walked after that, I cannot say. He was
tired already and stopped often to rest, the way was hard, and each
time he took a hundred strides it seemed to him that he had traveled very far.

At last he came upon a naked old man who was gnawing on a
human foot. The old man looked up at the sound of his approach,
and the man with the black sword saw that he was blind, his eyes
as white and blank as boiled eggs. "Get back!" this old blind man
shouted, and he snatched up a rusty knife and flourished it.

"I must go past you," the man with the black sword told him, "but I will not harm you."

At the sound of his voice, the blind man stopped slashing the air with his knife. "You, you're alive," he said. And he groped for the man with the black sword, although he was well out of reach.

"I am," the man with the black sword said. "Are you afraid that I'm an inhumi? I'm not."

"Same thing happened to me," the blind man told him. "Lost every drop of blood. They thought I was dead and threw me down here."

"Was that long ago?" the man with the black sword asked, and the blind man replied, "I think so."

He no longer knew his name, or the name of the city that had sent him and his companions to Green, only that he had believed someone who had told him that they must go, and that they had fallen into the hands of the inhumi as soon as their lander set down. The man with the black sword ordered him to stand, and when he stood tried to make him straighten up, because he wanted to see how tall he was; but he was no longer able to stand straight.

"I can't help wondering whether you are Auk," the man with the black sword told him. "Auk, a man I used to know, murdered another man called Galada. I never saw Galada but he was very much like you, except that he was not blind."

"I'm not blind," the blind man protested.

"The gods do such things. Does the name Auk mean anything to you?"

"No." The blind man seemed to think for a time.

"Chenille. Do you recognize that name?"

"Chenille?" The blind man turned it over and over in his mouth, muttering, "Chenille. Chenille." At last he said, "No."

The man with the black sword explained his task.

"I can show you," the blind man told him eagerly, and shuffled ahead of him. "It's bad. Very bad." He cackled to himself, and the man with the black sword recalled the mad laughter of certain animals he had known in a similar place.

"Bad," the blind man repeated. "You can't get at the good ones." Abruptly he halted. "You want to get at the good ones, don't you? The nice fresh ones?"

The man with the black sword held the light he had been given so that it shone on the blind man's face then, hoping to read its expression; but it had been gnawed by cancer and evil, and was so hideous that he closed his fist around the light at once.

The bodies of men and women and children filled the waterway to the top, which was much higher than a tall man could have reached. Some were swollen with decay, others rotted almost to skeletons. "They drain them and I take them," the blind man muttered, "but there's no life in them."

The man with the black sword swung it at the leg of a dead woman, and the black blade severed it cleanly at the knee; leg and foot fell at his feet, and he kicked them into the water. To the blind man he said, "They dropped you into this sewer thinking you were dead. I understand that, but why did you remain here?"

The blind man did not reply, pushing past him to finger the clogged corpses, his rusty knife waving like the feeler of some sightless, boneless water creature.

"Take what you want and go," the man with the black sword told him. "I have work to do."

"I want to be here when it happens," the blind man said. "I want to see it."

The man with the black sword made him stand back while he hewed at the corpses, finding that his sword would split the pelvis of a grown man as an axe splits kindling, chopping and slashing until his arm dripped with the reeking fluids of dissolution. At last, when it seemed to him that he had cut to bits at least a hundred corpses, the water that had only seeped and sweated began to trickle and spurt. It was not clean water, yet it seemed clean to him; and laying aside his sword and the light he had been given, he washed his hands in it, and bathed his face.

"It's what's past," the blind man said. "You see that, don't you? It's the past holding on."

"More water's getting through now," the man told him as he took up his black sword again. "A little more water, anyway."

"Water always does."

"This is new water—better water, I think." The man with the black sword picked up his light, which seemed to weigh nothing.

The point of his sword pried free a faceless, battered corpse; it fell upon the walkway on which they stood, and he pushed it into the river with his foot. "I believe that I understand what you mean. It may be that I understand it even better than you do. In the past, this whorl we call Green has belonged to the inhumi. These people came here and supplied them with human blood. That must change." He slashed again and again, laying open the rib cages of his human dead, splitting their skulls and severing their limbs. "The future must be set free here."

As he finished speaking, he felt the blind man's fingers on his back, and knew what they portended. He spun around as the rusty blade drove toward him. He tried to counter it with his black sword, and was struck from behind as the tangled dead gave way at last.

Very far he was carried by the boiling surge, and nearly drowned. When he was able to gain the riverbank, it was a bank lined with trees so immense as to defy description, trees to dwarf towers, whose mammoth limbs and innumerable, whispering leaves hid the towers of the City of the Inhumi from his sight, and whose topmost leaves were among the stars.

"That was no story to tell at table, Incanto," Inclito's mother informed me. "I could scarcely eat a mouthful." She cut a piece from her slice of veal with unnecessary violence, then cut that into two smaller pieces.

I apologized very sincerely.

"Was it just a story?" Mora demanded. "Do you just make it up?"

I was hungry, and until then I had been unable even to taste the food Inclito had heaped onto my plate. I shrugged and began to eat.

"No one said that all the stories tonight had to be true," his mother told her granddaughter. "It was just that your friend Fava began with a true one."

Fava herself smiled charmingly. "All stories are false, and none are falser than those that are supposed to be true. The lie adds a second lair of falsity."

Mora turned to look at her. "Even yours?"

"Even mine, though I made mine as true as I could. The question somebody ought to ask is why Incanto chose to tell that particular story tonight." Fava raised a fragment of boiled potato to her mouth and put it down again. "I'll ask, if no one else does. But it would be better if your father did it."

Inclito grunted, chewed, and swallowed. "What about yours, Fava? Why'd you tell us about that poor sprat you found in the mountain stream?"

"Because it was the best that I could think of just then," Fava told him, "and I was first and had to think quickly. Your strego had plenty of time in which to think, and he's much too clever to tell that story merely to win the game."

Inclito's mother said severely, "It's very impolite of you to call Incanto a strego, Fava, when he's denied it. He is our guest."

Mora said, "If Papa won't ask, I will. Why did you tell us that story, Incanto?"

I sipped my wine as I considered my answer. "All the stories tonight have been about duty, or that was how it seemed to me. You were miserable in your palaestra, and Fava thought it her duty to help you, as she did. In her own story, she thought it her duty to rescue the child from his mother, and to look for him when he disappeared."

Inclito nodded. "Mano did his duty, and he was a man who would murder his own brother. There's something I want to ask Fava about that story of hers, though. The boy, Fava. What was it you called him? Bricco. At the end you said he'd never come back to his family?"

Fava nodded.

"But those other sprats, the ones he used to play with, they saw him every so often. They said the Vanished People had stolen him?"

Fava nodded again.

"Well, when they saw him, did the Vanished People bring him back?"

She laughed—a good, merry laugh that left me feeling entirely certain that she was more mature than she appeared. "I should have asked them that. I don't know. Perhaps he escaped from them every now and then, and tried to return to his family and his old life."

"But he couldn't," I remarked. By that time I felt certain I had been right about her.

Inclito pursued the topic. "There was one of them with the man in Incanto's story. This Bricco sounds like one himself, like he had joined them, almost."

Fava nodded. "That was why the other children associated him with them, I feel sure."

Mora said, "There aren't any, are there, Papa? That's what you always say."

"There are stories." He helped himself to more veal. "We heard one tonight."

"There are the old houses," Mora said. "Not like ours, but old houses of theirs that nobody wants." Her slow speech may have given her words more weight than she intended. "People see those, and at night they see travelers camping in them, and they imagine there's a town full of them that we can't find."

"Incanto believes in them," her father declared. "What do you know about them, Incanto?"

His mother reached across him to prod my arm. "Do eat something. Why, you've hardly touched your food."

To satisfy her I swallowed another bite. "I've been fasting up until this meal. What I've eaten already is more than enough for me."

"You didn't talk about my story." It was her accusatory tone again. "You said all the stories had been about duty. Mine was about ghosts and witchcraft."

"In that case I was mistaken. I apologize, humbly and contritely."

Mora asked, "Do you believe in witchcraft, Incanto? In stregas and stregos, like my grandmother? In ghosts?"

"I believe in ghosts." I recalled Hyacinth's ghost and its effect upon Pig very vividly, but I chose not to mention that memory. "The best man I've ever known told me once, long ago, that he had seen one, the ghost of an elderly man with whom he had lived and whom he had assisted. He wouldn't have lied to me—or to anybody, if he could help it—and he was a careful observer."

I spoke to Inclito's mother. "It was Turco's ghost who did his duty, or that was how it seemed to me. Turco felt that it was his duty as your husband to protect you from Casco, and from two men whom he feared were like Casco, or might become like him. You didn't see that in either of them?"

She shook her head, and I said, "The dead must look at people differently."

Inclito nodded. "I think so too. Men and women, it's the same. A girl is crazy about some man. Her mother likes him too, but she won't say so. Her father knows he's a loafer and a thief. I see it all the time."

Mora told me, "You haven't answered Papa's question about the Vanished People yet, and you haven't said anything about witches. If you believe in ghosts, you have to believe in witches, too."

"I believe that there are people who are called witches by others," I said. "Some of them may find it to their advantage to help the belief in witchcraft along."

Mora said, "Then you believe in witches but not in witchcraft," and Fava tittered.

"You may put it like that if you want. I think it's fair. May I ask you a question about your story, Mora? You said that the giant's daughter did badly in her lessons, I believe—or at least you seemed to imply it. Did she do badly in all her subjects? Or only in some."

"The story's over now," Mora declared.

Fava put in, "I know a girl who gets the answer before the teacher does."

"In arithmetic? I thought so. There are people who do not know all the good qualities they possess. Mora is one, I believe."

Seeing that Inclito's mother was about to speak again, I added, "The man who warned Casco was a strego, a male witch, if you like. How he got into the orchard I do not know, but from what our hostess said it certainly cannot have been difficult. As for warning a man about to desecrate a grave, no great amount of wisdom is required to know that no good can come of such things. If the adder had not bitten Casco, he would have been ostracized when what he had done became widely known."

There were nods all around the table.

I said, "I've been called wise several times tonight. I know that I am not, but I'm wise enough to know that strong emotions of any kind often make people act very foolishly. I include myself. When the emotion is a good one—love, for example—they are often foolish in admirable ways. Anger, hatred and greed lead to acts of the kind we heard about in our hostess's story."

Inclito nodded again and swallowed. "Greed for foreign cards, you mean."

"That and food," I told him. "I had resolved to eat very little tonight, and look at this." While we had been talking, I had practically cleaned my plate. "And various other things as well."

He pointed with his table knife. "You believe in the Vanished People."

"Because I put one in my story? It was only a story, as I told you from the beginning."

"Because Mora keeps trying to get you to say you don't, and you won't."

I conceded that he was right. "There's another continent on the other side of the sea. Do you know about it? I realize that we're far from the sea here."

"Must be," Inclito said, "or the backside of this one." He traced a circle through the gravy on his plate.

"People there call the Vanished People the Neighbors. They

are conscious of living beside them, and the name they give them reflects that."

I drew breath, conscious of having eaten too much, and conscious, too, that there was more food to come, although I was resolved not to touch it. "As for me, I have walked with them, and sat with them around their fire. Thus I know that they exist. They have gone elsewhere—found a new home circling another short sun. But they have our permission to revisit this one whenever they choose."

Fava's eyebrows went up. "Who gave them permission?" At that moment I was only too conscious that those full, fair eyebrows were in reality nothing more than smudges of color drawn across her forehead.

"I did."

"Have you been there?" Mora wanted to know. "To the continent on the other side of the sea?"

Studying her broad, coarse face, so earnest and intent, I realized that she was not nearly so unhandsome as I had at first thought. Her features suffer in comparison to Fava's, and she is more than a trifle over-fleshed even for her not inconsiderable stature; but there is a hint and more of her grandmother's beauty behind the big, hooked nose and the wide mouth. "What difference does it make whether I say that I have or that I have not?" I asked her. "If I've lied to you about sitting with the Neighbors at their fire, I would lie about my travels, too, wouldn't I? Fishermen lie about their fish, and travelers about the foreign towns they have visited—or at least we travelers certainly have that reputation."

Fava burst out, "What were you called before you came here and became Incanto?"

"Rajan," I told her. "I've had other names, but I think that's the one you're looking for."

She leaned toward me, so intent on impressing me with her sincerity that she actually allowed her blue-green eyes to glitter in the candlelight. "I'm not looking for you, Incanto. I mean that."

"You *are* a strego!" Inclito's mother exclaimed.

I said, "I am not, madam. But I intend to cure you if I can. If someone will furnish me with paper when this excellent meal is over, I'll write out some instructions for you. They will not be difficult, and if you follow them exactly as I set them down I believe that you will soon notice an improvement in your condition."

What happened next was so farcical that I hesitate to tell it. Oreb darted through an open window, circled the table, and settled on my shoulder, croaking, "Bird back!" and "Bad thing!"

5

IN GREEN'S JUNGLE

Atteno the stationer has let me stay in his shop again tonight, and furnished me with a pallet he bought today for my sake, a pillow, sheets, and three blankets; but I slept so much yesterday (in a barrel in the alley when the shop was open) that I find I am unable to get to sleep tonight. Unable as yet, I should write.

So here I sit in my usual place in the shopwindow, burning Atteno's oil in his lamp and writing on paper I have appropriated from him, having used up all he gave me earlier while I finished describing Inclito's dinner of night-before-last. It was the most I have ever written in a single sitting, to the best of my memory. Even when my wife and I were composing our book about Silk, I never wrote so long a time without some sort of break or interruption, or wrote so much.

Not a lot has happened since Oreb burst in upon us, although I have received two letters. My friend the shopkeeper (I have got to find some way to repay him for the paper I have taken) was delighted. "People of quality write letters," he declared as he endeavored to conceal his pleasure. "It's the mark of quality, and a good education." No one in Blanko can set pen to paper without putting the little squares of silver they term "cardbits" here into his pocket, and he is very conscious of it. Since I began this rambling account of my journey back to the *Whorl* by copying what I remembered of the letter from Pajarocu into it, I will copy them out here as well.

Two young men with huge dogs on leashes just walked past the shop; seeing me behind these panes of bull's-eye glass, they saluted. They had slug guns slung across their backs in the fashion I saw our troopers in Gaon use. I returned their salutes—and at once, without the mumbling of a single spell or the offering of some poor, sad monkey's life to Thelxiepeia, I was fifteen again, and by no means the youngest of General Mint's Volunteers. Once a trooper, always a trooper. No doubt Spider felt the same way, or much more so. We ought to have put something of that in our book, but it is too late now.

War looms—not only for Blanko, but for me. To give myself due credit, I never imagined that by leaving Evensong and her pretty little boat on the Nadi I would throw them off indefinitely. A week? Ten days, perhaps, although it seemed much longer. Very well, I have fought them before, and in place of a slug gun and the black-bladed sword I have Hyacinth's azoth. Let them beware.

I have drawn the three whorls just as I used to in Gaon. Not because I have been away, or slept, or made love to any woman. No, merely because I ceased writing for an hour or so to play with Oreb and wrestle my conscience. But midnight has come and gone—I heard the clocks strike.

How much do I owe my devil-son? I swore I would not tell, and I will not. But what constitutes telling? If I were to take down the big bar on the door and go out into the street, stop a passerby, and explain everything to him as I would like to, that would be telling beyond all doubt. But what if I were to write it here? Who would ever read it?

Fava's letter was badly folded and sealed with a blurred

impression of a flower. If this were New Viron, it would surely be her name-flower. Here I cannot say. A wide-petaled, short-stemmed flower badly stamped into pink wax. She did not trust poor Mora to do it for her, clearly.

She is a fellow-pupil at Mora's palaestra, they say, and a very bright one. No doubt she is, but she cannot do well in penmanship, unless she has discovered some cheat beyond my imagining. Both of them wear masks for Mora's family, I believe: Fava is by definition brilliant in all of their classes, and Mora is by definition slow or worse. But it cannot be that simple. Mora would write a small hand, very neat, if I am any judge of women's characters.

She came to the barrel in which I slept in a simple gown, such as she must wear to her palaestra; and yet she wore such small and childish jewelry as she had, and scent, too. What ran through her head as she thus dressed herself to visit me? I can only guess.

First the gown. It was a palaestra day, and she was not quite sure that she could nerve herself to miss her classes. Alternately, she hoped to find me quickly and come late to palaestra. She would merely have been marked tardy in that case, perhaps.

Perhaps. It was a favorite word of Patera Silk's, and I try to avoid it for that reason. What right have I (I ask myself) to Silk's words? Yet I have striven to pattern myself on him in many other ways, most of all in his way of thinking. Can I think like Silk without employing the words he did? If in fact I thought more like Silk, I would have thought of that much sooner. It is nothing to say, "I will be logical." It is everything to be logical, provided that I act from good motives.

Good motives cannot excuse bad actions, as I told Mora. I was stern—I hope not too stern. I know what she is going through, poor child.

And she is a child. "I won't ask you to disrobe," I said, "because it doesn't matter whether I know. You'll know if I'm right, and that's enough."

She nodded solemnly, sitting cross-legged on the bare ground in front of my barrel, with her clean blue gown spread over her knees. Several persons saw us talking there. What must they have thought?

"The time of maturity varies between individuals. For a few it may be as early as eleven, and there are a few for whom it comes after eighteen. In general, the larger the individual the slower the onset."

I paused to let that sink in.

"In speaking of the size of the individual, I mean weight as well as stature. You are of large stature. You are aware of it, from what I've seen." (I dodged the word *perhaps.*) "You may even be too acutely aware of it. You are also fleshy, as I am. I try to fight it, though for other reasons. I am not telling you that you must fight it, too. If you are satisfied—"

She shook her head.

"Then you can correct it. If you succeed, you will be a woman sooner. Talk to your grandmother about what it means to be a woman. There will be a flow of blood, and if you are not prepared you may find it deeply unsettling."

She nodded. "Do you think someday I might . . . ?" She dropped her gaze to the ground between us.

"Good girl!" Oreb assured me.

"You're still too young to be concerned with marriage," I told her. "But yes, I do."

She looked up, and her shy smile was gold.

"Mora, you envy beautiful women. That is natural, but—"

"Like Fava."

"Fava is not a beautiful woman, or even a pretty girl, which is what she pretends to be. You and I know what Fava is."

I waited for her to protest. When she did not, I said, "It is only natural for you to envy them. It's foolish, but it does no harm. You must be careful, however, that your envy does not turn to hatred."

She nodded, her face serious. "I'll try."

"Bear in mind always that they may envy you."

"My family, you mean. My father." Her voice held an edge of bitterness.

"You believe that you would be happier if your father were not rich, if you were not his only child, and if he did not love you as he does. Believe me, Mora, you are wrong."

"He wants you to stay with us."

"I know. He pressed me to last night."

"Why didn't you?"

"Because I wasn't sure I would be welcome."

"Grandmother thinks you're wonderful! Probably you didn't see it, but she kept telling Papa to make you stay, the way she looked at him and the things she said."

"I did see it, Mora. And hear it, too. It wasn't your grandmother's welcome that concerned me."

She was baffled. "Papa's going to write you a letter. He said so."

"I would prefer one from you."

The solemn nod again. "When I get back home."

"Fava will try to dissuade you, I feel sure."

"I won't tell her." She fell silent, then burst out, "They'll burn her if they find out."

I tried to make my voice noncommittal. "In that case, she is foolish to remain."

"Are you going to tell Papa? He'll burn her himself. He hates them."

"Most people do. I may tell him, or I may not. Certainly I won't unless I find it necessary."

"Don't you hate them, too?" Beneath their heavy, dark brows her eyes were puzzled.

"No," I said. "Mora, I have been to Green, and I have come back. I know that's hard for you to credit, but it is the truth. I have."

Trying to be helpful, Oreb added, "Good Silk!"

She ignored him. "They say the inhumi kill everybody that goes there."

"I know they do. They're wrong. Haven't you asked her about it?"

Mora's voice fell to a whisper. "We don't talk about that."

"You don't talk about her real nature?"

Mora shook her head, unwilling to meet my eyes.

"How is it that you know?"

"I guessed."

"Have you ever seen her when she wasn't—Fava?"

Mora's "No" was whispered, too. Much louder: "*I don't want to.*"

"I don't blame you. Mora, there was an inhumu who was a son to me. Can you believe that?"

"No," she repeated.

"That, too, is the truth. For a long while you did not so much as suspect what Fava was, and for still longer you must have been unsure. It wasn't like that for me. I was in real and imminent danger of death, and he helped me and let me see him as he was. I was so badly frightened that it did not seem strange to me."

"I was in trouble, too."

"I know you were, and that's one reason I don't want Fava burned. One of many."

"It's hard for me to think of you being afraid of anything. Were you really?"

I cast my mind back to the pit; it seemed very long ago. "I was resigned to death by then, I believe. I had lost hope, or almost lost it, yet I was very frightened."

"You said I had to make her go away."

I nodded.

"But this one helped you."

I nodded again. "Then and afterward. He stayed with me, you see. With us. Others saw him as a boy about your age, Mora. I saw the inhumu. That was a part of our agreement—that he would not deceive me as he deceived others. When my real son and I went aboard the lander that would carry us to Green, he boarded it too. I hated him then, just as I had come to hate him while we were on my sloop. Brave men taunt the things they fear, Mora, and he did too."

"She's not afraid of me."

"She should be. You said that if you told your father, he would have her burned alive."

"He'd burn her himself, only she knows I won't. How did you find out?"

"From the story she told, first of all. There was an undercurrent in it, a stream of things left unsaid. Your father sensed it just as I did, though he may not have been conscious of it. He was puzzled because the little boy in the story did not go back to his family, remember?"

Mora nodded.

"We were supposed to believe he was afraid that the mother who had set out to kill him in her desperation would try to kill him again. That didn't ring true, and your father rejected it out of hand, as I did. A boy too young to know his own name could have had only the vaguest notion of his mother's intention, and would have forgotten the entire incident in a day or two. Then Fava suggested that he got away from the Vanished People, who periodically recaptured him. That was ridiculous and made the real answer obvious, as ridiculous solutions frequently do."

Mora nodded again.

"What was the real answer? I won't tell you, Mora. You have to tell me."

Tears coursed down the big, rounded cheeks. "I don't think it happened at all."

Oreb muttered, "Girl cry."

"I think Fava made it up!"

We sat in silence for some time after that. At last I said, "You have a good mind, Mora, and when someone has a good mind it can be painful not to use it."

She sobbed openly then, into her hands at first and afterward into a clean handkerchief, far too small, that she took from a pocket of her gown. When her shoulders no longer heaved, I said, "Krait, the inhumu I loved as a son, told me once that we are their cattle. It's not true, but on Green they have tried to make it true. It doesn't work very well. We milk our cattle, and butcher them when it suits us. But we don't milk them to death in our greed. Last night someone asked why I told the story I did."

"It was Fava." Mora wiped her face with her handkerchief,

and when that proved ineffectual, with her sleeve. "You told it so she'd know you knew."

"I did not, because I wasn't certain then. I told it—in part, at least—to find out whether anyone else suspected Fava as I did."

Mora shook her head.

"You're right. No one did. Your expressions told me that you knew and that Fava knew you did, and that neither your father nor your grandmother, whom your friend Fava has been slowly killing, suspected her of being what we know she is."

Mora had whispered earlier. This time her voice was softer than a whisper, so soft that I cannot be certain that I heard her correctly. I believe that she was saying, "I'll be all alone now."

I tried to be as gentle as I could. "There are much worse things than being alone, Mora. You're living through one of them at this moment."

Having written that, it occurs to me that this was why the Outsider sent the leatherskin when I was alone on the sloop and prayed for company. He wished me to learn that loneliness is not the worst evil, so I might teach it to Mora.

How lonely it must be to be a god!

When Krait lay dying in the jungle, I offered my arm, telling him that he could have my blood if it would strengthen him, or even if it would just make death easier.

"I never fed from you."

"I know." My eyes were as full of tears then as poor Mora's were this afternoon. I felt myself an utter fool.

"It would make you weak," he told me, "without making me stronger."

Then I remembered that Quetzal had been full of blood when he had been shot by Siyuf's troopers, but had died just the same about two days later.

"Do you know why we drink blood, Horn?"

"You must eat." That, at least, is what I now believe that I said, with something about the short digestive tract. I may also have said that every living creature must eat something, even if it is no more than air and sunshine. I believe I did.

"On the night we met, I drank your hus's blood."

"I remember."

"It made a beast of me until I fed again. We feed to share your lives, to feel as you feel."

"Then feed of me," I said, and I offered my arm as before.

The tips of his fingers slid along its skin, leaving thin red lines that wept tears of blood. "There's another reason. Swear. Swear now that if I tell you, you'll never tell anybody else."

I promised I would not. I am not sure now just what it was I said.

"You've got to swear . . ."

I leaned closer to hear him, my ear at his mouth.

"Because I have to tell you, Father, so I can die. Swear."

And I did. It was the oath that Silk had taught me aboard the airship. I will not set it down.

Krait told me, and we talked together until I understood the secret and what had happened almost twenty years ago; then Krait, seeing that I understood everything, clasped my hand and begged my blessing before he died; and I blessed him. I recall his face very clearly; it was as though Sinew himself were dying, forced by some mad god to wear a serpent mask. I saw the serpent face, but I sensed the human face behind it.

At the moment of death, it seemed to me that the mighty trees bent over Krait as I did—that he was in some sense their son as well as in some sense mine. I was conscious of their trailing lianas as female presences, wicked women in green gowns with gray and purple moths upon their brown shoulders and orchids flaming in their hair. Looking up in wonder, I saw only vines and flowers, and heard only the mournful voices of the brilliantly colored birds that glide from tree to tree; but the moment that I looked down at Krait again the green-gowned women and the brutal giants who supported them returned, mourners sharing my sorrow.

If ever you read this, Sinew, you will not believe it, I know. You have nothing but contempt for impressions at odds with what you consider simple truth. But my truth is not yours any more than your mother's is. Once I watched a mouse scurry across the floor of a room in the palace I occupied as Rajan of Gaon. To the mouse, that room with its cushions, thick carpets, and ivory-inlaid table was a wilderness, a jungle. It may be that as Krait lay dying the Outsider permitted me to share Krait's thoughts to some degree, and to see Green's jungle as Krait himself did.

To see it as our blood allowed him to see it.

That insight was never again as strong as at the moment of his death, but it never left me entirely as long as I remained on Green. You feared that jungle, I know; so did I at times. Yet what a beautiful place it was, with its capes of moss and trickling waters! The boles of the great trees stood like columns—but what architect could give us columns to stand as those trees do in their millions of millions, individual and despotic, ancient and majestic?

After writing that last, I blew out the lamp, let Oreb fly and reclosed the window, and slept for a few hours. Now it is morning. Early morning, I believe, since the shopkeeper has not yet come down. Dawn's clear, cool light fills the street outside. I would take up my staff and stroll the avenues of Blanko now if I could, but I would have to leave the shop unlocked, which would be a poor return for the owner's kindness; so I have taken up my pen instead.

Wait while I reread what I wrote last night.

There are various matters left unfinished, I see—most obviously, the letters; it was late and I was tired. Here they are. Inclito writes large, his broad-nibbed quill swooping and slashing as it lays a thick trail of jet-black ink.

Incanto, My Dear Brother—
You did not believe me when I told you I want you to

stay with us. Mother says for me to urge you. Is this urging
enough?

Stay with us. I say it, and so does she. She has prepared a
room for you with her own hands. She will drive me mad.

So pack your things and come—

Anyone in town will bring you, or lend you a horse.

If you are not here by afternoon, I will come after you
myself.

Inclito

Fava writes a shaky scrawl, some words too distorted almost
for me to make out.

To Incanto at the stationer's on Water Street
Rajan,

What I said last night is true this morning. You know me
better than anyone, that is why I hate to quarrel with you.
Wait outside the academy this afternoon and tell me that we
are friends. I will be so happy!!! If you like, you could even
ride out to Mora's with us, there is plenty of room and
Inclito and Salica will be delighted, and you could reassure
yourself. She is following all of your instructions, but there is
no need of it. Do you understand me, Rajan?

Your loyal
friend forever,
Fava

I have given a good deal of my conversation with Mora, but in
bits and pieces; I had to do it like that because some of it was
so personal (I mean, for her) that it would have been wrong
for me to write it down. Just the same, it is choppier than it had to
be, and there are things I should have set down that I have left out.

She said, "Grandmother goes on and on about what a miserable thing marriage is and how terrible it was for her. She's been
married five times and outlived all her husbands. Papa's father
wasn't even the last one. To hear her tell it, it's awful being mar-

ried and being widowed is worse, and I know she's saying all that because she thinks I'll never be married and she doesn't want me unhappy. But I'm unhappy anyway."

I told her, "Married couples must endure a great deal of unhappiness, Mora. So do single people. There is also a great deal of happiness in both states. That being so, what is the point of blaming the married state or the unmarried state? Or praising either one?" As I spoke, I thought of Maytera Mint; but I said nothing about her.

"I want to get married."

"Do you, Mora? Really?"

"Yes, as soon as I can. I want somebody who will love me always."

"Good girl," Oreb remarked.

"Your father and grandmother love you, but you blame them for your unhappiness."

She was silent for some time after I said that; I could see that she was thinking, and I let the silence grow.

"If I were more like the other girls, the town girls, they'd like me more."

"Or less. If you lived here in town, as they do, your size and strength, your slow speech and quick mind, and the strong, sensual face that you will possess when you are a woman would affront them at every turning. Your father likes me, and because he does, all the townsfolk treat me with respect. Would I be respected as much if I had been born three streets from here?"

She shook her head.

"You don't feel that life has treated you fairly. That is not a question. Everything you've said this morning confirms it. Your mother died while you were still an infant, I know, and that is hard, very hard. I sympathize with you deeply and sincerely because of it. But in every other respect your lot is far above the average."

"I don't think so!"

"Naturally you don't. Almost no one does. What would be fair, Mora?"

"For everyone to be even."

"Everyone is. Listen carefully, please. If you won't listen now, you may as well go. Last night someone told me that you could outrun all the other girls, that when you run races at your palaestra you always win. I suppose that it was Fava—"

"Bad thing!" (This from Oreb.)

"Who must run very poorly."

Mora said, "She doesn't run at all. There's something the matter with her legs, so she's excused."

"Are the races fair, and do you win them?"

Mora nodded.

"What makes them fair?"

"Everybody starts even."

"But some girls can run faster than the others, so they're bound to win. Don't you see how unfair that must seem to the losers? Mora, there is only one rule in life, and it applies to everyone equally—to me, to you, to all the girls at your palaestra, and even to Fava. It is that each of us is entitled to use everything we are given. Your father was given size and strength, and a good mind. He used them, as he was entitled to, and if anyone is the worse for it, he has no right to complain; your father played by the rule."

"Papa helps poor people."

"Good man!"

I nodded. "That doesn't surprise me. Some of them resent it, but he helps them anyway."

Her eyes opened a trifle wider. "How did you know that?"

"When some people are in pain, they strike out at any target within their reach, that's all. If you haven't learned it yet, you'll learn it soon. We all do."

"Have I been doing that?"

"That is for you to decide. I have been a judge, Mora, but I am not a judge here. Before I talk to you seriously—and I have serious things to say to you—I want you to consider this: Suppose that instead of being as you are, you were the small and pretty girl whom Fava appears to be. Don't you think it's possible that your father might doubt that you were really his? And that your life would be a great deal less happy if he did?"

She was silent again, the large, plump hands motionless in her lap, her head bowed. At last she said, "I never thought of it."

"You will think about it now, I know."

To say what I wanted to say next was to risk the life of the girl before me, and I knew it; I waited until I felt certain I could suppress the tremor in my voice.

"Mora, I used to know a woman named Scleroderma. She was quite short. You are already much taller than she was. She was also fat, a great deal fatter than you are, and not at all good-looking. People made jokes about her, and she laughed the loudest at them, and made jokes about herself—about others, too, to tell you the truth. All of us thought that she was very funny, and most of us liked her and felt a little superior to her."

"I'd feel sorry for her," Mora said.

"Perhaps you would. War came, and Scleroderma acquired a needler. I don't know how, and it doesn't matter. She did. And when we who had lived in the Sun Street Quarter had to fight, Scleroderma fought like a trooper. It isn't good for a trooper to be over forty, or short, or fat. It isn't good at all, and she was all of those things; but she fought like a trooper just the same."

As I said that, something came into Mora's eyes that told me I was in fact running the risk I feared.

"There were many women with us who had known her all their lives, and some of them were shamed into fighting too, though none of the rest showed her determined courage. I was almost precisely as old as you are when all this happened, and there was a girl named Nettle there with me who was my own age. Nettle had fought earlier—we both had—and she said then what both of us felt, which was that General Mint might easily have put Scleroderma in command of fifty or a hundred troopers."

"Women don't fight here," Mora told me, "or not very much."

I smiled. "They fight only with their husbands, you mean. I know they must, because women everywhere do that. Scleroderma did more than fight, though I have mentioned the fighting first because it was what she did first. The troopers we were fighting were brave and well trained. They had slug guns, and some had armor. It wasn't long before some of us were dead and many of us were wounded. It was Scleroderma who went for our wounded under fire and bandaged their wounds, and carried or dragged them to a safe place. I know that very well, Mora, because I was one of the wounded she rescued."

"I'd like to meet her."

"We will both meet her in time, I hope. She is dead now. But long after that fighting was over, when we were here on Blue and I helped her and her husband build their new house, she told me her secret. It's a simple one, but if you'll make it your own it may serve you well. She said she thought about what there was to do. What would be hardest, what next hardest, what followed that, and so on. Then she decided which level was within her reach, how difficult a task she could manage. Mora, do you understand what I'm saying? She ranked the tasks mentally."

"I think so."

"She might decide that dragging the logs to the spot where her new house was to stand was the hardest, for example. That felling the trees was next hardest, and so on. And that both those would be too strenuous for her. Shaping the logs and boring the holes for the pegs were both too difficult, too; but she could cut small limbs for pegs and smooth them with a knife. That wouldn't be too hard for her."

Mora nodded. "Sometimes I do that, too."

"Then she went to the level above that one, and bored the holes."

The next nod came slowly, but it came.

"Blanko will be at war very soon, Mora. Your father thinks so, and he's got a level head and a good grasp of the situation here. I'm not going to tell you that you'll be loved as you wish if you do as Scleroderma did, or even as Nettle did. You may not be—and I honestly believe you'll be loved like that no matter what you do. But if you do what Scleroderma did, you'll deserve to be, which is something quite different. It is far easier to get all the good things that our lives have to offer than it is to deserve them. We seldom have much joy of them, however, unless we deserve them."

"I don't know if I could," Mora muttered. Then, "I'll try."

"You'll be risking your life. I'm sure you understand that. What is far worse from my viewpoint, I am risking it just by talking to you as I am now. You may be killed. But Mora . . ."

"Yes?"

"You may be killed no matter what you do. Not everyone who runs risks dies, and many who try very hard to avoid every risk are killed anyway. You're the daughter of one of Blanko's leaders—"

"He's the Duko. They don't call him that, but he is."

"Things won't be easy for you if Blanko loses. Now go to your palaestra. You're very late already, I'm sure. My blessing goes with you, for whatever it's worth."

Oreb seconded me. "Go now. 'Bye, girl."

"About Fava . . . Does she really, *really* have to leave?"

I nodded. "For your grandmother's sake, for her own sake, and for yours."

Reluctantly, Mora rose. "She's the only friend I've got."

"Yes, I know. And as long as she is with you, she's the only friend you can have. Possibly you haven't thought of it like that; but Fava has, you may be sure. Another friend might guess the truth, as you did. Fava will see to it that no one gets that close to the two of you. Isn't she doing it already? You must know, and the story you told last night indicated that she is."

As I watched Mora go, it came to me that I was watching a woman who did not know that she was a woman or had not yet come to terms with the knowledge, a woman whose womanhood was reckoned not in years but in weeks or months—perhaps only in days.

★

★ ★

When we were on Green and I was searching the river for the sword and the light I had been given, I walked up and down the banks of the river for most of a day. I found and saw a great many things without being much affected by any of them. I was looking for my light; I was looking for my sword; and since those other things were neither of them, I paid them little heed. They took their revenge on me just now, waking me wet with sweat. I have dried myself with the towel Inclito's mother gave me, lit the candle, and opened my door. I would like to have company, but Oreb is off exploring and everyone else seems to be asleep. If any of them are awake, perhaps they will drop in for a talk. There is no one in this house, not even the cook, whom I would not like to talk to. The gloomy chambermaid would be best, I believe. Her name is Torda, but Torda is probably too much to hope for.

In the meantime, I am going to write about what I saw and what I dreamed, which comes down to saying the same thing twice. By writing about them, I will subject them to the discipline of my conscious mind. At least I hope so.

The corpses were the first and the most obvious thing. They floated past upon the slow water the whole time I searched, mostly singly, but sometimes by two and threes. I have already written about the first, the one I saw in the water while the Neighbor was still with me. There would be no point in recording the same facts about the rest. I had cleared the blockage enough to raise the level of the river noticeably, and the opening I had made was permitting the water in the sewer to erode dead men (and women and children) as any little flow of water washes away grains of sand. A few of them floated face up. Most were face down, and I was glad of that.

Nothing has happened, except that I have sat here thinking, trying to recall something that I heard Patera Pike read from the Chrasmologic Writings long, long ago. Something about the people Pas put into our Long Sun Whorl multiplying until they were as numerous as grains of sand. Patera Remora has a copy of the Writings, I know. He probably has the quotation by heart, too; it would not even be necessary to ask him to look it up. But what a sad thing it is to try to live by a book written for another time and another whorl! The gods to whom he prays and sacrifices are far away.

Yet he is one of the few good men in New Viron. One of the few good men left, I ought to say. Who is worse off, we who have lost faith in his book, or he who keeps it, faithful without praise and without reward? We are, beyond all question. Better to be good without reason than to be evil for a hundred good reasons.

Can Great Pas really have meant for all this to happen when he inspired one of the Chrasmologic Writers to pen those few words about grains of sand? Can he have foreseen the blocked sewer on Green, and the corpses bursting free in the wave that nearly drowned me? In my dream, the floating corpses motioned to me and spoke, saying the things they had said in life, urging me to buy nails or boots, cheap clothing, and meat pies, blessing me in the names of various gods, and wishing me a good morning, a good afternoon; and it became clear to me that the dead cannot know that they are dead, that if they know it they cannot be dead. Thus all those dead men and women behaved in death as they had in life. It seemed certain that I was dead as well—that it was only because I too was dead and did not know it that I could hear the dead as I did, that I could see them move and speak.

Let me leave my dream for a line or two. I have wondered a good deal about the actions of the Neighbor who released me, gave me my sword (and no doubt the light), and set my task. Why did he want the sewer beneath the City of the Inhumi opened? And why did he want me to do it, and not some other? Why did he not do it himself?

Most important, why would he not permit me to take Sinew with me?

This last is the easiest, I feel sure. I had reached my conclusion long before nightfall, and have never changed it. He wished me to return to the City of the Inhumi and free everyone who had been held with me. If Sinew had been freed too, the two of us would have been much less likely to return for the others, and would, moreover, have shared their gratitude if we did. Freeing them made me their leader.

I had no desire to be, and still less did I wish to risk my life a second time in the City of the Inhumi. I decided, very firmly, and as I thought irrevocably, that I would not return—that I would not allow myself to be so manipulated. Sinew had detested me for years; very well, let him free himself or die. As for the others who had been our companions on He-hold-fire's lander, I did not care a straw for any of them except Krait, who was safe. I resolved that when night came I would abandon the search and make my way down the river until fatigue overcame me, putting as much distance as possible between the City and myself.

The sky, which is nearly always dark on Green, grew darker; and the slumberous silence of river and jungle was violated again and again. I heard splashes and snorts as animals, newly awakened from their day-sleep, came to drink, and from across the river (which was by no means wide) the breaking of bones as some beast fed upon a stranded corpse. With my mind's eyes, I saw the blind man crouching on the bank, an arm between his jaws.

And I set off downriver, as I had resolved to do.

In my dream tonight, however, that moment never came. I had found gems, or at least smooth stones that seemed gems, in the sand in the hollow of an abrupt bend in the channel. After pocketing a few I ignored the rest, having hoped to find my light there. In my dream they were jewels indeed, jewels as big as pullet's eggs, sparkling from a hundred facets. At the opposite point, where the strengthened current washed away the earth of the bank, I had glimpsed squared stones and shards of pottery among the roots. In my dream, these became strange machines and gleaming weapons, objects of unthinkable power and mystery. The dead children taunted me, and begged, "A cardbit, sir? Just one cardbit," urged on by Scylla.

Or at least, I believe now that those strange machines and weapons must exist only in my dream tonight, as fictive as Scylla and the speaking dead. It may have been, however, that they were actually present, that I saw them and ignored them, refusing to recognize them for what they were; but that my memory has stored them up, and now recalls them to torment me for my neglect. What might we find if we were to dig for those treasures near buildings such as this rambling house of Inclito's?

Tonight, when we told stories around the dinner table, I discovered to my utter astonishment and her consternation that I could enter into Fava's, seeing everything she described and more, and changing the course of her tale. (I must remember to describe all that here.) If there is more to tales than I have ever believed, may there not be more to dreams, too? I will not say that there are treasures in the ruins here because I dreamed them. Madness lies in all such assumptions. But may not they be there, just as my sword was concealed in a wall? (Better yet, as the silver cup must have been hidden somewhere in the ruined Neighbor house near Gaon.) And may I not find some because of my dream?

For a moment at least I had the company I have been wishing for. The kitchen maid, fully dressed, with tousled hair and the indescribable expression of a woman who has been satisfied in love, appeared in my doorway to ask whether I would not like something to eat. Without answering her question, I demanded to know why she was awake at such an hour.

She said that it was necessary for her to rise very early to help the cook make bread, so that we could have freshly baked bread at breakfast, which my host's mother insists upon whenever there is company.

I remarked that she could not get much sleep in that case, asked where she had slept. It struck home. She colored, her cheeks (fuller even than Mora's) blushing so dark a red that I could not miss it even by candlelight, and said that she slept in the kitchen. "I'm going there now."

I refrained from asking from where.

"So I can get you something very easily, Master Incanto, if you want anything, sir."

I told her that I did not, and she fled. The other maid is slender and more attractive.

*   *   *

I have tried to sleep again, but it is perfectly useless. The nightmare river waits in my mind, ready to pounce the moment my eyes
close, its dead people voicing their dead greetings and its dead
children crying out to me for help. I do not mean that I dreamed
it again. I cannot have, since I did not sleep. But it filled my
thoughts most unpleasantly.

Not half a minute after I sat up again, in came the kitchen
maid with this tray. This time I was able to speak with her somewhat longer, although she seemed more frightened than ever. Her
name is Onorifica, she is the fourth child of seven, and her father
owns a smaller, poorer farm nearby. He has bought three heifers
(Onorifica says very good ones) from Inclito, and is paying for
them with three years' labor from his daughter.

"It's not near as bad as you're thinking, sir. I get plenty to eat
and my clothes, and presents sometimes." She showed me a silver
ring and a bracelet she thinks is gold. It is actually brass if I am any
judge, and was probably made in Gaon, where you can see a thousand like it on any market day. "And I'll get in a nap after breakfast, sir. Cook and I both will."

I asked her about the others. Decina, the cook, is a permanent
servant, paid in foodstuffs that she trades for whatever other
things she may require. The coachman and the other farm laborers
are paid in the same fashion, and all take a wagon into Blanko once
a month to trade for whatever they want or need.

Torda, the other maid, is a distant relation of Inclito's. "A
cousin?" I suggested.

"She'd like you to think it, sir. Madame's brother's son was
married to her mother. I think that's the way of it. Only he got
killed in a war, and she married somebody else, and that when
she"—she meant Torda—"got born. It's some story like that, sir.
Anyhow she came here in rags, that's what cook says, expecting to
be treated like Mora, you know. Only they was always fighting.
That was how it was when I came and I've got to go."

This tray she brought me holds a cup and saucer, a little pot of
very good tea, sugar whiter than I was accustomed to in Gaon,

half a lemon, and enough cherry tarts for four or five persons. I am drinking the tea, but I intend to leave the tarts for Oreb. That business about fresh bread for breakfast suggests a substantial meal.

Looking back over what I wrote an hour ago, I find my speculations on the motives of the Neighbor on Green who recruited me to clean his sewer. Let us try another, one I think deeper and more difficult.

Why (I asked) *did he not do it himself?* I am going to propose two theories; neither or both may be correct. The first is that the Neighbors find it hard to move some kinds of objects. So it seems to me after the dealings I have had with them. I do not think that they are *here* in the sense we are, even when they are standing beside us. This is only speculation, but I believe they may be able to move natural objects such as sticks and stones, and things that they themselves made when Blue and Green were their homes, better than other things. The silver cup they gave me (which I am very sorry I left behind), the door the Neighbor opened for me when I was confined on Green, and the sword and light he gave me are all examples. We human beings are native to the Long Sun Whorl, and not to Blue or Green; and so the tangled corpses of so many hundreds of us would have presented a Neighbor with great difficulties, if I am correct.

Second, he wished me to see (and to smell and touch) those bodies. He might have freed me in many ways, and made me the leader of my fellow prisoners in many ways, too. But I cannot think of any other way in which he could have been half so effective. The horror of the inhumi that I had when I set out from the Lizard had been blunted by living with Krait on the sloop. If the Neighbor wanted to renew it as much as it could be renewed, he chose the most effective possible way of doing it.

I believe, however, that his true goal was to give me a realistic understanding of what we faced.

Before moving ahead, I ought to double back to the time after Mora left me. I've written nothing about that.

When I received the letters, it struck me that if I was going to ride out here with Mora and Fava it would be of value to know at what time their palaestra ended. I asked directions and walked over to it, and finding the coachman already waiting for them, I wrote Inclito a note thanking him for his invitation and saying that I could not come that day but hoped to come the next, and asked him to tell his coachman to allow me to ride with Mora and her friend.

The owner of the stationery store had invited me to share his supper; it was a simple meal of bread and soup, and I surprised and pleased him and his wife by eating little of either and amusing them with stories of my journey to Viron with Pig and Hound. Before we ate (as I should have said in the beginning) they asked me to invoke the gods. I blessed our meal in the name of the Outsider, making the sign of addition as solemnly as I would have when I was a boy, and talked about him for a few moments afterward. There is a great hunger for the gods here on Blue, I believe; but without their presence it lacks a focus.

Onorifica came back, perspiring from her bread-making but with her hair in better order. She had appeared frightened when she carried my tray in, her eyes darting around the room; I had thought that she was afraid of Oreb and had assured her that he was gone. This time she seemed more resolute; I made her sit down and offered her one of her own tarts.

"Cook was like to die at me for that, sir." She sat gingerly, picked up a tart in both hands, and nibbled at it like a fat squirrel.

I remained silent.

"She's afraid of you, sir. Swears she won't show her face in the kitchen door as long as you're here."

Of course I said that she had no reason to be, although I wondered how true it was; it seemed barely possible that his cook was the spy Inclito felt certain he was harboring.

"They're afraid of you in town, too, sir. Terrible afraid's what I hear."

I asked whether she had been there, and when she said she had not, how she knew.

"Coachman says, sir." She paused, worried (I believe) that she might be getting her informant into trouble. "He's got to come straight back after he drops them off in the morning, sir, and he does."

"But in the afternoon he has time to—" *Gossip* clearly would not do. "Talk to people there, assuming that he arrives a little early."

"That's right, sir."

"When I rode out here, Onorifica, Mora and Fava told me that their teachers had been quizzing them about me all day."

She chewed and swallowed. "I think so, sir."

"They also said that they'd given me a good character, and told everyone I was perfectly harmless. That last is quite true, and I'd like to think that the first is, too—though I know better."

"Is that all they said, sir?"

I shook my head. "They said quite a lot, Fava particularly. But that's all they told me that they had told their teachers."

"Mora wouldn't lie to you, sir."

"I'm delighted to hear it." I would have been even more delighted if I had believed it.

"But that Fava! Don't you trust her, sir."

I promised I would not.

"Looks like butter wouldn't melt in her mouth. Well, Master don't trust her, let me tell you. I've heard him jawing away sometimes, and she come in the room and that's the end. After that he talks about as much as a sti—" As Onorifica spoke, she caught sight of the staff that Cugino had cut for me. In a markedly different tone she asked, "Does your stick talk, sir?"

I smiled and said that it had not done so recently.

"It has that little face on it, though, don't it, sir?"

"Does it really? Show it to me."

"I'd rather not to touch it, sir, if it's—would you want me to fetch it, sir?" Her eyes pleaded with me to refuse, so I got up and got it myself.

She pointed, her trembling finger a good cubit from the wood. "Right here, sir."

There was a small hole where a knot had come out. Above it, a minute protuberance that might be called a nose, and over that two small, dark markings, that could—with a cartload of imagination—be taken for eyes. I rubbed this "face" with my thumb, dislodging a few dry scraps of inner bark. "Do you mean this, Onorifica?"

"Don't touch it, please, sir." The color left her cheeks. "Don't make it talk."

Suppressing a smile, I promised not to.

"What I got to ask you about, sir, is—is . . ." Her lips twitched soundlessly.

"Whether I really am a strego, as your mistress calls them? A magic worker?"

Her expression told me I had missed the mark, but her head bobbed.

"No, Onorifica, I'm not. No one is."

I waited for her to speak.

"Nobody is. There is no such thing as magic, in the way you mean it. Things we don't understand, ghosts and sudden storms for instance, make us think that there might be. But ghosts are merely the spirits of the dead, and though I don't know what causes sudden storms, I know they aren't raised by magic. It's true that certain people can predict the future, but they do it by drawing upon insights that they don't know they have, or because they're informed by the gods."

I smiled again, trying to reassure her. "Long ago I was the friend of someone who became a sort of god, an aspect of Pas. He gave me a lot of information and advice, and all of it was valuable. But wise as he was, he taught me no magic. He couldn't have, even if he had considered such a thing desirable."

"Like tonight, sir."

I thought she was referring to Fava's story. "Strange things happen, Onorifica. Nevertheless, it is no explanation to call them magic." There was a tap at the windowpane, and I got up and opened the window to let Oreb in.

"Good girl?" He eyed the good girl (who seemed on the verge of fainting) doubtfully.

"A very good girl," I assured him.

"I told him we shouldn't with you in the house," the good girl blurted, showering me with crumbs.

"Bad thing," Oreb warned me.

I started to ask whom she intended by "him," thinking that there might be an inhumu here, then realized the true state of affairs. Speaking very softly I said, "The friend to whom I referred was spied upon once when he was shriving a young woman. He told me that because the young woman had kept her voice very low, the spy had learned little or nothing." More loudly I concluded, "We should do the same."

"Yes, Master Incanto." From her expression, Onorifica had not the least idea what I was talking about.

"You happened to pass my room tonight on your way back to the kitchen, and very kindly asked whether I needed anything. And I, without in the least meaning to, frightened you by asking where you slept. Isn't that so?"

She seemed almost afraid to move her head, but managed a nod.

"I have no business interfering in my host's affairs, save those in which he has asked my help, and no business interfering in yours at all."

In a hoarse whisper she asked, "Are you going to do anything to me?"

"Punish you? I can't. And wouldn't if I could. He's given you a ring, anyway."

"Only we're not, you know, sir, married."

"You couldn't be, since there are no proper augurs here. My wife and I were united by Patera Remora, who is an augur, so we're really married. Without one, giving a ring is about as much as anyone can do. You might have a child, however. Have you thought about that?"

The fear vanished and she glowed. "I want one, sir. He'll take care of us. I know him."

I rose. I cannot have been impressive in Inclito's borrowed nightshirt, but she seemed impressed. To further impress her, I grasped my staff. Oreb hopped from my shoulder to the angled handle. "I don't have an augur's power to forgive wrongdoing," I told Onorifica, "but I can bless you, and I will. By Great Pas's generosity, anyone may bless." I traced the sign of addition in the air, and asked Pas and the Outsider to look with favor upon her and any children she might bear.

When I finished, she rose smiling. "Thank you, sir. Can I— would you like anything else?"

"Only a couple of very minor items," I told her. "You were going to tell me what the coachman had learned in town. What was it?"

"Everybody's afraid of you, sir." She licked her fingers. "They won't go near the shop where you're staying when you're there, only when you're gone they all come wanting to hear about you, only he won't tell them anything unless they buy. Cook'll be after me the same way, sir."

"I understand. What do you plan to tell her?"

"Nothing, sir."

"Nothing at all?"

"Well, maybe something." She smiled again, and for the first time I felt that I understood why Inclito was attracted to her. "But not very much."

I said, "That would be wise, I'm sure. But before you return to the kitchen, would you please find the other maid—wake her up if you must—and tell her I need to speak to her?"

"Yes, Master Incanto. Right away."

"And on your way out, you might ask Fava to come in. She's waiting in the hall, or she was."

As soon as I had spoken, Fava entered. Less boldly, Mora shuffled behind her. Both were in their nightdresses.

6

THE GUESSING GAME

There are times when enlightenment comes suddenly, as it did on the ball court; I never think of these sudden illuminations without recalling my second night on Green. I had spent most of the broiling day searching for the gifts I had received from the Neighbor, and had thrown up the task as hopeless. I was ready to justify the worst things that Sinew had ever said or thought by leaving him and the men who had been with us in the lander to their fate. I set off down the river, that river of death that was a sewer when it ran under the City of the Inhumi, determined to put as much distance between myself and its horrors as I could.

For half that night I made my way cautiously through the darkness along its banks, somewhat cheered when the flying dot of sapphire that was Blue crossed the sky, but infinitely saddened by the sight of the faint, unsteady spark that was the *Whorl*. I should have been up there searching out Viron and its caldé, when instead—

I was going to write something about tramping along the riverbank. The truth (which I have only just recalled) is that for a long time after I caught sight of the *Whorl* among the crowding stars I did not. I sat sweating on a log instead, swatting insects and watching the reflections of those stars on the smooth, oily flow

that had succeeded the foaming flood that had carried me so far
from the City. At times it seemed to me that a thousand inhumi
must have been lurking beneath the water, and that the points of
light I saw were their glittering eyes, softened by ripples; but every
few minutes a dark shape would pass among them like a floating
log, and I would realize yet again that it was we, not they, who
populated the water.

Nor was that all I saw. Great hairless beasts, on two legs and
four, and six, came to the river to drink or to course our floating
corpses as bears pursue fish, and I recalled the strangely named
bear with which He-pen-sheep had exchanged blood, and wondered whether such bears sought carrion beside the rivers of
Shadelow.

Most vividly I remember the enormous snake I saw swimming
swiftly upriver, a snake whose head was as big as a man's coffin and
of the same shape. It held up its head and looked around it as it
swam, and its head was higher than mine would have been if I had
stood upon the log. I was seated, as I wrote a moment ago; I
remained completely motionless, and it passed by me. For a long
time after the head was out of sight up the river, I watched the
progress of its great body, and listened to the gentle slap of the
waves that its long, slow curvings created.

Then there was nothing left to do but to stand up and walk
again. As I think back on that night, it seems to me that I cannot
have taken a hundred steps before I caught sight of the light, shining forth from the mud at the edge of the water. Incredulous, I
went down the bank to it and picked it up, and squatted to wash it
off. I had given it up for good, and now held it in my hand as
before. Many strange things have befallen me, in the Long Sun
Whorl, on Green, and here upon this smiling whorl of Blue; but
none have ever seemed more miraculous than that did at that
moment. Once I slid from the prow of the Trivigaunti airship, and
had begun the half-league fall to the ground below when Silk
seized and saved me. That is the only thing to which I can liken
the finding of the light.

While I was washing it in the shallows, I discovered that it floated, and in fact floated as high and buoyantly as a cork, something I surely ought to have anticipated from its sensation of perfect weightlessness. Floating as it did, it had naturally been carried much farther by the flood than I had; with that sudden insight, the illumination of which I spoke, I realized what a fool I had been to search for it for hours near the spot where I myself had been cast up by the water. Furthermore, that my sword, which could not possibly have floated at all, must necessarily be much nearer the point where I had dropped it than the point where I had struggled out of the river and lain panting on the bank, vomiting foul water—that it was quite likely, in fact, that it was still beneath the overarching pavements of the City.

I knelt in the water then and forced the light beneath the surface, reasoning that if it had not been extinguished by the flood it could not be by immersion to the depth of two fingers. I found to my delight that when I pushed it under, it illuminated the bottom.

But I began tonight with the idea of writing about the ways in which we come to knowledge, and am in danger of losing sight of my original purpose, as I frequently do. Without Oreb to remind me, I might very well forget to eat and sleep.

Sudden enlightenment can be wonderful, as wonderful as the sight of the Neighbor's light flashing through the dense foliage of the bank had been to me. But wonderful though it is, it is not the only way in which understanding comes. A full day after that (I still remember how hungry I was by then), when something moved in the bone-littered filth of the river bottom, I jerked my hand away, sure that it was a venomous worm like the one that had risen from the cut I made in the first corpse we saw. The silt it had stirred up darkened the water, blinding me for a minute or two until the current carried it away; then I saw the pommel, and saw too that the sword was struggling to reach my hand; and stretching my arm down I held my breath, but could not keep my eyes open in that vile water, and groped blindly for the grip that was groping blindly for me. And at last I closed my hand about it and felt it grasp me from within.

That, too, is how understanding comes at times. I told Mora

something about my sword on the first night I spent here at Inclitor's farm, but I will try to give that in the proper order.

We three rode out from Blanko together, Mora and Fava and me; and the coachman, too, although I do not believe he was listening to our talk, or that he made a part of our company to a much greater degree than his horses did.

"It's a treat to have you with us," Fava declared. "Mora and I take this ride twice a day, and we play games and act silly just to pass the time. Besides, it was nice of you to talk to Mora the way you did. She told me all about it."

Mora's expression said plainly that she had not told Fava everything.

"I want to talk with you, too," I told Fava, "when we can speak privately."

An airy gesture with her open parasol indicated the open coach in which we rode. I shook my head.

"Mora won't tell. She knows everything you do."

"In that case," I said, "you don't have to talk to me. You can talk to Mora instead."

"Wouldn't you like to play a game with us? I mentioned them because I hoped you'd ask to."

"Bad thing," Oreb croaked. "Watch out."

"Incanto?" Mora cleared her throat. "I don't want to play. You and Fava can, if you like. I'd like to talk to your bird. Can you get him to come over here?" She and Fava were side by side in the seat facing mine.

Oreb fluttered nervously. "No, no!"

"Give him some time to get used to you," Fava advised. "He might peck."

I told Mora, "He doesn't like the company you keep."

Fava ignored it. "I want to play the guessing game, and I'll make the first guess. I guess that Mora isn't going to play, though she could if she wanted to. Now I have a point and I get to ask you a question, Incanto. I know the answer and I don't think you do, but if you guess it right you score a point. Most points when we get to Mora's house wins."

I nodded; Oreb repeated, "Watch out!"

"Why do you think that Mora and I were more popular today than we have been since I came?"

For a few seconds I pretended to consider my answer, rolling up my eyes and stroking my beard. "Because you brought your most beautiful parasols today."

Fava looked disgusted. "Are you hinting that you want more shade? Mora can lend you hers, she's not using it."

"Bird shade," Oreb announced, and hopping onto my head, spread his wings.

"Another guess," Fava demanded. "I won't tell you unless you guess seriously."

"Very well. It must have been because Mora had talked to me this morning."

"They didn't know that," Mora said. "I didn't tell them."

Fava simpered. "That gives me a wonderful question, but you get to ask next, Incanto, after I give you the answer. It was because everybody knew you'd been to Mora's for dinner."

"How could they know that?"

"Is that your question?" Fava asked.

I nodded.

"Humm . . . Your bird's been telling?"

"I don't believe so."

For a few seconds, Fava hid her face behind her ruffled pink parasol. "You think I told. Well, I didn't! I hardly speak to any of them. Ask Mora." The parasol went up until its fringe was above her face again, and Fava gave me a wicked smile.

I pretended to misunderstand. "She heard the question and may answer, if she wants to."

"Then I've got one point," Mora said. "My father's been telling everybody. He said you were staying with us before I wrote to ask you to, even."

"Perhaps he has, but that wasn't my answer. Do you know the shopkeeper I was staying with? His name is Atteno. I told him where I was going before your father came to get me."

"Mora has half a point," Fava ruled. "Now here's my wonderful question. Mora said she didn't tell the others. Who did she tell, besides me?"

"I have no idea."

"The teachers. Wasn't that brave of her? And silly?"

"She's a brave girl, though I doubt she's a silly one. Do I get a point for that?"

"No. That wasn't a question in the game. It was just something I do when I'm talking."

"A rhetorical device."

"Thank you. You're so wise that I'd think you could win easily."

"I'm wise enough to know I can't," I told her. "Is it my turn now? Why are you staying with Mora?"

"Because I like it and she said I could. Isn't that a good enough reason?"

Indicating the coachman, who could not have seen her, Mora said, "Her mother's dead, just like mine, and her father's a trader. He's away a lot."

"I have two points," Fava declared. "Mora has a half point, and you don't have any. My turn. Mora and I didn't have to go outside and play games today. Why was that?"

"You never do, Fava."

"That's right, but she does. Answer the question. I was trying to make it easy for you."

"Your teacher wanted to talk to Mora, I suppose."

"Not nearly good enough. It was all the teachers, and they talked to me more than they did to her. They wanted to know everything about you, and since I told them the most I got the most questions."

"What was it they were most interested in?"

"You can't ask unless you know the answer. Do you?"

I shook my head.

"Then it isn't a fair question."

I looked out at the fields of crisp stubble and the maples and sycamores waving in the wind like so many pillars of flame, and I thought of the green-uniformed men who had saluted me. "Let me revise it. Did they ask you what I was going to do to help Blanko against Duko Rigoglio?"

Mora's eyes widened. "Yes, they did."

"That's another point for you, Mora. You have a point and a half."

Fava nodded above the high lace collar that concealed her neck. "Incanto, you really are discerning. I've met stregas and stregos before, or people who said they were, and it was all tricks and lies. You're the real thing. Whose turn is it?"

"Mora's," I said.

"I suppose I'm playing after all." Mora sighed. "All right, this one's only for you, Incanto. What does your name mean?"

"A great many things, including a drinking vessel and a container for ink."

"Wrong. Papa's still trying to borrow back that book he read last year, so I don't know what your name was before you came. But here, your name's Incanto. Papa's name means 'the famous.' Did you know that?"

"Your grandmother mentioned it."

"Yours means 'the enchanter.'" Mora adjusted her position on the deep leather seat to talk to Fava. "Each of you has asked two or three already. Shouldn't I get one more?"

"If Incanto doesn't object."

"I don't think he will. Incanto, I could be wrong about this, but I think that Papa probably suggested your name before the two of you got to our house. If I'm right, why did he tell you to call yourself Incanto?"

"Because it was the name of his brother, who died in infancy."

"Wrong again. I have three and a half. It was because he wanted to brace up the ideas so many people here have about you. He wants them to think we've got a powerful witch on our side, so they'll fight Soldo instead of giving in. They're afraid. I think even Papa is, a little."

I said, "He and they have good reason to be afraid. I've seen war."

Fava put in, "We told the teachers you were the most powerful strego in the whole whorl, but very good and a very good
friend of Inclito's. Didn't we, Mora? And then I said Inclito gave a
secret signal to bring you here in our hour of need. Mora didn't
approve, but they thought it was because I wasn't supposed to say
anything about the secret signal. If I knew the answer, I'd ask you
right now exactly how you plan to destroy Soldo without firing a
shot."

Oreb bobbed on my head. "Good man!"

Fava smirked. "He'd better be."

"I haven't the least intention of destroying Soldo," I told her.
"I'm sure there must be many innocent people living there. Many
and perhaps most of them must be poor people, too, bled white
by their Duko and the inhumi. Can't we agree that they have sor-
rows enough without the death and destruction of war?"

"You'd better ask a game question instead, or Mora will."

"Bad thing!" Oreb eyed Fava with disfavor.

I told her that I had no objection to Mora's asking game questions, and added, "You know, I've just realized why it is that the
inhumi attack the poorest people so often."

Mora snapped, "Because they're stupid!"

"They aren't, and in fact they can't afford to be. I grew up
among very poor people, Mora. My own family was poor, though
not in comparison to many others. There was enough money to
send me, and my brothers and sisters, to the palaestra—but only
just."

Fava said sweetly, "*We* call it the academy."

I shook my head. "Mora and her father and grandmother do,
I suppose. You wanted another question for your game, so tell
me—why did Mora's grandmother call her first child Incanto?"

"Not fair! You've got to know the answer."

"I do. Do you?"

Oreb dropped to my staff to bob up and down. "Silk win!"

Mora asked, "Is that your real name?"

"No." I tried to explain. "Silk has never really been my name.

But when I first acquired Oreb I used to ask him questions about a man named Silk, and he picked it up."

I waited for one of them to speak. When neither did, I said, "My question wasn't for Fava alone. You may answer it if you can, Mora."

Her speech is always slow; this time it seemed slower than ever. "I want to think about the inhumi and the poor people first. We're not poor."

"It isn't an invariable rule; but I've traveled a bit, and in every place I've been it's the poor whom they attack most."

That is everything of any importance that was said. Not long after that, we were admitted by the sullen chambermaid.

And now I have other things to write.

7

SECOND STORIES

We played the storytelling game again at dinner. This time Mora's grandmother went first.

Salica's Second Story:
Stuck in the Chimney

This is a true story, something that actually took place in Grandecitta when I was a little girl. There was a terrible strega living among us then. She was old and ugly, but she knew so much magic that everyone was afraid of her. When I was about old enough to walk, she fell in love. The unlucky young man's name was Dentro, and he was a quiet, handsome fellow you'd think would be frightened to death if you so much as told him that a strega wanted to speak to him. But the strega could change her appearance whenever she wished, and whenever Dentro was around her, which was more and more often as the weeks passed, she became a beautiful young woman with a ravishing smile and a voluptuous figure. It did no good to tell Dentro that the fascinating young woman he saw was a wicked hag. The people in our district, who liked him and felt sorry for him, were at their wit's end.

After goodness knows how much dithering and arguing

among themselves, they resolved to lock him up, thinking that if he couldn't see her he'd cease to love her, and hoping that she'd go away in search of him. Some men his own age went to his house pretending they were on a friendly visit, overpowered him, tied him up, and carried him to a room that had been made ready to receive him. It was comfortable enough, but herbs and spells had been hung on every wall to keep the strega from finding him as long as he was in it.

She didn't, but she very quickly found out what they had done. Soon the luck of the whole district turned bad. If a man fell down, he broke both his arms. No woman could make a stew without burning it. If one child threw a stone at another, he put out his eye. Houses caught fire for no reason at all, and fires that had been doused with four cisterns sprang up again by magic. Things got so bad that they had to produce Dentro again and let the strega marry him. As you can imagine, they liked her less than ever after that.

Well, one evening a man who lived in a house near ours happened to ride past hers. He was in a hurry, but he could not help noticing Dentro, as black as any printer, standing on her roof and poking a broom down her chimney. She had him cleaning her chimney himself, you see, instead of hiring a sweep to do it.

Such parsimony made our neighbor angry, and he clapped his spurs to his horse, as angry people always do, and fairly flew down the road until he came to a graveyard. Then out popped the strega from behind a gravestone and into the road, where she stood like this and stopped his horse so abruptly that he was nearly thrown, calling, "What's your hurry, loafer?"

It made our neighbor angrier than ever. "I'm going for the doctor," he told her. "Your Dentro's fallen into the chimney and can't get out. If you ask me, he's dead."

She turned as white as boiled icing and limped out of his way, and when he met his friends at the tavern, they had a good laugh about the trick he'd played on her.

Now up there in the *Whorl*, as Incanto here will tell you, the wild storms we had were the work of devils, who mixed and served them up to us in the same exact fashion that Green does down here. Stregas can make devils do their bidding, and this strega waited until our neighbor was called out of the city on business, and then had them make one for him that flattened half the houses in Grandecitta. It did so much damage, in fact, that he heard about it in the foreign city where he was and hurried home to see if his own house still stood.

He had nearly reached it, when who should he meet trudging down the road but the strega. She stepped into his path and stopped him as she had before. "Hurry home, loafer, your wife's stuck in the chimney."

He laughed, because his wife was a great, heavy woman, exceedingly fond of her plate and not at all inclined to move from her chair for any reason, and he thought that there was no chimney in all of Grandecitta big enough for her to get stuck in. But when he got home, he found his house half demolished and no wife. It was about this time of the year, when nights are liable to be chilly, so as night drew on he picked up some sticks of broken furniture and built a little fire in the fireplace of what was left of their bedroom. The chimney wouldn't draw, and I think you can guess what came out of it the next day, when he and my father climbed up to the top and dropped a broken timber down it to clear it.

And how much damage the devils had done to her, pulling her up into there.

"Violent storms can do surprising things," Inclito said. "I've seen splinters driven into trees like nails."

Fava nodded. "I've seen that, too, and worse. Why don't you arrange for a storm to flatten Soldo, Incanto?"

"If I could, I'd consider it. Unfortunately I can't do anything more to harm the Duko than you can—which may be harm enough. We'll see."

"Good thing?" Oreb inquired.

"No. But she may become one."

Mora addressed her grandmother. "You've told us over and

over that Incanto's a strego. Are you saying that he's wicked? That's impossible!"

The old lady flushed, and the faint touch of pink that rose to her cheeks gladdened my heart. "No, not at all. Not all stregas are wicked. You mustn't read such meanings into every old story you hear."

To me she said, "I didn't intend to offend you, Incanto, really I didn't. I would never treat a guest like that, and I've felt ever so much better since I've been sleeping with a fire in my little fireplace and bolting my door and both the windows as you told me."

I picked up a dish of dumplings that chanced to be near my place and passed it to Fava, saying, "Have some. They're tender and savory, and you must be hungry." She gave me a murderous look.

"I went first tonight just as I promised I would," the old lady told us. "Who'll go next? How about you, Mora darling?"

Mora's Second Story:
The False Friend and the True Friend

Once very long ago, there were two little girls whose houses were only a few steps apart, but were far from any other houses at all. This was soon after the first landers, I suppose, when there were only a few people here and everything was unsettled. One little girl was very good and very kind, but the other little girl was a liar, a cheat, and a thief. Just the same, the two played together nearly every day. They had to, because there was nobody else for either of them to play with.

More people came, but the girls were used to each other by that time. They played together as before, no longer as little as they had been, and seemed closer than ever. No one could understand it, because the one was so very nice and the other was so very, very bad.

But they did it just the same.

A little settlement that was nowhere near them grew to a town and broke out in politics, as it seems towns always do. The good little girl's father got involved in it, and when the other side won, the town took his land and told him that he and his family had to move away. The good little girl was so brave and strong then that even people who hated her father admired her and talked about her "noble spirit."

But the bad little girl wept bitterly and would not be consoled. She helped her friend's family pack, working harder than anybody, and showered everyone in it with presents. Some of the pretty things she gave them she was really giving back, because they were things she had taken from them to begin with. But many others were her own dearest possessions. When they left, she walked beside their wagon crying, and when night came, and they got ready to camp next to the road, she embraced her little friend for the last time and started back home.

She was already tired, so she walked slowly. The night passed and the sun came up again, and she was not home yet. An old woman who knew both families was going out to milk her cow just then. She saw the bad girl, and how terribly tired she was, and got her to come inside and sit down, and shared her breakfast.

"I've known you all your life, Mora," the old woman said after they had talked a bit, "and you're as mean and selfish a child as ever I saw. What's gotten into you?"

"I'm very, very selfish, exactly as you say," the bad little girl replied, "and she was the only friend I had."

"I've heard that story before," Fava told Mora firmly.

"Bad thing!"

"But it was the other way 'round. You've got the parts mixed up."

Mora shook her head. "I've told the truth. Even liars like me tell the truth sometimes." She has a mole or wart in the middle of her left cheek; unless I am vigilant I find myself looking at it instead of her expression, and that can be a serious mistake.

My host's mother said, "I like it the way Mora told it. So often the people in stories are either completely bad or completely good.

Mora's saying that even bad people can be good sometimes, and I agree." It was clear that she had no idea what her granddaughter had been talking about.

Inclito asked, "How about you next, Fava?" Seeing her reluctance he shrugged. "Or I will, if you rather do it that way."

She nodded eagerly.

Inclito's Second Story:
The Mercenary's Employer

There are lots of stories I could tell, but Mama and Mora have heard them. Fava has heard a lot of my stories too by now. Even you, Incanto. I told stories when I drove you that I should have saved. So what I'm going to tell tonight is one I just heard from somebody else today. Not even Mama has heard it.

These days there's all this war talk. I wouldn't want to scare Mora and Fava, but they know it already. Even if nobody said anything out here, they'd hear it in town.

In a war there's no such thing as too many men. Too many to feed, maybe, but never too many to fight. You got enough, maybe you won't have to fight at all. The Duko's been hiring mercenaries to fight for him and to scare us, we think we should get some too. For us there's never enough cards, but we got a few.

So today I'm in town to talk to some and look them over for us. One of them tells me this.

The last time he fights, it's for this big town down south. When a lander comes here, mostly it sets down in just the one place. Everybody knows that. And the people, they take out all the old supplies that were in it. Then they say, "I'm here, what do I need with this lander now?" So pretty soon the cards are all gone out of it, and lots of the wiring. Sometimes I go into other people's houses and sit down, and it is a couch out of a lander. There's steel and titanium, all that stuff, and the people it brought think they need it.

This town down south is different. A god tells them they got to leave their lander like it is, just take supplies and nothing else. That's what they all say, he says. Maybe somebody just says a god said it. Who knows about that stuff? Anyway, they take the supplies and leave the rest. This is all years ago.

So after a while it goes back up. Wonderful. It goes back to the Long Sun Whorl and gets more people from their city up there and comes back. It keeps on doing that.

Things are bad there, like in Mora's story. People fight and steal. There's no justice. You want to win your case, you pay a big bribe. The biggest bribe wins. So pretty soon they say, "This's no good. Let's some of us go back with the lander next time. We'll find somebody real honest and wise up there and make him come back here and straighten everything out." This mercenary never heard of anybody doing it before and neither did I. But he says that's what they said they did.

So they went and got the wise man they needed, a real tall man. His beard is white like new snow, he's only got one eye and it's the color of deep water. He's still there when the mercenary comes, and this is the man that hires him when he gets to that big town down south. Before, another man that was working for this wise man had talked to them and put them on a boat that took them there.

This is a real good man, the mercenary says. Soon as he talks to him he knows he can trust him. He's living in a house the town gave him, a big one with floors up above each other, maybe three or maybe four. I remember houses like that in Grandecitta and so does Mama, she lived in one like that a long time ago. But this mercenary was born here. He never seen a house with more than two before. He's younger than I am, younger than anybody here but Mora and Fava.

This big house is full of carpets and all kinds of furniture and pictures, the kind of things Duko Rigoglio has in his house. But when he talks to them, this wise man, the mercenary knows none of it means anything to him. He has silk clothes and jewels, and gold cloth around his head, but they don't mean anything to him. Walking on carpet or grass is all the same to him. After he has talked to all of them a little, he asks each one what he wants the cards he's going to pay them for. This mercenary says he got to know the others on the boat, and there are some real good liars there, but when they try to lie to the wise man they only say, "I-I-I . . ."

Like that.

Some want the money for good things and some for bad. He talks to all of them, no matter what they want his money for.

This mercenary I talked to, he wants to buy a little piece of good land. All the good land where he was born, somebody owns already. So he wants to get hold of some cards and buy enough that he can build him a little house and get married. He's got a girl back there he hopes will wait for him.

When this wise man is through talking to them he hires them all, and this mercenary goes away to fight for him. Pretty soon they win, and he goes to the enemy town to hold it. The wise man, he sends his own people back to their farms and uses his mercenaries for that. Then he's gone, and nobody knows what happened to him. They got this young general, he loves him like his father, and he searches everyplace. He thinks somebody killed him and hid the body.

Then somebody in the enemy town where the mercenary is sees the wise man's wife. He tells the officer taking care of things there, and this mercenary is one of the ones they send to bring her in. They ask lots of questions, and he gets to hear some of it.

She and the wise man are going to go away and never come back, she says. They get a boat and go down a river that they got down there. Not our river. There's inhumi after him that want to kill him, and his wife is real scared. He tells her not to worry, they only want him, not her. They stop on a island and cook and eat, and there's inhumi all over. Then they get back in their boat and go to sleep. The wise man has this pet bird—

Oreb interrupted Inclito's story here, exclaiming, "Good bird!"

It talks, and the wise man says it will wake them up if the inhumi get too close. She's very scared, but he holds her and after a while she gets to sleep.

When she wakes up, it's still night. This wise man is gone, and the inhumi too. The boat's still tied to a tree or something on the little island, but she sees him over on the bank. He's taken off the head cloth he used to wear, and she sees his white hair shining in the dark. He's going away, and pretty soon she can't see him any-more, so next day she takes their boat and sails it back up the river to the enemy town and sells it.

This mercenary I talked to is one of the men that took her from the enemy town to the big town where this wise man was so the young general can talk to her. But when he gets her there, the young general pays him off and lets him go because they're cut-ting back now. That's when he comes here. So this is the end of his story, or anyhow it's the end for right now.

Mora gave her father a quizzical look. "Why did the wise man want to go away when they had won the war?"

Inclito's big shoulders rose and fell. "Somebody like Incanto could tell you, maybe. I'm just a farmer. You want to know about pigs and cows, ask me."

"Incanto?"

I shook my head, and Inclito sighed. "All right, I asked the mercenary the same thing, why did he go? He didn't know either. Then I asked about the big town that hired them, and he said things were good there. I said, they don't fight each other any-more? Or steal? And he said no, it was a nice town with honest people, only big. As big as a city inside the Long Sun Whorl is what he said, but how would he know? As big as Grandecitta? I don't believe it!"

Inclito turned to me. "My whole family has told, Mama and Mora, and now me. There's only you and Fava."

I said I would prefer that Fava precede me, and his mother thrust a platter of fresh pork at me. "You haven't eaten anything tonight, you or Fava. How about some bread? Decina baked this morning, and it's our own butter."

I took meat and a slice of bread to satisfy her.

"I'm leaving tomorrow morning," Fava told Inclito's mother.

"Mora knows, and so does Incanto now. I'd like to tell a long
story tonight, since I won't be doing this anymore, and I want to
make up a specially good one. Anyway, Incanto got to go last
when he was here before."

She turned to me. "May I go last this time, Incanto? And will
you tell us another one about Green? I'm going to lay mine there
too, I think."

8

MY SECOND STORY: THE MAN WHO RETURNED

On Green, at the time of which I speak, there was a band of a hundred bad men. A few had slug guns and almost all had knives. With these weapons they fought off the inhumi, and fought among themselves as well, only too often.

Their leaders were a certain man and his son, and though they thought themselves better than the rest, they were much worse because they hated each other. The others did not hate one another, though they fought and sometimes killed one another. It was only that they were proud and reckless, and that each one wanted to be thought very brave.

If they had been wise, they would have tried to recover the lander in which they had come to Green, but they were foolish, and because they feared the inhumi and did not know where in the City of the Inhumi it was, they would not. They felt sure there were other men on Green, and women, too; they wanted very much to find women.

Their leader, the man I spoke of, tried to persuade them to retake the lander; but when they refused, he foolishly agreed to lead them in search of colonists from the Long Sun Whorl. He led them north through the heat and the terrible jungle, feeling that the landers would have chosen a more temperate climate for the colonists they carried.

They traveled a long way, or at least they thought it long, and found a small settlement; but the settlers drove them away, then fled when they returned and attacked. Far though they traveled, it was never far enough to escape the jungle, its fevers, and its insects.

At last their leader gathered his men about him and told them frankly that their only hope was to reclaim the lander in which they had arrived. "If you will not come with me," he told them, "I will go back alone and take it by stealth, if I can, or die trying. If we continue as we have begun, I will die in any case. I promised the people of my town that I would do my utmost to return to the *Whorl*. If I am to die here, I prefer to die with honor." They talked long after he spoke to them, eight or ten in support of him and a dozen or a score opposing him. Their wrangling continued for hours . . .

Here I stopped to listen, for I heard Hyacinth singing to her waves. "What is it?" my host's mother asked me.

"A woman singing in the sea on the other side of the whorl," I told her. "I doubt that you can hear her, but I do."

While they wrangled in that fashion, I counted them over and over, and the result was always the same, one that I had come to know well since Ushujaa died: sixty-nine. At last even they grew tired and slept, agreeing to settle the matter by a vote in the morning.

As I lay sweating in the darkness, I foresaw what morning would bring. It was neither delusion nor enlightenment from any god; I knew them well by then, how foolish they were and how quick to anger. They would vote, and the sides would be very nearly even, though they could not be precisely even. The winners would demand that the losing side do everything they wished. The losers would defy them, and the sides would fight.

I rose as quietly as I could. We always had a fire, and two sentries; but the sentries, though they were awake, were as tired as the rest, and they had let the fire sink to embers. I crept away unobserved, not using the light that the Neighbor had given me until I was completely certain it could not be seen from the camp.

The next day, and the next, I made my way back toward the City of the Inhumi. It will seem vainglorious when I say that I lived by eating the creatures that attacked me, yet it was so. Their flesh was foul, for they were predators and carrion eaters; but I lived upon it and upon half-eaten fruits and nuts dropped by the great green spiders.

On the third day, Sinew joined me. Three more came on the morning of the forth, and six after night had fallen—six who had found us by my light, which shone a long way through the jungle, thick though it was. Then more and more, until we were forty-six men.

Forty-six we regained the City. I am proud of that, as proud as Patera Remora was of having brought Maytera Mint to confer with the Ayuntamiento. We had lost more than half our force since we set out; but we had learned a great deal in the losing of it, and I had brought these back without losing even one more.

"Poor Silk," Oreb muttered on my shoulder. And again, "Poor Silk."

"My name is not Silk," I explained to the people seated beyond the clear white glow of my light. "It has never been Silk. He once belonged to a man called Silk, and uses that name for me now."

The white light died in my hand as I spoke. A big man with a kind, ugly face that made me want to smile said, "Was this you for real, Incanto? Were you on Green? By Echidna's babies, I think you were!"

I shook my head and told him it had been someone else, a man whose name I have forgotten, a man who wore a ring with a white stone. My own name is Horn, no matter what Oreb may say.

They stole into the City of the Inhumi by night, moving through the sewers at first, then through the cellars and the lower floors of the ruinous towers, the way having been scouted for them by their leader's son. Eventually, however, they were forced to go out into the neglected, rubbish-strewn streets, in which the inhumi take the shapes of men and women to act out their ghastly parody of human life.

An hour passed, and another; they had to fight, and fight they did, cunning as felwolves and fierce as Mucor's lynxes. Onward and onward until they found the place where their lander had put down. It was not there, and when they saw that it was not, the heart went out of them.

Two had been lost in the advance. Their leader tried to count those who died in their retreat as well, but they fell too fast. At last they reached the sewers again, and the fighting slackened. He counted them then, and counted twenty-seven with his son and himself; but as they made their way along a narrow, slimy walkway above the water he tried to name them and found he could name only twenty-six. Other names occurred to him, the names of dead men and of certain men who had not rejoined him in the jungle. He knew that the twenty-seventh man could be none of those.

He had feared that the human slaves of the inhumi would be waiting for them where the sewer left the city, and so it proved. There was a hot fight there, in which he was wounded. His son carried him back into the darkness under the City; and when his son had returned to the fighting, and he felt a trifle stronger, he sat up and watched the battle as one who sits at ease in a darkened theater watches the play, his men crouching and firing, or wriggling and creeping near enough to use their knives. Among them fought a young man whom he had never seen before, a young man with a needler who fought as bravely as the bravest.

Night came, and they got away. Wounded, he was no longer their leader; but they carried him with them, and he loved them and wept. The young man with the needler was wounded too, with many others; but when their wounds had begun to heal, his (which he would allow no one to treat) grew worse each day. He had been on another lander, he said, and had been hiding in the City of the Inhumi until they came.

The slaves of the inhumi pursued them, armed men and

women in chains, with empty eyes; and when he could no longer walk, the men who had fought beside him left him beneath arching gray roots, where he lay as if in the Grand Manteion—and the man who had been leader lay there beside him.

"This is too hard for you, Incanto," my host's mother said kindly. "You don't have to go on with it if you don't want to."

"It would be worse not to finish it," I told her, "but I'll make the rest as brief as I can. I've talked too much already."

The young man lay on the ground, upon the naked black soil of Green, for little can grow between the monstrous trees. The man who had been leader lay beside him, and it seemed to him that the trees and vines leaned toward them to overhear their talk, and wept. I will not tell you how tall those trees are, or their thickness through the trunk; you would not credit anything I said. But I will say this. The trees you have seen are bushes, and the roots of many of the great trees on Green could heave the soil of this big farm from one end to the other and from one side to the other, making hills and valleys of its flat land. There are animals that burrow in the bark of those trees that are larger than we.

"You don't recognize me," the dying man said. "I knew you wouldn't."

The man who had been leader shook his head.

"I promised I wouldn't deceive you as long as we were on your boat," the young man told him, "but we are no longer on your boat. I am your son Krait." Krait was an inhumu. The inhumi seem men and women to us when they wish to—but no doubt all of you know that.

Mora and Fava looked at me strangely. Inclito said, "I've never seen one I couldn't tell after a minute or two."

Our hostess spoke of devils, saying that witches can command them, and they raise storms. I do not know whether either assertion is true. Perhaps they are, though I am prone to doubt it. But

I realized long ago that the devils about which poor, ignorant people talk in the Long Sun Whorl, those malign beings who, it is said, crept into the *Whorl* without Pas's permission, were only inhumi by another name. At the time of which I speak, Krait revealed the secret that has permitted me, at times, to command them, the secret that they dare not let us learn, thinking that we could employ it to ruin them.

I do not believe we can. I tell you that openly and fairly, all of you who hear me now, and all of you who will read the account of our dinner that I intend to write. It is a great secret, truly. If you will, it is a great and terrible weapon. That is how the inhumi themselves see it, and I will not call them wrong. But it is a weapon too heavy for our hands. The Neighbors, whom you name the Vanished People, knew it; but they could not wield it against the inhumi, who drank their blood in their time as they drink ours today. If they could not wield it, there is little hope that we human beings can. Or so it seems to me.

Here I must pass over many things if I am not to keep you all night. After coming near death more than once and more than twice, the man who had been leader rejoined the men he had led. They traveled very far together and saw many strange things about which I will not speak tonight, until they found a deserted settlement, in whose center stood a ruined lander.

(Silk had thought the lander Mamelta showed him a tower underground; this was a tower indeed, its nose high as the tops of the tallest trees and its sleek lines radiating a strength it no longer possessed. I can see it now, that slightly canted tower gleaming dully in the reddish light of the stifling afternoon. Like a rotting corpse, it showed ribs where some sideplates had been taken. How we shouted in our delight, thinking it would save us!)

There were cards as well as bones in the wretched huts, the cards that were our money in the Long Sun Whorl and that are too often our money here as well—the cards that let a lander think and speak. We restored them to the lander, and directed by its monitor we tried to restore the lander itself, raiding the few settlements we could locate, and sometimes carrying heavy parts from other landers for scores of leagues. Then the leader's son found a woman in one of those settlements and turned against his father for good, helping the settlers fight him and his men.

And one by one they died, those men. Some fell prey to wild beasts, and some to rotting wounds and fevers. Some were killed by the settlers, some killed or captured by the inhumi. Always, it seemed to them that a few more parts would be enough, three more, two more, one more—only one more!—and their lander could fly again, and return them to the Whorl of the Long Sun.

Until at last there were only two left with the man who had again become their leader, and their leader lay dying.

They deserted him, taking both the fell black sword and the light he had been given. Perhaps they still hoped to find the wave-guide coupling they needed. Perhaps they merely hoped to be accepted by some settlement. I only know that he lay dying in the lander, and that he silenced its monitor so that he might die in peace.

A terrible yearning for the life he was to lose came upon him when the monitor had gone. He took off the ring Seawrack had given him not so very long before, and clasping it between hands that had been thick and strong implored every god he could call to mind to send a Neighbor to heal him.

None came, and his legs were cold and dead. He felt the thirst of death, and it seemed to him at that moment that he had been cheated, that all his sons should be at his deathbed, and Nettle, who had been his wife, and Seawrack herself. And he raised . . . He raised—

Fava gave me her handkerchief, a little square of cloth scarcely larger than a pen wiper, trimmed with coarse lace; and Inclito pressed his soiled napkin into my hand.

He raised Seawrack's ring and put it to his eye, peering through its silver circle because a fathomless darkness was closing in. He saw the whorl then as something small and bright, receding into the night beyond the stars; and for senseless reasons felt that the ring's bright round might hold the night at bay.

Through the ring a Neighbor saw him, and she came to him in his agony. He told her what was in his heart; and when he had finished, she said, "I cannot make you well again, and if I could you would still be in this place. I can do this for you, however, if you desire it. I can send your spirit into someone else, into someone whose own spirit is dying. If you wish, I will find someone in the whorl in which you were born. Then there will be one whole man there, instead of two dying men, one here and another there."

That was all I told Inclito, Mora, and the rest that night; but I consented, and found myself upon my knees beside the open coffin of a middle-aged woman. My hands and arms and face and neck were bleeding, and an old, worn knife covered with blood was by my hand. There was no one else in the poor little house in which I knelt, and almost nothing in it that was not torn or broken.

I rose, and leaving the dead woman in her coffin opened the door and walked out into the whorl. It was a little after midday then, as well as I could judge from the narrowing line of the Long Sun.

9

FAVA'S SECOND STORY:
THE GIRL ON GREEN

Incanto set his story on Green. It was an unhappy one, as I think we can all agree. For me the saddest part was the death of the leader's son Krait. Incanto never told us how the two came to know each other, or why he had adopted an inhumu. That will be a very good story, I feel sure, and I am sorry I will not be here to hear it.

I am going to use that setting, too. Since none of us have ever been there, it will let my imagination play in any way it wants, and be a fit locale for a story as fanciful as mine.

On Green there was a little girl who lived happily in a warm, dark place. She could see nothing because the place was so dark, but she knew nothing about "seeing" anyway; so she did not miss it. She could hear only a little, though she could hear some noises now and then, and even wondered about them. There was food in the warm, dark place, of which she drank whenever she was hungry.

Her food dwindled away, and the warm, dark place grew more and more cramped until her arms and back and head were pushed against its sides more and more uncomfortably. Nor was that all. The harder she was pressed against sides of the warm, dark place, the more she understood that though it was her whole whorl, there was another whorl, a strange, cold, and frightening whorl, outside it. Her ears heard a few noises, as I told you. Her mind heard more, sounds of lust and hunger, both of which frightened her very much.

She drank the last of her food, and knew hunger not as a noise outside but as a need within. The woman in Salica's story, the woman who was pulled up the chimney by the storm, had eaten as much as she wished for years, and no longer wanted to move. This little girl's case was the reverse of hers. Starving, she soon began to long for another place, one where there would be food again.

That, you see, is the way of the whorl. The well-fed remain where they are, if they can. The ill-fed wander on.

I do not mean to imply that I, who will leave tomorrow to wander through many foreign towns with my father, have not been well fed at your table, Salica. You have always been more than generous with me, not only with food but with your love, just as your son has been a father to me while I have been with you. Nevertheless, I am hungry for the sight of others of my own blood. I hope you will understand how I feel, and even sympathize.

"I certainly do!" my host's mother exclaimed.

And Oreb, from my shoulder: "Bad thing! Thing fly."

A time came when the little girl could not bear her hunger any longer. Gathering her little body, she pressed outward as hard as she could with head, hands, and feet. And when that availed nothing, she clawed frantically at the walls of the warm, dark place that had been home to her for as long as she could remember.

The walls gave way almost at once, and she found herself among rotting reeds and leaves. She did not know what they were, you understand. She had no name for anything beyond her own person. To her, they seemed a further wall, an extension of the warmth and darkness that had wrapped her for so long. She clawed at them, too, and eventually, fatigued and weak with hunger, burst forth into the sunlit brightness of a riverbank.

As I have implied, she did not know who she was or where she had come from. She knew only that she hungered. Seeing the green water, she sensed that it was liquid, like her food, and pulled herself over the mud with her claws until she plunged in.

Soon she discovered that there were hundreds of other babies with her in the water. What games they played! Now and again one of the others tried to bite her, or she tried to bite them; but no harm was done. And every day they grew stronger and fewer, for the fish on which they fed, fed on them.

She was perfectly happy there, until one day—

Here Fava interrupted her story to ask me, "May I use your leader, Incanto? Your man on Green? I won't hurt him much, I promise."

I nodded, hoping that no one other than Oreb was aware of my agitation.

Until one day, as she jumped to escape a particularly large and aggressive fish, she caught sight of Incanto's leader walking all by himself along the riverbank. As soon as she laid eyes on him, she knew that everything she and her playmates had been doing in the river was wrong, and pulled herself up onto the bank. For a time, she ran behind him on all fours like a dog. But that too seemed wrong.

Swimming and eating and swimming again through the calm, sunlit waters had made her much stronger. She stood up as he did, and toddled along behind him, leaving her baby footprints in the mud.

Though she walked as fast as she could, she could not keep up with him, and once a green grabber burst from some thick leaves and snatched at her with claws that were those of a big owl, but ten times larger. Grabbers are horrible animals without feathers or hair, and they change color in ways that make them very hard to see. Think of a bad child as big as a grown man, with a long tail and hands like owls' feet, and you will have pictured one. This grabber forced her to hide in the water for a long while, while the leader walked on.

*   *   *

As Fava spoke, I had been picturing the events in her story; and by the time her little girl had leaped from the green water and seen me, they were painfully vivid.

We had called the "grabbers" *colorcats* from their claws and the shape of their faces; and I could picture the colorcat at that moment much more clearly than Mora, Inclito, and his mother, or the curving wall of age-old ashlars and the fire in the big fieldstone fireplace: a bull colorcat as green as grass, humpbacked with muscle, splashing through the shallows with high-kneed caution, its snakey tail waving behind it like a detached liana, peering into the water, turning and peering again—and at length pouncing, its horrible claws stretched wide, and coming up with nothing more than a crumbling half load of mud. My hand groped my side for the sword I no longer wore, and found it.

The little girl I've been telling you about would have been left hopelessly behind (Fava continued, with a puzzled expression) if the leader had not turned back. Apparently he had caught sight of the grabber, or more likely had heard it grunting and splashing as it searched for her. I doubt that the leader can have known it was hunting a little girl, but he seemed determined to save that innocent creature, whatever it might be. As soon as he caught sight of the grabber, he drew his sword and advanced upon it fearlessly. At the sight of his resolute face and that slaughtering black blade, the grabber lost heart.

My host's mother could contain herself no longer. "This leader, Fava? Was he—"

"Grandmother!" Mora exclaimed. "You're not supposed to interrupt. You know you're not. You're the one who always objects when Fava and I do it."

"Interruptions are permitted in cases like this," my host's mother declared with great firmness. "Fava, I have to ask you about Incanto's leader, because Incanto never did describe him. Was he tall? As tall as Incanto?"

Fava shook her head. "That's funny. No, he wasn't. But almost as tall, though he didn't look it, and—"

Stocky. You can think of him as muscular if you like, and he certainly looked strong enough to fight and climb and the rest of it, but there was nothing heroic about him except his eyes.

The little girl whose adventures I have been recounting to you knew nothing about heroes and swords, or any such thing, but she was as curious as a monkey, and as soon as she realized what was happening she pushed her little head up out of the water, and as soon as the grabber was dead she overcame her natural shyness sufficiently to speak to the leader who had killed it and saved her, offering her timid thanks and after some hesitation venturing to say that she thought his was the best shape for everyone.

The colorcat lay dead, half in and half out of the muddy water, scarlet blood that looked no different from a man's or a hog's spurting from the gaping wound below its jaws. Dozens of young inhumi rose to drink it; wading in, I caught one by the nape of the neck and carried it to the bank with its tail lashing futilely and its arms and legs pawing air. "Can you talk?" I shook it.

It swung its head from side to side, then nodded. Already its lizard's face was softening a little, melting.

"You see that tree?" I pointed dramatically. "All I've got do is grab you by your tail and swing you against it, so you'd better do everything I say. What's your name?"

"Mee."

"You're changing your looks, and that's good, but you're making yourself too childlike. I want you older, so grow those legs. Are you a male or a female, Mee?"

"Girl."

"That's good too," I told her. "I think I'll keep you. I need a little help. If you'll come with me and do your job, I won't hurt you, and I'll see to it that nobody else does, either."

* * *

So he cut off a big piece of the grabber's skin for her (Fava continued), and scraped it until it was thin and smooth, and as flexible as grabber-skin can be made. She wrapped it around herself, and they picked flowers and pretty leaves for her to wear in her hair.

Incanto's leader had merely wanted her to frustrate the plans his son and a young woman were making in one of the human settlements. But without in the least intending to, he had made the little girl I have been talking about into a little girl from that day forward, a very good little girl, too, in her way, very fond of pretty dresses and playing nicely with other little girls.

Now I am tired and all of you have finished eating. I have a long way to go tomorrow, so I end her story here, and end it happily.

★

★   ★

Perhaps I ought not to have drawn the three whorls, for I only corked my little bottle of ink, wiped my pen, stretched, and talked to Oreb. Now here I am again, the same man in the same place, with the same ink, paper, and pen—though I have sharpened my nib a trifle, as you see.

As *I* see, I interrupted myself at the place where Fava and Mora came in here in their nightdresses last night, and went off storytelling. I hope to get back to that, but first I ought to say that Fava has gone, and that the two young men who are to carry the letters I wrote for Inclito had dinner with us tonight.

One is certainly the mercenary with whom Inclito spoke; when I entered the room, I saw him glance at Inclito and nod. His name is Eco, a fine, stalwart young man whose dark face and flashing teeth and eyes remind me of Hari Mau.

I have been trying to place him in the group I spoke with in the palace. To my left at the back of the room, I believe. He is quite tall, and I am reasonably certain that I remember him looking over the heads of those in front of him. No smiles then. I saw a very young man about to be sent into battle, and wondering whether he had the courage to bear himself well. From what Inclito said, I feel sure he did.

Indeed, I would be equally sure if Inclito had said nothing about him.

When Mora and Fava came last night, I sent Onorifica for the other maid, Torda, the sullen, good-looking young woman who fetched lap robes for us on the night that Inclito drove me back to Blanko. "I've been wanting to talk to you," I told her. "You are in danger—in deadly danger, in fact. I'm going to save you if I can. I had not intended to speak to you with Mora listening—"

I stole a glance at her; her heavy, coarse face told me very little, but her mouth seemed narrower than ever.

"Still, this may be the best way. And if Fava listens as well, it can do no harm and may do some good."

"You think you got me out of bed." Torda looked at me accusingly. "You think that—"

"I know I didn't. Onorifica brought you much too quickly for that. You were up and dressed, or dressing."

"I'm supposed to heat madame's bathwater. She bathes every morning. She'll be furious."

"Then Onorifica will have to do it."

"She's supposed to set the table for breakfast."

Fava tittered.

I waved the table aside. "Decina can do it. There can't be much involved in setting table for five."

"You thought I'd be scared and mixed up, but—"

I shook my head. "I hope to frighten you. I'm aware that you're not frightened now." (It was a lie; I knew she was.) "But I hope to frighten you for your own good. Women fear death, Torda, just as men do. If I can show you—and I think I can—that the Hand of Hierax is reaching for you even as we speak, you will be sensibly frightened and tell me the truth. If you do, things may not go so badly for you. Confusion is the last thing I'm hoping for. You must think clearly now, more clearly than poor Onorifica has ever thought in her life. You must see your peril, if you are to escape it."

"Poor girl!" Oreb cocked his head.

Mora nodded emphatically. "That's what I say too. If it weren't for—you really shouldn't bully her like that. I'm going to tell my father."

Fava's hand concealed her smile. "We came in here to talk to you about something entirely different, Incanto, and we were here first."

"I know what you want to talk about," (my voice was not more assured than I felt) "and it is the same thing. You say it's entirely different, but you don't know what I'm talking to Torda here about. Or do you?"

Fava shook her head.

"Torda is a spy," I said, and was careful to look at Fava as I said it. "Inclito has known for some time that there was a spy in his household. He asked me to identify her. I say *her* because it was clear to both of us that it had to be one of four persons: Decina, Onorifica, Torda, and you, Fava. It's Torda, and she can save us all some time by confessing."

"A spy? I am not!"

Oreb spat, "Bad girl!"

"I imagine everyone here knows your history," I told her, "so there can be no harm in re-hashing it. You came here as a poor relative—a relative only by courtesy. Your mother was supposed to have been a second cousin by marriage, or something like that. Something equally nebulous and impossible to prove. Came here from where?"

Torda shook her head and stared at the floor.

"Not from Blanko, because it wasn't said in that fashion. If you and your family had lived in town, Inclito and his mother—his mother particularly—would have known all about you. You came here from Soldo, and it's obvious who sent you."

"No!"

"You may actually be the sort of step-relative you claim to be. Who cares? The relationship is so tenuous as to be nonexistent anyway. Inclito took you and treated you as well as his daughter. All four of us know why."

I waited for her to speak, but she did not.

"You really are good-looking," I told her, "your profile particularly. Your face is a trifle too narrow, I would say, but it's not at all bad, and you have an admirable figure. When you smile you must be very pretty, and I'm sure you smiled a lot at Inclito, at first. Didn't you?"

She was glaring at me now, eyes blazing. "That has nothing to do with you!"

"Then something went wrong between you. Did he find you with another man? Or did you ridicule his appearance? He isn't a handsome man, and he seems sensitive about it."

Torda's face was set hard. "It's none of your affair. I told you."

Mora said, "He's acting for my father, or thinks he is." Her voice was flat with resignation.

"I would guess that you simply wanted too much. Was it jewels and clothes? Inclito had made a mistake when he treated you as well as he did in the beginning. You may even have tried to get him to marry you, and he doesn't want to remarry. He's hoping to leave everything he's got to his daughter and her husband."

Torda looked at Mora, and her eyes spoke volumes.

"He cast you aside, and you had to become the mere servant you'd been pretending to be. Any normal woman would have left then—"

"I had no place to go!"

Mora sighed. "Nobody here will, if you don't keep your voice down."

I nodded. "Why did you stay? Clearly because Duko Rigoglio would have been displeased. He would want you right here, as long as you could learn—"

"I'm from Novella Citta. I really am." Torda's voice was almost conversational, but a tear crept down her cheek.

I shrugged. "If that's the truth, perhaps I can arrange for your body to be sent there. I'll do what I can. Certainly Blanko won't want you where its own citizens find rest."

"Fish heads?" Oreb inquired.

"Breakfast soon, at least, though I doubt that there will be fish for you. Mora, would you be willing to go to the kitchen and see that Onorifica brings your grandmother's bathwater? Or perhaps even see to it yourself? It would be—"

She shook her head.

"As you like."

I turned back to Torda. "To repeat, it was clear that the spy was one of you four. Inclito suspected Fava and took care to say nothing that a spy might think significant in her presence. It was a reasonable precaution, and he took it; but nothing changed. The Duko seemed to know each plan he hatched. That suggested that Fava was not the spy, but he—and I, when he told me about it—remained understandably suspicious of her. She was not related to him, had no discernible family of her own, and had the run of the house. I talked to her and to Mora, hinting that her visit, welcome as it had been, had reached its natural conclusion. Mora wanted her to stay, but she herself readily agreed to leave at once, as you've no doubt heard. That settled it for me—Fava was no spy.

"Mora, how do they kill spies in Blanko? Have you any idea? At home they shoot them, but I've heard that in some places they're torn apart by four horses."

"Hang them, I think."

Fava said, "We burn inhumi. It depends on just what the person's done."

I nodded. "You were eliminated, as I said. That left Decina, Onorifica, and Torda here. Torda was clearly a rejected lover, so the answer was plain enough. I took time to inquire about the other two just the same. Decina has been working for Inclito and his mother since Mora was small; moreover, she rarely leaves her kitchen. I eliminated her, as any sensible person would. Onorifica's family lives nearby, and she isn't intelligent enough unless she's a superb dissembler."

I returned to Torda. "If you don't confess, you'll still be tried before the Corpo and executed. It's not the way I'd deal with this if I had a choice, but this isn't my house and Blanko isn't my town. What have you to say?"

"I didn't!" And then, in a whisper, "I love him."

"Poor girl!"

"Yes, Oreb. But a wealthy one if she could have made him believe it. Torda, I can only say that you have a strange way of showing it. If you confess—now—I'll do my utmost to see that there is no trial and no execution."

She shook her head violently.

"I hesitate to speak for him, but I believe that Inclito will as well. He'd prefer to keep your past relationship a secret, surely. Will you confess?"

"I didn't do it!"

I drew a deep breath and let it out. "Then there's no more to be done. Mora, will you tell your father we must see him as soon as he's up and dressed?"

"No." She spoke to Fava. "Go tell the other one about Grandmother's water."

I shook my head, and Fava said, "Really, Mora, I—"

"I mean it. Go now."

Fava stood, nodded, and left us, closing the door behind her. As I watched her go, I had to marvel at the perfection of the illusion. To my eyes (if not to Oreb's) she was a girl of thirteen or fourteen, rather small, with light brown hair that I knew must be a wig.

"Bad thing! Fish heads?" Oreb tugged at a lock of my own.

"No, breakfast isn't ready yet. Onorifica would have come around to tell us, I feel sure."

Mora began, "I am—"

I cut her off. "I know. First let me send Torda away."

Mora shook her head. "I am the spy. It was me."

"As you wish," I told her, and spoke to Torda. "Mora's been spying on her father for Duko Rigoglio. I accused you in the hope of making her confess. Do you understand?"

"It will . . ." Her face was stricken. "This will kill him."

"It will if he finds out, perhaps. A few minutes ago you said you loved him. Do you intend to tell him?"

She shook her head.

"Then perhaps you do. Will you tell your father, Mora?"

"No," Mora said. "I couldn't."

"In that case, neither will I. If we three can keep a secret, there's no reason it shouldn't be kept."

Mora began to speak, but I raised my hand to silence her. "Before you say anything about Fava—it may be we've seen the last of her. Do you realize that? It was why I didn't want you to send her away."

"I hope she's gone. That would make it easier." Mora slumped in her chair.

"Harder, I believe, and certainly less satisfying. She recruited you, isn't that right?"

After a lengthy pause, Mora nodded.

Torda said, "Then Fava is really the Duko's spy?"

"She is—or was—one of two," I said. "She got Mora to cooperate with her, and I imagine that Fava herself carried their reports back to Soldo."

Fava opened the door as I was speaking. "I did, and I got Mora to tell me things, that's all. I never said anything to her about spying, or telling the Duko. No matter what she's told you, that's all it was."

"That is all I ever thought it was. But after a time she must have realized what she'd been doing. If she hadn't before Inclito told her he thought there was a spy in the house, she certainly must have after that. Nevertheless, she didn't want you to leave."

Mora nodded.

"And she must have been very much afraid that you'd find a way to tell her father after you left—a letter to be found in your room or something of that sort. Most of you can't write, but you can, I know. Since you've been going to palaestra with Mora, it's not surprising."

Mora said, "She wouldn't have."

"She'll say she wouldn't have if you ask her now, I feel quite sure." I watched Fava resume her seat on my bed. "What was it the Duko gave you, Fava? Silver and gold? Cards with which to repair a lander? Not food, you seem to have had no difficulty getting that for yourself."

She shook her head.

"What was it, then?"

"I won't tell you!"

"Yes, you will." I strove to sound ruthless. "I'm giving you a chance to leave alive, but I'll withdraw it if I must."

Sullen silence.

"In a little while, I'm going to have to speak with Torda in private, because I want her to tell me a private matter. Yours is not. You must tell all three of us right now, Mora particularly."

"Torda too?"

"Yes, I think so. It's a bit late to leave Torda out."

I turned and glanced at the window. The Short Sun was rising, illuminating Inclito's broad fields and fat cattle. (Today I watched him stoop and pick up a clod of black earth, which is just now being plowed for winter wheat.) Gesturing, I said to Mora, "All that will be yours someday—no doubt he's told you. Yours, and your husband's."

"Good place!" Oreb assured us, and Mora nodded mutely.

"How did the Duko pay you, Fava, for the information you brought him? What did he give you?"

"Nothing!" She hesitated. "Jewelry, mostly. Jewelry and cards. I gave them away or threw them away."

"I can imagine—gold is heavy stuff. Since you didn't want the Duko's jewels or his cards, what did you want? You must have wanted something."

She shook her head. "Nothing."

"I know, you see, or at least I think I do; and I'll tell Mora if you don't. It will sound far worse from me."

"You know everything, don't you!"

"Certainly I don't know as much as I need to. I intend to consult the gods again, if I can persuade Mora's father to give me a lamb—"

"No cut!"

"Not you, silly bird. If Inclito will let me have a lamb or something of the kind to sacrifice, I'd like to consult the Outsider. Him, particularly, and perhaps the Mother, the Vanished People's sea goddess, though as far as I know the war brewing here has no connection with the sea."

"Then you'll pretend the gods told you," Fava declared.

"Certainly not. The gods won't tell people who do that sort of thing anything."

"We've been waiting for it," Mora explained listlessly. "Some kind of magic or enchantment. We were afraid, but we wanted to see it."

I nodded, and admitted that when I was her age I would have felt the same way.

Fava said, "Do we still want to talk to him about what we came to see him about, Mora? It will sound inane after all this."

"I don't care," Mora told her. "If you want to."

"Then I won't."

"I think we need to finish talking about your spying first," I said. "Mora will feel better when that's over, and so will I. While you were out of the room, I said that if the three of us—Mora, Torda, and I—could keep a secret, there was no reason for anybody else to know. Can you think of one?"

"Not if you can't."

"I can't. You're an intelligent young woman. Can you summarize everything you've told the Duko for me? Briefly, we haven't a lot of time."

"I think so. First there was the ammunition problem. Blanko had a lot of slug guns left over after the last war, but not much ammunition for them. Inclito was able to buy some in Aspis, and he got people from there to come here and show our people how to make it, so now there's a shop making ammunition in Blanko, and the town buys it from them as fast as they can turn it out.

"Then there was a lot of talk about fortifying. Some people wanted to make the town wall thicker and higher, and build more towers, but where was the money coming from? Naturally Inclito was against all that, and so were all the other farmers. He wanted to use the money, or as much as there was, to hire troopers who'd protect everybody, and that was the way it was decided after the farmers said they were going to start taking their produce someplace else."

Mora put in, "My father went around to a lot of the neighbors to get them to do that, and got some of them to go around like he was."

"I see."

"And I told him about you," Fava continued, "after you came here the first night. Inclito thinks you're a man called Silk he read about—"

"Good Silk," Oreb assured us.

"In some book. Only I don't think the people in books are ever really real."

"Nor do I," I told her.

"And that was the last one, two nights ago. I said you were supposed to be this very powerful witch who'd cast spells on him and Soldo so Blanko would win, and I thought there might even be some truth in it. That was because of the story you told us the first night. Then you told that other one tonight, and you got inside mine and started changing things. I told Mora this morning, and she said we should just go and see you and ask how you did it, as friends. I said you were her friend, not mine, but if she wanted to I'd come along."

"He's going to let you go," Mora told her. "He could get Papa to kill you twice over. You couldn't have a better friend than that."

"Yes, I could. I do."

"Before we talk about stories—"

From my shoulder Oreb repeated, "Talk, talk."

"Before we discuss those, I have a few questions about your reports, Fava. How many times have you gone to Soldo to talk to Duko Rigoglio?"

She muttered to herself, counting on her fingers. "Nine."

Torda burst out, "She said she went there night before last, Incanto. That can't possibly be true. She was here when you and the master went back to town, and here next morning for breakfast."

I nodded. "But let's pretend we think it's true, for the present."

"Nobody can ride that fast!"

"Thing fly!" Oreb demonstrated, circling the room. "Bad thing!"

"Come back, you silly bird.

"I was about to say, Fava, that you must surely have gained some information of value to Inclito on all those trips. How did you give it to him?"

"I couldn't, or not very much. He would have known."

"We both know you could, that you needn't always be Fava. How did you appear to the Duko?"

"Like I do now."

Without in the least desiring to, I pictured her as she must have appeared that night, her wig still upon her head, her arms, widened and lengthened to wings, straining the loose cotton stuff of her sleeves.

Torda was leaning forward to study her. I said, "In bright sunlight you might be able to make out her scales—it's why she carries a parasol. In this room I don't believe you will, unless your eyes are a great deal better than most."

"I've never seen one up close before."

"You're not seeing one now. Fava, would you like to show Torda—and Mora—your natural shape?"

"If you make me, I suppose I'll have to."

"I won't. I asked whether you would like to."

She shook her head.

"They can make themselves look very much like us, as you see," I told Torda. "They think like us as well. There is a stain of evil in them, however. Perhaps I should say that there is a streak in them that appears evil to human beings like us, an undertone of black malignancy with roots in their reptilian nature."

Fava began, "We feel—"

I raised my hand. "Think before you speak."

She nodded. "I was going to say that we feel the things we do are right, exactly as you and Mora feel that the things you do are right, even when they're wrong."

"That malignant stain kept you from informing Inclito, who

has housed you and been kind to you, as well as causing you to offer your services to the Duko. I hope to equalize matters a little, if I can."

"I'll help you," Fava declared.

Mora asked her, "Was that all it was? You threw away the jewels, you said. Is it just that you don't like us?"

"I like *you*," Fava told her.

I said, "If you really do, you will want to leave her for her sake. You have done a great deal of good here, I believe. You're beginning to do harm however, and it will only grow worse. Remember please that in a week or a month I will be gone, but Mora and Torda will still be here, and both know.

"Mora, you must understand that however much Fava may have liked you—I'm not qualified to pass on that—she resented the other human beings with whom she came in contact, not only your father and grandmother, but Torda and Onorifica, and all the people she met in Blanko."

Mora nodded reluctantly.

"She envied their humanity, and soothed her feelings by doing what she did, proving to herself that she had the power to destroy them—but we have very little time. The obvious question, Fava. Why didn't the Duko attack when you told him about the ammunition shortage?"

"He should have!"

"I agree, but he didn't. Why didn't he?"

"He said he wanted to train his people better, and get the crop in."

I nodded, wondering as I still do exactly how far I could trust her. "And hire more mercenaries, I'm sure."

"That's right, and equip everybody better for winter fighting."

I nodded again. "Does it snow here? I suppose it must."

Mora offered, "It snows a lot more up in the High Hills, and that's where my father wants to meet them."

"No doubt. Fava, when you told the Duko about Inclito's influence, how he had persuaded the town to fight outside its walls, it would be natural for him to order you to kill him—or so I would suppose. Blanko would certainly be much weaker without Inclito. Did he do that?"

"Yes," Fava said. "I wouldn't do it."

What power was in those words, I cannot say; but as she spoke them I felt once more the stillness of the steaming air between the colossal trees, dripping with moisture and thick with the smell of vegetable decay. Oreb surely felt it, too. Again and again he exclaimed, "Bad place! Bad place!," sounding half frantic with fear.

"He'd want me to kill you, too, Incanto." Her fangs came out, for her kind, like ours, appears about to eat when it is pleased. "If I were to go back there tonight, I know he'd tell me to. I wouldn't do that, either."

Mora and Torda were staring at her, Mora's slack jaw and open mouth rendering her less attractive than ever.

"I want you to go back to him," I said, and felt that she and I were sitting together on the damp, fecund soil. A moth with wings the size of dinner plates fluttered above the dark, stagnant pool between us, displaying staring eyes upon its wings before it fluttered up and up to vanish into the vaulted ceiling formed by the lowest limbs.

"You said you wanted to help me set things right here." I told Fava. "This is how you can do it. Tell Duko Rigoglio that Inclito is about to marry a woman from Novella Citta, and that both Novella Citta and Olmo have agreed to support his counterattack on Soldo once the war has begun. Will you do that?"

Fava nodded; her fangs had disappeared.

"If you do, and if you leave here today and do not return, you will have my friendship—for whatever that's worth. I won't reveal your nature to Inclito, or tell him that you have nearly bled his mother to death."

Torda grasped my arm and pointed at the idiot-faced, long-legged thing that had fallen from the tree under which we sat; its wrinkled, hairless hide was the brownish pink of human skin, and although it seemed stunned, its blunt tail probed the ground like a blind worm. "Don't worry," I told her. "They eat leaves, are not good to eat themselves, and are perfectly helpless and harmless. It would never have left its tree if it weren't looking for a mate." At the sound of my voice it lifted its head and stared at me, its eyes as dull as ever and its mouth working.

Fava leaned forward to admire her own face, studying her reflection in the water as she might have in a slab of polished jet. "Back in Grandecitta, where I lived as a girl—do you mind if I'm older now, Mora? It's been so hard staying young for you while I dined with your grandmother. I kept having to stop on the way to Duko Rigoglio's palace, or on the way back, to find another child. Incanto said I had no trouble finding food, and I heard him say once that we prey upon the poor as if it were an accusation. It's really just that we look for houses that aren't very solid and are poorly defended."

Mora gasped. "Are you doing this? Is this . . . ? Is it where you come from?"

Fava nodded. "But I'm not doing it." For a second her mouth opened as widely as a human mouth can, I would guess because she believed she was retracting her fangs. "Incanto is, I'm sure. How do you manage it, Incanto?"

I shook my head.

"Back in Grandecitta, it was fashionable to credit witches and fortune-telling, and all sorts of humbug. If you didn't consult a strega at least once a month, when your period came, you pretended you had and made the charm yourself to show your friends. I did that sometimes, and so did they I'm sure. Charms against the pain, and for love and good luck. When I remember them now, it seems to me that they never helped anyone, though they may have hurt a few of us."

Her face had become the smooth but delicately wrinkled one of a woman who had been beautiful thirty years ago. "I hope yours aren't like that, Incanto," she added. "Aren't we all friends here? If we are, anything that harms any of us hurts all of us. I hope you agree."

I said nothing because I was watching Mucor, who had coalesced from a shimmer on the dark surface. "There you are, Silk.

There you are, Horn. I've been looking everywhere for you. Babbie came back without you, and Grandmother's worried."

"Tell her I found an eye for her," I said. "I'll bring it as soon as I can."

There was a knock at the door, and a hoarse, muffled voice outside it.

Mucor had turned her death's-head grin toward Torda. "Are you sure you want to marry him? Silk will help you."

The door opened, and for a moment I saw the fat, middle-aged face of the cook, stupid with shock.

"B-b-breakfast . . ."

The colossal trees were fading as the small but comfortable bedroom my host had provided returned.

"Breakfast is on the table. The—the, uh . . ."

Oreb appeared to shrink. "Good place!" He practically crowed it.

And then, "Fish heads?"

10

Untamed Talents

Mora, Oreb and I went in to breakfast then. No doubt Torda went to her morning duties, whatever they were; I did not see her again until shortly before I sacrificed. Fava must have gone to Soldo, if she has not set off to gather more of her kind to hunt me down. Wherever she went, she certainly was not at breakfast with us today.

Here I ought to jump ahead to dinner. The two young men who were to carry the letters I had written for Inclito ate with us, and we were all much too interested in talking to them for anybody to suggest the story game. One was raised in Blanko; his name is Rimando—it means "delay," he tells me, and was given him because his mother carried him for almost ten months.

"If I'd known that," said Inclito, "I'd never have accepted you. You'll be half the morning just getting the saddle blanket on."

The other is the mercenary whose story Inclito told; his name is Eco, and I saw him nod to Inclito when I came into the dining room.

"They'll ride for Blanko to take my letters to Novella Citta and Olmo," Inclito explained to his mother and daughter. "It'll be dangerous. They know, and every god knows I do. But they're going to do their best to get through, aren't you, boys."

Both young men nodded.

"The Duko's troopers are on their way to fight us already?" my host's mother asked me. "That was what you saw when you sacrificed?"

"As I told you, madam."

"We've got to believe it," her son said. "But if the gods had told Incanto the Duko wouldn't move for another month, we'd have to believe his troops had started anyway. We can't afford the other. You got to stay off the main roads. You got to stay off the little side roads as much as you can. You want grass under his hoofs whenever you can get it."

Thinking of Green, I added, "And leaves above your heads."

"That's right. Stay out of sight. Move fast, but not so fast you wear out your horse." Inclito paused. "I don't think you're going to get a chance to change horses, but do it if you can. Lead him uphill wherever it's steep. Give him a little rest."

Speaking for the first time, Mora said, "They should be riding this minute."

Her father shook his head. "They rode out here. For today, that's enough. Let them get a good meal now and a good night's sleep. There's good big stalls and clean straw for the horses, water and oats and corn. Tomorrow they go as soon as the sun's up."

Turning to Rimando he explained, "Decina's going to wake me up. Decina's my cook. She goes to sleep right after dinner and gets up early. I'll wake you up, and you, too, Eco. I'll see you off."

They nodded, and I gave Inclito what I intended to be a significant glance.

"Both, we don't want you killed. We don't want you dead, understand? If they try and stop you and you can get away, fine. But if you can't—" He raised both hands.

Mora asked, "Do they have needlers?"

Rimando shook his head.

Her father said, "We can't spare even one for this. No needlers, no slug guns, no swords. They're too heavy anyway. We want them to get away, not fight."

Decina herself came in as he spoke and transferred the huge roast on the spit to a great pewter platter fit for it; she set it down ceremoniously before Inclito, who stood and took up a fork with which he might almost have pitched hay and a carving knife with a blade as long as my forearm. "Holy meat. Don't anybody swear or talk against the gods while you eat it, it's not polite."

Eco, seated between Inclito and his mother, asked me whether the victim had been a steer.

I shook my head. "A young bull, fawn with a black face. Do they sacrifice steers in your town?"

"I think so."

"Perhaps they may, customs differ. In my own—and much more in Old Viron—no animal that had been maimed in any way could be offered, just as no private person sacrificing at home was to offer a loaf from which a slice had been taken or wine after he had drunk from the bottle."

Salica said, "You're not a patre, Incanto? I know, I asked you before."

I smiled at her. "No, I'm afraid not. Nor am I an augur, which is what we call them. Our canons permit sacrifice by a sibyl when no augur can be found, however, and sacrifice by a layman—or a laywoman, for that matter—when no augur or sibyl is present. Such sacrifices are nearly always private, carried out before a small shrine in the giver's own house."

"I see."

"I felt that this one, which was to take place in your son's presence and on his property, with the sacred fire upon an altar of turfs I built myself, could reasonably be considered a private one."

"Only the family attended," Salica explained to Rimando and Eco. "My son, my granddaughter, and I."

Mora added, "And Torda."

"That's right, Torda to help Incanto with the knife and the blood."

Inclito had been carving a thick slice while we spoke. "You're the main guest, Incanto, and you sacrificed him for us. Hold out your plate."

I did not. "Half that or less. Less, as a favor."

"Rimando? Here you are." Inclito cut a smaller piece and gave it to me.

Eco told Mora, "In Gaon, where I was before I came here, they still sacrifice heifers to Echidna, but they won't eat the meat themselves."

"The gods got the head, all four feet, and some other stuff," Inclito remarked as he laid a thick slab of beef on Eco's plate. "They said that was all they wanted, and we could have the rest."

"The people of Gaon do not abstain from beef and veal because they think them unclean," I explained, "but because they think them too sacred."

Rimando paused in the act of cutting his meat. "But the gods told you that the horde of Soldo has already set out to invade us? That's the important point. What gods were they, anyway?"

"The Outsider and the sea goddess of the Vanished People," I told him. "I don't even know her name, and perhaps no one does now."

Mora smiled mischievously. "You could ask your neighbors."

I smiled back. "The Vanished People themselves, you mean? I'll try to remember."

"Fava didn't believe in them," Mora told Eco. "Fava's a friend of mine who was staying with us until this morning."

Rimando said, "I've got her old room. She seems to have left behind a good many of her belongings."

"She'll be back for them eventually, I suppose."

I added, "Or she'll send for them, Mora. I would think that more likely."

Mora nodded.

"Why did you choose those two?" Rimando asked me. "Isn't there a god for war?"

"A goddess," I told him absently, "and several minor gods, as well."

Salica said, "Don't make him talk, please. He doesn't eat enough as is."

Eco asked Inclito, "Didn't the gods have anything to say about us?"

There was a pained silence, broken at length by Rimando. "I believe I understand. One of us won't reach his destination. Or is it that neither of us will?"

"Fish heads?" Oreb had flapped through an open window to reclaim his post on my shoulder. I passed him up a scrap of meat, and Mora asked, "If I try to feed him, will he take it?"

"Probably. He likes you."

She cut a considerably larger piece from the slice on her plate and tossed it across the table to Oreb, who caught it in his beak and flew to the hearth to tear it into shreds of manageable size.

"I'd like to know," Rimando challenged us all with his eyes, "precisely what these gods, two gods I've never so much as heard of, had to say about us. I don't believe in them. Less even than your friend believed in the Vanished People, if that's possible." (This last was addressed to Mora.) "But I want to know. It's my right, and Eco's too."

Salica inquired rather timidly, "Why don't you believe in the gods?" Rimando snorted, and she gave me a pleading glance.

"You see," I told her, "as soon as you silence me, you find that you require my speech."

Eco tried to restore harmony. "I think I'd prefer not to know. It was a private sacrifice, they say. Let it stay private."

"I'm of your mind," I told him. "The interesting question isn't what I read in the entrails of this young bull. An augur with sufficient imagination can read whatever you like in the entrails of whatever beasts you choose, and predictions made at sacrifice fail at least as often as they succeed—more often, in my experience."

Rimando asked, "Is one of us to die? Which one?"

"No," Mora told him. "There wasn't anything like that."

"Nor is the interesting question why Rimando doesn't believe in gods," I continued. "It is why anyone should. Why didn't Fava believe in the Vanished People, Mora? The answer may prove enlightening."

"Because they have vanished. She knew that they were here once. I mean she'd seen the things people show that they say were theirs, things that have been dug up, you know. And last year one of Father's hands found a little statue when he cleaned out our well."

"I'd like to see it."

Inclito glanced up from his plate. "I'll show you right after dinner."

"Only she said they were gone, and that was why they're called the Vanished People. If they were still here, we'd know all about them and see them every day."

I nodded. "Anything that's seldom seen is assumed to belong to the remote past, even when it was last seen yesterday."

Rimando began, "I want to know—"

"Of course you do. This is my fault; I may have misread the gods' message, and in fact I probably did. I thought it said that only one of you would set out in the morning."

Inclito broke the silence that followed by picking up the small bell beside his mother's plate and ringing it. A smiling Torda appeared at once, and he told her, "I'd like a little horseradish. Would you ask Decina for some, please? I know it's not your job."

"I'll grate some for you myself, sir. I know right where it is."

Rimando cleared his throat. "It didn't say which one of us wouldn't go?"

"I don't know," I told him. "Quite possibly that was written there as well, but if so I was too obtuse to read it."

Mora said, "Wouldn't the gods know you couldn't, and not bother writing it?"

I shrugged.

"You want to ask why I don't believe in the gods, all of you," Rimando declared, "but you're afraid to ask me, or too polite."

"Not at all," I told him. "By this time you should have seen enough of our host to know that though he is extremely brave, he is never polite."

Inclito dropped his knife and fork, and roared with laughter.

"He has many excellent qualities. He's both intelligent and shrewd, for example, a rare combination. Mora, you love your father, I know. What is it you like so much about him?"

From his place on the hearth, Oreb croaked loudly, "Good man!"

"He is." Mora nodded. "But that's not why I love him. It's hard to explain."

"Do you want to try?"

"I think so. It's that he loves whatever he's doing. He made me a house for my doll when I was small, and he loved doing that, just like he loved building onto this house and then building more, or putting up a new barn. I played with his dollhouse, and you know how children are. After a while it didn't look as nice, so he fixed it for me and repainted it, and he loved doing that, even when he'd been working hard all day."

Torda returned from the kitchen with a saucer of horseradish and a spoon. Inclito took it from her and dumped half of it onto his plate, then held out the rest to us.

Only Eco accepted. "Your daughter mentioned a little statue, you were going to show it to Incanto. I'd like to see it myself. Would that be all right?"

"Absolutely," Inclito told him. "There are some other things, too."

"In Gaon they've got a cup that belonged to their rajan, the one that disappeared."

Inclito nodded.

"The Vanished People are supposed to have given it to him, and it certainly looks like some work of theirs I've seen. They say it cures the sick, and they keep it in the temple of their goddess."

Mora came in as I was writing *cures*. "Not in my nightgown this time," she said, and tapped her riding boots with her quirt.

"Nor with Fava," I remarked. "I like this much better."

"But with the same questions she and I had last night, and more." She paused. "I've been out in the stable just now with Rimando. He wanted to see about his horse, see that it was comfortable and had enough water. Only when he got me out there he had a thousand questions, just like me."

She seemed to expect me to smile, so I did.

"I couldn't answer most of them, but when I got back to my room and started to undress for bed . . ."

"You became curious yourself," I suggested.

"I was already. That's why Fava and I came last night. But I need somebody to talk to. That used to be Fava, but she's gone now."

"What about your father and your grandmother?"

"It wouldn't be like talking to Fava. Or to you."

She sat in silence for a few seconds while I finished the sentence I had begun when she knocked, and wiped my pen.

"That man Eco talked about, the man down south who was looking for his father. Do you have a son?"

I nodded.

"Because you thought he might be looking for you. That's the way it seemed to Rimando, and it seemed like that to me, too."

I asked whether she thought Rimando attractive.

"That has nothing to do with it."

Oreb croaked a warning: "Look out!"

"Of course it does. You went to the stable with him."

"I wanted to see their horses, that's all. Did you see them when they came?"

I shook my head.

"They've got wonderful horses, both of them. A chestnut for Eco and a bay for Rimando. Father got two of the richest men in Blanko to contribute a horse apiece. I'd like to know how he does that."

"So would I."

"Uh huh. You don't know anything, do you, Incanto?"

"At least, I know how little I know."

"Did you really think that could have been your son looking for his father down south?"

"No." It required a good deal of resolve to tell the truth. "I didn't think it could possibly be. But I hoped it was."

"I think the father that he said he was looking for would have been younger than you are. He didn't sound a lot like you, either."

I nodded.

"You don't know who it was?"

"I have no idea—none. You'll want to know whether Eco's description would fit my son. No, it would not. My son's name is Sinew."

"That's what you said."

"It is. He may be calling himself something else—I have no way of knowing. But the young man Eco talked about didn't sound like my son. You indicated that you came with many of the same questions you and Fava had last night; this cannot have been one of them. What are they?"

She waved their questions aside. "You wrote those letters."

"The ones that Rimando and Eco are going to carry to Olmo and Novella Citta? Yes, I did. I wrote them with your father's permission, and he read them before he signed them. Do you want to know what was in them?"

Mora shook her head. "Rimando's is in his saddlebag. I could go out to the stable right now and read it if I wanted to. I could, but I'd have to break the seal. Does that bother you? That I could read it?"

"Not in the slightest."

"All right." She leaned forward, her brutal, girlish face intent. "For just a minute, this morning just before Decina came, we were someplace else. Fava and I were, I think, and I asked Torda about it and she said she was too. Was that Green?"

I nodded again.

"You did it to turn me against Fava."

"I didn't do it at all. Not consciously at least."

"But you've been there? Is that what you call the jungle? What we saw and smelled and felt?"

"Yes, it is. I have not said so."

"At dinner yesterday you got inside Fava's story and changed things around. Did it really happen?"

"I suppose it did. I didn't do it consciously."

"Good Silk!"

For half a minute or longer, Mora studied me, her elbows on

her knees and her chin in her hands. At last she said, "I meant what Fava told about. Did that really happen? Did you try to use an inhuma to fool your son?"

"No."

"It was just made up?"

I nodded. "I've told you I don't know how I did those things, if I did them. That was the truth, but I've been thinking a lot about them, as you can imagine. Would you like to hear my theory? Telling someone else may make it clearer in my own mind."

"Go ahead."

"Suppose that the Duko were to build a road to facilitate the passage of his horde to the border. Might not troopers from Blanko use that same road to besiege Soldo?"

"I don't think I understand this."

"Neither do I, but I'm trying to. Have you ever seen a dead inhumu? One who had been personating a human being?"

"You told me that I hadn't seen one at all. I still haven't, not close up."

"I have, and more often than I like."

Those were magic words, although I had been ignorant of their power when I pronounced them. As a small boy I had heard the stories all children hear, and used to imagine that if only I could stumble upon the correct syllables a garden would spring up where our neighbors' houses stood, a place of mystery and beauty in which the trees bore emeralds that turned to diamonds as they ripened, and fountains ran with milk or wine. Eventually I came to realize that the immortal gods were the only spirits who granted the wishes of men, and that prayers were the magic words I had sought. It thrilled me, as it still does; but when I told my friends my discovery, they only sneered and turned away.

Now—very far from those friends, men and women I will never see again—I had stumbled upon words that were magic indeed. No sooner had I pronounced them than I found myself back in Green's jungles, squatting beside the young man who had joined us and fought beside us, as he writhed and bled beneath the arching roots.

"Tell me again why you hate the inhumi," he asked, as if we two were sitting at ease in my bedroom in Inclito's house, and had all the time in the whorl.

"I've never told you anything of the kind," I said, "or talked to you at all until this moment."

"You'll know me when I'm gone."

"They drink our blood. Isn't that enough?"

"No." His face was a mask of pain.

"Incanto?" Mora was concerned for me.

"What is it?"

"Are you all right?"

I nodded. "His mother—Krait's mother—she was the one, you see. We were as poor . . . You've been rich all your short life. You can't imagine how poor we were."

"I could try."

"We had shared out everything when we landed, we who had come from Old Viron and the new people, the sleepers, the ones who had slept three hundred years in the caverns of the *Whorl.* Do you know about them, Mora? Their memories had been tampered with, like Mamelta's, so they were confused in strange ways."

No doubt she thought I was one of them, for which I cannot blame her; but she nodded politely.

"The tools and the seeds and the frozen embryos, though there weren't many of those. No human embryos at all. They'd been taken, every one of them. Special talents, you see—untamed and unpredictable abilities that were supposed to help us; but they had been taken by those who had broken the seals. Taken and sold, long ago."

"No cut," Oreb advised me. "Good Silk!"

"Silk had been one of them. Silk had been our leader. That was his talent, leadership. People trusted and followed him, and he tried—I tried very hard, Mora, not to mislead them, not to lead them astray and betray them. But Silk had remained behind in the *Whorl* with Hyacinth, and it almost destroyed us."

"I see," Mora said, although clearly she did not.

"Our women were supposed to bear the animals, exactly as Maytera Marble's granddaughter had, bear horses and sheep and cattle and donkeys. Nettle couldn't, because she was carrying Sinew, and so we gave ours to a woman she had known all her life who promised to give it back to us when it was born. But she didn't, she wouldn't. She said it had been stillborn. Many of them were, but that one was not. She hid it from us until she thought we wouldn't know, and it was only a little, long-necked animal, like a little camel without a hump, after all. It wouldn't plow, and she and the man who lived with her killed it trying to make it plow, and so we were so poor—Nettle and I were so poor—because Silk had not come.

"We sold part of the land they had given us, and bought a donkey, but the donkey died. Eventually we sold the rest of our land and ate what little we got for it, and bought milk for Sinew when Nettle's dried up, and lived in a tent on the Lizard, a little tent I made for us from the skins of the rock goats I hunted. That was when she came, Krait's mother, and Sinew nearly died.

"My son's name was Krait, did I tell you?"

Poor Mora shook her head. "You said your son's name was Sinew."

"Yes. Yes, it was. But when he died—when Krait died there in the jungle—the illusion was last to die. I think it always is. The illusion of humanity. It is a thing of the spirit, you see, and so partakes of immortality. The spirit is the breath, Mora."

She nodded again, hesitantly; I could not tell whether she understood everything or nothing.

"They reshape themselves. That is the animal. That was how they lived and how they reproduced until the Neighbors came and found them, and were themselves found by them. It is the animal, as I said. A chemical woman like Maytera Marble carries within her half the plans necessary to build a new chem, and a chemical man like Hammerstone, the other half, did you know that? It was how they began to build Olivine. You've probably never seen a chem."

I showed her the eye I am bringing to Maytera Marble.

"The animal part is easy. We had lizards at home that could

change their skins to look like human skin, and there are bugs that shape themselves to look like other bugs, or like sticks, or the heads of deadly snakes. When an inhumu dies, it seems to be a human being—Krait seemed to be a young man there to the end, there in Green's jungles. A young man when he died and for some time afterward. When it was too late, I saw him as I had seen him on the sloop."

There was a mirror above the bureau; I went to it and stood before it trembling. "Do you see this face, Mora? Of course you do. It is the only face you can see. It is not my face, however. Come and look."

"I won't!"

"Poor girl!" Oreb flew to her, and would have comforted her if he could.

"Suppose that Fava were to die, Mora, and that you waited at her deathbed as I waited beside Krait. I had stayed behind, you see, because he had fought for us. I had been wounded too, but I tried to get some of the others to carry him. They would not, Mora. I ordered them to, but they only shook their heads and turned away, even Sinew; and in the end they would not carry me either. They left me just as they had left him, and I made myself stand and go back to him.

"You would hear Fava's last words, just as I heard his. Perhaps she would tell you the secret, the great secret they fear so much that we will learn. You would hear the rattle of Hierax in her throat, the rattle that he kept and would not allow his younger sisters to play with. In a second or two, she would cease to breathe. Do you understand, Mora? Am I making myself clear?"

She nodded.

"Still—still!—you would see the child you had known as Fava lying in her bed. Her face would appear shrunken, its full cheeks pale and not so full. Yet still Fava, a human being of about your own age."

"She got a lot older just before she went away," Mora said hesitantly. "Like Grandmother."

"Because so much of her food had been taken from your

grandmother while she slept. Foolish people think that they will see the marks of the fangs, and there will be blood on the sheets. The truth is that the marks are small and white, and do not bleed. An inhumu's fangs are round, you see, and the wounds made by all such round things close themselves, unless they are very large. In addition, I imagine that Fava was wise enough to bite your grandmother in a place where she couldn't see her wounds—on her back, perhaps, or on the backs of her legs.

"You would see Fava lying there dead, exactly as you had always known her. Then you would blink away tears, or look aside for a moment; and when you looked back at her, you would see something that did not look human at all, a beast dressed like a girl, its scaly face painted and powdered, and its hair a wig. Around New Viron, farmers like your father put up lay figures to frighten birds. Do they do that here, too?"

She nodded again.

"Have you ever seen one from a distance when you were out riding, and thought it a real person?"

"I think I understand, but I still don't understand how you took us to Green before breakfast."

"Because the illusion was there, and was strong—when I looked at Fava I saw a girl, though I knew better. She was impressing her reality upon my mind, just as the Duko wants to impress the governmental system of his town upon Blanko. But something in my mind seized the links Fava had forged between the three of us and herself, shouting its own reality, which was and is mine. There were bugles and trumpets all along the road, Mora, and the crash and rattle of marching men with slug guns. All of that was exactly as Duka Fava had intended, but the men were not hers."

"I think I understand," Mora said slowly.

"I hope so. I don't believe I can explain it any better than I have."

"Can I ask about the sacrifice? What you saw in the bull?"

"You may, of course. But I doubt that I can tell you more now than I did then."

"You said one wouldn't go. Does it mean that only one letter will, or—"

"I suppose so."

"Or are you just saying that either Rimando or Eco is going to stay here?"

"That's a good question." For a few seconds I was at a loss, trying to recall exactly what intimations I had received from the bull's entrails.

"Did you see whether the letters would be delivered?"

I shook my head. "I saw nothing about the letters. It's actually very rare for anyone to see anything concerning an object, as apart from a human being. I saw signs I took to represent the names of the messengers—that is to say, I saw a thorny branch, which I took to represent Rimando, in a dome, which I took to represent Eco. Only a single line departed from there, directed toward an *O*, which I took to be the sign for Olmo."

"Eco has the letter for Olmo. Rimando's is for Novella Citta. Is he going to get scared tonight? Too scared to go?"

"I have no way of knowing. If you're asking whether I saw anything of that kind in the victim, I did not. What about you? You've talked to him in private, and you're practically a woman, as I've said before. What do you think?"

"I don't think so. He said that it wasn't really going to be very dangerous, just a long, tiring ride. He wants me to suggest to Papa to let him keep his horse for a reward."

"I see. Are you going to do it?"

"I don't think so," she repeated. "You say I talked to Rimando, just the two of us. You wanted to talk to Torda like that yourself."

"I didn't intend to imply that there was anything wrong with your speaking to him, only that you had, and were likely to have more insight into his character than I do."

"You told Torda what she was supposed to do when she sacrificed our bullock. What else did you tell her?"

"Good girl," Oreb declared. "Bird hear."

Mora smiled.

"I think he means that you should be told everything I told Torda," I said. "He's probably right. You realize, I hope, that I can't tell you anything she told me."

"All right."

I sighed and leaned back in my chair, sorry to see the friendly relationship I had built up with Mora destroyed. "I acted against your interests, if you like."

"You mean you want Papa to marry her."

"If he wants to, yes."

"So I won't get the farm. I'll never be mistress of this house or rich. I know you think I'm rich now, but it doesn't do me any good."

"You think it does not."

"I know it doesn't. I'm not just the biggest girl in my class. There's more to it."

"I realize that."

"Do you know what I'm scared of? Really, really scared of? I want to say what I've been so scared of all my life, but it wouldn't be the truth. What I've been so scared of for the past year?"

"Not Fava, obviously, and not the war. That more inhumi would come? No." I shook my head. "What was it?"

"That I'd meet some man and think he loved me, and after we were married I'd find out he just loved this place, loved the idea that someday Papa would die and he'd be rich."

Her hands (large hands for a girl her age) tightened, grasping her legs above the knee. "I saw it start tonight. This was the first time ever. But I know—I know—"

Two big tears escaped her deep-set eyes to course down her broad cheeks; I left my chair to crouch beside hers, my arm around her shoulders.

"I know it's going to go on and on and on. . . ." Suddenly she turned on me, a fledgling hawk. "I'll kill him! You can make me promise anything you want, but I'll kill him just the same. What did you tell Torda?"

"The same things anyone in my position would." I stood up and returned to this sturdy, leather-covered chair in which I sit writing. "That I thought she loved your father and that he loved her; but that sullenness and sulking would never win him, no more than demanding that he marry her had made him marry her. That if she were cheerful and smiling instead, and asked for nothing, he would certainly give her a great deal and might even give her what she wanted."

"Would that work for me?"

I shrugged. "It might, if you were to find a man of the right sort, and had an opportunity to be around him for extended periods. It may not work for Torda—I don't know. And if the man is of the wrong sort it will not work at all for any woman."

"I ought to go now," Mora said pensively. "I ought to get a little sleep, but it will be hard with Fava gone."

"You certainly should if you intend to rise early and see the messenger off," I agreed.

"Just one?"

I nodded. "I think so."

"Well, I don't. But I ought to get to bed anyhow. When you and your wife—and your little son, is that right? Were on . . . What did you call it?"

"I probably said the Lizard. Lizard Island, off the coast."

"You lived by hunting rock goats?"

"Yes. And by fishing."

"Well, I'd rather live like that with a man who loved me, and live in a little tent of skins, than live here by myself or with a man who didn't. Why are you smiling like that?"

"Because after racking my brain for four long days I've finally realized who you and your father remind me of. I knew—I felt, at least—that I had met you both before. I won't tell you because the names would mean nothing to you."

"Were they good people?"

"Very good people." Without my willing it, my voice grew softer. I myself heard it with surprise. "People are always asking me to predict events to come, Mora. Usually I say that I can't, because it's so seldom I can. I try, as you've seen; but it's very doubtful stuff, like my prediction concerning Eco and Rimando."

She nodded as she stood up.

"Once in a rare while I really do know the future, however. When it happens—which is only rarely, as I said—I generally have a terrible time making people believe me. Will you believe me now, if I swear to you that what I'm about to tell you is the simple truth? The truth about the future?"

"If I can."

"Just so. If you can. You have been growing up with a number of assumptions, Mora, and all of them are wrong. You said a moment ago—please don't cry again, it isn't worth it—that you saw for the first time what it would be like to be pursued by fortune hunters."

"He wanted to know how o-o-old I w-was." Her voice was without any hint of emotion until it shook and broke. "So I said fifteen, to see if he'd—if he'd . . ."

She bit her lower lip to steady herself. "Because I wanted to see if he'd believe it, and he did. You have to be sixteen to get married in Blanko. Is it like that where you come from?"

"Probably not," I told her. "I don't know, but I doubt that there is any restriction at all."

"In Blanko it's sixteen, so I said fifteen and waited to see what would happen. He looked at me and looked away, and I could see it working in his mind. He asked me about my mother, and how many brothers and sisters, and everything I said made him worse."

"I understand. I, too, saw something for the first time tonight. I think it's very likely that it was the first time that it's ever been seen at all, by anyone." I paused to collect my thoughts.

"When a boy becomes a man, Mora, there must be a moment, a moment when the boy falls away never to be seen again. But before that moment come moments, which may be many or few, when one can glimpse the man who is to be, the man waiting behind the boy."

"I'm not a man, even if that's what they say at the academy. Or a boy either."

"I know you're not, which is why it came as such a surprise to me. I had known the other, you see; but I had never realized that it would apply equally to girls. Even when it took place before me, I was so busy recognizing her—I recognized the woman you will become as soon as I saw her—that I didn't think through the implications for a moment. You talked just now about finding a man who will love you."

"Maybe I can't." The hawk returned. "But by every god in the whorl, I'm going to try!"

"You will find many, and without much difficulty," I told her. "But be careful—be extremely careful, I beg you—that you find one you yourself can love as well."

"Man come," Oreb muttered.

"Your father," I told Mora. "Why don't you open the door for him?"

"How do you—?"

"I know his step."

He knocked as I spoke.

"And his knock, too. Please come in, Inclito. It's not locked." He did, and looked surprised to see his daughter.

"Mora will be lonely without Fava," I explained. "She wanted to talk to me about that, and some other things. She realizes, as I'm sure you do, that she won't be a child much longer. She's concerned about her course in life, as all such young women are. I've tried to help a little, though I haven't much help to give her."

"It would be a lot," Mora said, "if I could believe you." And then, impulsively, "Good-bye, Incanto! Good-bye, Papa!" She blew us kisses, and was out of the room before I could so much as consider what gesture I might make in return.

Inclito shut the door. "She's not in trouble with some boy, is she?"

I shook my head.

"Her mother had a dozen on her string. Nobody ever figured out why she picked me." Inclito sat down on my bed. "She wasn't a beautiful woman, but . . ."

"If I were more polite myself, I would say now that you're mistaken," I told him, "in part at least."

"You're not that polite?"

I shook my head.

"Me neither. Mama tried to make me when I was little, but it saves a lot of time. All right, not a dozen. Six I can name and me. No, eight."

"I wasn't referring to that. A dozen may be the figure for all I know—or twenty. But you lied when you said she wasn't a beautiful woman."

"You could see by my face, huh? I thought I was better than that. You're right, she was, and I was the only one that knew it."

"You are better than that. It was another face that told me you were lying."

"You saw her one time, my Zitta? Before you left the old whorl?"

"Tonight. What was it you wanted to see me about?" I went to the window, which was open already, and opened it more widely.

"The spy. It was Fava?"

I nodded.

"She ought to have been hanged."

"Then hang me. I arranged for her to escape in safety."

He shook his head, a head bigger than most men's, upon a neck far thicker than most. "She was only a sprat. It would have made me sick to watch it. I'm not going to say you did right, but I'm glad you did it."

"So am I."

"The Duko's marched already? That's what you said."

"No, I didn't. I said I thought so, and that if he had not, he would set out within a day. That is as exact as I can make it."

"We got to meet him in the hills." Inclito stood up, absent-mindedly wiping hands twice the size of his daughter's on his shirt. "He gets out into the bottomlands where he can spread out his horses, and it's all over. You weren't ever a trooper? It's what you told me once. But you fought enough to get yourself shot." He pointed toward my wound, though it was concealed by my robe and my tunic. "There in the side. In and out. It doesn't bother you?"

I shrugged. To write the truth—Nettle, you must never read this—I was listening to Seawrack's song as it floated across the waves a hundred leagues from where I stood.

"That man in the town down south? The one they called the rajan? It seemed like he ran a pretty good war. The other town had more men. That's what Eco says. He beat them anyhow, with brains and magic."

"Mostly by luck."

"Oh. You heard too? If you say so, but I'd like to have luck like that on our side. They say he's got six hundred on horses, the Duko."

My eyes must have shown the skepticism I felt.

"He had a spy here? I got spies there. Six hundred, they tell me. And Novella Citta. And Olmo. You know what I've got? How many horses? I'm trying to get two hundred. You know my men here? Well, I'm taking them, all three of them, on the carriage horses. After that if I can find just a few more, two hundred."

"Meanwhile, I am sending away two of your horsemen to carry my letters."

"It's right what you're doing. We haven't got so little we can't use any at all. Suppose they both get through. How good a chance they come over to our side?"

"Your estimate would be much more accurate than mine, I feel sure."

"One out of ten one will. One out of twenty for both. Each can bring a hundred and fifty on horses, maybe. Maybe a hundred. So that's eight hundred to get around behind us as soon as they get through the hills."

I said that my chief object in sending the letters had never been to win over Novella Citta and Olmo—welcome though that would be, should it occur—and that it was by no means impossible to be outflanked among hills.

"No, but it's harder, and they'd have to fight us, probably. If they get close, they can go straight at Blanko. You've seen it, the river and the walls. How long could they hold it against eight hundred men? That's boys, old men, and women."

I reflected. "A month, perhaps, if they were well led."

"Pah! A day. Maybe one whole day. Not two. And when our men found out the town had fallen behind them." He made a graphic gesture. "They're shoemakers and shopkeepers, farmers like me. The gods didn't say we win the war?"

"Nor that you will lose it."

"We'll meet them in the hills and crush them. We've got to. In the hills—" He waved toward my chair. "Sit down. You're making me all upset. Sit down."

I did, and he sat again.

"In the hills it doesn't matter so much how many men, it's how good they are. If you ask me, I've got to say the Duko's men are better. But we'll be better. We've got to be, so we will be. Tomorrow we march. I sent word this afternoon. It would take all morning to get everybody together, but we won't wait for everybody. We'll be gone before the frost is off the grass."

"Would you like me to come with you?"

Inclito raised one thick eyebrow. "It's not your fight."

"Nor will I be of any great help to you, I know. I may well be more of a hindrance than a help. But I would rather go with you and see the fighting than try to make my way back to the coast alone, in winter, with a war raging."

"I was thinking maybe you'd stay here and take care of Mama and Mora."

"I can if you want me to. Or I can come back with news of you, if I'm in the way." I am sorry that I said that now, but it is what I said.

I have sat here writing so long because I feel sure I cannot sleep so long as Seawrack sings. I have sent Oreb to beg her to be silent, although I do not really believe he can fly that far.

No, not if he were to fly all night, poor bird, and all day tomorrow.

I have shut the window now and closed the shutters—no doubt it will be days before Oreb returns, if indeed he returns to me at all. It was very hard to make myself do it, though it was freezing in here. It does not help at all, even though it nearly muffled the drumming hooves. I am going to pray and go to bed, and (if I cannot sleep) daydream about the first time I lay with Seawrack on the clumsy little sloop I built with my own hands and loved so much, and of lying with Hyacinth, too, in Ermine's on the night of our marriage.

How sweet dreams like that would be!

Let Inclito see off the remaining riders—both of them, if he can; I have carried this account to the present moment with these words, and I am going to sleep as late as they will let me.

11

IN THE FIELD

Our whole camp is sleeping now, but I am afraid of my dreams; I had horrible dreams last night, lost in Green's jungles again, and in the hideous city.

Besides, I am not tired or sleepy. Why should I be? The troopers walked, or at least most of them did, until they were ready to drop—I rode on horseback. From yesterday morning, then.

Inclito woke me, pounding on my door. Before I opened it, while I was still sitting up in bed yawning, I heard him exclaim, "She's gone! She's gone!" I knew at once what had happened; and I had known, or at least suspected, what Mora planned before she left my bedroom the night before, had surely known when I heard her gallop away. I had lifted not a finger to stop her—but then, how could I?

I advised Inclito to calm down and went outside with him. It was still almost dark, with a light snow falling. In the stable his hired men were milling around and getting in each other's way as all three tried to ready his horse. Rimando was stamping and swearing, and Eco saddling a tall chestnut gelding that looked as if it could run like the wind. "I'll get her," he promised as he swung into the saddle. "I'll find her, wherever she is, and I'll bring her back." I tried to tell him that if he could not he should go on to Olmo, deliver his letter, and search for Mora again on the way home; but he was galloping out of the farmyard and onto the road before I had said half of it.

Inclito's own mount was soon saddled, a good horse (it seemed to me), though not half so good as Eco's. He took me by the shoulders. "You'll have to do it, Incanto. Go into town and see that they leave. They can march as well without me as with me, and I'll join you in the hills as soon as I find Mora and bring her back."

Then he, too, was gone, and Rimando was demanding that Inclito's coachman give him the best of the remaining horses, which the coachman adamantly refused to do. I could see that the coachman would appeal to me eventually; and I leaned upon my staff, still half asleep, waiting for it.

It came sooner rather than later, even though the coachman had tried to get support from Perito and Sborso first. "I can't, can I, sir? They're not my horses, now are they, sir? I can't let somebody just ride away, just 'cause—"

"I'm going to find your master's daughter and bring her back," Rimando told him for the tenth time at least. "By Pas, if I had my sword I'd kill all of you!"

I shook my head and addressed the coachman. "Your master has left me in charge, Affito. You heard it. Do you dispute it?"

"No, sir." He was visibly relieved that someone else was willing to take responsibility. "I'll do whatever *you* say, Master Incanto. That I will."

"Good." I turned to the other two, asked their names, and received similar assurances from both.

"Now then, how many horses have you here, good, bad, or indifferent?"

"Four, sir."

"And a donkey. I know there is a donkey, because I've heard it bray several times since I've been here."

"Yes, sir. And the mules."

I nodded and spoke to Rimando. "Do you consider yourself a trooper, a member of the horde of Blanko? In Inclito's absence I am in command of that horde. I am to assemble it this morning and advance to meet the Duko in the hills that separate your town from Soldo. Inclito doesn't want the Duko's troopers burning farmhouses and despoiling the countryside, for reasons much too obvious to require explanation. You are an intelligent, spirited, young man of good family, and can be of great help to me. If you will obey me as a loyal trooper should, I will appoint you my second in command on the spot."

For a few seconds, he was able to meet my gaze. "I want to find the girl who took my horse."

"I know you do. If you insist upon setting off after her—on foot, because I cannot permit you to take any of our animals—I will not stop you. I will, however, report your insubordination when the four of us reach Blanko, and I will report it again to Inclito when he rejoins us."

He could no longer look me in the eye, but he hesitated still.

I said, "I won't threaten you with punishment. I doubt that you'll be punished at all, or that you should be; but when you're my age, and your fellow citizens speak of those who came forward bravely when deadly danger threatened Blanko, your name will not be among them. There will be questions, perhaps, and whispers. Wouldn't you prefer that your name be honored?"

"All right. Yes, sir. I would, sir." I heard his indrawn breath as he came to attention and saluted.

I returned his salute, touching my right eyebrow with the handle of my staff. "Some people here call me a strego," I told him. "I'm no magic-worker, but there are times when I have certain knowledge that is denied to others. This is one of those times."

"Yes, sir."

"If I had let you go after Mora, you wouldn't have succeeded in returning her to safety, or even in finding her. I'm not saying that to insult your abilities—I know that you're an able young man, and as a matter of fact I know it better than you do yourself. I say it because it is true."

"Yes, sir," Rimando repeated.

"Nor will her father succeed. Nor will Eco. I can only hope they do not lose their lives in the attempt."

Sborso asked, "Are we going to town, sir?"

"Yes, but not until we've eaten, and our animals, too. Do they have corn, or whatever you're feeding?"

The coachman said they did.

"Good. Come into the house, all of you. I know you don't normally eat at Inclito's table, but this is not a normal day. I need to talk to the women, and it will be best to do it with everyone present."

Once in the house, I called Decina and Onorifica out of their kitchen and sent Torda for my host's mother. When food had been passed around and everyone was seated at the table, I rose.

"Mora has gone to Novella Citta," I told her grandmother. "She took Rimando's horse and rode off during the night. Your son has ridden after her, and so has the other messenger. At present I don't know whether any or all of them will come to harm. I'm going to pray for them, and I advise you to do the same.

"And you, too, Torda. Decina and Onorifica should pray as well."

The cook could only stare. I got frightened nods from the other three women.

"As any of these men will confirm, Inclito put me in charge of this house, as well as the horde of Blanko, in his absence. I can't stay here, however, much as I might like to. To be more precise, we five men cannot."

To the coachman I added, "Rimando is my chief subordinate. I want you to give him the best horse."

He nodded, his mouth full.

"Inclito told me that he intended to put all three of you into his cavalry. Has he given you slug guns and other equipment?"

Perito and Sborso said that he had.

"Then you will come with Rimando and me," I told them, "and serve there until your master rejoins us."

My host's mother began, "Incanto, the farm . . ." Her voice quavered.

"You will have to take care of everything to the best of your ability," I told her. "You will require someone to help you, and for that I suggest Torda, though you are not bound to accept my suggestion."

Both nodded, my host's mother gratefully and Torda fearfully.

"I doubt that you will be able to get the winter wheat planted, but if you can, do it. If you can get only some of it planted, do that. Can any of you plow?"

All four women shook their heads.

"Neither can I," I told them, "but there may be old men or boys on some of the other farms hereabout who can. You might hire one to complete the plowing. Sowing the seed should be simple enough."

The coachmen asked, "You're going to let them keep the mules, sir?"

I nodded.

"They can use the seeder then, sir."

Sborso spoke to Torda. "It don't take but one mule. Bruna's the best, and won't kick if you don't treat her mean. Just pour in your seed and pull back on that handle soon as you're in the furrow. It's easy."

I have had a reunion with some old acquaintances, and Oreb has returned. This last may be more important than it seemed at the time; the leaders in Blanko were disturbed at his absence. I believe I might have had an easier time with them had he been with me. But I will recount that later, if I write about it at all.

Here I should say that this is still the night on which I wrote about talking to Torda and the other women yesterday morning. (Although yesterday morning seems a very long time ago.) I was away only a few hours.

One of the patrols I sent out when we camped here returned. I sat its leader down before this little fire when he said he had located the enemy, and told him to tell me everything, that he should consider no detail too small.

"There's not much to tell, sir. You've seen the road here."

I nodded.

"It just gets worse on north." He jerked his head. "It's not fit for wagons, sir. Only pack animals."

"How far are the enemy?"

He sat in silence, watching me finger my beard.

"I realize you had no means of measuring the distance," I said. "But how long were you gone? Four or five hours? You must know about how fast you walked."

"It isn't that, sir. We went about two leagues, I'd say, and going back the same. But these two hills . . ." A gesture. "You can't see them now, sir. It'll be a little better when Green comes up."

I nodded. "Tell me about them, so I'll know what to look for."

"There's a sort of saddle higher up, sir, but you can't get through it, or I don't think you can. It's all full of big rocks and thornbushes."

"I saw it."

"So the road goes on around." More gestures. "Over that way, and then around there."

"Around the flank of the eastern hill, so to speak."

"That's right, sir. Then it comes back this way, sir, bending around west again."

"I believe I understand."

"It wasn't as dark as this when we first saw the enemy, sir, and I kept on looking up at that saddle, here and there both. I think it's worse on their side, and it looked pretty bad on ours."

I nodded again. "But you couldn't escape the thought that if only we could go through there we might be able to take them by surprise."

He smiled, teeth gleaming in his dark and dirty face, and I liked him. "That's it exactly, sir. We can't do it, but you asked how far, that way it'd only be a scant league, maybe less. Suppose we sent twenty men up on those hilltops, sir. It's practically all rocks up there, just a few thornbushes. They could be shooting from up there while the rest came around by the road."

I called Rimando over, and explained what we had been talking about.

"It might help, sir." Rimando looked thoughtful. "I'd want to look it over first, though."

"So would I. So do I, as Lieutenant . . . ?"

"Sergeant, sir. Sergeant Valico."

"So do I, Lieutenant Valico. How many enemy did you see?"

"Not their whole horde, sir."

"Of course not. This will be their advance guard or a flank guard, and I wish I knew which. How many? A hundred? A thousand?"

"I counted twenty-two fires, sir. It seemed like there was seven or eight around each fire."

Rimando said, "Plus their sentries. They'll have put out sentries unless they're the biggest fools on Blue."

Valico nodded. "One shot at us, sir. I tried to get in closer and one shot, that was why we came back."

Rimando grinned. "Quickly."

"No, sir. I tried to make a little ambush for them, sir, thinking a few might chase us. Only nobody came."

Just reaching the cleft between the hills required a fairly stiff climb; and well before we did, I had decided that even if the rocks and thornbushes Valico had reported could somehow be cleared away, it would be impossible for horses and pack mules unless a road could be built.

"You should have brought your donkey, sir," Rimando told me.

"You're right, I should have. I was just beginning to wish that they hadn't let me have that horse in Blanko. Or that I hadn't taken it."

He gave me his hand to help me up a particularly difficult bit, and I accepted it gratefully.

"I could have ridden one of Inclito's mules, too, and that would probably have been the best solution of all. What was her name? Bruna? I suppose it must mean that she's brown. In any case she sounded just right for me."

From some small distance above us, Valico called, "This is about as far as you can go."

"I should have put a sentry up here," I told Rimando. "No, two. Two at least, well separated to keep them from talking. Do it when we get back down."

"Because Lieutenant Valico says somebody might be able to climb over the top?"

"Exactly." My legs felt weak, but with the help of my staff I was able to surmount the last rock, and even to stand upon it without falling. Green showed through the thornbushes from there, dim and blurred at first but brighter and more threatening with every moment that passed. Seeing it like that, between the peaks of hills that had once been a single hill and were divided now by this boulder-strewn and thorn-choked dry watercourse, it reminded me oddly of the front sight of a needler. I tried (as I am trying now) to keep that image in my mind and forget its jungles, its terrifying cliffs, and the swamps swarming with poisonous reptiles—the endless leagues of reeds, the eon-old trees, and the putrefying water in which the inhumi breed.

Rimando had gone ahead. He called back softly, "All right if I see how far I can go in there, sir?"

I managed to nod, I suppose. Perhaps I answered him.

Something, some slight turning of my head, had thrust the thornbushes aside. They clustered thickly to left and right, but down the center of the cleft, where the water ran in the rainy season, Green's gleaming disc shone like a bead of jade. I saw Rimando advance a few steps toward it, gingerly pushing thorny branches out of his way that he could readily have stepped around, and watched him halt and turn back in disgust.

I went to him, having once or twice to step a little to my left or right, and he goggled at me. "Go back now," I told him. "Don't forget to post those sentries, and don't forget that we are two leagues at most from the enemy. Rouse some men to defend the rest. If I'm not back by shadeup, you're in command until the people of Blanko decide otherwise."

I turned and climbed the gentle slope, then halted and waved to him and Valico, knowing they could not miss seeing me with Green behind me. Just then I heard Oreb crying "Silk? Silk?" above my head as he had when Silk deserted us at the entrance to the tunnels. I waved to him; but he was unable to reach me through the thorns until I held my staff up, grasping it near the tip so that the handle was high above my head. He settled upon it, and I drew him down to me and asked whether he had found Seawrack.

"No find. No sing."

"A beautiful, one-armed woman with golden hair?"

"No find," he croaked unhappily. "Big wet." And then, "Bird wet. No swim."

She has gone back into the sea, apparently, and I will hear her no more. I suppose I should be happy, but my heart aches as I write these words.

The enemy had camped some way up the northern slope. I halted where the thornbushes grew sparsely, and was able to study the few who remained awake at my leisure. Soon I saw what seemed a familiar face, then another. For a minute or more I tried fruitlessly to recall the names that went with those faces. One saw me, and I blessed them, making the sign of addition.

He came as near as the thornbushes permitted, his slug gun at the ready. "Rajan? Is that you, sir?"

"Yes," I said. "Have you left Hari Mau's employment?"

He nodded cautiously.

"He paid you? Did you get all your money? If not, I'll go back with you as soon as I can, and we'll get it."

"I got everything," he said.

By that time, another man was coming toward us; he seemed less suspicious, although he had his slug gun as well. It seemed clear that as long as I appeared afraid of them, they could not be expected to trust me; so I advanced until I was clear of the thornbushes.

The second man asked, "Do you remember me, Rajan? My name's Chaku."

It was a Gaonese name and he wore a cloth wrapped around

his head as all the men do there; so I said I certainly did, and asked what he, a Gaonese, was doing here.

"A lot of us are Gaonese, Rajan. There wasn't much work for us after the fighting stopped, so we decided to go along with these fellows and try to earn a cardbit or two."

The first man said, "My name's Gorak. You talked to us before we went to fight." Others were gathering around as he spoke.

"I recall your face very well," I told him, "and I believe I might have come up with your name if I'd had a little more time."

A third trooper said, "You stopped and talked to me once when you were inspecting the trenches, Rajan. It was raining like the gods were emptying a year's worth of slops on us, remember?"

I told him I would never forget it, and asked whether he, or any of them, knew Eco.

A trooper who had not spoken before said, "He's not here, Rajan."

"But you know him?"

He nodded. "He was in my bunker down south, sir. A good man."

"He's on my side now," I said, "fighting for Blanko. Quite a few of you are." Just then, by great good luck, I recognized a lanky trooper with a scar across his chin, another Gaonese. I called softly, "Thody, how are you? It's good to see you again," and his smile warmed me.

Gorak said, "We don't have much, but we can offer you some tea." Chaku added, "And cinnamon bread. I'll get it."

I lifted my staff and my free hand for silence. "Wait, brothers. You may shoot me in a moment or two. You are with the Duko's horde?"

Several nodded.

"Then you ought to, and there's no sense in wasting your good food on someone about to die. Do you have one of your own officers? Or is one of the Duko's in charge here?"

"A man from Soldo." Gorak pointed toward a tent some distance down the slope.

"This is going to be very bad," I told them. "Very difficult."

"We won't shoot you," the man who had known Eco assured me.

"Listen to me," I told him, "before you make any such rash promises. Are you the advance guard, by the way?"

He and others nodded.

I sighed. "I am in command of the horde of Blanko, you see, and we—"

Chaku interrupted. "We captured their general two days ago."

I nodded as though I had known it, and another trooper said, "Their general and his daughter."

"That's why I'm in command now. I was advising him, and with him unable to perform his duties the entire responsibility has become mine."

"Good Silk!" Oreb assured them.

"I had planned to crush you tomorrow morning. I didn't know who you were then, of course. Now. . . . Sacred Scylla, what am I to do?"

Oreb answered, "No fight!"

A moment or two later, Thody came and stood at my right hand, saying, "Anyone who would strike the rajan must strike me first!," and a chorus of voices declared that they intended no harm to either of us.

"Nor do I wish in the least to harm you," I told them. "In fact, I will go further. I will not fight you, no matter what happens."

For some time they whispered among themselves, seeming to sway like a field of grain stirred by the night wind. Chaku left them and came to stand on my left, his slug gun ready and his eyes upon his comrades.

"No fight," Oreb urged. "Come Silk."

"He's right," I said loudly. "Listen to me, brothers. I want to hire all of you. If you'll return whatever the Duko's paid you and come over to our side, we'll pay you the same rate you got in Gaon."

Someone said loudly, "The Duko's giving us a silver card every month."

"How much have you received so far?" I asked him.

"Nothing!" several voices answered.

"But you're getting good rations?"

"*No!*"

"What the Duko intends is quite clear," I told them. "He hopes to take Blanko before he's got to pay you. Then he'll invoke some technicality and give you a tenth or less of what's due you. A tenth, perhaps, if you're lucky."

Many nodded.

"I can't offer you that much or half that much, because Blanko will actually pay the entire sum promised."

Deferentially, Gorak asked, "All right if I talk to them, Rajan?"

"Of course."

He raised his voice. "Men! All of you know me. I've been doing this longer than most. It's my fifth war."

Those who had begun talking among themselves fell silent.

"These troopers," he pointed to Chaku and Thody, "they're going to side with him 'cause he was their rajan. That doesn't mean a thing to me, and it shouldn't to you. He hired me a while back, I got my pay, and that's over and done with. If he was just the head man in some foreign town, I'd just as soon fight against him as for him. But there was spells he cast in that war. Real spells that worked. I never saw any of that, and I misdoubt anybody here did. But I talked to prisoners, and they had a lot to say. You want to fight him now? Well, I don't!"

He turned toward me as the contending voices of his fellow troopers rose behind him. "A lot's asleep, Rajan. More than's here, and there's the officer from Soldo. Can you wait till morning?"

Reminded unpleasantly of Green, I said that I could and would.

"We'll talk it over then, all of us. If you see us coming with our slug guns hanging crosswise down our backs and muzzle down, don't shoot, 'cause we'll be going over to you. And if we're going to stay with Soldo and fight you instead, we'll say so first."

Thus it ended. Half a dozen of them would have come with me if I had permitted it, but I ordered them stay behind to influence their comrades. And now I must sleep for a few hours at least.

12

---◆◆✕◆◆---

AN EXCHANGE OF PRISONERS

What days the past two have been! Now I am free and Inclito is in command again, which is a great relief to me. In addition we have more than three hundred fresh mercenaries, whom I have pledged to pay. Tomorrow I am going back to Blanko to try to raise the money. In a moment I will write about everything; but first I should say that we are a formidable force now. A hundred and five of the troopers we left in Blanko joined us while I was talking with the mercenaries—my mercenaries, I should call them—and yet another group, I would think almost two hundred, arrived this morning. I was on the point of leaving then, and if an exact count was made I have not heard the total.

What happened after I wrote last was that the mercenaries sent Gorak, Chaku, and two others to talk to me a little after sunrise. Their own officers were meeting to decide what was to be done, they said, and they had disarmed their commander and put him under guard. I was invited to come and address their meeting—invited so urgently, in fact, that for a moment or two I thought they might carry me off bodily.

I told them that although I was presently in charge of the horde of Blanko, it would be better if two of its leading men treated with them as well as I, so that I could not be accused of overstepping my authority. (I should explain that I first summoned the two I had in mind, and they were in hearty agreement.)

Nothing had been said about that in their camp, so they returned to speak with their officers again.

They came back about midmorning, this time with a mercenary officer, one Captain Kupus. He is short and stout and looks, in fact, like anything but a military man; but he is a shrewd thinker from what I have seen of him. His men, whose respect he plainly has, say he is as brave as a hus.

He had brought a counterproposal, pointing out that our General Inclito was their prisoner and a leading citizen of Blanko. They would permit him, and his daughter as well, to attend the meeting. Surely, he said, I would agree that was fair.

Naturally I replied that I had no say in the matter, and asked the leading men I had chosen (their names are Bello and Vivo) for their opinions. They replied as I had hoped they would, that Inclito might be under duress—we had no way of knowing what threats had been made to him. They would be happy to have him present, and Mora, too. But they themselves would have to be present also. After an hour or so of generally circular arguments, this was agreed to provided that all three of us came unarmed and agreed to be searched.

To speed matters up, I loaned Captain Kupus, Gorak and the rest horses, which seemed to impress them. While these were being saddled and so forth, I was able to conceal my azoth—for obvious reasons I will not specify the place.

The meeting took place in the open amid softly falling snow, a circle of stones serving Kupus and the other four mercenary officers, Bello, Vivo, and me for seats. Neither Inclito nor Mora were present, so we asked at once that they be brought in.

It led to the first great surprise of that day, for the girl who was marched out with Inclito was not Mora but Fava. I tried to maintain my composure, and I hope managed my face better than Bello and Vivo did. We insisted that seats be provided Inclito and Fava—calling her Mora—as well, and this was done. The other mercenaries crowded around, and the meeting proper came to order.

We began by acquainting Inclito (and, of course, all the listeners around us, although we pretended to speak to Inclito alone) with the present situation. I went to Blanko on the morning that he left home, I told him, in accordance with his orders. I had expected, I said, to find the horde of Blanko assembled and preparing to march.

What I had found instead was fewer than a hundred men, more than half of them mercenaries. My second in command and I spent a good two hours conferring with various people, but our efforts added only forty-two more. We assembled the leading men of the town then, forcing some who were reluctant to attend to do so. I outlined the danger of defeat in detail, the grave danger that small groups of troopers, widely separated, might be decimated, one after another, by an enemy small when compared to their total, but large in comparison to each group.

I had warned them that we would march at once with what troops we had, challenge the Duko's forces—however great—and resist their invasion to the best of our ability. If we were overwhelmed (and I admitted frankly that it was what I expected) I counseled them to throw themselves upon the mercy of Duko Rigoglio, who might conceivably permit some of them to retain their houses, shops, and farms.

After which we had formed up, twenty cavalry and ninety-six infantry, and marched.

Frowning, Inclito shook his head. "You were taking a terrible risk."

It was very gracious of him to say so, I told him, but he knew as well as I that it is the business of troopers to undergo terrible risks in fulfillment of their duty. (This went over well with my hearers, I felt.)

Fava asked whether we had not gone slowly so that those behind could join us.

I shook my head. "We marched as fast as we could, with our horsemen riding ahead to scout, and to pick up whatever recruits they could persuade to join us at the farms we passed. By our fast march we nearly reached the last plowlands before we camped."

Bello added that we had marched until midnight to do it, and had risen the next morning with the Short Sun.

Vivo said, "My men and I left Blanko about three that afternoon. That's how we were able to catch up with Incanto when he stopped here. The rest wanted to wait and start in the morning, and I guess they did."

"We halted where we're camped now on the second night," I explained to Inclito. "Some herdsmen had warned us that the enemy was close, and we sent patrols ahead to find out where they were."

Kupus cleared his throat, looking at his fellow officers and then at us. "Last night you told some of these men that you intended to crush us. I wasn't there, but that's what I've heard. How many men did you have then?"

"Roughly two hundred and fifty," I said; it was true, although I had not known it when I talked of crushing.

"You thought you could do it with that many?"

"Or with half that many," I declared.

"How?"

I shook my head. "I've pledged myself not to fight against you, Captain, but you haven't pledged yourselves not to fight against me."

One of the listening men protested—Chaku, I suppose. Hearing him I added, "Except for a few friends among you. Certainly Captain Kupus has given no such pledge."

Fava said loudly, "You think that the men he's been talking about are his whole force. That's very foolish of you. Haven't I told you that my father and I were staying with you because Incanto didn't want us to go? He could have freed us last night easily, if he'd wanted to." Inclito gave her a severe look as if to silence her.

"Less than three hundred last night." Kupus returned us to the matter at hand. "How many now? I saw some back there who seemed to be just catching up with you."

Bello said, "About seven hundred infantry." I doubt that it was true.

I raised my staff, with Oreb flapping on it. "It doesn't matter. In the first place, you're perfectly safe—from us at least, though I can't speak for the Duko—as long as I am in command. I've pledged that we wouldn't attack you, and we won't.

"In the second, you would be in as much danger from the hundred and sixteen with which I left Blanko as from the seven hundred we have now—or from sixteen hundred, or five thousand. If we do fight you, you will be destroyed. That is what all five of us are hoping to avoid."

Kupus lifted an eyebrow. "But we'd be safe in your service?"

"Of course not. We're going to fight the Duko and sack his city—though the plunder will have to be shared with Olmo and Novella Citta, or so I imagine. Some of us, and perhaps many of us, will be killed. Some of you will be killed as well. If I were half the prophet people think me, I could tell you how many, perhaps. I can't."

One of the other officers (Karabin is his name) asked, "Can't you say whether we'll take your silver?"

"I prefer not to get into that."

Kupus repeated, "Can you?"

"If you're asking about your personal decision, Captain, I can't tell you. If you intend this company of yours . . ." I spread my hands. "I am here."

Referring to the Duko's officer, another lieutenant said, "I think we ought to bring out Sfido, too."

I told him I agreed.

The captive Soldese officer was led out, and when I saw that they had not troubled to untie his hands, and that no one brought him a stone to sit on, I knew that my decision had been correct.

"This is Captain Sfido, the commander the Duko set over us," Kupus told us. "Technically, I'm his second in command."

Some of the listening men chuckled.

"Captain, these three men are from Blanko. The one in the black robe is Inclito's sorcerer."

His eyes conveyed his query, and I nodded.

"When I first met him, he was Rajan of Gaon. They call him Incanto here, but in Gaon they say that his real name is Silk."

As I shook my head, Oreb croaked loudly, "Good Silk!" I ordered him to be quiet.

"These two are Colonel Vivo and Colonel Bello. They're probably shopkeepers with needlers, or farmers like General Inclito here. I don't know."

"You're trying to suborn these troopers from their duty," Sfido said to me; as soon as I heard his voice, I knew he was an antagonist to be reckoned with.

"Not at all," I declared. "I'm simply trying to persuade them that they should repay whatever they may have received from your Duko and take service with Blanko. Captain Kupus would notify you of the change, and we would let you go back to your Duko to tell him about it. We'd even give you a horse for that purpose."

"They've gotten no money from Duko Rigoglio yet," Sfido said. "Many have been with him for almost a month, however. If they do as you suggest, they'll forfeit a great deal of pay, money that they've earned and that they deserve."

Bello inquired, "Are you prepared to pay them now?"

"No." Sfido displayed his bound wrists. "Are you?"

Bello did not reply. I asked Sfido, "Are you saying you have the money here, hidden in your tent?"

He shook his head. "It will be sent from Soldo on the tenth of the month."

There was a stir among the listeners.

Inclito said, "We ought to take it, if we can, Incanto. That shouldn't be too hard for you."

I nodded.

Sfido smiled—he had a good, warm smile. "Next you'll say you'll pay them for the time they spent in our Duko's service. If there's anyone here stupid enough to believe it, you'll probably win him over."

"No," I said, "I won't."

An officer whose name I had not yet learned, a burly man with a fair mustache, announced, "I think this has gone far enough. If we stay with Soldo, we'll get the wages the Duko promised. If we sign with Blanko, we'll be starting over for less money. We've all seen the Duko's horde. Most of us haven't seen Blanko's. I haven't myself, but from what I heard just now, I think the Duko's going to win it."

Lieutenant Karabin said, "You weren't in Gaon."

"I would say the same if I had been."

The wrangling went on for some time. It would take every sheet I have to give it all, nor do I remember it well enough to set it all down; often there were two or even three persons talking at once.

At last I stood upon my stone seat and was able to quiet them. "You're about to fight among yourselves," I told them.

The two mercenary officers loudly denied it.

"Listen to me! If you decide to remain in Duko Rigoglio's service, the Gaonese among you, and a few others who were in Gaon, will fight the rest. If you come over to Blanko, nearly half of you will fight to remain with the Duko. There's not a man among you who doesn't know in his heart that what I've just said is true."

I waited for someone to object. No one did, and Oreb crowed, "Silk talk!"

"I said earlier that with a hundred troopers I could have crushed you. Now you see how easily I could have done it. What need did I have for troopers, when I could so very readily have set you to fighting among yourselves?"

They were silent and shamefaced.

"But I don't want to see you crushed. Far too many of you fought beside me when we beat the Hannese. Let me make the case for my side again; I promise to do it quickly, and to be as quiet as you like afterward.

"First, Blanko will pay you. Whatever Captain Sfido here may honestly believe, I know that Soldo won't—they don't have enough.

"Second, Blanko will win. A few minutes ago I spoke of sharing the loot of Soldo with Olmo and Novella Citta. Did you hear

anyone ask about that? Or object? I didn't. The Duko's allies are
our allies now."

Fava said, "I told everyone about their changing sides."

"There is the case for Blanko in a nutshell," I continued, "and
I believe that any of you who look at it squarely will see that it is a
very compelling one."

The burly officer snorted. "Not compelling enough for me."

"Hear Silk!" Oreb insisted, and I told him to be quiet.

"Many of these men will side with you, Lieutenant, I feel
sure. I would like to speak for a moment to those who would side
with me."

He stood and drew his needler.

So did Captain Kupus. Kupus said, "I don't think we'll allow
that."

"You have no reason not to," I told him. "All that I want to
say to them is that they must not fight their comrades—who are
also mine. It would be best if you fought for Blanko and justice.
But it would be better for you to fight against Blanko than for you
to fight among yourselves."

I spoke to Kupus again. "Captain, I would like to make you an
offer, one that will keep friend from killing friend. Colonel Bello,
Colonel Vivo, and I came here with you, unarmed and under a
flag of truce. I'm sure you won't deny that; you know it's true."

He nodded.

"Very well. I want to exchange myself for General Inclito and
his daughter. If—"

The burly officer with the blond mustache interrupted me.
"When you were listing your reasons for thinking your town
might win, you didn't say anything about your magic."

"It is not my town," I told him, "and I have no magic to
threaten you with."

That set off a buzz of talk.

Fava shouted to make herself heard. "My grandmother's an
old, old woman. She was nearly fifty when she came here to Blue,
and she knows a lot about stregos. She says Incanto's the greatest

strego she's ever seen." More loudly still, she shrieked, "Don't say you weren't warned!"

Kupus stepped near enough that he could speak almost normally. "You'll exchange for Inclito?"

I nodded. "And his daughter. I want to be with you to keep you from killing one another."

"Not the daughter." Holstering his needler, he took a slug gun from one of the bystanders and fired it into the air for silence. "She came on her own to try and get her father out, and we're keeping her."

That was how our meeting ended. Before Inclito left, he tried to have a word with me in private but was prevented by Kupus and the guards. He told Kupus, "Take a tip from someone who knows, Captain. It's over. You and your men will be part of Blanko's horde before long. You may not think so, but you don't know Incanto like I do." He kissed Fava before he rode off with Bello and Vivo.

Our hands were free until nightfall; then Sfido ordered us bound. Our guards took my staff, and chased Oreb away.

13

ESCAPE TO GREEN

O nce again I have let this account fall behind events. I am back in Blanko, and staying once more with my friends Atteno the stationer and his wife; he has let me refill this little ink bottle, and given me a great deal of paper—more, surely, than I will ever need. My task here is to raise enough money to pay our mercenaries, and I am finding it far from easy; but before I get into that, I should explain how we came to have them, although I can scarcely expect anyone who reads this to believe me.

They had no tent for Fava and me, the only tent in their whole encampment being the one Sfido had brought. The snow, which I had borne easily at first, became a sort of torture after sunset, wetting and chilling everyone. I huddled under some thornbushes with Fava; and although she may have gotten some warmth from me, I got none from her. For hours I lay there shivering while four troopers with slug guns stood guard over us, my freezing fingers grasping one another inside my robe; but eventually I fell asleep.

Or woke.

I was lying upon stone instead of stones, a level stone floor that felt blessedly cool although the steaming air I breathed might have come from a bathhouse. A man with a cloth around his head in the Gaonese fashion crouched beside me. He shook my shoulder, saying softly, "Rajan, Rajan."

I sat up, sensing somehow that the perspiring girl who lay at my side was a human being, although the light was so dim that I could only just make out the face of the man who had shaken my shoulder. "Yes, Chaku, I'm awake. What do you want with me?"

"Rajan, where are we?"

I had no idea; but I held my finger to my lips, fearing that he would wake Fava.

One of the troopers who had been set to guard us stepped over to stand next to Chaku. His name was Schreiner, and he asked "Have you done this to us?" in a voice that trembled with fear.

"Done what to you?" When I do not have the answer, I find it best to ask another question.

Chaku turned to him. "Am I dreaming?"

When Schreiner did not answer him, I asked, "Do you usually ask others whether you're dreaming in your dreams, Chaku?"

"Never!"

"Then I doubt that you're dreaming now," I told him.

The door was flung back by a burly human slave, and a small but handsome man in rich robes came in, followed by three naked muscular human slaves. Iron bands encircled their wrists, bands joined by heavy chains they swung like weapons. The robed master pointed to Chaku; sensing what was about to happen, I hurried over to stand before him with outspread arms.

The slaves hesitated; then the largest, a graying man with protruding ears and a lantern jaw, indicated Schreiner.

His master nodded.

Schreiner raised his slug gun, but it was knocked out of his hands before he could fire; a second blow from the big slave's chain followed like lightning, dashing Schreiner to the stone floor.

At once the robed master threw himself on top of him, and appeared to kiss his neck. His slave whispered, "You shaggy well better beat hoof, Patera."

Chaku fired as he spoke. The robed master's head seemed almost to explode, wetting my face with blood and brains flung hard enough to sting. From other parts of the huge room, others fired, slugs shrieking as they ricocheted from walls, ceiling, and floor. The slaves shouted and raised their hands, then snatched up their master's body and ran, slamming the iron door behind them.

Fava sat up screaming.

By then I had recognized the place. Overcome with wonder and awe, I muttered, "I am asleep and dreaming, and they are in my dream." Fortunately, Chaku did not overhear me.

The chamber that confined us was so dimly lit that I could scarcely make out its walls; but as well as I could judge, only Fava had changed at all. And even Fava had changed only subtly, for she had always seemed an apple-cheeked child just short of puberty, with long, light brown hair and a winning smile.

Thinking about this, and what had just occurred, and certain other things, I sat down upon the cool flagstones again, my right forefinger drawing circles on my cheek.

While I sat lost in thought, Schreiner, our guard, recovered consciousness; his head was bandaged with strips torn from his tunic, and then, because he seemed not to like my company, he was helped to his feet and led away. I saw these things, but they made little impression on me. The dream, I felt, must surely end soon, as our earlier dream of Green had when it was interrupted by the cook. The various difficulties that I had tried to think of some way of confronting as I lay beside Fava under the snow-covered thornbushes would be pressing again, and I struggled against them with little hope, while wondering whether I was not in fact freezing to death while I wiped the sweat from my face with the sleeve of my robe.

I wanted to prevent the mercenaries from murdering one another, and I could see no way to do it other than by bringing them all to Blanko's side, meanwhile stepping in to smooth such quarrels as I chanced to witness.

Very well, they had to be brought to Blanko's side—but it seemed out of the question until enough time had passed to show the falsity of the Duko's promises clearly—and by that time the war would more than likely have been lost. I reproached myself bitterly for pretending to agree when Inclito spoke of intercepting the mule-loads of silver the Duko had promised to send, since by nodding as I had, I had appeared to accept the idea that Duko Rigoglio had such a sum at his disposal and would pay it out. I had nodded so it would seem that Inclito and I were in agreement on all questions. Still it had been a mistake, and one I continue to regret.

(As I write, it strikes me that there is a chance, however slight, that Inclito was correct and I mistaken. The tenth is only three days distant. It would be well to send horsemen to intercept the silver, if it exists; but I have no horses here to speak of, and I feel sure Inclito will do it himself if he is not hotly engaged.)

How could Duko Rigoglio be persuaded to abandon his war? I had sent Fava with that hope, and had likewise written those letters to Olmo and Novella Citta, hoping that the messengers would be captured by the Soldese—all in order that Rigoglio, fearing that his allies were not as reliable as he had supposed, would cancel his invasion. Both my tricks had clearly failed, and as I sat on the stone floor of that sweltering room in which I could not possibly be again, I could devise no fresh scheme that seemed apt to succeed.

What was worse, Mora had made herself one of the messengers whose lives I had risked in the hope of securing peace. By this time she had presumably been captured and raped, I reflected, and was weeping in a dungeon much worse than this dream dungeon of mine.

Behind these lurked the greater problem: how could I make my way back to New Viron and you, Nettle, as I long to, without abandoning my friends here? All these problems plague me still, and none more than that.

Fava came to sit by me; and I, looking around at her and smiling, realized with a start that we had half the chamber to ourselves.

"I thought you might like some company." She returned my smile. "Somebody to talk to, even me."

"You think I'm your enemy." I shook my head. "I never was, Fava. While we were where we were, I could not be your friend; but I was never your enemy."

"That's what Mora said once."

"Mora was right. If we're going to be friends, tell me something now. Are you as young as you look?"

After a moment, she shook her head.

"I didn't think so. You're older, and very cunning—"

She laughed at that, and it was a girl's clear laughter.

"Too often, you let it show. Did you really try to free Inclito?"

She nodded. "He'd been nice to me. He let me live with his daughter in his house, and treated me almost as well as her. I'd hurt him and his mother, and if I could I wanted to make amends."

I smiled again, and tried not to let my smile become bitter. "Very few of us are that honorable."

"I'm not fooling you for a minute, am I?"

"To the contrary," I said. "I very much hoped that you were telling the truth."

"Well, I was. But I wanted to get even with Duko Rigoglio too. That message you gave me, I'll bet you thought I wouldn't deliver it."

"I hoped you would, and thought you very well might."

"I did. He had me arrested and was going to chop my head off for it."

I apologized and told her that I had not considered that he might react violently.

"You think I'm clever because you are. You think everybody against you must be clever too. If the Duko had been clever, he'd have wanted to keep me as a spy. I was counting on it, but everybody says he's more than half mad, and he got furiously angry when he thought I'd brought bad news."

I said that I would like to speak with him sometime.

"No you wouldn't." Fava sounded positive.

"So he was going to have you killed. I take it you escaped?"

She laughed again. "Did you think I couldn't? They put me in a little room with bars on the window, and as soon as they weren't looking, I went out between them. We can change our bodies a lot. You know that. I know you do, because you put it into my story that time."

I nodded. "I know you can lengthen your legs and widen your arms into wings."

"We can do lots of other things, too. Remember how Flosser tied my hands? I could have pulled them right out! Don't think I wasn't tempted to, either, just to see his face. We can even slip under doors if there's a big crack there. Want to see me make my neck long and open my hood? It's something we do here to make animals think we're bigger than we are."

I told her it was something that I would like very much to see, if she was confident that no one else would see it too.

"They're afraid even to look at you, and my hair will cover it. I'll only do it a little bit."

She turned to face me squarely, raised her head, and grinned. Nothing happened, and I told her, "We need not worry about their seeing that."

"I can't!"

"Neither can you fly," I said. I was guessing, but I was quite certain my guess was correct. "You can run and jump now, however; and if there were horses here, you might even learn to ride like Mora."

She stared. "What's happened?"

"I have fallen asleep, that's all. You and I sit talking in my dream, and you are as I think of you."

She threw her arms around my neck and kissed me.

When I had freed myself again I said that Krait had told me once that his life was a nightmare in which he was trapped in the body of a blood-drinking reptile.

"That's it! That's it exactly!"

"I don't think so, but I am not your judge. What you must realize—what we both need to realize—is that this really is a nightmare, whether it is mine alone or ours. Your mind has joined my own to produce it. I thought of you as a girl often, though I knew what you really were. And you must think of yourself as a girl frequently as well. Thus in our shared nightmare you actually—"

She had leaped to her feet and raced away, her long hair streaming behind her like a banner. I watched her, recalling how

Mamelta had run in the Hall of Sleepers, possessed by a girl locked in a small and stinking bedroom—a girl far too starved and sick to run even if she had been free.

A second more, and Fava had disappeared into the dim farther reaches of the chamber. Another, and she was returning. I had said that she could no longer fly, but she seemed to fly as she raced back to me.

"Some men—" She dropped breathless to the floor. "Are coming. They saw me kiss you. The Soldese—" She pointed.

I looked. "Captain Sfido and Captain Kupus, and another officer."

"Zepter." She gasped. "He doesn't like us."

Zepter was the burly officer with the blond mustache. I muttered that under the circumstances I could hardly blame him, but I am not sure Fava heard me.

Sfido called, "May we speak to you, Rajan?"

"You may speak with me, of course; but I would rather you didn't address me like that."

"What should we call you?" He was advancing hesitantly; even so, he was well in front of the other two.

"In Blanko, the people call me Incanto."

They halted, the three of them looking at one another. "Call him Dervis," Fava suggested impishly. "It's a good name, and I don't think he'll mind."

"We—" Kupus began, and started over. "The men . . ." He cleared his throat.

"Sit down," Fava told him. "He doesn't like your standing over him like that." (They were still half a dozen strides away.) "Neither do I. Papa's just the same, and I'm sure he hasn't forgotten all those times you made us sit on the cold ground and yelled down at us."

"No insult was intended," Sfido told her smoothly. "I let you sit as a gesture of respect."

"You made us sit because you were afraid he'd kick you again! He would've, too!"

I rose. "These brave troopers haven't come to quarrel with us, I'm sure."

All three nodded, Sfido vigorously.

Fava declared, "These brave troopers wouldn't have come at all if I hadn't shown them you didn't bite."

Kupus said, "We want to make a bargain. You'll have to trust us—"

Fava snorted.

"And you can. You came during a truce, and no one tried to harm you. You exchanged yourself for a prisoner we held legitimately. You proposed the exchange yourself."

"I came voluntarily too," Fava told him, "and Incanto wanted to exchange for Papa and me."

I motioned her to silence. "At that time, I didn't know you could escape whenever you wanted; thus it made no real difference whether you stayed behind with me or left with Inclito. Let's not argue about that. Captain Kupus, what is your bargain?"

Zepter interposed. "The men are saying you carried us here by magic. Did you?"

"No," I told him.

Fava stamped her foot, "Incanto . . . !"

"I didn't. Would you want me to lie?"

"You—" Her face was flushed with rage.

I spoke to Kupus. "Now that we have settled that point, what is your bargain?"

"Can you carry us back where we were?"

"To that barren hillside in the snow? I'm surprised you don't prefer this."

Angry as she was, Fava giggled.

"He was an inhumu, wasn't he? The man whose servant knocked down Schreiner."

I nodded.

"Do you know where we are?"

"I believe so," I said. "Do you, Captain? Tell me, what whorl is this?"

Kupus shook his head. "Are you saying we're actually on Green? I don't believe it, magic or not."

After a moment Zepter asked, "Do they really have human servants here? I didn't know."

"They have human servants on our whorl, too," I told him. "You're a mercenary, Captain?"

"Lieutenant." He drew himself up. "Yes. I enjoy that honor."

"You serve Duko Rigoglio for a silver card every—"

"Three," Kupus told me. "Two cards per month for a sergeant and three for a lieutenant."

Fava told him, "Four for you," and he nodded.

I asked Zepter, "How many would it take to persuade you to serve the inhumi?"

"I wouldn't!"

"You insist I'm a strego, a male witch; so let me turn those silver cards to gold. Three cards of gold every month, Lieutenant Zepter. Wouldn't that be sufficient?"

Sfido said, "It would. More than enough. Don't deny it, Zepter. I saw your face." He turned to me. "Do you really believe the inhumi may have human servants on—where we came from?"

I shrugged. "I encountered some once in a place called Pajarocu, and it should be obvious by now that they could have them here if they wanted them and had the gold—still better, real cards enough. Or even silver, I imagine."

Fava asked, "Are you applying for work, Dervis? How much? When we get back, I'll see if I can't raise it."

Zepter said angrily, "You're no inhuma, you dirty little sprat, and—"

"Mora! My name's Mora, and it's a better name than yours!" Fava lifted her gown above her knees and danced, comically at first but soon gracefully. "Look at these legs. They're an inhuma's legs, aren't they? Here." Stopping, she gathered her hair behind her as though she were about to tie it up, and pressed the whole hank into his hand. "It's a wig. Pull hard, and it comes right off."

Rising, I laid my hand upon her shoulder.

"No teeth, see?" She grinned at him, displaying two rows of

white and very even teeth. "That's because we don't chew. Just fangs to suck up your blood. Want to see them?" Held to her mouth, her forefingers assumed the role.

To me Kupus said, "We came to talk to you about a serious matter."

I nodded. "What is it?"

"We've already—" He paused and drew breath. "We would like to return to the barren hillside you reproach us with." He looked at Sfido and Zepter, and both nodded. "If you can do that—"

I shook my head, and Fava crowed in triumph.

"You can't."

"No," I said. "Not now, at least."

Sfido stepped nearer me. "Later you might be able to?"

"Conceivably."

"How?" Zepter asked.

"You are trying to bargain with me," I told them, "so you can scarcely blame me if I bargain with you."

Kupus nodded. "Go ahead. Let's hear it."

"If you will return my staff—my own property, taken from me for no good reason—and if all three of you will concede that we are in fact on Green, a whorl that to most of us has never been more than a colored disk of light in the sky, I will tell you how we may be able to return to Blue."

Sfido nodded. "One of the men may have it. I'll ask. For myself, if you assert we've actually been taken to Green I'll accept it. Do you, Rajan?" Seeing my face, he gulped and hurried away.

Kupus said slowly, "It's hot in here. Very warm."

"We inhumas love it," Fava announced.

He ignored her. "But we're in a room in a building, after all. I'm old enough to remember the Long Sun Whorl, Incanto. So are you, as anyone can see. I don't know how it was in your city, but ours had buildings that were kept warm by a big furnace in the cellar."

I nodded. "I think the Prolocutor's Palace in Viron may have been heated in that fashion, although the Caldé's was not. The floors of the Prolocutor's Palace were always warm in cool weather."

Grunting, Kupus bent to touch the floor on which I had been sitting earlier, and I assured him that it was cool in comparison to the air of the room.

"Are you saying that it's this warm outside?"

"No."

Zepter asked, "Then why are you insisting that we're on Green?"

"I'm not," I told him, "but I remember this room, and it was on Green. I think it more likely that we are there than that it has been carried to Blue. Don't you?"

Kupus began, "A duplicate—"

I sat down again.

Fava said, "It won't be as hot as this outside because it will be a lot hotter, that's what he means. This's the cellar. Can't you see that?"

"It looks like one," Kupus admitted grudgingly.

"It is. We're underground, and so it's cooler here. It should be very nice outside."

Zepter crouched to speak to me. "I'm sorry about your staff, Dervis. Captain Sfido ordered it, and he represents our patron. The rest of us were merely following orders."

"I understand."

Heavily and rather awkwardly, Kupus sat down beside me. "Do you need it to bring us back?"

I shook my head. "It won't help in that way—a slug gun might be more useful."

Zepter began, "Without Sfido's—" Kupus silenced him.

"I don't actually want one," I told them. "Or at least I don't think I do, and especially not on those terms. I haven't quite made up my mind about it. I was hoping you'd return my staff because I miss Oreb. He likes to perch on it."

Zepter raised his eyebrows. "Your bird?"

"Yes." I closed my eyes. "You chased him away, some of you back there. I think the staff might make it easier." I tried to visualize the staff and Oreb fluttering down to land with a thump upon its T-shaped handle, as he had so often during the past few days.

Fava said, "Here comes that Soldese officer again, but he hasn't got it."

"Once in a while," I whispered, "when I'm nearly awake . . ."

At times Sfido had an oily, almost feminine way of speaking that reminded me of one of the augurs at our schola; in it he said, "I'm terribly sorry, but your staff doesn't seem to have come with us, Rajan. I talked to Private Gevaar. He was the one who actually took it from you. He told me where he put it, but it doesn't seem to have been taken when we were."

I was thinking of the sun on Oreb's black wings, of Oreb as he had looked when he flew up in alarm from Scylla's shrine of twisting pillars on the cliffs above Lake Limna, and did not reply.

Fava asked someone, "Where did he put it?" and Patera Grig replied, "What difference does that make?"

A rougher voice with an undertone of cruelty in it: "Is he asleep?"

"No," the girl told him.

"Yes," I said; but I was not sure they heard me—Oreb fluttering up and away over blue water, a hint of blue upon one black wing. For a moment (if only for a moment) he seemed more real to me, the sable-and-scarlet bird flying beneath the slim golden bar of the Long Sun, than the hideous prison-room on Green in which I sat, or the snowy thornbushes under which I huddled with Fava. I may have heard the creaking of the hinges; now that all that horror is over and we have returned to Blue, I cannot be sure.

Certainly I heard the girl Fava's shout of surprise, and Kupus's incredulous "Gods doom!"

Then—*"Bird back!"*

I opened my eyes. Oreb was about the size of a child of four, with wings that seemed almost feathered arms; but he cocked his head at me as he always has, regarding me through one jet-black eye. "Good bird?"

"Good bird, Oreb. I'm very glad to see you."

"Good Silk!"

"He frequently calls me Silk," I explained to Kupus. "I believe it must have been the name of his former master, the man I set out to bring to my town of New Viron, but failed to bring. Silk is an aspect of Pas now."

Fava began, "He looks so different—"

"So do you," I told her.

Zepter asked, "Is that another inhumi?"

"I'm sure it isn't. Come over here, Oreb. You're too big to perch on my staff at present, I'm afraid. You'll have to walk for yourself, or fly. Can you still fly?"

"Bird fly!"

"I doubt it, but we'll soon see."

"Fish heads?"

Nodding, I stood up. "Certainly we'll need food if we're going to stay here indefinitely, and I doubt very much that the inhumi will feed us."

Fava rubbed her hands. "I'd like to eat right now. A small salad with some of that thick white dressing that Decina makes from eggs and olive oil, and maybe a slice of roast beef and some bread and butter." All that she was, was in her smile—the girl and the artful intelligence behind the girl's, and the torpid inhuma (dressed as dolls of painted wood are) who froze with me beneath leafless branches covered with snow through which there protruded, here and there, needle-sharp points of black.

"Girl thing?" Oreb was clearly puzzled.

"I would take that, too," I told Fava. "But if you're expecting me to conjure it out of the air for you, you'll be disappointed."

"Oh, no. I just wondered what you thought about the roast beef. Not terribly large and not too rare, if you please."

Zepter nodded, the nod of a man who takes food seriously. "I'm with you on that last one, Mora."

"I hope you'll be with her on a good may other things as well," I told him. "She supports Blanko and Inclito—"

"Papa? I certainly do!"

"To begin with. You oppose both, Lieutenant Zepter—or at

least you have been opposing them up until now. Sfido, I don't think it's wise for you to let your hand stray to your needler like that."

The burly lieutenant turned on him with a low growl that might have come from the throat of a large and suspicious dog.

"Your own loyalty to Duko Rigoglio does you credit," I told Sfido, "but you cannot keep these troopers loyal to him by force."

I spoke to Kupus. "When we had our meeting yesterday, Captain, there were four of your officers present. Lieutenant Zepter is here with us, which leaves three unaccounted for." I indicated the other side of the room by a gesture. "Are they over there?"

He nodded.

"Then call them. No, call everyone."

Kupus raised his left arm, moving his hand in circles. "On me!"

"We will reconvene that meeting," I told Sfido. "Has it occurred to you yet that this girl and I, and all the mercenaries of Captain Kupus's company might go back to Blue in some fashion, leaving you here?"

He stared at me without speaking, and at last shook his head.

"It will. You have seen nothing of Green yet, Captain. Nothing beyond this room. When you have slept in her swamps and jungles, and seen the City of the Inhumi, it will occur to you at every breath."

"I will not betray Soldo," Sfido declared.

"I would not ask you to," I told him.

Oreb sprang into the air, his clumsy wings flailing. "Men come!"

I waved to them. "Lieutenant Karabin? I don't know the names of your brother officers. Perhaps you could introduce them."

Kupus said, "I should have myself. Go ahead, Karabin."

"Yes, sir." Like Zepter he had a bristling mustache, but he was tall and rather slender, and his was black. "You and I haven't met formally yet, Rajan." He offered his hand, and I shook it.

"This is Lieutenant Warren, and this is Lieutenant Wight. They're from the same town. We don't have two officers from the same town very often."

I shook hands with both. "May I ask without offense how a mercenary becomes an officer?"

Wight said, "We're elected by our men, Rajan. We formed my platoon, and then we elected sergeants and a lieutenant."

"You?" Fava asked, and he nodded.

Kupus said, "We elected me captain once the lieutentants had been decided on. After that, the First Platoon had to elect one of the sergeants lieutenant, and choose a new sergeant."

By the time he had finished speaking, the men were all gathered around us, which had been my chief purpose in asking the question. Most were staring at Oreb, and I waited a moment more for them to assuage their curiosity, smiling and nodding to every man who wore a headcloth.

"Watch out!" Oreb muttered, and I nodded. What I planned to do, or at least planned to try to do, was fully as chancy as letting my legs hang over the prow of the Trivigaunti airship; but I needed to understand the extent of my powers in what I still thought of then as a nightmare that I shared with Fava, and this would delineate them as nothing else could have.

"Troopers," I began, "you deserve to know why I'm doing what I'm going to do, and what I expect from you. I'm going to explain all that, and it won't take long. To start with, we're on Green, the green whorl that you've seen in the sky since you were children. Green is the breeder of storms and the breeding grounds of the inhumi."

There was a rattle of excited talk.

"Some of you may doubt that we're really here. I won't argue the point—you'll be convinced soon enough. A minute ago, I was about to explain to your officers how I thought we could get back to our own whorl. I said I'd do it, if they'd give me back my staff. I'll make you the same offer: give my staff back, and I'll explain how we may—I said *may*—be able to get back home."

I stood silently then, concentrating, and let them talk. After some minutes, Gorak approached me. "We haven't got it, Rajan."

"Do you still consider yourselves troopers in the Duko of Soldo's horde, Sergeant?"

"If you're asking me personally, Rajan—"

"I'm asking about the whole company," I told him firmly. "Do you?"

At my elbow, Kupus said, "Yes."

His tone had been at least as firm as mine. After looking for a moment into that hard-featured, somewhat fleshy face, I shrugged and raised my voice. "In that case, I'm going to tell you nothing more, and leave you here." Closing my eyes, I extended my hands before me, and thought with all my might of the sword the Neighbor had revealed to me. I do not mean that I described it to myself in so many words, saying that the blade was black and keen, and all the rest. Instead, I recalled its weight in my hand, and the bitter edge that had killed so many inhumi and severed the head of the spitting horror.

I heard the hiss of a hundred indrawn breaths, and a little gasp from Fava. *To me*, I thought, *to me!* I extended my right hand as I had offered it to the lieutenants. And something hard, cold, and hauntingly familiar grasped it from within.

14

DUKO RIGOGLIO

I opened my eyes. The blade was somewhat darker, if anything; its curve may have been a shade less pronounced.

Sfido was goggling at me, his mouth gaping. "You have your needler," I told him, "and these troopers of yours, slug guns. Surely you won't begrudge me a mere sword."

Pushing past him, I began to tap the mottled gray flagstones with the point, willing one to sound hollow. "Here," I said at the third, "lift it for me, please, Fava. Help her, Oreb."

Together they did, struggling with its weight until Sergeant Gorak stepped forward to add his much greater strength to theirs. At once the stink of rotting flesh seemed to fill the whole chamber. Steep stairs, narrow and treacherous with slime, descended from the opening. I told Fava, "You had better precede me. It may be dangerous down there, but it would be worse for you to remain up here alone."

She nodded, hesitated, and at length took the first step, shuddering.

"You too, Oreb. Take care of her."

"Bird go?" he croaked doubtfully. (His voice was exactly as it had always been, though he had come to seem a sort of clumsy, feathered dwarf, and I had seen undulant arms wrestling with the flagstone as well as his now-armlike wings.) "Bird save?"

"Yes," I told him firmly. "Bird save. Protect her as much as you can. Go on, Oreb."

Fava's head sank out of sight below the level of the floor. Oreb started forward, flinched in a way I found very human, then dove after her, spreading his stubby wings almost before they were clear of the rectangular opening.

"Good-bye," I told the mercenary troopers peering into it. "This is a hard road and a dangerous one, but in the end it may lead us home. You will be safe here, I believe, until you die."

"Rajan!" Twenty hands at least reached out to stop me.

Kupus pushed his men aside, aiming his needler at my head. "You are our prisoner."

"No." I stepped down. "There cannot be a prisoner of a prisoner, Captain. We are prisoners, you and I—the prisoners of the inhumi who rule this whorl. But I intend to escape them, if I can."

Fava's voice reached me, distant and hollow. "Incanto! There's a man down here!"

Thinking that she had come upon the blind man I remembered, I nodded and went down into the opening.

Querulously, a voice behind me ventured, "Rajan . . . ?"

Recognizing it as Sfido's, I turned. "Yes? What is it, Captain?"

"May I . . . ? May we come with you?" He was crouching at the edge of the opening.

"No," I told him. "But they may go with you, to the place to which you go. You're their leader. You are Duko Rigoglio's representative, and their commanding officer."

Oreb sailed past, his tubby body and stubby wings suggesting an airship in miniature. "Man come!"

I stepped off the narrow stair, which disappeared as my foot left it.

"Rajan!"

It was Sfido again; I stopped and looked back up at him. "I thought I'd asked you not to call me that. I can tolerate it from the men I knew in Gaon; but when you use it, it puts us both in false positions."

"This hole." I watched him choke back the title he wished to give me. "It's getting smaller."

I waved, told him that I wished them all well, and left him.

A new voice called, "It's me, sir. Lieutenant Valico."

Darkness had closed about me with Sifido's last, despairing cry. Very much afraid of falling, I halted and opened my hand. The light the Neighbor had given me gleamed in a crease in my palm; as I focused my attention upon it, it grew stronger. I held it up and looked around me.

The sewer was a flattened oval, its thick obsidian walls cracked and near collapse. A trickle of water ran along its bottom some considerable distance below the narrow walkway on which I stood; a man's rotting corpse sprawled there, half in and half out of the dark water, a patient traveler waiting for a current strong enough to move him.

"Incanto!" It was Fava, the fact confirmed by Oreb, who sailed past me calling, "Girl say!"

Holding my light higher, I caught sight of her some distance down the sewer.

"He says we're all asleep!"

Valico himself called, "It's true, sir. I—I mean that's how it looked."

I nodded to myself. "Can you see the opening from where you are, Lieutenant?"

"No, sir."

It was night in that case, I thought. Night, or we had far to go.

As I drew nearer, Fava said, "He was looking for us, Incanto. Inclito sent him. I mean, Papa did."

Valico nodded. "Are you really the general's brother, sir?"

"Why do you ask?"

"It's what a lot of people were saying when he came back and you stayed in his place, sir. They say you're his older brother, and you stayed behind with your father when him and his mother left Grandecitta, and you've come to Blanko to help him out."

I smiled, although I doubt that Valico saw it. "And what does General Inclito himself say?"

"Nothing, sir. Colonel Bello asked him point-blank, but he wouldn't talk about it."

"No doubt that's wise. Let us be wise, too, Lieutenant."

"Sir . . . ?"

Fava said, "He can't understand how you brought him here. Neither can I, Incanto. How you do this?"

"We brought him," I told her. "Or at any rate I believe we did, that both of us are necessary for it to take place. I want to talk to you about that, and about the Vanished People, when we're alone. Meanwhile, you must remember what happened in Inclito's house, shortly before you left."

"I didn't understand that, either, or how you got into my story."

Overhead, Oreb called, "Thing come! Bad thing!"

"That will be an inhumu, I suppose," I told Valico. "You have a slug gun, I see. Be prepared to use it." I heard the jingle of the sling swivels and a faint click as he pushed off the safety. "I was wrong," I told him. "It's not an inhumu."

"That's good," Fava said; narrow though the walkway was, she was walking beside me and pressing herself against me, as children often do when they seek protection.

Valico ventured, "You'd better let me go first, sir."

"So that you can have a clear shot."

"Yes, sir."

I shook my head. "Fava said you didn't understand how you came to be here. I'm not at all sure I do, either. Will you tell me? What occurred, from your perspective?"

He cleared his throat. "General Inclito sent us, sir. He told my men and me what happened when you and those two colonels went to try to make a bargain with the enemy, sir, and how they thought his daughter's friend was his daughter, and all that."

"In back!" Oreb had returned.

Far down the sewer, I caught sight of something faint that moved. At almost the same instant, Valico's slug gun boomed behind me; I whirled, nearly knocking Fava off, and was in time to see a long-fanged beast whose naked body was as wrinkled and repulsive as the white-headed one's neck fall from the walkway.

Before the echoes died away, Valico turned to face me, his gun still smoking. "I'll try to keep a better lookout behind, sir."

"And I, a better lookout ahead." The white thing I thought I had seen had vanished, if it ever existed.

"Bird find," Oreb announced proudly; I asked him to fly ahead and tell me what he found there.

"General Inclito said to get in as close as we could, sir," Valico continued, "and see how they were treating you, and to try to get you out if we could. We waited till about midnight before we started off, me and six men."

"You came as close as you dared. Then you yourself went forward alone. Isn't that how it was?"

"Yes, sir. They had sentries out, sir, just like you'd expect."

"But you slipped past them and got in among the sleepers?"

"Yes, sir." Valico paused. "The sentry I came closest to was asleep too, sir. That was the first thing that surprised me."

"What was the second?"

"Everybody was asleep, sir. Just like the sentry."

Oreb returned to report. "No see."

"When it's cold, sir, you've just about always got a few that can't sleep. And unless you make them, there's some that won't even try. But these mercenaries the general told us about were all asleep, and their fires died down to just about nothing, sir. Some just ashes and smoke."

"I understand. How did you find us, Lieutenant? They wouldn't allow us a fire, and there can't have been enough light for you to see our faces."

"I didn't, sir. I was just going from fire to fire," Valico paused to gulp, "and something smelled just . . . just so awful, sir. And the fires went out, it seemed like, but all of a sudden I was hot."

I nodded. "Fava, you know more about the inhumi than most of us. I hope you don't mind my saying that."

"It's all right."

"Good. Many people fear that the inhumi may begin to breed

on Blue as well as Green. Quite some time ago, I theorized that they could not, that their eggs were hatched by the heat of the Short Sun, which is not sufficiently intense on Blue. Was I correct?"

"I think so."

I halted, conscious that something was lying in wait for us only a few steps farther on, whether Oreb could see it or not.

Pressing closer still, Fava asked, "Is that good enough? A good enough answer? I could just say you were right, if it would be better."

"Fava . . . ?" My mind was racing.

"What is it?"

"You saw me create this sword."

"Yes, but I still don't understand how you did it."

"Neither do I, but I may be getting closer than I was a minute or two ago. This is a real place, this sewer. I've actually been here. Have you?"

"Have I? You mean before this?" The light in my hand revealed the confusion in her face. "No . . . No, I couldn't forget this."

"Good. Remember the jungle? We went there from Inclito's. Did that seem familiar? I may well have been there myself, I mean there in that particular spot, but I can't say with any certainty."

"Yes, I was, once. I remembered the little pool."

"Better and better. These are real places. I was held a prisoner in that room up there, for example, and I recall it very vividly. You agree that they're real?"

She nodded. "I suppose so."

"So do I. You told me the Duko had wanted you to murder Inclito, but you refused, remember? Your refusal made me think about my adopted son, who had died in that jungle."

I glanced back to see whether Valico was close enough to overhear me, and lowered my voice. "Then you showed your fangs and we went; but it was to a place you remembered, not to the exact spot where he died—a real place, though we ourselves were not actually there, and no more real than my sword. You've been in the Duko's palace?"

She nodded again. "What are you getting at?"

"Mora told me once that you didn't believe in the Neighbors, in the Vanished People. When she said it, I thought that was simply foolish of you; I myself have seen the Vanished People and spoken to them, and even been saved by them. Later, when I'd had time to think about it, I realized that it wasn't nearly so foolish as it looked, that the Vanished People I'd seen and spoke to here and on Blue were no more physically present than you and I in that jungle on Green."

"Do you think they might help us now, Incanto?"

"I doubt it very much. For one thing, I no longer have the ring Seawrack gave me. Fortunately, I'm not at all sure we need them."

Again, I glanced behind me. "Your . . . Never mind. The inhumi preyed upon the Vanished People once. You must know it. That was one of the reasons that they left these whorls, and it may even have been the principal one. When the inhumi prey upon us, they are like us. I won't be more specific now, but you must know what I mean. What do you suppose the inhumi were like when they were preying upon the Vanished People?"

"I've wondered about that. It must have been marvelous. Miraculous . . . For them, I mean."

"I agree. Let us suppose that some small trace of that remained behind, passed from generation to generation in some fashion. Do you see what I'm getting at?"

"I think so."

"Good."

I halted, waiting for Valico to catch up to us, then called to Oreb, who landed teetering at my feet.

"When we were lying under the thornbushes, Fava, I wanted desperately to be warm, and I must have thought of that room up there, one of the warmest places that I have ever been in. Do you understand me? I want to you to think now of the Duko's palace in Soldo—of his bedroom, if you've ever been there. He's probably in bed by now."

"I haven't." Looking up at me, Fava closed her eyes, her broad, smooth brow wrinkling with concentration.

My first impression was that nothing was happening, my second that the sewer had become larger, or perhaps that it had always been bigger than I thought.

"A window!" Valico pointed a trembling finger (I shall never forget this) toward the other side of the sewer. "Look! I can see the stars!"

"So can I," I told him. "Go over there, Lieutenant, and open it. I don't think you're going to get your feet wet." My voice cannot have been as joyful as I felt at that moment—no voice could be.

Gingerly, Valico tried to step off the slimy walkway; but there was no walkway. The slime had become wax, the filthy stone slabs beneath it a figured floor of gemwood and singing oak.

"Good place?" Oreb sounded doubtful.

"Perhaps not. But you may open your eyes, Fava. We're here."

She did, looked around her, then clutched my arm. "There are guards."

"No doubt."

Valico threw up the sash of one large window in a long row of large windows. From outside the palace, I heard excited voices and the rattle of sling swivels, then the unmistakable *snick-snack* of the bolt of a slug gun opening and closing on a fresh cartridge.

"There's some sort of disturbance out there," I told Fava, "one that we almost certainly shouldn't become involved in."

Seeing an elaborate chair upon a dais at the other end of the room, I asked her whether this was where the Duko held court, and she nodded.

"Where does he sleep?"

She shook her head. "I have no idea."

"It will be on this floor, I feel sure."

While we had been speaking, Oreb had flown to the end of the room, circling behind the throne. "Bird find! Here door!"

He was correct, and the door unlocked. We discovered a

reception hall, and a library with a very high ceiling and very few books, and eventually a door protected by a sentry who challenged us.

I stepped forward and offered him my sword (which he had no way to take, since he was holding his slug gun) hilt first. "We are from Blanko," I explained. "We have come at the request of the Duko to sue for peace."

"His Grandeur is sleeping!"

"I'm Fava," Fava said. "You must remember me, Marzo. Duko Rigoglio charged me strictly to report to him as soon as I got here, day or night."

There was a good deal more arguing, which would certainly have roused the Duko if he had in fact been asleep. Eventually the sentry went in to consult him, with me at his heels and Oreb sailing over both our heads to land upon the foot of the ducal bed.

"What is this!" The Duko was middle-aged and clean-shaven; for some reason I had expected a thick mustache.

Fava curtsied.

"That man has a slung gun! Take it from him!"

I told Valico to give the sentry his slug gun, which he did, and added my sword, suggesting that he put them in some safe place from which he could return them when we left. The new sword I created for myself as soon as his back was turned had a straight blade like Pig's. It also had gold chasing, which looked very nice against its black steel.

"Who are you?"

Fava looked demure. "This is Incanto, Your Grandeur. Inclito's sorcerer? I've told you about him, and I thought you might want to talk to him."

"I do." The Duko had recovered from his surprise. His full, round face was without expression, and his eyes reminded me unpleasantly of a sacred serpent that I had at first believed a part of Echidna's image in Gaon.

I said, "And this is Lieutenant Valico, of the Horde of Blanko."

Valico bowed.

Duko Rigoglio ignored him. "You gave my guard your sword.

Now you've got another one. I do not permit anyone weapons in my presence."

"Then you should have taken your guard's slug gun," I told him.

Fava said, "This isn't going to get any of us anywhere, Your Grandeur. It's just like locking me up for telling you the truth, can't you see that? You'll take Incanto's sword again, and he'll make another one, or something worse."

Oreb added, "Silk talk!"

"He means me," I explained to the Duko. " 'Incanto' is a bit long for him, so he calls me Silk."

"Good bird!"

Duko Rigoglio said, "Your child companion, whose status here is that of an escaped criminal as I should warn you, has described your pet to me. She indicated something a good deal smaller, however. A more conventional bird."

I acknowledged that Oreb's present appearance puzzled me as well.

"He is fat. He looks as if he were about to burst."

"No cut!" Oreb retreated to a windowsill.

"Is he the source of your occult power, Incanto?" The Duko studied him. "He seems to have very little himself. I don't suppose I could persuade you open him with your sword?"

Employing the feathers at the tips of his wings as a boy would have used his fingers, Oreb unfastened the window catch and pushed out the swinging casement, admitting a gust of icy wind.

"Certainly not." I explained that Oreb had been intended as a sacrifice, but that Patera Silk has spared his life—if indeed this was the same Oreb.

The Duko's eyes glittered. "You failed repeatedly to honor the gods as is their right."

"No doubt."

"You wakers on the *Whorl*. In Nessus the gods walked among us, lords and ladies of Urth, even unto Shining Pas."

"Scylla!" Oreb croaked angrily. "No god!" (Or perhaps it was "Know god!" I should ask him.) "Wet god!"

I said that if he meant that the gods and goddesses we had
known in the *Whorl* were figures of clay, I quite agreed with him;
and Fava wanted to know whether "Nessus" had been the same as
the Short Sun Whorl.

"Nessus is our city," He fixed her with that glassy, unblinking
gaze. "A city larger than the whorl on which it stands."

"He's mad," Fava told me matter-of-factly.

"No, never!" He sprang from his bed with agility surprising in
so massive a man of middle age. "My child! My child! Hear me."

Startled, Oreb fled through the window.

"Hear me." Duko Rigoglio crouched before Fava in his
embroidered nightshirt, his big face intent. "A whorl, my child . . .
A whorl, any whorl, is only flat. Don't you see that? So much land
and so much water?" His hands molded a plain around them.
"Here on Blue, I'm going to claim it all. In time, hmm? In time.
But it's really not so much, now is it? Not so great an area. You
must have . . .

"No, you, sir. The sorcerer. Incanto? That's your name?"

I said that he might call me Incanto or Horn, as he wished.

"But you were in the void, the emptiness between the stars,
the mirror sphere? You looked down, down upon this Blue whorl,
and you saw it all, didn't you? The seas, the continents and islands,
just we looked down on Urth from the *Loganstone*. We saw land
and Ocean, as we had seen green Lune in the night sky. And it was
not so very big."

He turned back to Fava, taking her by the shoulder. "Also we
beheld Nessus, the undying city. But we did not see Nessus. No
one save Pas, whose true name was known to us all in those glori-
ous days, could behold Nessus."

"We came hoping to make peace," she whispered.

"Exactly," the Duko whispered in return. "Precisely so. Listen
now, while I explain. There were many buildings there, countless
houses of one and two and three and even four stories, and countless towers of twenty and thirty and three hundred. Of three thousand. Do you grasp it? Why, no one ever succeeded in counting
the towers in the Citadel alone. That's what they say, though I

never tried, or met anyone who had, and the Citadel itself . . . I lived near it. Did I tell you?"

Fava shook her head.

"I did, near the river, south of the Necropolis, which was unfortunate because its infinite dead polluted the water after each rain, a sort of sticky black, like tar, that might float or sink. We used to say the women floated and the men sunk, but that was a joke. Only a sort of joke. I doubt that it was true at all."

Valico touched my arm and pointed to the open window, from which a clamor as of contending voices issued. I nodded and put a finger to my lips.

"But one could have walked all around the Citadel in three days, or four," the Duko was saying. "It was only a small area, really so small that people from distant parts of the city, of which there were many thousands, actually doubted that it existed at all. Then underneath all our buildings were cellars and sub-cellars, dungeons and caverns and tunnels without end. The wall around the city, which was taller than its tallest towers, was honeycombed with passages, chambers, gun rooms, barracks, shelters, galleries, armories, cells, chapels, retiring rooms, and compartments of a hundred other sorts. One has only to sum the areas of all these, and the damp mines under Gyoll. But no one could."

I said, "We had hoped, Your Grandeur, to reach some mutually satisfactory arrangement by which our Corpo, while acknowledging your supremacy, might retain some local control over strictly local matters. That, coupled with your guarantee that property rights would be respected, might be the basis of a lasting peace advantageous to both parties."

The Duko laughed, rose, and walked over to lay a hand as clean and well groomed as any woman's on my arm. "Do you know the definition of peace, my friend?"

"Not the one you are about to quote, I'm sure."

Beyond the Duko, I saw Oreb flash past the windows—and heard him, too: *"Here Silk! Silk here!"*

"Peace, as you intend peace, is but the slice of cheese in a sandwich, a period of cheating between two periods of fighting.

Your peace would endure only until Blanko felt strong enough to throw us off, probably when we were deeply committed elsewhere. No, my friend, Pas would agree to no such peace, and neither will I. Would your Blanko consent to surrender all its weapons, every big gun, every slug gun, every needler, every sword and every knife?"

I said that I did not know, but that I felt sure the Corpo would at least consider such a demand.

"Then I make it. I make it because after you have complied with it, I can do whatever I wish."

Soon there was a hubbub in the hallway outside, over which I heard the voice of the sentry, followed by four or five shots.

"It's time for us to leave," I told Fava urgently. "Think of the hillside, of the snow. Concentrate!"

She closed her eyes, and I would have closed mine as well; but the door burst open, admitting Oreb and a dozen wild-eyed troopers I did not at first recognize as Kupus's mercenaries. One leveled his slug gun at the Duko, and fired. The slug struck the slime-draped wall across the creeping stream of fetid filth into which about a third of the mercenaries had fallen, and ricocheted again and again, echoing and re-echoing up and down the sewer as it screamed through the reeking air.

When Inclito sent me here, I expected to face a great many difficulties; but never the worst that I have encountered, which is simply that the mercenaries themselves are not here. Because they are not, I am unable to ask them, either collectively or individually, what they might be willing to accept in place of the promised silver. By forming my own auxiliary corps, I have raised a good deal of money. A fortune, although it may seem that I am boasting.

But what confusion! Much of it is in silver—of various grades and alloyed with a variety of other stuffs, generally nickel. Some of it is gold, more or less alloyed with copper and lead. It ranges in hardness from a buttery little ingot contributed by Cantoro (may the Outsider smile upon him, now and forever), to three broad disks as hard as flints.

Nor is that all. There are real cards, too, such as we used to use in the *Whorl*. How much silver is a card worth? How much gold? I have asked half a dozen merchants, bankers, and moneylenders thus far, and received a full dozen replies. That is scarcely to be wondered at, and not all the cards in circulation here are in serviceable condition. (To think that we used to chop them up into a hundred cardbits, never once considering that they could never be reassembled!)

And how good is the silver you want to change them for, Incanto? Let me see it.

Well, I would if I could.

I've jumped far ahead of myself, however. Let me say here quickly what our situation is. Then I will write more about all that befell Fava, Oreb, and me on Green, and how Kupus's mercenaries discovered the corpse hatch and followed us to Soldo. I still do not understand why they did not disappear into some dream of their own when Fava and I left, or why all of us returned to the sewer we hoped to have left behind us forever; but I find so many other mysteries there that I am scarcely troubled by that one. (Why did not the Duko accompany us? And was he shot, and what was the result of that shot, a visionary slug fired by an unreal trooper from an equally chimerical slug gun.)

It is only too easy to ask whether we were actually on Green— I should know, since I have been asking it ever since I returned. But what is meant by *actually*? Our physical bodies were not there: Valico saw them asleep in the snow. Equally, something else was or imagined it was. Our minds? Our spirits? Both, and some third and fourth things as well? At what point did Fava (I cannot, will not, write "poor Fava") die?

When I arrived, I had little idea how I might raise the large sum we require. Inclito had suggested that I assemble the leading men

of the town, and provided me with a list. I did; but the topic of
our deliberations was quickly changed to how we might best cheat
the mercenaries of the money Inclito and I had promised them, in
spite of all that I could do to prevent it.

At last I rose and slammed the table with my staff. "You are
thieves," I told them. "I had thought you worthy of respect. The
more fool I! You have made yourselves rich by robbing your fellow
citizens—"

They protested this so loudly that it was a full minute at
least until I could continue. Doubtless that was for the best; I
felt my hot rage turn icy cold while they shouted and pounded
the table.

"You think you have escaped the gods and the punishments
gods mete out to such as you. You are mistaken. The Outsider is
sitting among you unseen, and he has given his judgment. He has
appointed a scourge fit for you. I will not call you together again,
and it may be that no one will ever summon you a second time. I
think it very likely. If you wish to speak with me again, come to me
singly. Perhaps I'll find time for you, if you do. Perhaps not."

I went out of Ugolo's house then without a thought in my
head, and saw five boys in the street playing trooper, and two old
men laughing and advising them. I called all seven to me and
introduced myself, although I soon found that all of them knew
very well who I was. I said nothing to them of money; it was clear
enough that none had much. But I told them in some detail how
desperate the battles in the hills were liable to be, and spoke as elo-
quently as I could of the need to defend Blanko should the enemy
break through. Then I showed them the keys to the armory and
ordered them to come with me.

The people laughed at us at first, a straggling company of boys
and old men; and they laughed louder still when I enlisted
women. There came a moment, however, when I had to order my
troops not to fire upon a jeering crowd unless they offered us violence. That quieted them, and I was able to arrest the ringleaders.
We have driven spikes into the walls of the dry sewer Inclito told
me of—a much more comfortable place, certainly, than the sewer

I opened for the Neighbors—and chained them to the spikes. Ugolo is there now with a few of the others.

In the Long Sun Whorl, bio troopers were called auxiliaries because the fighting forces there had originally been composed of soldiers alone. They were the *Army*, which is to say the arm of the city. The armed bios enlisted to assist and augment them were designated auxiliaries, and their assembled strength (which in Viron included my Guard) the *Horde*. Together, the army and the horde composed the *Host*.

Even there, hordes increased in importance, while armies dwindled as their soldiers perished. Here the horde—Inclito's for example—is the entire force. Surely then I can take that term *auxiliary* for my old men, women, and boys.

As I have.

Only the largest boys arc of use to us, as I soon found; the smaller ones cannot manage a slug gun, not even with the lightly loaded cartridges. In the same way, only the largest, strongest women; and poor young women who have had to work hard are by far the best suited to fighting Duko Rigoglio.

15

BEFORE THE BATTLE

Have I a solitary evening before me? I hope so. The town is celebrating, as well it should; this is not a night for speeches, especially speeches from me. Perhaps I'll be able to get some writing done.

If I were to speak to these citizens of Blanko, I am afraid I would talk mostly about Chaku and Teras, who perished in the sewer fighting the white worm, yet were alive again and walked, speechless and dazed, among us when we woke. Who can plumb the mind of the Outsider, or search out all his ways? Our riches are his dross, and our gods his toys.

The townspeople are shooting off fireworks, and I am sorry to say that a few of my troopers seem to be firing their slug guns into the air. The sky over Blanko is no place for Oreb tonight, and he knows it.

All this because a courier from Olmo arrived at shadelow, a tired man on a blown horse. I cannot help wondering whether either are getting any rest. Perhaps they are—they seemed fatigued enough to sleep through anything. The news, and it is wonderful news indeed, is that the Duko has turned against Olmo, and that Olmo has turned to us in its extremity. We are offered an alliance: Olmo will fight against Soldo and Duko

Rigoglio—indeed, Olmo must, since Duko Rigoglio has laid siege to Olmo. Olmo asks only that it be permitted to retain its independence, and begs Blanko's aid.

Eco was captured or killed, and the letter he carried believed; there can be no doubt of it. How I wish Fava were still alive so that I could send her to Soldo to try to secure his release! If the Outsider wills it, Eco should remain safe (although imprisoned) throughout the rest of our small and foolish war. We will free him when it is over. Was Mora killed or captured too? It seems likely.

I had intended to write about Chaku and Teras, and our joy at waking in the snow and seeing them, whom we had buried upon Green and prayed over, wake with us; and how we had discovered that they could neither speak nor understand what was said to them. It would all be true, but I cannot forget poor Fava. All human semblance was gone; she was an inhuma in a girl's flowered gown, a dead inhuma painted and decked in a wig—nothing more. I covered her as quickly as I could and demanded that the mercenaries who had not allowed us a fire lend me a pick and shovel. A dozen strong men would have helped me, and gladly; but I sent them away and buried her myself near the crest of the hill, beneath a flat stone on which I scratched her name and the sign of addition, not knowing how else to mark it.

Fava, who was well and very happy on Green, is dead here on Blue; and Chaku and Teras, who were dead on Green, are alive here if they have not been killed in one of Inclito's battles.

"Man come," Oreb mutters. I have opened the door and looked outside, but there is no one. I asked him whether it was a good man, but he only clacked his beak and fluttered his wings. Those are generally signs of nervousness, but he was doing both before he announced our visitor, and with all the fireworks and shooting he has more than enough to be nervous about.

I should say here—or at least I certainly ought to say somewhere—that Fava, Valico, and I halted when we heard the mercenaries behind us in the sewer. Oreb did not halt, Molpe bless him, but flew back to investigate.

Several prostrated themselves, which was embarrassing. I told them that I would not talk to them until they bound Sfido and gave me his needler, which they did at once. "We lifted the stone," Kupus explained to me. "There was a sheer drop under it. One by one we jumped, and found ourselves on a dark street in Soldo."

I nodded.

Fava (I intend the human girl whom I have been calling Fava) laughed at him. "Incanto is a strego, didn't I tell you? The best any of us have ever seen."

"I never believed in any of that raff," Kupus said. "It's you women that believe it, mostly. But you women are right, and Kupus wrong."

He drew his sword and raised it, grasping it by the blade, point downward. "I and those who follow me will follow you, Rajan, working and fighting for you wherever you may lead us, loyal as long as the last rogue breathes. We require no pay from you, beyond your good will."

I asked how long they bound themselves for, and he and dozens of others answered forever. More would, I think, but those farther back on the narrow walkway cannot have heard what we said.

"Will you still serve me when we return to Blue?" I asked Kupus and Lieutenant Zepter, who was looking over his shoulder.

"Anywhere," they declared; and Zepter used a phrase I had not heard before: "In the three whorls or beyond them." You who will read this in the years to come may call me a fool, but I detect the Outsider's hand in it.

After midnight, and so a new day.

My visitor arrived. It was Sfido. We talked for an hour or more, and managed with all our talk to rouse my host's wife, who had abandoned the celebration and wisely taken to her bed. She has found a bed for him, and warmed a bowl of the bean soup. He said that he was too tired to eat, but looked half starved and managed to finish the whole bowl quickly enough, dipping the soft white bread that is so much valued here into it and eating like a lost hound.

Let me go back to the beginning.

There was a knock at the door. At first I did not answer, fearing I would quickly have a dozen drunken revelers to deal with; he knocked again, pounding the panels like a man in fear. "Rajan! Dervis!"

No one here calls me either, so I opened. At first I did not recognize him, unshaven, starved and frenetic as he looked; in the ten days since I had last seen him, the dapper officer had vanished. I told him brusquely that Atteno's shop was closed, and asked what he wanted.

"I must talk to you, Rajan. I call you that because it won't put us in a false position now."

I knew him then, but it took me a second or two to recall his name. "Sfido? Captain Sfido?"

"Yes." He drew himself up, heels clicking and shoulders squared, and saluted me. I suppose I must have asked him to come in and sit down; certainly I got out the old wooden chair that my host keeps by the till for him.

"Poor man." Oreb regarded him through one jet-bead eye and snapped his crimson beak as though to say, Behold the straits to which the wicked have fallen!

Sfido tried to smile; I have seldom seen a grown man appear so pathetic. "You have your little pet back, I see."

I told him that Oreb was under no restraint and had returned to me of his own will.

"None save your magic."

"I have none; but if I had any, I surely would not use it for that."

"None at all." It was not a question.

"No. None."

"You transported us to Green in the twinkling of an eye, then to Soldo, then to Green again, and brought us back as soon as it suited your purpose to do so." He sighed. "That sounds as if I'm arguing with you. I suppose I am, but I didn't seek you out to argue. Have you ever heard of a man called Gagliardo, Rajan? He's a citizen of my own Soldo."

"I don't believe so."

"He's rich and can live on his rents, so he studies the stars, which interest him, and he's had some strange instruments built for that purpose. You gave me a horse and sent me home, remember? I was to inform our Duko that Kupus and his troopers had turned coat."

"Certainly."

"I tried to see Duko Rigoglio at once, but he was too busy; so I went to see Gagliardo and asked how far it is to Green. When it's as close as it ever comes, it's thirty-five thousand leagues. I can't understand how anybody can measure a distance that great, and Gagliardo admits he may be in error by a thousand leagues or so, but that's what he said."

I thanked him, adding, "I've wondered about that from time to time, and I'm glad to get the information."

"Talk, talk," Oreb commented dryly.

I said, "It's astonishing that anybody should be able to make such a measurement, I agree; but I find it still more astonishing that the inhumi should be able to make the crossing from their whorl to ours, hurling their naked bodies thousands of leagues through the abyss."

"Green's nowhere near its closest now," Sfido said. "It's more than eighty thousand leagues away."

I shook my head. "They don't dare attempt such distances. They come only when the two whorls are at their closest, and even then many perish—or so I've been told."

"Bad things," Oreb declared piously.

"No worse than we are," I told him. When Sfido did not speak, I said, "It's true that there are inhumi in the Long Sun Whorl; but they made the trip on board returning landers, apparently."

"You carried a couple of hundred men across eighty thousand leagues, four times, in the winking of an eye." Sfido sighed. "That's what I told Duko Rigoglio. I said that he had seen you himself and had to know that as long as Blanko had you on its side it was suicide to fight."

"Did he agree to peace?"

Sfido shook his head.

"So he sent you here to kill me," I hazarded. "When will you make the attempt?"

"No cut!" Oreb exclaimed.

Sfido took up the word, after a momentary pause repeating, "No."

"Then he will send someone else, I presume. He tried to have Fava poison Inclito."

"I wanted him to bribe you, that was my suggestion. I told him that I doubted you could be killed at all, and an assassin would just lose his own life and whatever part of his reward the Duko had advanced him. But I said that you might help us for gold and power, and that he should offer you a great deal of both. Women, horses, troopers, and whatever his emissary sensed you wanted. A throne in Blanko or Olmo."

"You were wrong," I said, "since I have already died once. But you proposed that Duko Rigoglio offer me a throne?"

Sfido nodded.

"You're too old to have been born here. How old were you when you left Grandecitta?"

"Fifteen."

"That was my own age at the time I left Viron. You should remember boarding the lander and crossing the abyss, exactly as I do. Were any of you rich?"

He laughed, the weary laugh of one who has witnessed the ironic conclusion of his efforts. "We thought then that some of us were, Rajan. And there were others that we thought were. Neighborhood rich. Do you know what I mean?"

"I think so. My father owned a little shop very much like this in a poor neighborhood."

"That's it. Some of us were as rich as this."

"How long ago, Captain Sfido? Twenty years?"

"Not quite."

"And now we, who complained so bitterly about the rich when we were poor, have taken up every practice and custom we hated in them. Thrones! One for Duko Rigoglio and another for me. I can't begin to tell you how many complaints I heard about the rich when I was growing up, Captain."

"Don't call me that anymore, Rajan." He smiled bitterly. "It puts us in a false position."

I smiled back at him, while laughing to myself at myself.

"Certainly I've put myself in the reprehensible position of keeping a tired man talking because I wanted to. You've come to me for help, obviously, and I'll give it to you if I can. How can I help you?"

He squared his shoulders again and threw his head back. "Sfido needs no one's help. I'm here to help you."

I said that it was good of him, and waited.

"General Inclito will be defeated. You may deny it, but it's true."

"I believe it's true that you believe it. Can we leave it at that?"

"No. I've been in the hills and watched the fighting. I have no supernatural powers, but I've an eye for war. It was not for nothing that I was chosen to command our advance guard."

I said truthfully that I had never supposed it was.

He sat in silence for a moment, struck by a new thought. "You, with all your magic, Rajan. You should be at the front with the troops. Why are you here?"

"To raise the money I promised the mercenaries. I have enough now, or nearly enough. For one month's pay, that is."

"They offered to serve you for nothing. I was there, and that was when you ordered them to take my needler . . ."

"Yes?"

"I had it again when we returned to this whorl. You had them take it from me a second time. And those troopers, the great worm tore them to bits. Horrible! But they were alive again, and the General's daughter was dead."

"You said you had come to help me," I reminded him.

"Yes. Can you foresee the future? That's what one of the men from your own town told me."

"Not always."

"But sometimes. Often, I think. Do you agree that Blanko's horde will be defeated?"

I said (patiently, I hope) that he had said so, and that I deferred to his greater knowledge of military matters.

"Girl come," Oreb cautioned us.

"That will be my host's wife," I said. "I hope we haven't disturbed her."

"Who will win the war? You must know! Tell me quickly and truthfully." Sfido swallowed. "I do not plead. Never! Not even when our Duko condemned me. But tell me, Rajan, if you will, and I'll be in your debt till Hierax takes me."

"Blanko."

I had already heard Volanta's feet on the stairs going down into the shop. She came in before I could say more. "Incanto? Is this man bothering you?"

I shook my head. "I'm bothering him, I'm afraid. I've been keeping him from the rest he needs."

"Fish heads?" Oreb suggested.

"And the food too, you're right. I doubt that he can buy anything this late, but a lot of people are still celebrating. Someone might give a hungry man something, if he were approached in the right way."

Volanta had started for her kitchen before I finished. "There's some soup left, I'll heat it up for him. Bread and soup, that's the best supper."

"I'm too tired to eat," Sfido murmured, and licked his lips.

For the first time I was able to make out the narrow mustache that had almost faded into his sprouting beard. I declared that he would have to eat something, a few bites of bread and a little of the soup, so that Volanta would not be disappointed.

"Blanko will win? You're quite sure?"

I shrugged.

"Our best troops are at Olmo. Do you know about that? Olmo was plotting to turn against us, and in war one takes the weaker enemy first, so he can't put his knife in your back while you're fighting the stronger one. Besides, sacking Olmo will steady Novella Citta."

I explained that a messenger who managed to get through the Soldese lines had told me this afternoon that Olmo was besieged, and that was why the town was celebrating.

"We're not going to starve them out." Sfido spoke like a man certain of his information. "The assault must be nearly ready, if it hasn't already begun. Your horde can't hold the passes. They've been driven back twice, and General Morello's merely amusing himself while he waits for the Duko and our professionals. Those are just conscripts your Inclito's been fighting, and he can't hold them."

"It certainly sounds bad," I admitted.

"Why are you paying Kupus's mercenaries?"

"Because I said we would." I had not yet wiped my pen or put away this untidy collection of loose sheets. I did both while I collected my thoughts. "You say that I carried them and you—and Oreb, Fava, and Valico, I suppose—to Green. Fava was the girl you called Mora."

He raised his brows. "She wasn't really General Inclito's daughter?"

I started to explain, then shook my head. If Mora had been captured, as I have been assuming, it seemed likely that Sfido would have learned about it when he returned to Soldo, especially since he had apparently been kept waiting for some time.

"Good girl," Oreb told us. I suppose he meant Mora, but I would like very much to think that he intended Fava.

I told Sfido, "If I had the supernatural powers you credit me with, I wouldn't have taken advantage of them in the way that you propose. They were desperate and believed, quite understandably, that I was a miracle worker who could save them.

"Besides, they fought very well when we cleared the ancient city of inhumi—or at least it appeared to me that they did. You have an eye for strategy, and I'm sure you must know far more than I about every aspect of warfare. What did you think of them?"

"I was proud of them."

"So was I. They earned a better reward than I can give them."

Volanta called to us from the kitchen, and Sfido stood up. "I would have led them, if I could. Thanks to you, I had to watch them with my hands bound behind my back. But I told myself that whatever might happen to me, for a few days Sphigx had given me some of the best troopers who ever squeezed the trigger."

We went into the kitchen, and seated ourselves at the little table there. "I'd carry my soup into the store for Incanto," Volanta informed Sfido severely, "but not for anybody else."

"He won't be staying here," I muttered.

"Well!"

"It would be too great a burden on you and your husband. On you, particularly. He may not wish to remain in Blanko at all."

As Volanta set his soup before him, Sfido murmured, "You are an employer of mercenaries, Rajan."

"Blanko is." (The steaming bowl was followed by a loaf of new bread, a big, curved knife, and a chipped blue plate nearly filled by an immense pat of butter.) "Technically, I act for the town."

He nodded, sipping the smoking soup, then dipped his spoon back into the bowl. "You're collecting funds to pay them, you say, and since General Inclito has sent you to do that, it's an operation of considerable difficulty. Getting money always is."

"I supposed not. But there have been a few setbacks here, I admit."

"Knowing no trade but the trooper's, I am a mercenary now myself." Sfido indicated his own chest with the butter knife. "Will you employ me?"

"Are you serious, Captain?"

"Entirely, Rajan. Also brave, loyal, and experienced."

I smiled. "I'll certainly consider it. Your Duko was going to execute you?"

He nodded again while he chewed his bread and swallowed. "He did not say so, he merely imprisoned me. But that would have been the upshot. You fear that I am a spy."

"I have to consider the possibility."

"Good man," Oreb remarked conversationally. "Fish eggs?" Sfido held out what was left of the slice, and Oreb swooped to snatch it from his fingers.

"What do your arts say, Rajan? Wouldn't they reveal it if I were?"

"I have none," I told him, "and I'm getting weary of saying so. I doubt that you're a spy, but I can't be absolutely certain that you're not."

"Then keep me with you, under your eye. I've seen men my father's age with slug guns here. Women, even. Couldn't you use a good officer?"

I admitted I could.

"As a mercenary colonel," he spooned up soup that looked too hot to swallow, and swallowed it, "I will be entitled to five times the pay of one of your private troopers. I'm going to ask you for much more than that, but you won't have to give it to me until the war's over."

I waited, watching him eat.

"My house and my lands. Our Duko will confiscate them. He probably has already. I'll drill your troops and fight for you as long as this war continues, on your promise to restore them to me when Soldo surrenders."

It was my turn to raise my eyebrows. "Nothing more, Colonel Sfido?"

"Such loot as may fall my way, and that's all." He grinned, white teeth flashing in his dark beard. "I've lost everything, Rajan. All that I worked and fought for here. It didn't seem like a lot when I had it, but I find that it was riches beyond counting now that it's gone. I had a house in town and three farms. May I rely upon you to deal with me as honorably as you are with your other mercenaries?"

I nodded, and we clasped hands.

"I need sleep. If I can't stay here—"

"Urbanita will take you," Volanta volunteered, pointing. "Right next door. I'll go over and talk to her about it, if you want me to."

I said, "Please do."

"I'll tell her Incanto said so," Volanta added as she bustled out.

"She'll be getting the poor woman out of bed, I'm afraid," I remarked to Sfido.

He grinned, and spooned up more soup. "Everyone must make sacrifices in war, Rajan. Can you get us troops from your town, by the way?"

"From Gaon, you mean? It's not my home, though I guided its people for a while. I suppose I probably could, but I won't."

"Because you don't think we need them."

I shook my head. "We do, and badly. Because they don't need us. I could ask them to come here and risk their lives, and I believe that at least a few might come willingly; but one in ten or one in twenty would be killed, and many more wounded. Killed and wounded for what? For my thanks when the war was over?"

"When that woman comes back, I'm going to let her take me next door and sleep." Sfido was buttering another slice of bread. "When I wake up, I want to look over the defenses of this town of yours, if you'll let me."

I said I would, but that this was not my town either—that it was Inclito's, if anyone's.

"After that, I'll tell you what we ought to do. You probably think the town's well fortified already, and it may be. Just the same, there's always something more that can be done."

I myself must go to bed now. It is very late. Good night, Nettle. A good night to all of you.

16

A Young Man from the South

When we had gained the jungle at last, and the mercenaries had seen our human dead scattered all along the sewer and crushed in the streaming jaws of huge and deadly river-beasts, I called them together. "Once I tried to destroy the City of the Inhumi," I told them. "I had fewer than a hundred men, braggarts and cowards for the most part, untrained, badly disciplined, and worse armed. I dreamed then of leading troopers like you against it, and I am going to do it now."

To my surprise, they cheered.

"I'm not going to try to tell you how to fight. You and your officers know far more about that than I. But Lieutenant Valico and I will fight beside you, and help you however we can.

"Fava, if you'd like to leave us and warn the City, this is the time."

"I'm no inhuma! Look at me!"

"As you wish," I told her, and turned back to Kupus's troopers. "The inhumi have human slaves, as you have seen. Don't kill them unless they resist you."

Several nodded.

"When the last inhumu is dead," I promised them, "we'll go home."

Fava, Valico, and I went with Kupus and the other mercenary

officers when they reconnoitered the city. "We'll have to fight from building to building," Kupus told me. "It will be an ugly business. Are you in a hurry?"

I shook my head.

"Then I suggest we wait till morning. We're going to need all the daylight we can get for this, and it will be an all-day job."

"Or more," Zepter added gloomily.

I protested that I had no food to give them, and was told that the men carried emergency rations, which Fava, Valico and I might share.

Not even in the pit have I spent a more nightmarish night. You may say if you like that I did not spend that one at all, that I was in fact hugging Fava's icy corpse under the arching canes of the snow-laden thornbushes; but I recall every moment of it, and find that I still cannot write about it without a shudder. After the rest had laid themselves down to sleep, I went around our impromptu camp warning everyone about the insects. (They are not like the insects of the Long Sun Whorl or the somewhat different insects here that are so often blind; but I know not what else to call them.) I had hardly begun when I was stung by one of the scarlet-and-yellow creatures that we called firesnakes—a flying worm, like a little viper with a scorpion's tail.

Thereafter I spoke to one small group after another, and it seemed to me that there was always another waiting, and sleepers, too, whom I had not yet warned and could not warn without waking. And I went from sleeper to sleeper, examining their faces as I had so many years ago in the tunnel, always looking for His Cognizance and always hoping—although I knew how absurd it was—that I would find Silk, that Silk had left Hyacinth and would be going with us after all, that Silk had rejoined us when I was inattentive, talking to Scleroderma and Shrike, and lagging behind the slowest walkers to talk to His Cognizance, whom I sought without finding on that nightmare night under the cloud-capped trees that outreach all our towers, so that at last I called out softly "Silk? Silk?" as I walked among the sleepers until Oreb grasped my hand with fingers that were in fact feathers, repeating, "Here Silk. Good

Silk," and I took my own advice and found the numbing fruit, cut one in two with the gold-chased black blade of the sword that I had imagined for myself and pressed a half against the sting on my arm, weeping.

But none of that is to the point, except for being a part of the story I have set myself to tell, my own long story of the tangled paths by which I failed to find the hero Marrow and the others sent me to find.

What is to the point is the way in which the mercenaries attacked and cleared the buildings of the City of the Inhumi the next day, working in pairs or in paired groups, so that one group occupied the inhumi with their fire while the other advanced to a place from which it could fire more effectively. We have been teaching that to our troopers, Sfido and I, for the past two days— along with much else, and drill, and some marksmanship, although we are too short of cartridges to spare many for that.

I should say, too, that scarcely a day has passed on which we have not received a request for food and ammunition, blankets and clothing from Inclito, a request delivered by some weary officer or sergeant who has brought back mules insufficient to carry the eighteen or twenty or thirty loads of whatever it is that he has been sent to get, but who knows just as we do that it does not matter since we have not half as much as his letter asks us to give him.

"You can spend some of that money you raised to pay Kupus's troopers for pack animals and food," Sfido told me when we met today.

I told him I already had—nearly all of the true cards I had worried so much about earlier—and asked why he said it.

"Because the dead need not be paid. This fellow" (by which he meant Rimando, who had carried Inclito's most recent letter) "won't admit I'm right, but I am. So are you, Incanto. There may have been two hundred mercenaries with Kupus once and a hundred or more hired separately, but there aren't nearly that many left alive by now. When Olmo falls—"

"Olmo has fallen," Rimando told us.

"Then it won't be long."

I held out Inclito's letter. "That's what the general says, too. Do you want to read it?"

"Later."

I dropped the letter on Volanta's table. "This is Captain Rimando. He was my chief subordinate when this wretched war began, and the general has sent him back to us to help us prepare the town to stand a siege."

Rimando nodded affirmation.

"He and I have been discussing tactics, and I've called you in, as our best tactician, to get your advice. You were in the hills for several days after you escaped from prison in Soldo?"

Sfido nodded, and seeing Rimando's curious glance said, "Nothing daring, Captain. I was a rich man once, and I bribed my jailer."

"Show him the map, sir," Rimando suggested.

I did, turning Inclito's letter over to reveal the crude diagram that Rimando and I had sketched on the back. "While you're looking at that, Colonel, I want to ask you about Eco again. Are you quite sure you didn't see him while they had you locked up?"

"I wasn't there very long, and I didn't see many of the other prisoners, as I told you that first night. He may have been there." Sfido stroked his little mustache thoughtfully. "I have no way of knowing."

"Tall and strong," Rimando said. "Quite dark. He smiled a lot, or at least he did when we rode out to the general's farm. Clean shaven, about my age."

I explained that Rimando had been the other messenger who was to ride with Eco, but that Inclito's daughter Mora had taken his horse, and asked Sfido about her as well.

He shook his head. "There weren't any girls or women in there at all, as far as I know. Or anyway the jailer said there weren't. . . ."

Seeing the change in his expression, I said, "You've thought of something. What is it?"

"He said there had been one just before I came but she and

her lover had escaped. He wanted more silver for my own escape because of it."

Rimando turned to me. "I don't understand."

Sfido said, "The Duko had been furious. Another escape would cause a lot of trouble, or at least he seemed to think it would."

"Had they bribed their jailer too?" I asked.

He shrugged. "I don't know. I don't think so."

Rimando asked, "Did he describe the man?"

"No, he didn't tell me anything much about either one of them, except that the woman had gotten out of her cell somehow and let her lover out. She was a big, strong woman, he said, as big and strong as a man." Sfido turned the diagram so that I could read it more easily.

"Now about this map." He pointed to the series of thin rectangles that Rimando had drawn at my direction. "These are our troops?"

"The old men and the women," I told him. "The boys in reserve, back here."

"And this double line is the road south? Your town is somewhere down here?"

Rimando nodded.

"You want my opinion of this?"

"No," I told him. "Not yet. We want you to tell us how Duko Rigoglio and General Morello will attack it."

"Pah!" Sfido looked disgusted. "This's child's play. The left flank, here, is against the river. But there's no support for the right at all. This space is what? Fields? Farms?"

"Yes."

"Morello will engage the front with his infantry." He glanced at Rimando. "Do you know the term, Captain? It means troopers on foot."

Rimando colored, reminding me again of how very young he was. "Certainly."

"Incanto did not, until I told him. They will shoot at us and we will shoot at them. They will advance and retreat, if we let them. Meanwhile the cavalry will make a wide circle here," he traced it with his forefinger, "and attack from behind and the flank, then chase us back to this town of yours. If we take the best horses, we three may escape them." Sfido shrugged again. "Some of the boys may, too. The boys run very well."

He slapped our map down on the table. "You asked me how the Horde of Soldo would attack those positions, Incanto, and I've told you. Now you have to ask me what I think of them, before I explode."

I nodded and smiled. "You know how highly I value your opinion, Colonel."

"They're childish. I don't criticize you, Incanto, because you're not a trooper. But," Sfido leveled his finger at Rimando, "if you're a captain, it's no wonder—"

"I told him!" Rimando burst out. "I said it was insane. It's exactly what the general said we were not to do."

I explained what I planned then, and thanked Rimando for the pack mules and mule drivers he had brought us, which we needed so badly to carry our cloth and rope, and the fireworks, and explained that we would have to scour the nearby farms tomorrow for oxen to pull the guns, and women and children to drive the oxen.

I have no more time to write.

★

It has been a very long day, but I must write something. I sent Oreb out tonight to look for the enemy, and he has just come back: "Men come! Bad men!"

Which I knew, of course. I have been trying to find out whether he thinks they will be here before morning. He says, "Come slow," and "Sun come. Men come."

In Green's jungles we were surprised more than once by the inhumi and their human slaves. This time I have taken steps to prevent surprise, posting little groups to the north as far as the first hills. We have no horsemen worthy of the name, but our northernmost lookout—I do not remember what Adatta called her—has a little boat, with oars and a small sail, moored where the river leaves the hills. I don't know whether she can get back to us in it before the first Soldese troopers reach us; but Adatta says she will kill herself trying, and Adatta I find a good judge of other women.

Our ditches are dug, for the most part. The women have sewn thousands of sacks for the soil, and most of our walls were half built this evening, or so they appeared to me. If the Outsider will, as I have devoutly prayed, grant us just a few hours of daylight tomorrow before the enemy's advance guard comes into view, we may be, if not ready, nearly ready at least. The walls are scarcely shoulder high, but they are thick enough to stop a slug everywhere. I have tried to recall the one over which I clambered on Gold Street so long ago and tell our people how it looked; but that was a better wall than any of ours, I am afraid.

I am still far from certain about the pigs, but Atteno is enthusiastic. He has ten or twelve pairs, savage old boars for the most part.

Inclito's wounded are coming back, hundreds where we used to see a dozen or two. A few who cannot walk are in panniers, one carried on each side of a mule. The effect on our troopers is very bad—on the women, particularly. They look from face to face for their brothers and husbands, weeping, often, although they have seen neither.

One group of walking wounded was escorting eight Soldese prisoners. Their hands had been tied behind them so tightly that the skin looked like a dead man's flesh. I ordered them cut free and found a little boiled barley for them, and some wine, although we are nearly at the point of eating Atteno's boars. They told me how they had looted Olmo, and burned it afterward. The burning was on their Duko's orders, they say. They are confident of a victory that will free them within a day or two; I do not believe it will be the victory they expect, but wish I were as sure of it as they are.

The last of the big guns has arrived. We hid it in a haystack just now, and are roasting the oxen that brought it. Everyone says how good they are and urges me to eat; but I know that it is only hunger that lends those roast oxen their savor, and I am too tightly strung for that. How long has it been since I have slept more than an hour at a stretch? Three days, I believe? I am all right as long as I keep moving, but sitting like this and trying to write, I can do nothing but yawn.

Wonderful news! It has begun to snow!

I lay down—for only a minute or two, I told myself—and slept until late this morning. No one woke me. When I got up there was two fingers of snow on the ground. Now there must be four or five.

Sfido and Rimando have performed wonders while I slept. The walls are all complete, and our troopers are building themselves huts from the remaining sacks of soil and whatever else they can lay hands on.

But the snow is the best, except that it has slacked off our trip ropes. I have set a few reliable men to retightening them. The fireworks are stacked in the solaria of this farmhouse to keep them dry; the chief danger now is that we may not get them out and into position in time.

The old woman who lives here brought me an apple and a mug of sweet cider. Apples and cider are about all she has left, she says; our troopers have taken her chickens, ducks, and geese. Her husband is dead, her sons in the hills with Inclito. She said she felt sorry for me, but I feel sorrier for her. I've told Uscita I want as good a supper as she can find me tonight, and I intend to share it with my hostess.

We are seeing unwounded troopers now. So many have thrown their slug guns away that I sent a party up the road to salvage what they can. I got a group of about twenty of these beaten men together this afternoon and talked with them for nearly an hour, then asked them to stay with us voluntarily and defend their town. Not a hand went up. Inclito would have had half of them swearing they would fight to the death, I'm sure; but I am a poor speaker.

It is interesting to walk up the rutted, snow-covered road a few chains and approach our defenses as the enemy will. Our walls do not appear very formidable, and the ditches in front of them (which are filling with snow) can easily be overlooked. I have been telling our troopers that the enemy will be here tomorrow afternoon, speaking as though I knew it. "In a day," I tell them, "it will be over." It is always a matter of hanging on for one more day, after all.

The old woman refused to share my dinner, swearing that she had just eaten. There is something familiar about that thin, wrinkled face. For a time I told myself that I must have seen her at Cugino's, but I spotted him among the new men Colbacco brought up from the south; and although I described her carefully, Cugino could not identify her. He had only his axe to fight with, but I have gotten him a slug gun. He was happy to see my staff, and surprised that I still have it.

A regular formation of unwounded men has passed through our line a little after dawn, still under discipline and making an orderly retreat. I had no opportunity to count them, but I would guess there were between fifty and a hundred. They would have been a valuable addition to our strength, but the officer in charge had been ordered to march to Blanko, and rejected my authority. (Which is scant enough, I must admit.) He said that Inclito is with the rear guard. I asked how many, and he told me three hundred; but he was lying—I knew it, and he knew that I did.

Inclito is here! He has been making a fighting retreat with his horsemen. I've seen his coachman and Perito, one of the other men who worked for him. I asked about Kupus's men; they should join us here within an hour.

★

★　★

It is over. Over!

Midnight, I suppose, but I cannot sleep. The woman in the boat arrived just after I wrote about Perito. I knew it could not be long then, and supposed that it would be under an hour.

That hour passed, and I sent Oreb, who returned so quickly that I knew the enemy was almost in sight.

Before continuing I should tell you who will read this, whoever you may be, that we had posted small parties along the road, in most cases three boys commanded by a man. Their orders were to fire as soon as the first Soldese troops came in sight, and retire to our lines. Most seem to have remained at their posts longer than we intended; there had been scattered shooting for some time before I sent Oreb to scout.

I should tell you, too, about something else—although it probably means nothing at all. The fireworks party came, and there was a young man there who reminded me poignantly of Hoof and Hide. I called their corporal to me and asked who he was.

"I don't know, Master Incanto sir. I saw him wandering

around and asked whose squad he belonged to. He couldn't tell me, so I put him to work."

"You did the right thing, I'm sure. What is his name?"

The corporal, too young even to be a trooper in Inclito's horde, picked absently at a pimple on his chin. "I don't know, sir. He told me, but it's . . . I don't remember."

"Find out for me, please, and bring him to me whenever you have the time and can spare him. I'd like to talk to him."

The corporal said he would, saluted, and left, turning back after he had taken a step or two. "Cuoio, sir. I knew it'd come to me."

But Cuoio and his corporal have not come to me as I asked; and it may be that one or both are dead, although I dare to hope it is not so. Tomorrow, perhaps. No doubt they are exhausted, just as I am.

Tomorrow—tomorrow night, I suppose—I will write all about the battle, giving it an entire evening. By that time I will be rested and will have received the reports of others. I should be able to offer a rational account.

Attacked again, but we have beaten them back.

Seawrack is singing. I can hear her through the windows and the shutters and the crackling of the fire. I feel I must go to her, but I cannot.

17

◆━◆✕◆━◆

THE BATTLE OF BLANKO

I was so tired last night that I actually believed I would be back in my snug bedroom in the old farmhouse tonight, writing at the little deal table by lamplight while Sfido snored on his pallet. In reality I am (as I should have foreseen) in these barren, snow-covered hills again, hunting down stragglers from the Duko's horde, a defeated and broken horde that crashed like a wave upon the small, hard rock of Novella Citta after the battle, and appears to have shattered into spray. But more about that at the proper time.

We still have not found Mora and Eco, but I have high hopes for tomorrow. It is possible, of course, that they are already with Inclito. I pray that is the case.

And now I would like to launch into my account of the battle, which had interest, excitement, and heroism enough for every quill in both Oreb's wings; but first I must mention (and truthfully, although it is difficult to be truthful here) what happened just before I went to bed last night.

I had promised you a rational account of the battle and risen, and was corking the ink bottle and wiping my pen when the old woman knocked as she did every night that I stayed in that house to ask whether we wanted anything and announce that she was about to retire.

I told her we were fine, much better off than those who had

fought so gallantly and lacked the comfort of her roof. She thanked me and began moving about the room, straightening small items as women will, snuffling to herself and coughing much as I do, but moving (although it did not strike me at the time) gracefully nonetheless, so that I was reminded vaguely of you, Nettle; and then more vaguely still of Evensong, Tansy, Seawrack, Hyacinth, and various others—or perhaps simply of all the women—or of all the young women, at least—that I have known at various times in diverse places, and fell to thinking (as I pulled off my boots and removed my robe) that it was a pity, a great pity, that we had no daughter—although it was so often all that we could do to feed the children we had, boys but good boys all of them, at least until Sinew was older.

All that we could do, and more.

And then I thought about Sinew and Krait, and the time—I hesitate to mention it, knowing it will pain you—when the house was building and the inhumu got into our little tent and drank blood from our child. The inhuma, I really ought to say, although at the time you and I assumed it had been male.

"I'm keeping you from undressing," the old woman said when I had washed and dried my feet.

I slid between the sheets and closed my eyes, seeing at once the flashes of Soldese slug guns. "I have been going to bed in my trousers and tunic every night," I told her, yawning, "and spreading my robe over me for additional warmth." I had given all my bedclothes except one old quilt to others who were forced to sleep outdoors, or in unheated sheds, and needed them much more than I did.

She muttered something in reply, wished me a good night, and blew out the lamp; and I, without thinking, said, "Thank you, Jahlee." It was a strange thing to say, surely, but even now I am not entirely certain I was wrong.

For two hours that seemed whole years, the new advance guard of the Horde of Soldo ranged up and down the wide U of our walls and ditches, firing from time to time and taking our measure; then a Soldese officer advanced carrying a flag of truce, and Inclito sent me out to talk with him.

He smiled and offered me his hand, saying, "I'm Colonel Terzo."

I accepted it, and we shook hands. I introduced myself and explained that I was not formally a member of the Horde of Blanko, merely a friend of its commander trying to give him what help I could.

"You are a combatant, eh? Do you fight, Incanto?"

"Not so far; and I have no slug gun, though I admit I have directed others who have fought you." It was all true, although as I spoke I was very conscious of the azoth in my waistband.

He shook his head, looking very gloomy indeed. "It will go hard with you if you are captured."

I said I would endeavor not to be.

"There are times, Incanto, and I speak as one who has seen a great deal of war, when one can't avoid it."

I told him I understood that, and explained that back in the *Whorl* I had once been captured by the Trivigauntis.

"Ah, you saw them? You fought them?"

I nodded.

"In Grandecitta we thought they were legendary. Women troopers? Not even Pas would attempt such a thing! That was what we said."

"They fought very well," I told him. "I realize now that they fought better than I did, although I wasn't aware of it at the time. We—Nettle and I and many others—had been fighting our own Civil Guard before, and they'd been very good fighters indeed, so that when we came to fight Trivigauntis we were only conscious that these new opponents were not quite up to the measure of our old ones."

"Someday you and I will speak of this all afternoon over a bottle of wine," he told me solemnly. "I have a place on the Bacherozzolo, and grow good grapes there. South-facing hillsides, eh? But at present it is my unpleasant duty to require your surrender, upon the authority of the Duko."

I pointed out that since I was not in Soldo and was not a citizen of Soldo, its Duko had no authority over me.

"Not only you." Terzo shook his head sadly. "Not just you, Incanto, but those pitiful grandfathers I see, and those unlucky women. The boys, too. You have boys? We dislodged a few on our march."

I confessed that our reserve was made up largely of those boys.

"Then you have no reserve." He spread his hands, appalled at our weakness but unable to help us. "Your women will run screaming as soon as the fighting is serious. I have never seen women cut down with the saber, and do not wish to see it. There will be sickening bloodshed. Incanto . . ."

He attempted to put his arm over my shoulders, but I shook it off.

"I like you, Incanto, and I'll try to do what I can for you. You have a horse?"

I confessed that I did not.

"I see a few country louts on horseback behind your line. Six, seven? How many?"

"We are short of cavalry," I admitted.

"Borrow a horse from one anyway. Surrender, and ride off as soon as we begin disarming the poor women that scoundrel General Inclito has forced out of their kitchens. I will see to it that you escape."

I thanked him for his good wishes, but repeated that we had no intention of surrendering.

"Incanto, you are unfamiliar with the rules of war."

"Yes, but I have two friends, one a very experienced officer, who advise me."

"You have three. I am the third, and you need all of us more than you know. It is one of the rules of war that untenable positions may not be held. Do you understand? Suppose, and I saw this only today, that some graybeard fool and three children attempt to hold a little mud-brick shed against an army. That is an untenable position, since the four greatest heroes mankind has ever seen could not maintain such a place against a hundred ordinary troopers. Do you understand me, Incanto?"

"Very well," I said.

"But they are stubborn, eh? Even fools can be heroes, just as the greatest heroes can be fools. We invited their surrender, they refused, and we stormed their little cowshed. Soon I was handed two little boys, boys of twelve or thirteen, which is about the age of my younger son, bleeding and weeping. You would have bandaged their wounds, eh? Waved your hands through the air and recited spells of healing?"

"Prayed over them, perhaps," I told him.

"Exactly. But I am a trooper, and I had no choice. They have tried to hold an indefensible position. You see what I'm getting at, eh? I had to shoot them both, and I did."

I was too shocked to say anything.

"I would hate to shoot you, Incanto. Possibly I would try, but I don't think I'd have the stomach for it. I'd call in some subordinate and have him do it, and turn my head away. I beg you not to give me so much pain."

I shook my head. "You're not completely serious in what you say, Colonel—"

"But I am!"

"And I am, too. You must know our Colonel Sfido."

His face froze.

"He is one of the two friends I mentioned. He was in command of an advance guard, an advance guard of two hundred mercenaries, before you. Those mercenaries have come over to us—no doubt you know that, since you've been fighting them in the hills. So has Sfido. If you'd like to speak to him, I can ask him to come out here."

"No." He would not meet my eyes.

"Duko Rigoglio was going to have him shot for reporting the truth, because it was a truth that the Duko did not like hearing."

"A dream," Terzo muttered. "A bad dream."

"He came to us, and we fed him and found him a place to stay, and gave him employment. When Soldo falls, we will give him his property back, so that he may live in his own house with his wife and children as he did before. I sincerely hope that nothing of the kind will ever happen to you. It isn't likely, since your Duko will be deposed soon. But if it does, don't be afraid to come to us. You'll receive a fair trial, I promise."

He drew himself up. "You will not surrender? May I report that you will fight to the death?"

"Why no," I said. "We'll run, I suppose, if the fight goes against us. But we're not going to run now, when it has hardly begun."

I had thought that he would order an attack as soon as he returned to his own line, but he did not. We waited tensely for a time, and I had what little food was available passed out to the troopers along our walls.

"This better work, Incanto," Inclito said, studying them as they leaned against the earth-filled bags or crouched in the snow to eat.

"Will Pas drive us from this whorl if it doesn't?"

He looked around at me, surprised. "I don't think he's even here. We left him up there with the Long Sun."

"In one sense he wasn't there, either. In another he is here with us at this moment, because I am."

Inclito said nothing for a time, but I am not at all sure how long a time it was; I was lost in thought. At last—"Because you pray to him, that's what you mean. He hears you praying."

I nodded. "I hope so at least."

"Me too. You think they'll attack soon?"

I told him I did not know, that a few minutes before I had felt certain that they would attack at once; but that I felt almost equally certain now that they were going to wait for the main body of their horde. "Colonel Terzo spoke so contemptuously of us that I thought he believed what he was saying, and would rush at us when we refused to surrender. It seems he will not."

It was Inclito's turn to nod. "Would you?"

"No. But if I governed Soldo I wouldn't try to conquer Blanko, either."

"Colonel Terzo doesn't govern Soldo, but that's a good answer just the same. Incanto . . ."

"Yes?"

"Usually when I ask what you're thinking about—"

"Men come!" Overhead Oreb sounded the alarm. "Bad men! Come fast!"

I lifted my staff for him, and he dropped down onto its handle. "On horseback?"

"Come horse! Bird see!"

"That's what he's waiting for." Inclito nodded to himself. "Their cavalry, and somebody else to give the order. You scared him, Incanto, just like you scare me. What did you really mean, when you said that about Pas making us go?"

"Only that he wouldn't, or at least that I don't believe that he will. I've been asking myself what will occur if we lose."

He chuckled dryly. "If she's still alive my Mora will be an orphan, for one thing. They're supposed to ask you nicely if you want a rag tied over your eyes, and you're supposed to say you don't. But I don't think it matters much by then what you say."

I could not help thinking then of Pig, and of everything that had befallen Viron while I had been away. "Soldo will dominate Blanko for a generation or two," I told Inclito, "then Blanko will throw off its domination, and more people will be killed. After that, something else will happen, and still more people will die, and the inhumi will come in the night to drink our blood, carousing upon our hates and fears and lusts. After which still more people will die for other reasons, and no one will be even a little bit wiser."

I took a deep breath. "Inclito, our mercenaries have been with us almost half a month. You have them in back with the reserve, the ones who are still alive?"

He nodded. "A hundred and thirty-seven. That's the number I remember, anyhow. Could be a few less."

"I want to pay them. Half a month's pay before the battle starts. May I do that?"

"You've got the money?"

"Four times enough. May I?"

"Sure, go ahead. You think it'll make them fight better? They've been fighting real good already."

"It will make me fight better," I said, "because I won't dislike myself quite so much for fighting."

"Good man," Oreb assured Inclito.

"I try. I want to promise those who are attempting to earn enough to buy land that we'll try to provide farms for them after the war. The rich in Soldo own a great deal of land—that's the impression I get, at least."

"Sure." Inclito stroked his jaw. "That way they'd stay right there in Soldo. I see. And if the Soldese—all right, go ahead and tell them, Incanto. I'll make it happen if we win."

We were going to, I knew, although I did not say so then. I found Sfido, and the two of us brought out the chest that we had hidden when we arrived. I gave every mercenary thirty silver bits, half of the sixty that we had paid every four weeks in Gaon, and told them about the farms Inclito had promised them.

Captain Kupus took me aside. "You're giving every man one? Enough land for a man to feed a family?"

"That's correct," I told him. "The Duko's chief supporters seem to own a great deal of good land around Soldo. It will be taken from them, of course, and Inclito has decided to give it— some of it at least—to your mercenaries, who have fought so valiantly for Blanko and suffered so much."

Atteno interrupted us to report that all his pigs were tied and positioned at last. When he had gone, Kupus asked, "Four for me? Four farms?"

I shook my head. "This is a bonus, not the promised pay. I'll try to see to it that you get first choice, however."

He is not a man who smiles often, but he smiled then. "I didn't think so, but I hadn't thought about first choice. They can't be exactly equal, after all, can they?"

I admitted that I did not see how it could be done.

"But we've got to beat them first. What was that little fellow saying about pigs?"

"Boars in pairs. A mature boar is a dangerous animal, nearly as dangerous as a hus."

He nodded.

"With a long rope stretched between them—" Just then, I sighted the first cavalry, tiny figures in wine-red jackets sifting down through the dry brown hills behind them. Sunlight winked on what I took to be silver cap badges but later found were plumed helmets of polished steel, on the blades of the officers' swords, and on the black well-oiled barrels of their slug guns.

Kupus snorted. "Not as dangerous as they look, if a man will just stand up to them and shoot." When I did not reply, he added, "What about these women of yours? You think they will?"

I fingered my beard, recalling the telescope I had on my boat, two lenses united by sliding tubes of brass and wood. I had accepted it reluctantly in trade for paper, and had never valued it as I should have; but I would have given a good deal of our chest for it at that moment.

"Well," Kupus muttered half humorously, "they haven't run yet, so the war goddess be thanked."

I nodded, trying to push aside the thought that I might take our lookout's little boat and follow the river to the sea. "I had not considered that Sphigx was our goddess of war under the Long Sun—thank you for reminding me of that. To answer your question, the General wrote me a letter a few days ago in which he said that Blanko's women and over-age men might fight from behind its walls but would not if I marched them out of the city. I'd seen enough by then to know that the men would fight very stubbornly to hold a position, though they would be slow and even hesitant in attacking an enemy position.

"And it occurred to me that Inclito was probably correct about the women, but that Blanko's walls were not the only walls in the whorl, that walls might be built almost anywhere."

"No fight," Oreb muttered nervously.

"You need not," I told him. "No one will accuse you of cowardice if you fly to a place of safety."

"So you came out here and built these."

"Yes. My first thought—I'm sorry I didn't have you to advise me then, Captain—was to build a sort of fortress, a square of temporary walls with ditches before them, but Rimando pointed out that our enemies would simply bypass it and go on to the town, and I saw at once that he was right."

I shaded my eyes with my hand. "The horses are slipping a little in the snow, I believe."

"They always do. They'll slip more if those fellows charge our flank."

"They will. I said that Rimando had said they would bypass our fort and ravage the farms on their way to Blanko, but *flank* was the word he actually employed. It reminded me that in open farming country such as this we would have to be prepared for flanking movements. I once had General Mint say in a book that one could always outflank the enemy in a desert. General Mint was a woman, and I believe she was the bravest person I have ever known."

"I wish we had her here."

"So do I, but that was an aside, and one I shouldn't have made. What I should have said is that farms and fields of grain make almost as good a battlefield for cavalry as a desert. The Trivigauntis had a great deal of cavalry. I think I've mentioned them to you before."

Kupus nodded, and pointed to the sky.

"Yes, back home. Their Generalissimo was a cavalrywoman too, and it was a long time before I understood that they had specialized in cavalry and cavalry tactics because so much of their territory was desert or semi-desert, and that they had succeeded as well as they had because their women troopers were lighter than men."

Rimando reported that our gunners were in position and ready to go into action, and asked permission to open fire on the cavalry massing on the slopes to the north.

I shook my head. "We would only scatter them. Don't fire, don't let even a single gun fire, until I give the order."

Oreb reinforced it: "No shoot!"

Kupus cleared his throat. "I hate to say it, Master Incanto, but that cavalry of theirs is the worst risk we face right now."

"We face many worse things than a few hundred men on horses, Captain. Our own fears may be the worst. You asked me about the women. Men can be panicked as well."

"I try never to forget it."

"The women will stand and fight as long as they are behind their walls, and some would stand and fight without them, for which we should be exceedingly grateful. A few—Sphigx is the god of war, as you pointed out, Captain. We say 'the goddess' to be polite, but the principal war god we have. I wonder why she chose that, chose war as her domain."

Kupus pointed. "Here they come!"

He might rather have said, "There they go," for it appeared at first that the horsemen were riding away from us, trotting eastward in long, thin columns of crimson and brown.

He touched his cap. "If you'll excuse me, Master."

I nodded, and he trotted back toward the troops who made up our reserve, waving his arms and shouting instructions. In a moment more, the boys who had formed our original reserve were moving into position to resist the cavalry, guided and stiffened by his own mercenaries and the troopers who had retreated under Inclito's command.

"Men fight," Oreb muttered unhappily.

"Boys, too," I told him, "and women. Horses and even pigs— or so we hope. You have been fighting too, Oreb, and you've been of considerable help to us."

"Bird fight?"

I nodded solemnly. "Now I'd like you to help a little bit more. Lieutenant Atteno—the man in whose house we stayed in town— is in charge of the fireworks." With my free hand, I pointed to the straggling hedge well to our right rear behind which Atteno, his fireworks, and the boys who had volunteered to set them off were hidden. "I want you to remind him that he is not to light the first fuse—"

"No bang."

"That's right, no bang until the cavalry reach the long ditch."

"Horse come," Oreb croaked thoughtfully. "Come hole."

"You've got it. Now make absolutely certain that Atteno has it too, please."

I gave him a little lift by raising the handle of my stick, and he flapped upward, vanishing almost at once against the dark sky. It was only an hour or two past noon; but quite dark, as it almost always is when it snows. The fireworks would show up well, I thought, unless the snow had wet them—in which case they would not show up at all.

For the first time it struck me that the young man who had so closely resembled my sons was with the fireworks detail, and would be in considerable danger from the fireworks themselves and from any cavalry troopers who were able to wheel their mounts and charge their tormentors. No ditch protected the hedgerow, nor had there been time to dig one even if I had been willing to risk the enemy's observing it. Angrily I reminded myself that a dozen other boys who did not in the least resemble my sons were at equal risk, and I did not have the right to get the one who did out of harm's way while leaving the others where they might be killed.

Inclito strolled over. "Well, we've done our best."

"Have we?"

He shrugged, then wiped his nose on his coat sleeve.

"I keep thinking—"

"That you should have sat tight in town like I told you to, and Hierax help the farmers. Incanto, there's going to be a hundred people a lot smarter than you are second-guessing you if we lose. Don't make it a hundred and one unless you can't help it. Remember the brothers I told you about? One killed the other one."

"Yes," I said. How often I had feared that Sinew would kill one of his brothers or his mother! Or that he would kill me, or try to kill me so that I had to kill or cripple him in self-defense. None of which had happened.

"I got second-guessed about that by everybody for two days' ride, and not a one of them had given me a single word of warning or advice before it happened." Inclito spat. "Mora's a good rider. Very good. You know that?"

I said Fava had mentioned it.

"Who do you think taught her? Taught Mora?"

"You?"

Inclito nodded. "If I hadn't, would she still have taken that horse and gone off with your letter like she did?"

"Yes," I said, "but if I had never written those letters, there would have been no horse for her to take."

"You're lying. How many times since then do you think I've wanted to kick myself for teaching her to ride?"

"A thousand, I suppose."

"Eight or ten. But believe me, eight or ten was bad enough. I never commanded our troops in a war before, did you know that?"

I shook my head.

"I was always under somebody, trying to carry out his orders. This is different, and I always thought it would be better, but it's worse. You know?"

"Very well indeed."

"I trained our troopers, and I got them the best equipment I could. I decided on the plan, holding the hills against Soldo, moving around and trying to block them no matter what way they tried to come.

"Then the war. It was like you're out in the field, and you see a big thunderstorm a long way off. You ever do that?"

"My field was the sea," I told him, "but, yes, I have."

"Same thing, probably. You see it and it's so much bigger than you that you can't even guess, and unless you plowed right it's going to wash away your topsoil and wash out your seedlings, and maybe it will even if you did, and it's coming on fast, and there's lightning in it, and you know there'll be big winds and you want to run but the sprats and the women are scared already. That's how I saw the war coming at us."

"I was frightened myself," I admitted. "I kept telling myself that I ought to leave you and Mora, and if things had been only slightly different, I'm sure I would have."

"That was why you stayed? For Mora and me?"

I nodded.

"I want to ask you about that sometime." He pointed. "They're moving again. This is it."

"They're not galloping," I protested.

"Trotting. They won't gallop until they're up close. Did you think they would?"

I nodded. "It would be better if they did."

"That's why they don't." He nudged me to make sure I understood that he was joking. "You've never seen a charge?"

"I have, but they were much closer."

"They will be."

I started for Kupus's uneven line of men and boys with slug guns, but Inclito caught my elbow. "The women and sprats are scared already, remember? The men are, too, and I mean you and me. So walk."

He was right, of course. I walked slowly toward our right flank, and even permitted myself to limp a little. From the top of a stile I studied the field of green, snow-spotted winter wheat, and the crimson, brown, and silver cavalry approaching it, spirited horses and expert riders obscured by wind-driven snow. From our viewpoint, it would have been better beyond all question had the rippling wheat been higher. I could see Atteno's pigs moving through it, and even the long waves when a pig's motions twitched the finger-thick rope that united him to his partner. They were mature boars for the most part, and big ones. I had been afraid that they would fight each other, bound together as they were; apparently the lack of sows and the length of the ropes had prevented or at least postponed it.

Something—some stir, perhaps, among the women and elderly men along the walls—made me turn and look north. Soldese infantry were advancing from the hills, only fitfully visible through the snow. Looking at those dark trickles of marching men, I felt I understood how Inclito had been forced out of a whole series of good defensive positions. There must have been a thousand troopers there for every hundred Blanko possessed when the fighting began; and from the top of that stile, I was tempted to believe that there were a thousand now for every ten.

"Master?" It was Adatta, with snow in her hair and on the lashes of her remarkable eyes. "Colonel Sfido sent me. He'll send some of our people to strengthen this flank, if you want them."

I pointed to the hills.

"Yes, sir, I know. So does he, I'm sure."

"I have been studying them, Adatta, and wondering where you people in Blanko ever found the courage to defy them and their Duko."

She hesitated so long that I concluded she would never reply and turned my attention to the swarming infantry again. At last she said, "We make our own laws, sir. In the Corpo. Lots of us are old enough to remember how it was in Grandecitta, when we didn't."

I turned once more to face her. "Are you, Adatto? You don't look it."

"Yes, sir."

"I don't believe you. Twenty years ago you can hardly have been old enough to walk."

"Thank you, sir. Sir . . . ?"

"What is it?"

"General Inclito's going up and down the walls, sir, talking to everybody. It might help if you did that, too."

"Did he or Colonel Sfido ask you to ask me?"

"No, sir. I just thought of it."

By a gesture I indicated the long thin line of men and boys in ragged coats. "We have no wall here, Captain."

"Yes, sir. Just this fence and the long ditch."

"Exactly, just the fence and the ditch. Colonel Sfido is offering to send them reinforcements deducted from your own rather slight strength. There would be women among them, I assume, as well as men. Would you go, Captain, if you were ordered to? Stand here at the edge of the long ditch with your slug gun, waiting for charging cavalry to get near enough to shoot at?"

(When I said that—I shall never forget it, Nettle—my heart sunk within me; the leading line of the Soldese cavalry were past the first trip rope, I felt sure, which meant that they had seen it in the wheat and cut it without my having observed the operation, and could very well have cut the others in just the same way.)

"Of course, sir."

I swallowed, knowing that it was useless to try to forget the crimson horsemen who would so quickly overwhelm us. "Suppose that I were to order you—you alone—to do it now. Would you, Captain Adatta?"

"Of course," she repeated. "My son's there, sir."

"I see. You don't need me to go along the walls behind General Inclito, Captain. Do it yourself. No better example of courage is to be had."

The silver notes of a bugle sounded far off.

Adatta unslung her slug gun. "Here they come, Master. You'd better get down."

The cavalry surged forward, and almost at once a score of horses fell. Rimando was waving to me frantically, but I shook my head while sympathizing with what he must have felt. I heard Adatta say "Shoot! Why don't they shoot?" under her breath.

The first trip rope had been cut or broken. More crimson-and-purple horsemen surged forward. Some were slashing at the winter wheat with their swords, and I saw one horse leap a fallen horse and rider magnificently. Two fell together almost at once; the indignant squeals of Atteno's pigs carried across the wheat field to us as clearly as the bugle.

The boys fired, a ragged crash followed by the rasping rattle of hundreds of fore-ends pulled back to expel hundreds of empty cartridges and pushed forward again to bring hundreds of fresh rounds into hundreds of chambers.

Adatta tugged at the leg of my trousers to get my attention. "Can I now, sir?"

I nodded, meaning that she should return to the walls; but before I could stop her, she was running down the line of boys, shouting encouragement and patting shoulders.

For a minute or more it seemed that the cavalry might never actually reach our long ditch. The trip ropes delayed it as I had intended, and in fact broke the legs of scores of horses. Against the greater charge of the Soldese cavalry, Atteno's boars made their own lesser charges again and again, working one another into a foaming fury that had many of the horsemen reigning up to shoot at them even as their fellow troopers fell from our fire.

Then a valiant trooper, virtually alone, broke from the rest and charged our line at full gallop. His horse jumped the last of our trip ropes only to plunge headlong into the snow-filled long ditch.

As it did, the hedgerow seemed to explode. Stars flew from it, and devils of red and blue, orange and yellow fire careened among the horses, whining, whizzing, shrieking and howling, lurching, and swerving before detonating in clouds of colored smoke and flying sparks.

"Make bang." Oreb announced self-importantly as he settled upon my staff. "Horse come. Come hole." Or at least that is what I think he said—it was hard to hear him over the noise of the fireworks.

Nor did I greatly care what he had said just then. Grateful for its new warmth, I pushed Hyacinth's azoth back into my waistband; and seeing Rimando running toward me, climbed down from the stile and walked calmly (I hope) toward him, careful to swing my staff and plant it solidly with every step, so that Oreb fidgeted and flapped on the handle, and at last abandoned it for my shoulder.

"May we open fire, sir?" Rimando called.

I waited until we were nearer, then said in a low tone, "Lieutenants may run, Captain. Captains walk."

"Yes, sir." He halted, drew himself up, and saluted. "Shall we open fire, sir?"

"You are sighted on the area behind the line of infantry facing us, as I instructed you?"

"Yes, sir."

"In that case, you may open fire as soon as the enemy's cavalry has been stampeded well into that area, Captain."

"They're in there now, sir." He pointed.

"Then you may open fire."

He spun about and dashed back toward the haystack gun, shouting; even so, it seemed to me a very long time before it spoke, and its first shot set the hay on fire so that half the crew had to fight the fire before it reached the ammunition, leaving only two men to load and fire.

The gun in the barn fired soon afterward—I got the impression that its crew had heard the first shot, and verified its elevation and direction one final time before pulling the lanyard. Almost at once, the gun in the wood by the river, the largest and most distantly sited of all, thundered forth so deeply that it seemed to me that I could feel it shake the ground.

After that, I paid little attention to which gun happened to fire at which time, or which was having the greatest effect on our enemy's troops. Inclito had an officer in the tree in front of the farmhouse, from which he was signaling about such matters with a yellow-and-black flag on a stick; and although I had been told what the two waves overhead meant, and the four waves down, and the rest of it, I had forgotten most of the code already. Whatever signals were sent, our shells were bursting among the enemy, striking stony ground and throwing up geysers of ocher dust and flying rock that only looked small to me as I hurried forward to our walls of earth-filled bags lined with women and elderly men; they were enormous and very dangerous, I knew, to thousands of terrified Soldese troopers, and to hundreds of horses already frantic with fear.

"More bang," Oreb muttered; and a young woman with brawny arms and a broad grin said, "Looks pretty good, don't it, Master Incanto?"

I nodded and told her, "We have to destroy that cavalry before it can make a second attempt," speaking as seriously as I might have to Inclito.

"They know our tricks now, I guess."

"That's so, and there can't be many fireworks left." As I spoke, I was looking for a way to climb over her wall as I had climbed Mattak's on Gold Street, but there was no helpful, murderous sergeant on the other side of this one to give me a hand up, only a deeper ditch full of snow.

Another woman exclaimed, "We've won!"

I shook my head and frowned at her. "Not yet, though we will win."

Like ghosts, I could see their corpses at the foot of the wall, dead women with open staring eyes, and dead men, their gray beards (their white beards) dyed with their own blood. Auk had taken off his undershirt to hang it out of the window of the Juzgado; but that undershirt had been as red as the old men's beards, and I had none, red or white, although a woolen undershirt would have been a comfort that day in that wind.

Another woman said, "They'll still come at us, won't they?," and this woman had her hair bound up in a white cloth and stood beside a wooden case of slug-gun cartridges. I got her to give me her cloth and tied it around my staff, and went to the end of the wall, where at Sfido's insistence we had left a narrow space between walls and between ditches.

Someone—I think the first woman to whom I had spoken—called, "They'll shoot you," and Oreb muttered uneasily, "No bang."

Each step was harder than the last. I reached the point I had marked with my eye as the midpoint and realized that it was not, and advanced step by uneasy step after that, waving my flag to signal one thing and one thing only, over and over. Had Maytera Marble felt like this while I, from a place of relative safety, watched her advance with steady strides toward Blood's villa?

"I have her new eye in my pocket," I told Oreb. "Maytera Marble's. You recall Maytera Marble, I hope?"

"Iron girl."

"That's the one. If I'm killed, you are to take her new eye to her."

I got it from my pocket to show to him, and he said, "Man come. No shoot."

Colonel Terzo was advancing toward me. He had a needler in his hand instead of a flag of truce. "You are killing our men," he said, "killing our horses."

"We will gladly stop," (I am afraid I sounded apologetic) "as soon as you give us any reason to do so."

"I should shoot you where you stand!"

"I have been shot before," I told him, and it affected him more than I would have anticipated; the hand that held the needler shook visibly, and although he was still too distant for me to be certain it appeared to me that he turned pale.

I advanced until we stood face-to-face, as two men might talk in the street. The sound of the bursting shells was louder there, and reports of the big guns that fired them hardly more than distant thunder. I cocked my head, hearkening to Seawrack's seasong in that field of stubble, smoke, and death.

"The Duko didn't send me out here," Terzo said angrily. "Neither did General Morello. I came out of friendship for you."

I nodded my thanks.

"You've brought your artillery outside your town, in violation of the laws of war. If you're captured you'll be shot, and I thought I should tell you."

"I didn't know that there was any such law," I said. "Where are these laws written, and by what courts are they enforced?"

"Everyone knows!"

"You mean that you make some excuse to shoot those prisoners you wish to kill. No doubt you always have."

"We're going to attack you within an hour, Incanto. You'll be—" He fell silent, staring at me. "Can you hear something I don't?"

"Sing song," Oreb suggested; and I did, following Seawrack's own intonation and pronunciation to the best of my very limited ability. The lapping of the waves was in her song, and the eerie cries of seabirds, and the lonely whistling of the wind.

"That is in the language of the Neighbors, whom you call the Vanished People," I said when I could no longer sing for weeping.

"I can—" Terzo began. Then again, "I can almost hear it myself." He fell silent.

I put my hand upon his shoulder. "Listen, and you will hear her. Those who truly listen do."

He heard the music then, I know; he stared at me with bulging eyes.

"Seawrack is singing in the place that lies beyond this place. Listen there, and you cannot help but hear her." With her I sang a few more words in the language of those whom Mora had once called the People of That Town. " 'In our small house with shining windows, I waited till the tide brought your wreck through. Lie here beside me in the darkness. I'll wake to life the corpse I say is you.' That isn't exactly right, but it's as close as I can come in the Common Tongue."

I spoke the final words to his back as he sprinted for his own lines.

★

★ ★

A representative from Novella Citta has reached us! The news is so good that I hesitate to record it. His name is Legaro, and he is a tall and very dignified man with graying hair, an assessor (he says) of his town, which is governed by such assessors.

"So you're Master Incanto," he ventured when we had been introduced, and seemed almost afraid to accept my hand. "Donna Mora and her consort have told us a great deal about you."

"You have her?" I asked. "I know she's still alive, but is she well?"

Oreb added his voice to mine. "Girl safe? No shoot?"

"She is well and safe in our peel house in Novella Citta," Legaro declared. "But I should be telling all this to the Duko, her father. Is he here?"

"He went out with one of our patrols," I explained, "but he should be back within an hour." And I told Oreb to find Inclito and tell him that there was someone here with news of his daughter.

"You're his brother, Donna Mora's uncle?"

"If she awarded me that honor, it would be uncivil of me to refuse it. A tall, sturdy girl, quite dark, with a mole here?" I touched my cheek.

He nodded. "A very stately and forceful young lady. She has made a distinct impression on everyone." He leaned toward me and his voice became confidential. "Duko Inclito is marrying a woman from Novella Citta?"

"He intends to, certainly. The ceremony will not take place until after the war."

Another nod. "Naturally. I understand."

"Her name is Torda; but beyond the fact that she is both gracious and beautiful, and a distant relation—a second cousin by marriage, or something of that kind—I really know nothing about her. Inclito has been a widower for many years. No doubt Donna Mora told you."

"Oh, yes. And I should tell you that though I came alone save for my servant, our horde is not far behind me. We have four hundred and fifty under arms. It's a small force to you, I understand. But it's a well-trained and well-armed one, I assure you."

I thanked him, and said we welcomed whatever reinforcements Novella Citta could provide to us.

"We expected to find Blanko besieged, and hoped we might accomplish something by taking the besiegers in the rear." He rubbed his hands and smiled. "You can imagine how we feel now that you've won. Will you tell me about your victory? I've been talking to troopers on both sides, you see. I had to convince every party we encountered that I wasn't a Soldese or a Blankonian, and in the course of our conversations I've picked up a good deal of information. You and your brother were in command?"

I tried to explain that Inclito was our commander, and that I had merely deployed the fresh troops I had brought up from Blanko and endeavored to assist him.

"The guns, too. You brought out your guns?"

"I have been told that it is contrary to the usages of war, but—"

"It's too dangerous. I mean that it's usually judged to be. No one can argue with victory, of course. Now tell me everything that happened, please. Every detail. I've been learning about it in bits and pieces, and I'm as anxious to have a rational overview as a man can possibly be. You shattered the Dragoons and wiped out the Bodyguard?"

And so I described the entire affair for him, finding the partial account I had written here already a great help. I will finish it when next I write, and perhaps find room somewhere to add a few words about my experiences on Green, which is what I am supposed to be describing, after all.

18

THE END AND AFTERWARD

The next Soldese attack came a quarter of an hour after Colonel Terzo and I separated, a wave of troopers running, throwing themselves flat in the stubble to shoot, and springing up to dash forward again until they fell. A second wave came behind the first, and a third behind the second.

There were no more after that.

Only a few weeks ago I watched a massed attack by the men of Han. The field of battle was black with them, and a trooper who shot one saw another appear at once in his place, and another in his and another his, man succeeding man as raindrops do. Because I had seen that, the Soldese troopers seemed less dangerous, perhaps, than they really were. I would never deny their courage and discipline; but I feared at first that they were no more than a diversion; and when at last I realized that there was to be no other attack, I felt a vast relief. Our veterans could no longer run and jump like the young men they had once been, but they could and would stand behind the walls and shoot all afternoon if need be. Some of our women still shut their eyes when they drew the trigger, as I saw, but it hardly mattered at that point; and although I saw tears here and there, I saw them through my own.

The second wave got as far as the deep ditches before our walls, and a few men leaped into them and tried to climb up the other side, but a more hopeless enterprise could not be imagined. I struck one on the head with my staff, and so saved him from having his brains blown out, which would have happened in another half second.

The third and final wave got no nearer than half a chain, I believe. For the space of a breath the troopers who composed it wavered there, firing and falling; then they turned and fled. Inclito led our reserve after them—such cavalry as we had, most of the boys, and the troopers who had been with him in the hills.

I watched them then, climbing up onto one of our walls as I had stood upon the stile and wishing again for the clumsy wood-and-brass telescope I had left behind on Lizard. The horde that had sifted through the hills was melting into them again, pursued not so much by our reserve as by striding shell-bursts from our big guns, distant dots of sullen black smoke and short-lived fountains of what at that distance seemed a yellowish water, like urine.

After that, there was nothing more to do except clean up. A few uninjured Soldese surrendered; they had to be herded together and searched for weapons. Our own wounded had to be bandaged and given what comfort and treatment we could muster. Two of the elderly men who had agreed to fight for their town one more time were physicians. The one who had examined and re-bandaged my own wound the day before the battle had been wounded himself, his right arm smashed so badly by a Soldese slug that it had to be taken off just below the shoulder. When that had been done, he helped with the rest, doing what he could with his left hand, and directing a woman he found who had an aptitude for the work.

If our own plight was bad, that of the Soldese wounded was far worse, for we could give them little attention until our own wounded were taken care of. Our wounds were to the head, arms, and shoulders almost entirely; that was fortunate, since many of our wounded women objected, in the most pathetic and ingrained fashion imaginable, to having their gowns and camisoles cut away, as often had to be done.

Our dead we laid out as decently as we could; and since we

could not spare blankets for the task, we covered them with straw, hay, and brush. By that time the short, dark day had ended, and the snow had ceased to fall. It was cold, the wounded (the Soldese wounded particularly) were dying with every breath, and we were all too tired, almost, to move. A few of us built little fires and ate rations taken from the Soldese dead. Most, and I was one of them, wanted only to lie down—anywhere—and sleep.

I was about to go into the farmhouse when the first party from the town arrived. It was made up of men who had been with Inclito in the hills, mostly. Of men, in other words, who had run, had in nine cases out of ten thrown away their weapons, and had taken refuge behind the walls of Blanko. Many, I do not doubt, had passed through our position or skirted it only a day or two before. There were a few officers among them, and I placed them under arrest, had their hands bound, and made them sit in the snow under guard with our Soldese prisoners. The rest I told to take slug guns (we had come into a plentiful supply) and join us.

No sooner was one group thus disposed of than another arrived, and by that time it had been disposed of as well, a third had come. Sfido and I went to the farmhouse at last, too weary almost to speak, and discovered to our great pleasure that the old woman had built a fire in our room. He slept at once; but I, finding that as tired as I was I could not sleep, sat up for a time and wrote about noticing the boy who looks like Hoof and Hide, then rose and went to the door of the old woman's bedroom, and knocked when I could not hear her breathing inside. But got no reply.

I was returning to our room, stepping as softly as I could manage across the bodies of the many sleepers who had thrown down their blankets and themselves upon her floors, when I heard distant shots, screams, and shouts. I gave the alarm and ran myself, when I had thought myself too tired to walk, and in that desperate fight in the dark wood by the river did what I could with my voice and the azoth.

As we learned later from our prisoners, fewer than a hundred men of the Ducal Bodyguard had found a point at which they could ford the river, wading in freezing water up to their necks while holding their slug guns and ammunition pouches over their heads. I cannot help thinking that if the leaders of the Horde of Soldo had employed that sort of enterprise and imagination against us while their horde was still intact, things might have gone very badly indeed for us. During the battle, I was constantly afraid that a second flanking attack would be attempted on our right, either by fresh cavalry (I could not be sure the Soldese had none) or by foot soldiers. Two hundred men there would have made things difficult indeed for us, and there must have been far more than that in each of the three waves that attacked our front.

I lay down a moment ago to look at the stars. How cold they are, how lovely, and how remote! Green, which is just setting, looks as cold as any and almost as distant; but I can never forget its steaming heat. Our wounded here were in danger of dying from shock and the cold; but wounds there are attacked at once by strange diseases. I remember far too vividly rotting wounds, and dead men whose rotting wounds still lived, seething with blue and yellow slugs, and striped creatures that resembled tiny squid.

Drinking rainwater from cupped leaves, and finding it alive already with the threadlike green worms.

The *Whorl* is high in the sky, yet another cold whorl of stifling heat, one in which I wandered through nights that lasted for days.

Nights in which neither these beckoning stars nor the skylands shone.

Nettle will never read this, I know—indeed, I would keep it from her if she were sitting at my right hand—but might I not communicate with Nettle if I chose, giving Oreb some message to carry to her? It is a thought I have had and pushed aside ever since he sought Seawrack for me. If I were to speak to her, I would not say that I was still alive, which could only fill her with false hope; rather I would say to her that the Outsider, the god who brought our race into being on some unthinkable short-sun whorl circling one of the myriad stars that I have been staring at, is no less present for her—or for me—tonight.

The Neighbors must have worshipped him here, under whatever name. When I sacrificed for Inclito's sake and was told that Mora was still alive (which Legaro now confirms), I was as eager for information and divine favors as Inclito himself. Tomorrow—or if not tomorrow, someday soon—I hope to learn of an altar of theirs in these hills. If not, I will build one and sacrifice to him there. Or merely worship him without offering any sacrifice, which I know that Oreb will greatly prefer.

★

★ ★

I have news good beyond hope, but before I write about it I should say (as I had planned to last night) that I faced some hard decisions on the morning after the battle. Whether I decided well or ill, I still cannot say. You may judge, Nettle—or whoever reads this may.

Sfido urged me to follow Inclito with our entire force. He argued, I think rightly, that a war is never really won until the enemy's ability to wage war no longer exists. He said that even if Inclito succeeded in overtaking our enemies and bringing them to battle, he might not be able to defeat and destroy them, and would very probably need every man and woman who could pull a trigger to do so.

Rimando urged me to send all the women back to Blanko with his big guns, since it would clearly be impossible to take the guns into the hills with us no matter how useful they might be there when we encountered the Soldese. Our guns would be of no use in Blanko, he said, without troopers to line the town walls; and the women would never attack the enemy with fortitude and resolution, no matter what orders I gave. They might well serve to protect the town, however, given leadership; and if the town were lost all was lost with it. In this last at least, he was indubitably correct.

I thanked them both for their advice and made the decision myself, as it seems I always must.

First I disposed of the rest of the money we had collected in Blanko. Since I hardly dared let it out of my sight, and the chest in which Sfido and I had kept it was weighty, I felt that it was clearly best to rid ourselves of it before we broke camp. I called our people together, explained that I had already given the mercenaries a half month's pay, and distributed the rest among all those who had fought the day before, giving officers double shares. Each ordinary trooper got almost as much silver as the mercenaries had.

Then I made a second speech, resolved to do better than I had in my first. The guns had to be pulled back to Blanko, I explained, and since we had eaten our oxen, they would have to be pulled by human muscles, unless more oxen or mules could be found. On the other hand, Inclito would surely need every possible assistance in cementing the victory that we had won yesterday. Those who wished to return to Blanko were free to do so. They would remain with Major Adatta—whom I was promoting on the spot—and Captain Rimando, help pull the guns, bring back our prisoners and wounded, and defend the town should the enemy defeat Inclito in the hills. "As for Colonel Sfido and me, we are returning to the hills to prevent any such defeat. Those who wish to come with us may do so."

All of the men who had come out from the town after the battle joined us, with about a third of the women and the boys Inclito had left behind, and two-thirds of the veterans. I can only say that all three groups surprised me. On the second day we overtook Inclito, and I have already recorded the rest. Or at least, recorded those events which matter most.

Here is my good news: We have captured the Duko, General Morello, and Colonel Terzo. All three were uniformed as ordinary troopers of the Ducal Bodyguard, but the behavior of the other prisoners toward them—one spat in the Duko's face—called Sfido's attention to them. He and I are taking them back to Blanko, escorted by four men on horseback. We are camped in the open tonight, but tomorrow I hope to return to the site of the battle; I would like to conduct an experiment.

* * *

I have been talking to the Duko. What an extraordinary man he is, and what a dunce I am not to have guessed that he must be long ago!

He was a sleeper, like Mamelta. I asked whether he had known her, but he explained what I would have realized without prompting if I had my wits about me. "I may have known your friend under that name or some other," he said, "but I have no way of telling. It was a long time, years in fact, before I understood that I did not remember everything, and that not everything I remembered had actually taken place."

"We had a great many of you with us when we left the whorl," I told him. "So many that we had to take two landers, and could barely fit everybody into those two. Those of us who had grown up in Viron wanted to stay together, so all of us got on the same lander. We filled the remaining places with sleepers like you, and the rest boarded the other lander. Our sleepers—I don't quite know how to say this . . ."

"They have come to resemble you, dressing and talking as you do. Believing whatever it is you believe in your town of New Viron."

It was not what I had nearly said, but I seized upon it eagerly.

"I have seen it myself, and in fact I have done it myself," the Duko declared. "Our memories are less trustworthy even than yours. At first we try to live in accordance with them, but sooner or later we learn very painfully that they lead us astray." He paused to look at his fellow prisoners, General Morello and Colonel Terzo, who certainly appeared to be asleep and probably were.

"I wouldn't want them to hear this," he said. "There is no good reason for it. All such things have ceased to matter. Yet I retain my pride, though I'd like to rid myself of it once and for all."

Oreb sympathized. "Poor man!"

The Duko pointed to him. "There is the chief reason that everyone thinks you're a powerful magician, Master Incanto. That, and your power to appear in dreams as you did in mine, and to take him with you. They had no such talking birds on the *Whorl,* and there cannot be many here."

I explained that Oreb had come from there, exactly as I had myself.

"All right, but they can't have been known in Grandecitta. Before your bird entertained us, I was about to say that the false memories Pas gave me had one final defeat stored up for me. But it's time that I stopped laying my own shortcomings at his door."

He sat in silence for some while after that, rubbing his big chin. With his noble head and broad shoulders, and the pronounced ridge of bone beneath his thick, black brows, he seems the last person in the whorl to try to shift the blame for his own failures to an external cause.

"I trusted Morello. He'd been here all the time I'd been pacifying Olmo. He said he knew you people, that he understood your capabilities. They have clever leaders, he told me, and if we try to out-maneuver them, we'll be doing what they want. Fence with them, and you fence all day. But if we go straight at them, hammer and tongs and the anvil, they'll break, he said." The Duko laughed bitterly. "You didn't break, and I should've known better."

I pointed out that General Morello had tried to outflank us.

"But openly. He let you watch us do it, thinking it would frighten you. Pas alone knows what he thought when your troopers met our horse in a long thin line that stood its ground shooting. That you'd put a spell on them." He laughed again. "Terzo's terrified of you. He's in agony of every time you speak to him. You must have noticed it."

"Poor man!" Oreb muttered sympathetically.

"There. Did you hear that?" For a moment I thought that Duko Rigoglio was about to smile. "You have a percipient bird, Master Incanto. Someone always wins, so someone else always loses. He repeats *poor man,* and doesn't need to bother his head about our conversation. Say *poor man* again, bird."

"No, no."

"More words of universal utility. What were we talking about?"

I said that I would be delighted to talk about any subject he wished to discuss, that the privilege of conversing with him was more than enough for me.

"Then let us consider the desirability of adding a few more sticks to our fire. I would do it if you compelled me. I would have to. But with my hands and feet hobbled like this, well, you comprehend my difficulty, I'm sure."

"Poor man!"

When I had added firewood, I held the wine bottle to his mouth again, and he drank deeply, contriving to wipe his mouth upon the shoulder of his coat. "Thank you. You've been decent. You don't have to address me as Your Grandeur anymore, you know. Your brother didn't."

"Inclito prides himself on his incivility," I explained, "and I think he might very well have called you Rigoglio while you sat your throne; it would be quite in character. If he were to call you 'Your Grandeur' now, he would intend it as an insult."

"He has enough common decency not to insult a man about to die? That's rarer than you might think. He could simply have had me shot. I realize that."

"No cut," Oreb cautioned.

"You'll be tried by the Corpo, I suppose. I doubt that they'll sentence you to death."

"They'll have to." The Duko shook his head gloomily. "Not that I could return to power after this. And Pas knows—" He paused in the midst of his thought. "It is Pas, isn't it, here? Our god-in-chief?"

"No, it isn't, Your Grandeur. Or at least I do not believe so."

"Poor man!"

"I probed a nerve, didn't I? Let's talk about something else. You speak of me as Duko Rigoglio, I've heard you. It must have struck you by now that *Rigoglio* can't have been my name originally."

It had not, and I said so.

"My name was Roger. That's what was printed on my tube, anyway. Roger. I'd like it on my stone, if they let me have one."

I said again that Blanko had no compelling reason to take his life.

"Just the same, I want it, if you can manage it. They'll put Duko Rigoglio on there, and that's all right. But I'd like for it to say Roger someplace, too, if that's possible." The Duko sat silent again for a time, clearly lost in thought.

He shook himself. "A woman I knew called me Rigoglio, and other people took it up. Do you know how I made myself Duko?"

I said, "I've been assuming that you were chosen by your people in some fashion, Your Grandeur."

"They'd gotten used to having a Duko back on the *Whorl*, the Duko of Grandecitta. They were glad to get out from under his thumb here, or said they were. The facts were that they didn't know how to run things for themselves, or even how to try. I didn't like being called Rigoglio, so I started calling myself Duko. A man objected, and I knocked him down. In a day or so, I had half a dozen young fellows hanging around me, anxious to do the knocking down for me."

"I see."

"After that I settled quarrels. If you were a friend of mine, you won. If you weren't, I gave the nod to the weaker party, and chopped off your head if I could find an excuse. A couple of months of that, and everybody in town was a loyal supporter."

I nodded while making a mental note.

"I remembered Pas, or whatever his name was. It was pretty much what he'd done, only on a larger scale. He came in on the side of his friends, and when there was a war with one country stronger than the other, he was generally for the weak one, and you only lost a war to him once."

The Duko rubbed his eyes. "What did you put in your wine, Master Incanto?"

"Nothing, Your Grandeur," I said, "and I've been drinking it myself."

"It's not down in the fire—"

"Watch out!" Oreb spread his wings in alarm.

"It's up over it."

I looked where he had indicated, and saw Mucor's shadowy figure coalesce there as if seated upon the smoke. "Babbie's come back," she told me matter-of-factly. "I wondered if you still wanted him."

"Why, yes. Yes, I do, if I may have him."

"That's good, he misses you. I'll send him."

The smoke swirled as she vanished; and just as it had been in the old days beneath the Long Sun, I thought—too late—of a dozen things I ought to have asked her.

"Girl gone?" Oreb inquired. He clacked his bill and rustled his feathers. "Ghost girl?"

I told him she was, and made the mistake of adding that I wished she would come back.

"Bird gone!" He took wing and vanished into the night.

"He's a night chough," I explained to the Duko. "Don't worry about him, He can see in the dark much better than you and I can at noon."

"I wasn't worried about *him*," the Duko muttered.

19

SAY FATHER

I wrote late last night (too late, to admit the truth) and still did not set down everything I had intended. Now here I sit, writing once more while everyone else is asleep; and even though I have not gotten to make my little experiment, I have far more to write about than patience to write it.

Or paper, for that matter.

Oreb came back this morning, and remembering how I had boasted to the Duko about his acuity of vision I told him to find me a stone table.

Soon he was back, quite elated by his success. "Big table! Stone table. White table. Bird find! On hill. Watch bird!" With much more. I promised to watch, and off he flew due north.

I told Duko Sfido that I was going to retrace our journey for an hour's ride or about that, and instructed him to continue toward Blanko. "This is a good horse," I said, "and I should be able to catch up to you tonight."

Certainly there was nothing to worry about; but whether he was really worried or not, he seemed very worried indeed. "If this is absolutely necessary, I'd like to send a couple of troopers with you."

Oreb returned, flying in circles overhead and calling, "See god! Watch bird! See god!"

I said, "Its necessity is not the question, Your Grandeur. I am going to do it. It is a private matter, a matter of my private devotions, and I am not going to take away two of the troopers Inclito gave us to help guard his prisoners. Or one, or any other number." With that, I turned and rode away before Sfido could stop me.

I had said an hour's ride, because I had told Oreb that I was interested only in tables not far from us. To give him his due, the altar he found for me would have been less than an hour distant if the ride had been over level ground. In the event, my horse was forced to pick his way across rocky little gullies and up and down the barren, windswept hills, which made my ride closer to three hours than one. With Hyacinth's azoth virtually out of reach under my greatcoat, robe, and tunic, my mind dwelt apprehensively on wild beasts and stragglers from the Horde of Soldo, without my actually seeing the smallest sign of either.

The cold and the wind were more immediate enemies. I pulled my looted greatcoat tight about me and muffled my face against the wind, just as I had when I rode with Sfido, but it seemed colder than it had ever been before, perhaps merely because I was facing into the wind, or perhaps merely because winter had advanced another step that morning. Those who live largely in houses or in warm climates, as I have, do not know cold. On my long, lonely ride today, cold and I at last shook hands—mine, of course—and exchanged unpleasantries that left me with the cough that is keeping me awake tonight. When I rode, my feet froze. Dismounting and leading my horse warmed me somewhat, but slowed our progress.

The altar Oreb had found was on a hilltop, as I expected, and the climb was difficult: up the side of a flat-topped hill whose gentlest slope was practically straight up, until at last, perspiring in spite of the cold, I was able to pull myself over the edge, and stand upright on smooth rock more level than your kitchen floor.

I had expected that the altar would be a mere flat stone not much diferent from the one beneath which I had laid Fava to rest, a rough slab of fire-blacked slate resting on three or four boulders. What I found instead was a wide rectangle of some white mineral so fine in grain it might almost have been a kind of glass, supported by twelve graceful pillars of a metal that I am going to call bronze until we can speak face-to-face. The Neighbors had danced around it once; I knew that as soon as I saw it and the floor of living rock that they had leveled and smoothed with so much care. They had danced, and their watching gods, with their feet upon the stars, had smiled and bent in honest friendship to accept a morsel from a table fit for gods.

Sinew had found an altar of the Vanished People in a wood, and had tried to persuade me to visit it without exposing himself to the humiliation of my refusal. Now I wonder what wonders I missed by my surly rejection of his implied invitation. Was it an altar like the one to which Oreb guided me today? If not, in what respects did it differ, and why? Did Sinew himself worship there? If he did, did he experience what I experienced today, or anything of the kind? Have you visited the place, Nettle? I am eager to talk to you about all this.

Sinew is still on Green, assuming that he is (unlike his father) still alive. On Green and so unreachable, as Sfido's friend Gagliardo would doubtless tell us. But I and others will visit Green's jungles tomorrow night if my experiment succeeds. If I can locate Sinew, I will ask him about the altar he found in order that we can find it ourselves, assuming that Hide and I succeed in returning to the Lizard; if it is as remarkable as the altar to which Oreb led me, it will be well worth visiting more than once.

Ever since my boyhood, it has seemed to me that it is a species of insult to the immortal gods to pray at their altars without sacrificing, provided that sacrifice is possible. If I still had the long, straight, single-edged knife I used to carry when I was Rajan of Gaon, I would have thought seriously about sacrificing Oreb. I do not believe that I could have nerved myself to do it, but I cannot help wondering what the result would have been. My horse would have made a sacrifice worthy of the Grand Manteion, to be sure; but I could not spare him, and I had no knife other than the azoth (as I said), and no means of getting him onto the hilltop.

There will be a barn for him tomorrow, poor creature. A barn and hay—corn or oats if I can find them, though I have little hope of that.

When I had rejected both sacrifices, my next thought was to
pray as I would have at a shrine. I tried, kneeling on the level living
rock with my head swathed in my scarf, and mumbling a few of the
prayers I have not yet forgotten. When I have failed in prayer in
the past, I have generally felt myself ludicrous, like the little boy in
the story who prayed that Hierax would fly off with the larger boy
next door and drop him on the head of some evildoer.

Not so today—my prayers were beneath even Comus's good-
natured raillery. When I was in the schola, I once asked why those
spirits who had been thrust from the Aureate Path could not save
themselves by prayer; and I was told that they could not pray—
that although we, the living, might pray for them, they themselves
could only mouth the words of prayers, words that left their lips
without effecting any interior change. So it was with me, as I knelt
before that cold altar and felt its hunger. I was like a barren
woman who longs to conceive, but cannot conceive although she
lies with three-score men.

At last I rose and lifted my face to the dark winter sky. "I have
no knife for a sacrifice," I said, and I spoke aloud as one man does
to another. "Even if I had my old knife back, I would not give you
Oreb, who has led me here to you. You will reclaim us both
quickly enough. But you did not condemn me—or at least I dare
to hope that you did not—when I sacrificed for Olivine."

I opened the leather burse that Volanta gave me when we left
Blanko, found the piece of Soldese flatbread I had put there before
setting out, and struck by the idea of sharing the simple meal we
shared with our prisoners at midday, climbed down and fetched
the last of my wine from my saddlebag. The second climb should
have been worse than the first, yet it was not. I was tired, my ankle
pained me; and my fingers, which had been cold from the beginning, were colder than ever. But all the emptiness I had felt when
I had tried to pray, had vanished so completely I could almost
believe they had never been. I was happy and more, and if an old
instructor had appeared and demanded to know the reason for my
joy, I would only have laughed at him for needing causes and
explanations in so simple a matter. I was alive, and the Outsider—

who knows very well what sort of creature I am—cared about me in spite of all.

"This is what I have," I told him, and raised my bread and my bottle, displaying them to the low, gray clouds. "I beseech you to share them with me, and I pray that you will not object to me and my animals sharing them with you." Then I broke the bread in two, laid half of it upon his altar, and poured wine over it, cautioning Oreb not to touch it. After that, I wet a bit with a little wine and gave it to Oreb, ate a bite myself, drank deeply from the bottle and recorked it, and put away what remained of the bread.

He came, and stood behind me on the hilltop.

I have been preparing myself to describe that the whole time I have been writing, and now that the moment has come I am as wordless as my horse.

I knew that he was there, that if I turned, I would see them.

I also knew that it was not permitted me, that it would be an act of disobedience for which I would be forgiven but whose consequences I would suffer.

Just now I got up to think, walking around our camp. Oreb is off looking for something to eat. "Bird hunt," he said. It recalled Krait, flying away from our boat after Seawrack and I had gone to bed.

Both Dukos are sleeping. So are Private Cuoio, General Morello, and the coachman and the rest of the troopers. Only Colonel Terzo was awake, staring at me with frightened eyes before pretending to sleep.

None of which matters.

That, I believe, is what I ought to tell you, although it is by no means exact. In the presence of the Outsider, I was conscious of another whorl. Not a remote one like Green or the Long Sun Whorl that you and I grew up in, but a whorl that is as present to us as this one, a place all around us that we cannot see into. Many would say that it is not real, but that is almost the reverse of truth. It is the things of this whorl that are unreal by the standards of that one.

Think of a picture. Do you remember the wonderful pictures

in the Caldé's Palace, and how we went through all those empty rooms taking off dustcovers and looking wide-eyed at the rich furniture and the pictures? Surely you must.

We are there still, Nettle, as Silk and Hyacinth still kneel by the pool in Ermine's.

There was a picture of a worried man writing at a little table while his wife crocheted, remember that one? Was the man actually present?

He was present in the picture, there can be no doubt of that. If he had not been, we would have seen a picture of a young, unhappy-looking woman crocheting alone.

That is how it is for us. The hill on which I found the altar was really there—in the whorl that we are so prone to believe is the only whorl; but it is no more real than the table at which that man wrote, and for as long as the Outsider remained with me I knew that.

No, I know it now. I was directly aware of it then.

Think of a man who sees a picture and thinks it is real. Here on the wall is a painted door, open, and beyond it another room, in which a ragged child stands weeping. He goes to the child to comfort it, stops, and reaches out until his fingers brush the painted plaster. So it was with me while the Outsider was with me; my fingers touched the plaster, and the illusion lost its power over me.

I cannot explain it better than that. I have tried to think of something more, of some way in which I can tell you what it is to walk with a god and know that the god loves you, as Auk did; and as I did there upon the hill. Perhaps something will come to me later. If so, I will set it down.

Before I proceed I should tell you that although my horse was where I had tied him, and unharmed, I saw the tracks of some great beast all around him in the snow. I was not huntsman enough to identify it, but it was very large and had big soft feet with seven toes. A baletiger? We coursed them in Gaon, but it seems that they are more apt to course men in this part of the whorl. Whatever it was, it had walked about my horse several times, and had left him trembling and sweating, but had not harmed him.

I took out the remaining bread, which was not very much, wet it with wine, gave it to him, and mounted and rode away. I have never left a friend with so high a heart.

Our son is here, as I believe I may have said already. He has been calling himself Cuoio—but let me begin at the beginning.

I found Sfido and the rest scarcely a league from the place where I had left them. I had told them to continue our journey, as you will remember; and so they had, but not very far. They were very glad to see me, or at any rate Sfido was. He called to Cuoio, who joined us and saluted. Sfido said, "Inclito's given this young fellow a horse and sent him to us. He says you wanted to see him."

I acknowledged that I did, and invited him to come with me. "I'm sorry to take you from the fire," I told him as we walked away from it, "but I want to ask you various questions. They are innocent things, but it isn't wise to let other people overhear conversations that do not concern them. You were one of the young troopers behind the hedgerow, weren't you? You set off the fireworks?"

"Yes, sir."

"And shot at the cavalry attacking us, after the fireworks were gone?"

"No, sir. I didn't have this," he indicated his slug gun, "until after the battle."

"I see. You came out here from Blanko?"

"Yes, sir."

"Were you born in Blanko?"

"No, sir."

"In Grandecitta?"

"No, sir."

"In Olmo then? Or in Novella Citta? Were you born in Soldo, by any chance? Duko Sfido wasn't either, he was born in Grandecitta, I believe. He has lived most of his life in Soldo, however, although he's been fighting against it."

"I didn't know he was Duko Sfido, sir. I've been calling him Colonel Sfido. That's what General Inclito called him."

"I feel sure he doesn't object; he would have corrected you if he did. Where were you born, Private Cuoio?"

"A long way away, sir." His voice was so soft that I could barely hear him.

I turned and looked back at the fire. Sfido and the rest were huddled about it so closely that it could scarcely be seen. Our horses waited, patient and miserable, their heads to the wind.

"We will find no comfort here," I said. "Not even the slight comfort of blankets and a fire. Winter is no time to fight a war."

Oreb leaned fluttering from the handle of my staff to offer Cuoio his advice. "Boy talk. Talk now."

"Yes, speak, Cuoio. You can dodge my questions for a long time, no doubt." I coughed. "But not all night. Would it help to know that I am not your enemy? Sinew thought I was his—"

Cuoio looked at me sharply.

"But we were friends at the end, even when we fought. What was your name before you came to Blanko? What name were you born with?"

"Hide, sir."

"Thank you, Hide. It seems a good enough name. Why did you change it?"

"Nobody would tell me anything, sir. I mean before I got into town. There was a place, a little village, like, and when I said my name was Hide they sent me to talk to the shoemaker. I mean they told me to talk to this certain man, and he could probably tell me. So I went around looking for him, and he was a shoemaker. He laughed at me, but he helped me anyway. He said to say my name was Cuoio, and showed me how to eat the way they do, and these people were a lot friendlier after that."

"Good! Good!" Oreb bobbed on the handle of my staff.

"They told you what you wanted to know?"

He nodded with his head cocked, listening. "Did you hear that, sir?"

"I didn't hear anything except the wind. What did you hear?"

"A big animal, I think, sir. Not a horse."

"It's a baletiger, I believe, though it seems almost too large for one. I saw its tracks this afternoon—or at least I saw the tracks of a similar animal. You said that the people told you what you wanted to know, after you changed your name. What was it you wanted to know?"

"That isn't exactly right, sir." Hide unslung his slug gun as he spoke and pushed the safety catch off. "But they tried to help me, and they were nicer to me."

"I have found them very friendly."

"Isn't your name really Incanto, sir? It sounds like one of their names."

I ignored the question. "What was it you asked them?"

"I'm trying to find my father, sir. Or a town called Pajarocu, because he went there."

"And has never come back. I see."

"Yes, sir."

"Don't you know where Pajarocu is, Hide?"

"No, sir. Do you?"

I nodded.

"Will you tell me, sir? I—I certainly would appreciate it, sir."

"I may. We'll see. You've been honest and forthright, Hide, and I'm grateful. Before I ask you anything more, I want to assure you that nothing bad is going to happen to you as a result of your honesty—that I wish you well. Do you accept that?"

"Yes, sir. You said Sinew, sir. He thought you were his enemy."

I nodded again. "Sinew was a young man who was with me in Pajarocu, Hide. He cannot have been your father, however. Sinew cannot have been more than nine or ten at the time you were born."

"He's my brother, sir. I mean, I've got a brother named Sinew. It might not be the same person. He's pretty tall, and he's got black hair like mine, sir. Big hands?"

"Many thousands of men would fit that description, Private Hide." A fit of coughing overtook me. "Describe your father."

"His name's Horn, sir. He's about as tall as me, maybe a little bit taller, and kind of stocky. Just about bald."

I untied my scarf and let my hair blow free in the wind. "Like this?"

"No, sir. You've got a lot more hair than he does, and yours is white. His is kind of a dark gray, and there isn't that much of it."

"As tall as I am?"

"No, sir. More like me, like I said. Sir, don't you think we ought to go back to the fire?"

"If you wish, Hide. I intend to ask you a great many more questions, however." I started up the hill to our left. "Will it trouble you to talk where the others can overhear us? I'm going to ask you about the place you came from, your mother and your brothers and so forth. Will you continue to be open and honest with me then, with Duko Sfido and the rest listening?"

"Yes, sir. I'll try, sir. Only . . ."

"Only what?"

"They'll know I'm a foreigner then, sir."

He was hanging back, and I motioned to him to follow me. "They will. But if I call you Cuoio, and you continue to eat as they do and speak as they do—you didn't mention that, but it's the most important thing of all—it will make very little difference. Besides, I'm going to adopt you. You've searched here for your father without finding him. Will it trouble you to call me Father?"

He hesitated, but when we had walked a short distance more he said, "No, sir."

"Good boy!" Oreb bobbed his approval.

"Does he understand everything we say, sir?"

"Call me Father, Cuoio."

"All right. Father, the camp's back that way. Why are we going up here?"

I slipped on a snow-covered stone, saved by my staff. "Because it's shorter. That's one reason, at least. I want to ask you about your mother and your home, Cuoio; but I can do it when were sitting at the fire warming ourselves. I want to ask about your father, too; and I had better do that now, since we're going to tell others you're my son. What sort of man was he?"

"He's a good man, sir."

I shook my head.

"Father, I mean. He always worked really hard so we'd have enough to eat, and he protected my mother and my brothers and me. Things are pretty bad where we live. People stealing and killing. Only nobody ever tried anything like that when he was around, and he didn't do it himself, either."

"Did you love him, Cuoio?"

"Yes, Father."

"Good boy!" Oreb hopped from the head of my stick to Hide's shoulder.

"For duty's sake? To make your mother happy?"

"No, sir. Father, I mean. He was my father, and I just loved him. He used to take me out in our boat sometimes so I could fish, even when he was really tired."

"I see."

"He was always pretty strict with us, but that was because Sinew got bitten by a inhumu when he was real little and almost died. After that he was really worried Hoof and me would get bitten too, and so was Mother. Then there was people from New Viron that would come out to the Lizard sometimes. That's where we live. On the Lizard, Lizard Island."

"I want you to sling that slung gun you're holding, Private Cuoio. First engage the safety. You may sling it behind your left shoulder, if you don't want to disturb my bird."

"All right." The click of the safety was followed by the rattle of sling swivels.

"Try not to make so much noise. Listen to me now—listen very carefully."

"Yes, Father."

"I've been trying to get you to walk beside me, motioning for you to catch up."

"Yes, Father. It's just that I'm kind of tired after riding all day."

"I'm tired too. Can you hear me when I speak this softly?"

"Yes, Father."

"Good. You have good ears. I no longer want you beside me.

Do you understand? Stay well behind me. Oreb, it might be best for you to go; but if you insist on staying here, you must be completely quiet."

"No talk."

Hide chuckled softly.

"That's the way, Oreb, but quieter than that." I had an idea then, and said, "I'm going to hold my staff in back of me, like this. Take hold of the end and follow me."

He did. "Father?"

"What is it?"

"It's all thorns up there where the hill's sort of split. I don't think we can get through there."

"The worst thing we could do would be to turn back here. To turn our backs. He wouldn't harm my horse this afternoon. Perhaps the god-spell hasn't worn off yet, and he won't harm us tonight."

"Sir? Father?"

"Keep your grip on my staff," I said as we stepped into the crowding thornbushes; and then I saw him. I had expected him to crouch, although I cannot tell why. He was standing instead, with all eight feet solidly planted, so large that his great green eyes were on a level with mine. Catching the starlight, they seemed luminous, shining in the darkness like gems malign as Green itself.

"Sir . . . ?" Hide was pulling the staff so hard he almost took it out of my hand.

"Be quiet. Winter is hard on animals. He's very hungry."

Hide let go of my staff. I heard the faint jingle of his sling swivels, and said as sharply as I dared, "Stop that!"

The baletiger came toward us, slipping between the thorns step by slow step. I ought to have been terrified, but I was merely weak and sick. I pitied him, and now that I have leisure to look back upon that moment, I think it likely that he pitied me.

"Is Mucor there?" I whispered. "Is it Mucor?"

There was no reply save the merciless winter wind's. I heard Oreb stir on my shoulder, fluffing out his feathers.

"Yes," I whispered to the baletiger, "make them come to us."

He sniffed the hand that grasped my staff as a huge dog might. For a moment his mighty body rubbed against me, and I could feel his muscles slither beneath his thick, soft winter fur. A second later he was bounding down the slope past Hide, and was gone.

"Come up here," I told Hide. "I want you to sit beside me on this flat stone. We won't be going back to the fire for another hour or so."

"I can't, Father." (I could hear his teeth chatter.) "I can't even move, sir."

"The thornbushes?"

"Yes. F-Father. That animal?"

"What about it?" I went to him and took him by the sleeve.

"Was it a—a . . . ?"

"I believe so, yes. Come with me, Cuoio."

He did, and sat upon Fava's grave when I pointed out the stone. I sat down beside him; instinctively we huddled together for warmth, father and son.

"Bird talk?"

My nose had been running all day, and was running worse than ever. I had it in a rag that one of the troopers had given me the day before, and did not reply. Hide said, "I think so, only not loud."

"We're going to shoot game here, Oreb," I explained when I could. "He's going to drive it toward us, if he can find any; and we're going to shoot it for him. I should say Cuoio is. I promised he would, so he must."

Hide nodded; I felt the motion rather than saw it.

"Are you a good shot?" I asked him.

"Pretty good, Father. My father, I mean my real one, had a needler he'd brought from the Long Sun Whorl, only he took it with him when he went away."

"To Pajarocu."

"Yes, sir. It gets kind of complicated."

I nodded. "We have time. Will you tell me, Cuoio? I'd like very much to hear about it."

He cleared his throat softly. "If you'll tell me a couple of things too, sir. I've told you a lot, and you haven't told me anything."

"What I've said would have told you a lot, if you'd been paying attention. Just a couple?"

"Maybe more than that, Father. Please? Like, why'd you want to see me?"

"Isn't it natural for a father to want to see his own son, Cuoio?"

"Really, I mean."

"Do you imagine that I asked my question in jest? I was completely serious."

"You're not really my father!"

"If you say so where the others can overhear you, we will be in difficulties."

"All right."

"Where is Hoof, Cuoio?"

"Out looking for our real father. He was supposed to go north and I was supposed to go south. I did, too, or pretty much. How did you make the baletiger do what you told him?"

"I didn't. Because he had spared my horse, I agreed to do as he asked. You and Hoof left your mother alone?"

"She made us," Hide said miserably. "She made us both go out and look for Father."

"You didn't want to."

"We did, only we didn't want to leave her by herself like that. Hoof wanted to go and tried to get me to promise to stay, only I said for him to stay and I'd go. She made us both go."

"Leaving her there alone."

Hide nodded wretchedly.

"How long has your father been gone?"

"About three . . . Did you hear that, sir?"

"No. What did you hear?"

"He's roaring, way off somewhere. He roars, and then he stops, and then he roars again."

Oreb bobbed agreement. "Bird hear!"

"He's trying to frighten game. Greenbuck, I suppose. He isn't fast enough to run them down, you see. He has to lie in wait and spring at them, and they don't move around very much in weather like this. There is little food for them anywhere, and they try to find shelter from the wind."

"Sometimes they die, too. My brother, my other brother, I mean—"

"Sinew."

"Yes, sir. Sinew. He told me one time he'd find them in the winter sometimes, starved to death or else frozen. He'd skin them and take that, but there wouldn't be any meat."

"They'll be poor soon," I agreed, "and few."

"I left my slug gun with her," Hide said. "Not this one, I got this one here. I was supposed to take it, and Hoof took his. Only I left mine where she'd find it. These people would come out from New Viron after Father and Sinew went away, and take things and make us do whatever they said. So Mother traded for slug guns for Hoof and me, so we could fight."

"No cut!"

"I wasn't going to cut anything."

I said, "He means you are not to shoot him. You wouldn't anyway, I know.

"He's going to shoot food for the baletiger, Oreb, and perhaps for us as well. Fish heads.

"Go on, please, Cuoio."

"Shoot good?"

"Sure," Hide declared. "She got them so we could fight if they came anymore, only we didn't have to. Hoof shot at them a couple of times while they were still on their boat, and they went away. Only I'm afraid they'll come back now that we're gone. Mother knows how to shoot, though."

I nodded, recalling the fighting in the streets of Viron, and our desperate battle with the Trivigauntis in the tunnels under the city.

"We figured to go over to the big island and hunt the way Sinew used to, and we did. We didn't have much stuff we could trade for cartridges though." Hide laughed softly. "So after we'd missed a little we learned how to get up real close and put the slug right where we wanted it." He sighed, and I knew that he was thinking of past hunts. "You know why they call these greenbuck, sir?"

"Say Father. You must learn to do that, just as I must learn to call you Cuoio."

"All right, Father."

Now I, too, heard the baletiger.

"Do you think he'll give us some, Father? There's not much to eat back at the fire, and I didn't bring much." He raised his slug gun to his shoulder as he spoke.

"If you can get enough for him and us too."

Oreb croaked softly, wordlessly, as the first game came in sight.

I told Hide, "Not now, my son—wait until they're closer." He nodded, his head scarcely moving as he squinted down the barrel.

20

BACK AT THE BATTLEFIELD

I am writing this in bed, in the little bedroom with a fireplace, and one brick wall, and one window, that I shared with Sfido. I have just spoken with Jahlee. Oreb is hopping about the little table they put beside my bed and eyeing the breakfast on my tray. I told him to take whatever he wanted, and he seems to be trying to decide. He would like a fish head better than any of it, I feel sure. Hide has gone to fish through the ice in the river, which is what everyone seems to be doing at present except for our prisoners and Inclito's coachman, who is guarding them.

And Jahlee, Oreb, and me. I must rest.

I have been ill. Perhaps I can begin there. A strange sort of sickness—no pain, just very tired. We brought the fourgoat back to camp, Hide going ahead to be sure no one fired. It was very welcome and was skinned and eaten at once. I ate some of the meat. Much less than the others, but they were not sick.

No matter. I was ill, I feel quite certain, before we reached the fire.

Jahlee came in again to chide me for not eating. "You can't live as we do, you know!"

I asked whether she had been feeding from my veins. She

denied it, but conceded that another might have, and examined me for the punctures of fangs, finding none.

Or so she said.

"We don't bring all sickness. Besides, you have a fever. We don't do that."

I agreed, recalling Teasel. How cold her skin was!

I should have written down our earlier talk as well. I see that I did not. In summary:

She asked why I had not betrayed her. I tried to explain.

"But you hate us!"

As a group, I said, because you nearly killed my son and for the hideous conditions on Green where my son is.

She pointed out that I could have told my troopers, who would have shot and killed her, and burned her body.

I conceded that it was so.

"Would you rather see me the way I looked in Gaon?" She began to change as she spoke—taller, her face lengthening, and so on. I said it might be hazardous for her.

"Somebody might try to rape me, you mean. It's been tried before."

I was—am—surprised. That lean, wicked, famished, thin-lipped face would not have appealed to me even when I was Hide's age.

My head aches.

★

★　★

"Silk well!" proclaims Oreb, which would seem to mean that I must write again. To confess the truth, I am far from well, too weak almost to stand; nevertheless, I certainly feel better. I have an appetite again—I wanted no food at all while I was so ill and for some time before I realized I was. I ate a little of the fourgoat, I remember that. Hide would have been hurt if I had not. I feel better now than I did when I conducted my experiment, and I thought myself much better then. No doubt I was.

First I should explain that I was eager to see whether I could make use of another inhuma to visit Sinew on Green. With Jahlee present, and as friendly as these creatures ever are, it seemed too good an opportunity to miss. Naturally I could not tell anyone else what I intended; I merely asked Sfido to bring our prisoners and our troopers, including Cuoio, to my room, saying that I wished to speak to everyone at once and that I was still too weak to leave my bed. It was quite true as such things are ordinarily judged, but what irony!

He brought them all, filling the room almost to bursting. I asked him to fetch the old woman then. He was surprised, but went for her. He had hardly left the room, however, when we heard the clatter of horses' hooves. Oreb flew to the window at once. "Girl come. Boy. Good girl!"

There was a knock at the front door a moment afterward, followed by Jahlee's hurrying footsteps. "We have company," the Duko remarked dryly, to which Hide added, "A man and a pretty big lady."

The Duko said, "You can't know that."

"She has a pretty deep voice. I never saw a little lady with a deep voice like that."

I had a presentiment then but kept it to myself.

Crowded though he was, Morello managed a bow. "I want to ask you something, Master Incanto. I've already asked this boy who was with you, but he won't tell me anything."

I warned him that I might not tell him anything either, and was applauded for it by Oreb: "Wise man!"

"On the night before we came here, the boy—"

"Cuoio," I said. "He has a name, General, and there's no reason why we shouldn't use it."

"Private Cuoio came back to the place where we were sleeping. Everyone was asleep except the sentry and me. He warned the sentry not to shoot, no matter what he saw, and tried to persuade him to take the cartridges out of his slug gun, which he would not do."

Rimo protested. "It's against regulations, sir."

I nodded. "I understand."

Morello said, "He challenged you and you told him who you were, and then he and Private Cuoio helped you drag the four-goat. Who was it that Private Cuoio thought the sentry might shoot?"

"We didn't want him to shoot anyone," I said, "very much including me."

For the time being at least, I was saved by Jahlee, who looked in at that moment. "A nobleman and a noblewoman to see you. She says she's—"

"Inclito's daughter." I raised my voice. "Come in, Mora. Is that Eco with you?"

"Bird glad!" Oreb crowed.

They joined us, Mora in furs, boots, and trousers, and Eco gleaming with gems and wearing a big saber with a golden hilt under his greatcoat. Between the deference accorded her and the area required by his broad shoulders and long blade, they made the room unbearably crowded.

She waved a cheerful greeting. "I'm sorry, Incanto. We've interrupted something."

"No, not at all," I told her. "We haven't begun. I've been ill—"

"The woman outside told me."

"Jahlee." From what Mora had said and the way she had said it, I knew she thought Jahlee human.

"Jahlee said she'd been taking care of you, but I'm going to take care of you myself. Grandmother and I took care of Papa when he was sick. Besides, she looks like a whore." She had elbowed her way to my bedside by that time; she pressed her wrist to my forehead. "You're feverish. How do you feel?"

"Wonderful."

"You'd say that if you were dying."

She swung around as she spoke, and I saw that she wore a sword with a shorter, lighter blade than Eco's, as well as a needler.

"People!" She raised both hands as well as her voice. "Get

out! All of you! I know you mean well, but you're making him worse. Outside, everyone! *Out!*"

When we were alone except for Oreb, I said, "I wouldn't have thought you could do that."

She grinned. "Neither did I, but it was worth trying. Anyway, my husband would have chased them out for me if I couldn't."

"I didn't—I'm very happy for you. For you both, Mora. He's a nice young man, and a brave one. I'd ask you to give him my congratulations, but I'll do it myself in a minute or two."

"When you go on with your meeting, or whatever it was?"

I nodded.

"Then you're going to let him sit in? May I sit in, too? Only I'd like to talk to you for a minute first."

"And I would like to talk to you. I'm very anxious to, in fact, though it will be painful."

"You want to scold me. I know you must have been worried, and Papa worried half to death, and I'm sorry. Really and truly I am. Only I didn't think about it until later. All I thought about was—"

I raised my hand. "I know what you thought about, and I excoriated myself again and again. We were terribly worried, exactly as you say—and so proud of you we nearly burst, both of us, and went half mad trying to hide it from each other. No, I'm not going to scold you, Mora. That's your husband's task, if it is anyone's."

"You said it would be painful. Is Papa . . . ?"

"Perfectly healthy, as far as I know, and at the head of his troops."

"Then let me go first. All right?" She found the spindly chair Sfido and I had sat in to pull off our boots, and sat down. "You're going to want to know a lot about where I went and what I did, so I'll say something about that before the other. You know I took the short messenger's horse? I forget his name."

"Yes. Rimando."

"That's it. I took it because I knew Papa's letter was in the saddlebag, and I didn't want to start changing tack. You always have to adjust something for the new horse, and sometimes it takes a while to find out. I wanted to die like a hero."

She smiled. "I kept thinking how I'd be wounded and I'd come galloping up to Novella Citta dripping blood and find out who was in charge and hand over Papa's letter and fall dead. Only it was the horse. Rimando's. They shot it and it died under me. There were a few seconds there when I was riding a dead horse."

"They didn't hit you?"

"No. I had Papa's needler. Did they tell you?"

I shook my head.

"I did. I knew he slept with it under his pillow. I went in and got it without waking him up. Only I never used it. I thought I'd shoot a lot of them and they'd shoot me, and I'd ride through their ranks and off I'd go, but my horse was dead and I'd have been dead too. I held up my hands instead and I yelled don't shoot. I wasn't brave at all."

"You were sensible."

"I hope so. So they got me, and about an hour later they got Eco, too. They'd been watching the road, I think."

"Their Duko and General Morello are both here. You can ask them."

"Those men with their hands tied? I saw them. That's great!"

"We think so. They took you and Eco back to Soldo and imprisoned you there. Isn't that correct?"

She nodded. "They took Papa's needler and sent our letters to their Duko, that's what they said. And they locked Eco up in a cell with some other men. I got a cell of my own because I was the only woman there. Do you mind if I call myself a woman?"

"Why should I? You are a woman."

She nodded again, solemnly. "My tits are starting. Want to see?"

I shook my head.

"Mostly I was just in the cell at night. During the day they let me out to work. I scrubbed floors and emptied slops and a lot of other stuff I'd done before we got Onorifica. I could've gotten away from them pretty easily, but I wanted to get Eco out too, and it was a while before I could get hold of the keys."

I said, "That was very brave," and she blushed like the girl she had been.

"May I ask where you were married?"

"In Novella Citta. They had . . . You know. They did it to me when they caught me, and then they caught Eco, and then they did it again that night, four of them."

"I'm sorry, Mora. I'm deeply, terribly sorry."

She shrugged. "You know how it is when you get thrown? You jump right up if you can, and you jump right back on. Because if you don't, if you let yourself have time to think, you'll never be any good. So I kept thinking I've got to get back on, I've got to get back on. That was after the first time. Incanto, this isn't even what I came here to tell you about."

Oreb commiserated with her. "Poor girl!"

"I think it is very probable that this is more important than whatever matter you originally wished to confide to me."

"Yes, but I don't need advice about this. They caught him too, and he was so brave. When they did it to me again he called them names and tried to get loose, and they hit him with their slug guns. They hit me, too, but only with their hands."

"They will be found and punished. I realize that won't help you, but it may save someone else."

Mora nodded, although I do not believe she had been listening. "He was so nice while we were going to Soldo and then when he was locked up there; and I said to myself, that can't have been what Grandmother got married over and over again for, and I've got to get back on. I could imagine what it was like when it was love. They hated me. That wasn't love, what they did."

"No, it was not."

"So I stole food for him in the jail, and he kept telling me not to worry about him, to get away if I could. But I opened his cell, and we stole horses—only there was no way we could get Papa's letters back or his needler. We rode a lot slower the second time, being a lot more careful, and we got through and I told them I was our duko's daughter, and Eco said I was too. And I talked about how we were going to win. They knew they had to give us to the Duko fast or come in on our side, and that's what they did. They gave us cards and jewelry, and swords and needlers and new horses, so on the second night we sort of slipped away and found this place and got one of the holy patres there to marry us. I'm glad you're smiling."

"How could I not smile?"

"Papa's going to be mad because Eco's a foreigner, I think. Only I don't know. You never can tell about Papa."

I remarked that Torda was a foreigner as well.

"Not from Grandecitta, I mean. Only Grandecitta's a long, long way away now, up in the sky somewhere, and nobody will ever see it again. We were afraid the patre would ask us a lot of questions, and he did. Only not the stuff we were afraid he'd ask about, like how old are you and where's your father? He was afraid we didn't love each other and wouldn't stay together. We had to tell him over and over that we did and we would. And we will."

"Good girl!"

"So he married us with two other patres for witnesses, and everybody kissed the bride." She smiled. "That night wasn't like the other times at all, only when I went to sleep I dreamed about Fava."

I nodded. "Was it unpleasant?"

"No. It was nice. I was little again and we played with dolls and things like we used to, only she wasn't . . ."

"An inhuma."

"That's right. When I first met her, Incanto, I thought she was just a little girl like me, and in my dream that's what she was. I kept thinking how could I have been so wrong about her? The next night it was the same thing, and the night after that one. I don't mean we did the same things or said the same things, only it's been me and Fava playing every night. I have other dreams, too, but one is always playing with Fava. It's nice, I like the dreams, only I think something must be wrong."

"I believe that something must be right, Mora."

"You don't think it's dangerous some way?"

"I doubt it," I said. "Also, I envy you. I would like very much to be a small boy again in my dreams. I'd give a great deal for that, if I had a great deal to give." Which was nothing less than the truth.

She nodded thoughtfully.

"Do you want me to stop the dreams, Mora? I may be able to, if you wish it; but I warn you now that I won't be able to restore them, should you want them to return. If I try to stop them and succeed, they will be gone forever. Do you understand?"

She nodded again, her face solemn.

"Consider well, but you must make your decision quickly. I won't be here much longer." Seeing her expression, I added, "Oh, I'm not going to die, or at least the gods haven't told me that I am, and I've been talking with a goddess in my own dreams almost every time I sleep. I only mean that since the war's over or nearly over, I'm going home. I should also warn you that these dreams may cease sometime of their own accord."

She straightened up, squaring her shoulders. "If you don't think they're dangerous, I'm going to keep having them as long as I can."

"Good girl!"

"That's wise, I believe. You had a very short childhood, and you were eager to leave it behind you, I know. I'm happy to see that the Outsider, who is far wiser than either of us, has found a way to prolong it." I fell silent, fingering my beard.

Mora inquired, "What's the matter?"

"You liked Fava, didn't you? Even when you knew what she was."

Mora nodded. "She was the only friend I had. But even if I'd had dozens of others, I would have liked her the best."

"You will never see her again, outside dreams."

"She's dead? You didn't kill her, did you, Incanto?"

"No. I tried to save her life and failed."

"It—" Mora plunged her fingers into her short, dark hair. "This is so crazy. I was playing dolls with her last night."

I nodded.

"Was I really? Was it true?"

"I think so. It's the interior person that survives death, Mora. Fava was an inhuma, as we both know. We both know, also, that her interior person, her spirit, was not. When you yourself die—and we all die—you will be the interior person, and there will be no other. To put it a bit more accurately, that interior person will be the only *you* in existence."

"So I'd better make sure the interior person's somebody I can live with?"

"Exactly. I think you've done very well so far, but you've only begun. May I tell you a secret, Mora?"

"If you think it's something I ought to know."

"I think it's something that everyone ought to know. I know another secret of that kind, but I may not tell it because I gave my word to a dying man that I would not. This one I found out for myself, so it's mine to do with as I choose."

"Go on."

"The Outsider has arranged our whorl in such a way that there is far more balance than at first appears, with gain involving loss, and loss, gain. Your father is rich by the standards of Blanko, and it is a very good thing to be rich; but as a rich man he has certain responsibilities—and is subject to certain temptations—that his poorer neighbors do not. Do you wish to argue?"

"He's a good man, whatever they say."

"He is. I forgot to mention his neighbors' envy, which is one of the chief disadvantages of his wealth, though there are others. I do not mean that he would be better off poor, though many men would. I am merely saying that he and his neighbors are much more nearly at a level in life than either may believe."

"All right, I see that."

"This matter of the interior person is similar. We mourn, we weep, we tear our clothes and our hair when a child dies; but the child's interior person was far superior to ours in most cases. In all, if the child was quite young. The longer you live the more difficulty you will have in keeping your interior person someone you can live with. My own difficulties have been so great that I would hesitate to say that I've succeeded."

"Good Silk!" Oreb assured me, and I smiled. "Good bird, too," I said.

"Is that your real name? Silk? Are you the man in the book?"

"I don't think so."

Mora stared at me, then looked away.

"Before you and your husband came, I called everyone in our party together. It made it too crowded in here. You saw that."

"Sure."

"There's no room in this little house that wouldn't be equally crowded, or worse; and I don't think it would be wise for me to go outside for another day or two. There is an old woman here and a young one. Both may be addressed as Jahlee. Will you do me a favor, Mora?"

"You've done me a lot of them, and I wouldn't want to ugly up my interior person. What is it?"

"I'm merely being curious now. Do you still consider the external one ugly?"

She shook her head. "Eco says I'm beautiful. I know that's not true and won't ever be, but I lost weight while I was away. Did you notice?"

I nodded.

"I need to lose some more. I'm going to try. I know I'll never look like Torda or even come close, but there are things I can do about the way I look and the way I dress," she touched her loose silk blouse, "and I'm going to do them."

"In a year or two, Torda will have to admit ruefully—to herself at least—that she will never be able to look, or act, or speak like you."

"Thanks. What's the favor?"

"I still want to have my meeting, but I am going to have to limit the number present. Bring either of the women called Jahlee, please, but not both."

"All right."

"All three of our prisoners, I believe, and we'll have to include the trooper guarding them. In addition, Duko Sfido, Private Cuoio, and your husband. You yourself are welcome to attend as well. You said you wanted to."

"I still do. Thanks."

When she was gone Oreb asked, "Bird come? Good Silk!"

"You know what I'm going to do, clearly—what I'm going to try, at least. Do you approve?"

"Good Silk!" he repeated.

Hide was first to arrive. I explained to him that since there was only one chair it would have to be reserved for General Inclito's daughter, and said that he might sit on my bed, or on the floor if he preferred.

He shook his head. "Is the old lady coming? She was looking for her."

"Perhaps."

"She shouldn't have to stand up in her own house. I'll bring in another chair for her."

Duko Rigoglio, General Morello, and Colonel Terzo arrived, guarded by Inclito's coachman. I told the last that I was glad to see him, since he, as well as Inclito's daughter and son-in-law, could stand in for Inclito himself.

"He wanted me to go back and take care of the place, our livestock and wheat."

"He must be worried about his mother, too, Affito."

"He thought you'd see about them, sir. You know, all those womenfolk."

Cuoio returned with another chair, and a youthful Jahlee. "My aunt is unwell, Master Incanto. Will I make an acceptable substitute?"

I indicated that she would.

"This man you call Incanto has been a friend to me," she told Duko Rigoglio. "Without his friendship I might be dead today, or as good as dead, and buried. I've tried to repay his kindness."

The Duko smiled, and said he wished that he might say the

same someday; while he was speaking, Mora, Eco, and Colonel Sfido came in together.

"Silk talk!" Oreb croaked loudly, and they fell silent.

I thanked them all for coming. "I would have liked to speak to everyone," I explained, "but we don't have room for everybody, so those of you who are here will have to tell the rest. I hope that some of you will also tell the people of Blanko, Captain Atteno and his wife especially. I don't want to lay too many duties upon anyone, but I think Duko Sfido may very well want to talk to the troopers that he and I trained there, Adatta and all the others."

Sfido nodded.

"Eco is a mercenary. No doubt some of you learned that while I was talking to Donna Mora. He can convey my farewell to Captain Kupus and his troopers—to Thody and Gorak, particularly."

"I will," Eco said.

"And tell Captain Rimando, please. If you would. I'm very sorry that he's not among us."

I paused to look from face to face. "Donna Mora will tell her father, of course. It was truly providential that she and her husband arrived when they did."

Jahlee said, "You're not dying, I hope."

"Do you really hope I'm not?"

"You know I do! I could have—"

My nod silenced her. "Of course," I said.

"Talk, Silk!" Oreb commanded.

"He means that I've wasted too much time already upon preliminaries, and he's right. I have several things to say to you, and I should get to them.

"First, I've been ill, as you know. I'm better now, and feel that I'll soon be well enough to travel, if the gods permit it. I've decided that there's little point in my returning to Blanko with you—or even to your father's farm, Donna Mora."

There was a buzz of talk.

I tried to clear my throat to silence them, but ended by coughing. "You will have ample time to discuss everything I say in a moment, and I promise to be quiet and let you do it. Please let me finish.

"Since I'm not going to Blanko or to Donna Mora's father's, there's no point in Duko Sfido and his prisoners waiting here for me to recover. Nor, of course, is there any point in Donna Mora and her husband waiting. If either party chooses to leave this afternoon, I wish it good speed. It seems very clear to me that neither should delay beyond tomorrow morning.

"That was my first point, and I have made it. The second concerns my identity, about which certain foolish rumors have circulated. I was born in the *Whorl,* more often called the Long Sun Whorl. My mother was not Inclito's as well, nor was my father his father. I would have thought that our faces would have ended the speculations of that kind before they began, but they have not, and so I wish to end them now. I will not presume by saying that Inclito and I are brothers in our regard for each other—but we regard each other highly.

"Though I was born in the Long Sun Whorl, my home is in a coastal town to the west called New Viron. Here you think that holy men should not marry, and you may well be right; but I am not a holy man, and I have a wife there, a woman I've loved since we were children. We have been separated, for reasons that are of small importance to you. It should be sufficient for me to say that we have been separated for years, though I have been striving to rejoin her. When I am well enough to travel again—in a very few days, I hope—Cuoio and I will set out for New Viron."

Hide began to protest, but my voice overpowered his. "He is recently come from there, and should be able to guide me. He can continue the errand that brought him to Blanko afterward, if he chooses to and his mother agrees. Cuoio, you see, is my son, the youngest son of three."

I spoke to Mora. "I'm sorry that my wife and I were not blessed with daughters. I have envied my brother Inclito his ever since I met—"

Terzo exclaimed, "She's singing!"

"I know," I told him. "I've been trying to speak in spite of it.

I suggest that you try to keep silent in spite of it, for the present at least."

Jahlee asked, "Who is?"

"Someone only Colonel Terzo and I can hear. It doesn't really concern him, and it certainly doesn't concern the rest of you." I fell silent for a moment to listen to Seawrack's song, the beating waves and the cries of the seabirds.

Duko Rigoglio said, "I told you once that you had no magic powers."

"Did you? It's certainly true."

"I know better now. You've put some sort of spell on Terzo here, and I saw the witch sitting in the smoke."

"I know you did."

"Terzo says that you had a baletiger carry your meat, and that he put it down and went away when you told him to. The man who was on guard then says the same thing."

Inclito's coachman nodded.

"Private Cuoio wouldn't tell us anything. I understand that now better than I did the last time I spoke to him. This seems to be the last chance I'll get to talk to either of you, so I'd like to ask you something. Not whether you have those powers, because I know the answer. But how you got them, and what you set out to do with them."

When I said nothing, Mora declared, "The gods favor him. If you had been a better man, they might have favored you, too."

Jahlee added, "He's on good terms with the Vanished People, they say, and—"

Her voice was lost in a babble of others, including Duko Rigoglio's. I shut my eyes (I was very tired, which may have helped) and while attempting to fix her tones in my memory, I tried to recall Green's jungles and Sinew. Sleep rushed upon me, sending me spinning through an endless night.

21

THE RED SUN

I tried to sleep after writing those words about sleep, telling myself that it was an appropriate place to do so, and that I could push this account ahead a bit more in the morning. With everyone gone, the house is so quiet! Its silence should lend itself to sleep, but it does not; I am apprehensive, and grateful for the least sound from Oreb, for the small noises Jahlee and Cuoio make.

I want very much to describe the Red Sun Whorl in such a way that you can see it, Nettle—to do it so well that whoever reads this can. Have I made you see Green's jungles? The swamps and their dire inhabitants? The immense trees and the lianas clinging to them like brides? Or the City of the Inhumi, a grove of disintegrating towers like a noble face rotting in the grave?

No, I have given only scattered hints in spite of all my efforts.

What will be the use of trying, in that case?

We stood in an empty street, Nettle. Empty, I say, although it knew a certain traffic of broken stones, which fell from the crumbling houses lining it, rolled into the street, and lay where they had ceased to roll, attended by a guard of rank weeds.

"Look." Mora pointed.

I looked up and saw a shining crimson disk, so large a sun that when I stretched forth my arm, my hand could not cover it all. Stars gleamed all around it, and I felt that the Outsider was trying to convey some message to me by it and them, that this great ember of sun I saw had tumbled from a ruin as the stones had, and that the stars I saw by day here had sprung up around it like the weeds. But I cannot depict the vast city of ruins for you. If I were an artist, I might draw it here, a sketch in my friend the stationer's good black ink upon his thin gray paper. Imagine that I have, and and tell me what would you see in it? What could you? A few hundred ruinous houses, a few hundred dots in a gray sky that is in fact a dreaming purple, and the black sun (for it would have to be black in such a drawing) overlooking everything and seeing nothing.

To understand, you must visualize its sky and hold the vision above you. Not my words. Not my words. Not the smears of ink upon this paper. The sky, a sky purple or blue-black rather than blue, a sky whose skylands were always as visible as those at home, though vastly more remote and colder. It was warm there in the deserted, ruined street; but the dark sky made it seem cold, and I felt sure that it would be cold soon, would turn cold, in fact, before the actual setting of the crimson sun.

"How did we get here?" Hide demanded.

And Mora, "Where are we, Incanto?"

I shook my head and kept my silence.

Inclito's coachman snapped, "Don't do that!" and I turned to see to whom he was speaking. It was to Jahlee, and she was taking off her clothing. "Look!" she exclaimed. "Look at me!" The last worn garment dropped around her feet. She pirouetted, displaying hemispherical breasts, a slender waist, and narrow hips.

Mora muttered, "Is there some madness here?"

"Yes." It was Duko Rigoglio. As he spoke, he fell upon his knees before me. "Free my hands. That's all I ask, free my hands, please, as you love the Increate."

It was a new term to me. I could only peer into his eyes and try to guess what he meant by it.

"I'm a proud man. You know that. I'm begging now. Have I begged you for my life?"

"Your Grandeur—" Morello began.

"I'm begging, Incanto. This is more than life to me. Whoever you are, whatever you are, have pity on me!"

I motioned to Hide. "Cut his bonds."

Sfido exclaimed, "No!"

"Are you afraid he may escape, and remain here?" I asked him. Without waiting for an answer, I told Hide, "Free him, and the others, too. For their sake, I hope they do."

Hide tore his eyes from Jahlee, drew a knife smaller than Sinew's, and cut the cords that had held Rigoglio's hands behind him; Rigoglio rubbed his wrists, muttering thanks.

"You know this street," I told him. "You recognized it at once. You're a proud man, just as you say—too proud to enjoy feeling gratitude for anything. Share your knowledge with me, and I will acknowledge that you have settled any debt."

"I can't be sure," he said, and stared about him with wide eyes. After a moment, a trickle of blood ran from his mouth, so that I wondered if it were possible that he was an inhumu, and had deceived me; but he had merely bitten his lip.

"It's so quiet here," Mora said. Her hand was on the hilt of her sword.

Eco had a needler, and was studying each empty, staring window in turn. I told him, "I believe you're right, someone is watching us," and he nodded without speaking.

Jahlee ran long-fingered hands down her slender body. "This is your doing, Rajan, it has to be. Do you like it? I do!"

I shook my head. "You must praise—or blame—Duko Rigoglio. There is a city somewhat like this on Green, but we are not on Green; these houses would be the towers of the Neighbor lords there. Where are we, Your Grandeur?"

"We've come home . . . To Nessus."

Mora said, "You can't have lived here. Nobody alive now can. Just look at them."

He started to speak, but stopped.

"Big place!" Oreb dropped onto a pile of rubble, looking as he had on Green—a dwarfish man in feathers. Until that moment I had not been aware that he had come with us, far less that he had left us to scout.

"You asked us to free your hands," I told Rigoglio. "They are free. What do you intend to do with them?"

He indicated the house before which we stood. "I would like to search it. May I?"

"For weapons?" Sfido inquired. "I doubt that you'll find a stick."

"For something . . ." Rigoglio turned to me. "They forced me to board the *Whorl* and put me to sleep. I told you."

"Poor man!" Oreb studied him through one bright, black eye.

"If I could find something more, something I recognized . . ."

I asked whether he did not recognize the house.

He pointed to the roof. "There were arches up there, and statues under the arches. . . . I—I'm sure of it. They . . ." He wandered toward the house, bent, and rooted in the rubble banked against its wall.

"I was trapped in a pit in a ruined city of the Vanished People once," I remarked to Mora. "Have I ever told you about that?"

She shook her head.

"I've been thinking about it, and about the City of the Inhumi on Green. Those were ruins left by the Neighbors' ancient race; these were left by ours, I believe—we are as ancient as they, or nearly. How long have these been empty, do you think?"

She shrugged. Eco said, "A hundred years, perhaps."

"Longer than that, I believe."

I went over to watch Rigoglio, and in a moment more found Jahlee clinging to me like the lianas, her body warm and damp with perspiration (as those of inhumi never are), and fragrant with some heavy, cloying scent. Long sorrel hair that proceeded from no wig draped us both like the vines of Silk's arbor.

When I tried to free myself from her, she grinned at me. "I've got teeth here. Real teeth, Rajan. Adieu to my famous tight-lipped smile! Look what I can do now." She grinned again, more broadly than ever.

I suggested that she do it to someone else.

"Your son? He was flirting with me before we came into your bedroom. He isn't very good at it yet—"

Rigoglio straightened up, holding up a broken stone hand about half the size of mine. "Statues," he said. "Up there, underneath the arches. I told you."

"So you did. Statues of whom?"

"I don't—the eponyms."

"And who are they?"

He shook his head. "May I search the house?"

I nodded, then hurried after him. Seeing me run, Sfido shouted, "Stop him!" But I was not afraid that Rigoglio would escape, and in fact I would have welcomed it if it could have been arranged without my culpability. As soon as he left me, I knew that he was going into danger.

Nor was I wrong. Ducking under the lintel, I heard him fall, and his muffled cry. In what must once have been the solaria, he was struggling with a skeletal, nearly naked assailant. I saw the dull gleam of steel and snatched at the filthy wrist as the knife came up.

My fingertips only brushed it.

Rigoglio's gasp as the knife went home was followed at once by the boom of a slug gun, close and deafeningly loud. The skeletal attacker stiffened and shrieked, empty hands raised before his filthy, bearded face.

"Don't shoot him," I told Hide, and was seconded at once by Oreb, who was flying in tight circles above our heads: "No shoot! No shoot! No shoot!"

Looking up at him, I thought for a moment that it was a painted ceiling I saw beyond him; but it was the sky, a clear, star-spotted sky so dark that it seemed practically black; the roof and upper floor of the house had fallen in, leaving only its walls standing.

"I missed him?" Hide sounded disgusted with himself.

"Don'. Don'." Hesitantly, Rigoglio's attacker was getting his feet.

"Man run," Oreb warned us.

"You're right," I told him. "He will run, and Hide will shoot and kill him, and we will have lost him." I caught him by the arm as I spoke.

We tied his hands behind him with what remained of the cords that had bound Rigoglio, Morello, and Terzo, and contrived a hobble for his ankles that allowed him to take small steps. He seemed to have lost the power of speech almost entirely—it is no exaggeration to say that Oreb could talk better—and was so clearly mad that I was very happy indeed that Hide had not killed him. I had seen the tunnel gods that Urus and his fellow convicts had called bufes, and had killed several of them before Mamelta and I were apprehended; this new prisoner of ours recalled them so vividly that when I was not looking directly at him, or was pre-occupied with my own thoughts, it seemed to me that we were accompanied by one, starved, vicious, and desperate.

Rigoglio was badly wounded, as we found when we had ripped his shirt away. We bandaged him as well as we could with strips torn from it, and I promised that we would let Morello and Terzo carry him as soon as we found materials from which to contrive a stretcher.

He managed to smile as he struggled to his feet. "I can walk, Master Incanto. For a while anyway."

"Leave him here with the boy to guard him," Morello suggested, "while the rest of us look for help."

Mora sheathed her sword. "What if we don't find any?"

"There are more of them here," I told her. "More who are watching us, and listening as we speak. I feel their eyes, as your husband did earlier."

Sfido nudged Eco and whispered, "Having a nice honeymoon?"

Overhearing him Mora said, "It's had its good and bad, but I've got to admit this is the low point so far."

"For which Jahlee, the Duko, and I are all to blame," I told her. "I was about to say that if we were to leave Rigoglio and Cuoio here, they would be attacked—probably as soon as we were well away, certainly after nightfall. No, His Grandeur must come with us, walking if he can, carried if he cannot."

I had begun walking myself as I spoke, and they followed me, Morello and Terzo beside their Duko to assist him.

"Oreb!"

He dropped to the ground at my feet, neither bird nor dwarf.

"Have you seen people in this place? Not people like this man we've tied up, but normal people, people like us?"

He bobbed his head. "Flock men! Flock girls! See god?"

"No, not there. Lead us to them, please. The Duko requires a physician."

"Big wet! Come bird!" He flew.

One ruined street led to another, and that to a third. Eco and Mora hurried ahead after Oreb; I lagged, staring horrified at that desert of abandonment and decay, and soon got the position I wanted, beside Hide and behind the Duko, Terzo, and Morello.

Jahlee joined me there, naked still save for her long hair. "You did this, didn't you?"

I shook my head.

"I'm not angry, I'm very grateful. You have a wonderful, wonderful father, Cuoio. I'll never be able to repay him for all he's done for me."

Hide nodded, his face guarded.

"But you said it was me and you and Duko Rigoglio, Incanto. I don't think he had anything to do with it, and I know I didn't. I've never lied to you. I hope you know that."

I told her that not being a complete fool I knew nothing of the sort.

"All right, once or twice, maybe, when I had to. Will you lie to me if I ask a straight question?"

"Not unless I must."

"Fair enough. Could you take us back? Right now?"

Hide turned to look at me, startled.

"I don't know," I said. "Perhaps. I believe so."

"And I—?" Jahlee glanced at Hide.

"You're prettier now," he said.

"You will be again what you were, unless I am very much mistaken," I told her. "I cannot be certain, but that is certainly my opinion. Hide, you must remember that there were an old woman and a young one living in the farmhouse in which we stayed."

He nodded.

"The old one was presumed to be the farmer's mother, and to own the farm. You brought in a chair for her, saying that she should not have to stand in her own home."

"Sure."

"I may have told you that both were called Jahlee. I know I told Mora that."

Hide nodded. "Everybody says the young one was named for her grandmother."

"They are the same person—the person who is walking with us—and an inhuma."

Jahlee hissed. "My secret! You swore!"

"I swore I wouldn't tell unless I was forced to. I am forced to now. Hide is my son, and you will seduce him if you can. Don't deny it, please. I know better."

Giving her no time to reply, I spoke to Hide. "Honesty compels me to tell you that Jahlee is not an inhuma at present. She is a human being here, exactly as we are, and I believe for the same reason. But if we return to our real whorl, and I believe that we will, she will be again what she was before we came. Someday soon you will take a wife, as I did when I was younger—"

I felt a strange confusion, and having no mirror looked down at my thick-fingered hands, turning them this way and that.

"You look different." With more penetration than I had ever given him credit for, Hide had discerned my thoughts. "Maybe we all do."

I shook my head. "You don't."

"You really look a lot more like my real father here. You're taller than he was and older, but you look more like him than you used to."

"You were lying when you called him your son! I should have known!"

"He is my spiritual son," I told Jahlee, "and I was not lying—though he himself believes I was. I was going to say, Hide, that you will soon marry. I was a year younger than you are when your mother and I were married. Go clean to your marriage bed. It is better so."

"Yes, Father." He nodded slowly.

I turned to Jahlee. "I can take us back, or at least I think it likely that I can. If I do, I believe that you will be what you were. Do you wish me to do it now?"

"No!"

"Then watch your tongue, and put on clothing when you can find some."

Oreb sailed over our heads, a miniature airship. "Big wet!"

"He's right." Jahlee pointed, and I caught the glimmer of water ahead.

It was a mighty river, the largest I have ever seen, a river so large that the farther bank was nearly invisible. A wide and ruinous road of dark stone ran beside the water, which lapped its edges in places, leaving the great, dark paving blocks slimed and filthy in a way that recalled the sewer on Green. Guided by Oreb, we followed this ancient road, walking upstream as nearly as I could judge and forced to adjust our steps from time to time by wide gaps in its spalling, rutted pavements.

In a troubled voice, Hide said, "If we went back, we could take the Duko to a doctor in Blanko, couldn't we?"

"No!" Jahlee caught his arm. "Please, Cuoio. Think of me."

"He's trying not to," I told her, "but finds the effort futile. We could indeed take Duko Rigoglio to a physician in Blanko, Hide, a daylong ride for a well-mounted man. Will he still have his wound if we return to Blue, do you think? A knife wound he can show to a physician?"

He glanced quickly at me, surprised, then looked away.

"We are spirits here. Watch." I extended my hand, and my black-bladed sword took shape, floating before us until I reached out and grasped it—and felt it grasp me in return. "My staff has been left behind," I told Jahlee, "and it is better to have something, perhaps."

Hide slung the slug gun with which he had been guarding our prisoners and touched my arm. "If you can do that, Father, can't you heal the Duko?"

"I doubt it, but I will try."

Rigoglio must have heard us; I saw him look back at us—by then he was walking with his arms over his friends' shoulders—and the pain in his eyes.

"Would you want him back on Blue," I asked Hide, "with his spirit wounded and bleeding inside him, invisible to us and beyond our help? That is what befell certain mercenaries, who fought for me in the City of the Inhumi."

"I don't understand any of this, Father."

"It's very likely no one does." I softened my voice still more. "I wanted to take us to Green, where Sinew is. I wanted to see him again, as I still do, and I wanted you others—you and Duko Sfido particularly, and Mora and Eco as well, after they providentially appeared—to see what real evil is, so that you might understand why we on Blue must come together in brotherhood before our own whorl becomes what Green already is."

I fell silent, forced to think myself about what I myself had just said.

22

THE BARBICAN AND THE
BEAR TOWER

H ide and Jahlee came in together while I sat here wondering how to begin the next stage of my account. I asked them to summarize what we had seen and done.

"I learned why women weep," Jahlee said; and Hide, "We took the Duko home to die."

I could not do better, and in all honesty most of my notions were worse. "We visited the hill of ruined landers" was the best of mine, perhaps; but it did not satisfy me.

Far from it.

To elicit their opinions I had to explain what I was doing and display my manuscript to date—six hundred sheets and more, with both sides of every sheet covered with the writing as fine as Oreb's quills and I can make it. "Bird help!" he informed Hide proudly. "Help Silk!" And I explained that he presents me with any large feathers he happens to molt from his wings and tail.

"I had a perch for him in my bedroom in Gaon; and because he left me for close to a year, I got into the habit of using his feathers, which I had picked up off the floor. I missed him, you see, and didn't want the women who came in to sweep and dust and so forth to throw them away. I kept them in my pen case, since no one would be so stupid as to throw out the feathers in a pen case even if it were left open."

Hide said, "Sure."

"After that, it seemed reasonable to point them with my little knife as well, which I did while puzzling over one of the matters of law I had to judge. After that . . ." Too late, I fell silent.

"Are you embarrassed for my sake?" Jahlee asked. "It's true I don't know how to read and write, but I'm not sensitive about it. If you want to mortify me, quiz me about cooking."

"It's just that what I had intended to say next would have sounded very arrogant. Hide's mother and I wrote an account of Patera Silk's life up to the time we parted from him. And it seemed to me that by writing an account of my search for him—which is what I've been doing here, or at any rate what I like to tell myself I'm doing—I would be continuing it. So I began with the letter from Pajarocu, and talked about meeting with some of the leading people from our town, and the need for new strains of corn and so on. I brought a little seed from the *Whorl*, by the way, and picked up more in Gaon.

"What we really need, Hide, is not a way of returning to the *Whorl*, but more and better ways of exchanging goods and information among ourselves. If all of the towns here on Blue would share the plants and animals they brought in their landers, much of the pillaging of three hundred years might be undone."

Hide asked, "Is that how long people up in the Long Sun Whorl were going down into those tunnels Mother used to talk about? How do you know?"

"I don't. I only know that it has been about three hundred years since the *Whorl* left the Short Sun Whorl. A bit more than three hundred and fifty, really—three hundred and fifty-five, or some such figure. I was assuming rather carelessly that the pillaging had begun as soon as the voyage, which isn't actually very likely."

Hide scratched his ear. "If it's been three hundred years, or about that . . ."

"Yes?"

"I was thinking about the Duko's old house. Where I shot at the man that stabbed him?"

"The omophagist," Jahlee suggested. "That's what that first man we met beside the river called him."

He had seemed an ordinary-enough man, though we thought him fantastically dressed. He saw that our captive's hands were bound and his feet hobbled, and asked whether we were bringing him to the peltasts. Since I had no idea who those might be, I asked what they would do to him.

"Cut his throat for him and throw him in the river." The stranger laughed, seeing that our prisoner had understood him.

I suggested that he be arrested and tried for stabbing our companion.

"He's an omophagist, sieur. What would be the use of all that? You may as well kill him yourselves and rid the city of him. Where are you from, anyway?"

Terzo, Morello, and Sfido named Soldo; Mora and I, Blanko; and Hide, New Viron.

"I never heard of any of them. Down south, are they?"

With a readiness of wit that surprised and delighted me, Hide said, "We don't think so."

The stranger was eyeing Jahlee. "If women like that one don't wear clothes wherever it is, I'd like to go."

She smiled at him and moistened her lips.

"These peltasts—" I spoke loudly to regain his attention. "Do they administer justice here, and enforce the laws?"

"They're soldiers, sieur. See, the autarch takes them out of the line when they've fought enough and are getting worn down with it. They come back to pick up new men and train them, and meantime, they keep the rest of us respectful, collecting taxes and tolls, and breaking up riots and the rest of it."

"I see. Where might we find some, and a physician?"

"Around here?" He shook his head. "You can't, sieur. There's been nobody much in this part of the city for, well, a good long while."

"How long?" I asked. We had begun to walk again; and he with us, watching Jahlee from the corner of his eye.

"I can't rightly say, sieur." He pointed up the river. "See that white house sticking out? Looks like it's in the water, or just about?"

I shook my head. Hide said, "I see it, Father. It must be three leagues at least."

"Four," Eco declared. "Four, if it's a span."

"My grandfather's," the stranger declared. "He lived there till he died, and that was . . ." He paused, reckoning. "Sixty-odd years ago. He was one of the last thereabouts, and when he went Grandmother moved in with us. Folks say the city loses a street every generation. I'm not saying that's right, but it's close. Five or six streets in a hundred years, depending. So how long right around here? I can't say exactly, but it's bound to be a long time."

"There are seven thousand steps in a league," Sfido muttered to me. "From what I've seen here, the streets are seventy or eighty double steps apart. Say a hundred to be safe. If Eco's correct in his estimate, four leagues, they've been falling down for about two thousand, five hundred years. If your son is, three-quarters of that should be one thousand, nine hundred, unless I've made an error."

Mora looked at Duko Rigoglio, then at me, and raised her eyebrows.

I nodded. "Old though these houses clearly are, I can't believe they're as old as that. No doubt the rate at which they're abandoned was much higher at one time; but if we accept Cuoio's estimate and the error is fifty percent, they're still a thousand years old, roughly."

Jahlee had taken the stranger's hand, and was walking beside him. "I've been thinking about a city we both know, Rajan."

I nodded.

"It's not exactly abandoned. The slaves fix the old buildings a little when we—when they're made to."

Oreb landed some distance off. "Long way! Go fast."

"He says we must hurry," I interpreted for the rest. "If we have to walk even two leagues before we have any chance of finding a physician, he's quite right."

★

★   ★

Although I thought myself well enough to travel, I find I am very tired now, after a short day's ride. We have stopped for the night with a good deal of daylight left. Hide is taking advantage of it to build us—to build me, I should say, since it is clear it is my well-being he has in mind—a little shelter of sticks and pine boughs. We are still in Blanko's territory, I feel sure.

While we ate I read him what I wrote before we left the abandoned farmhouse, for I hope to inspire him to read the entire account eventually, and to that end it cannot be harmful for him to know that he himself figures in it now and then. He was quite curious about the City of the Inhumi, and asked many questions, among them some I had great difficulty answering.

"How old is it?" It was the second time for that.

"As I say, I have no idea, though it must surely be very ancient. There are trees that we here would call large growing from the sides of many of the towers."

"A real big tree's a hundred years old. About that. If you cut it down you can count the rings."

I agreed.

"Say it was a hundred years before one took root—"

"Many hundreds. Those towers were built by the Neighbors, who built everything far better than we men build anything."

"You mean the Vanished People?"

I nodded, watching him as I spooned up the ragout I had made. We have silver cards enough for our needs, and were able to buy mutton, turnips, flour, butter, apples, and salt at a farm we passed.

"How do you know so much about them?"

With another nod I indicated this manuscript. "It's all here. It would require a weary evening to tell you everything, Hide, and in the end you would find out that I actually know next to nothing, though I've spoken with the Vanished People more than once."

"They built that place on Green? Then went away and let the inhumi have it? Why?"

"Because they preferred giving it up—giving both of these whorls up—to living with the inhumi as we do now."

"Why?" he repeated.

I shook my head.

"Don't you know?" He put down his bowl to study me across our little fire.

"No. I think I could guess, but guesses are of little value."

"I'd like to hear it just the same."

I shook my head again.

"All right." He picked up his bowl. "This is pretty good. What's the hot stuff?"

"Ginger."

"You didn't get that around here."

"I got it out of my bag, having brought it from Blanko when Duko Sfido and I left there with our troopers. I'd had more than enough camp food when I was in the hills with General Inclito, so I bought some spices there and took them with me—ginger, red pepper, basil, oregano, and a few others."

"You don't eat much. While I've been with you, you've hardly eaten at all."

"I eat far too much. I try constantly—perhaps I should say I try to try constantly—to keep it in check."

"The spices sound like my father, but that doesn't. Do you like fish?"

I smiled. "Much too much."

"What would you put on it?"

"Lemon juice and black pepper, I suppose; but no one seems to have black pepper here. We had lemons in Gaon, but I don't think I saw a single lemon in Blanko."

"At home. Suppose we were on the Lizard."

"Seawater and vinegar." I shrugged. "It depends on the variety of fish, somewhat. Oil or butter on the kind we used to call white trout—though it wasn't really trout, of course. It tends to be dry no matter how you cook it." I heard his spoon scrape the bottom of his bowl, and added, "There's a bit more in the pot if you want it."

"I'd rather see you eat it."

I shook my head.

After that we sat in silence for a time, and I began to review what I had already written.

"You know, sometimes I think you really are my father."

"I am."

"Sometimes you talk like him, and sometimes you don't. But he was always writing. He'd work all day in our mill, and eat supper. And then he'd write while the rest of us talked or played games. Sometimes he'd get up while it was still dark, and write until the sun came up, then go out and work."

"I was writing Patera Silk's history," I explained. "His life, insofar as I knew it. When I remembered something fresh while I was working, or when I woke up, I wanted to set it down while the impression was still vivid. Don't forget that your mother wrote too—wrote more than I did, in fact."

"She was making clean copies of what you wrote, mostly."

"She knew many things that I did not—what was said in Patera Silk's final meeting with Councilor Loris, for example, and more than once she suggested ideas and approaches I hadn't thought of."

"Have I ever told you my father's name? Or Mother's?"

I lifted my shoulders again, and let them fall. "I don't recall. What difference does it make?"

"I know I told you I had a brother named Sinew, and a twin brother, and since I told about him I probably said his name's Hoof."

"You may have. It's quite likely."

"Only I don't think I told you Mother's or Father's."

"Your mother's name is Nettle. Mine is Horn."

Hide spooned the last of the ragout into his bowl. "You really are my father, aren't you? Something's happened to you to make you look different."

The happiness I knew at that moment is really indescribable; I managed to say something on the order of "That's it exactly, Son," but I cannot be certain just what it was. I may have said, "My son." Perhaps I did.

"You looked a lot more like him in that other place."

I nodded. "There was a mirror in the guardroom of the barbican—I suppose the guards there used it to shave. Didn't you realize when you saw me there in the Red Sun Whorl that your search had succeeded?"

"Jahlee looked like a real woman there."

"She was a real woman," I told him, "there."

"A bad woman."

"Because she tried to seduce you? You have to understand that she has been doing that sort of thing for much of her life, inviting men. Promising much more than she could ever give them. She could never let men see her naked, for example, as we did, or even let them come close when she stood in a strong light. We went to the Red Sun Whorl, and suddenly everything she had pretended so long had become the truth; she was giddy with it. Try to put yourself in her place."

"All right."

"Seducing you would have been an evil act, and would have had a bad effect on your moral and emotional balance; but she did not know it. She knew only that she could actually give the love she had pretended she would give scores of men. I hope I'm making myself clear."

"Then she isn't really bad?"

I shook my head. "She is an evil creature, exactly as you said."

"You talked like she was your friend, but she was going out at night, flying—"

"Fly good!" Oreb seemed to feel that he had been excluded from our talk for too long.

"Out of the window of her room to drink people's blood. She said so. She told me so."

"Did she? I didn't know. I knew she must be doing it of course, but I didn't know she had confessed to you."

Hide looked uncomfortable. "It was after we got back."

"I see. She felt obliged to make her restored nature clear to you."

He could not meet my eyes. "Yeah."

"A grave disappointment."

He did not reply, and when he had finished his meal he stood up and began to build this little shelter.

★

★   ★

There is a marsh here. Hide says he knew of it, but had hoped the ice would be thick enough for us to cross. It is not, and we will have to go around. Quite large, he says. A great man-killer stalks there two-legged like a man, green and quiet, with fangs longer and thicker than a strong man's arm—but only for me, and only when I do not look for it.

Tonight we talked about the Neighbors. I told him about the ruins on the island, and how I had fallen into the pit there, saying, "No wall was higher than my waist."

"You said there're towers on Green that go up and up, higher than the lander."

I nodded. "There are."

"When we were talking about the trees growing out of the walls, you said the Vanished People built better than we do."

"Better than we do thus far, at least."

"Then the place on that island must have been empty, a long long time."

I tried to read his eyes, as he was trying to read mine—tried to learn how much he knew and guess how much he guessed.

"What happened to them?"

I stared out over the marsh. It cannot have been for more than a few seconds, but the whole Red Sun Whorl seemed to rise before me: the starving, vicious omophagist; the cemetery gate through which wisps of fog wandered like lost spirits; the stupid, hard-faced guard before it who had represented our only hope of medical treatment for Rigoglio, and justice.

Surely we did not all speak at once, although it must have seemed so. Rigoglio himself was almost too weak to speak, the coachman had scarcely spoken since we arrived, and I believe Eco and Terzo held their peace. Perhaps Hide and Jahlee did as well—but Mora, Sfido, and I chattered away like monkeys.

The guard seemed not to hear anything we said, but leveled his long weapon at me. It was not a pike or spear, although it resembled both. "Are you a torturer?"

"What?"

"I said, are you a torturer? Are you in their guild?" He jerked his head to indicate something more distant than the cemetery that shingled the broad hillside behind him with stone.

I said no, not so much to deny it as because I did not understand him.

"The Matachin Tower?"

I shook my head and said that I had never heard of such a place.

"You've got that sword," he pointed to it, "and those clothes."

"I do, but I'm a stranger here."

Morello said, "The Duko's been stabbed." With an expressive gesture, he pointed out the wound. "We've bandaged him, but he's lost too much blood."

The guard nodded; if he had understood, nothing in his face showed it.

"He needs a physician," Mora declared.

Sfido added, "Or captors with sense enough to let him die."

Morello protested, and Hide stepped between them.

Colonel Terzo blurted, "If our Duko dies, he dies too!," and shot the omophagist a look of venomous hatred.

Mora's eyes flashed. "You're not master here!"

"Tie my hands then, and carry Rigoglio yourself. I say that if Rigoglio dies, he dies!"

Eco growled. His hand was on the hilt.

"I'd sooner set him free," Mora told Terzo angrily, "than let you kill him. I'd sooner give him his knife back and let him kill you."

The guard shouted for silence, Oreb croaked, "No talk," and Jahlee giggled.

"Nobody's killing nobody." The guard turned his strange weapon on the omophagist. "Not unless I give the order."

"Well said," I told him.

"And you—where's your sword?"

I held out my hands. "I have none."

Rigoglio raised his big head as though it were almost too heavy for him to lift. "Our friend is a witch, a strego. As you see."

"That does it!" The guard beckoned to Jahlee. "Are you with them?"

"Do you want me to be?"

He stared at her as if unable to think of a reply, cursing in a monotonous whisper.

"No die!" Oreb was speaking to Rigoglio, and I bent to listen to him, realizing that Oreb had heard something I had not.

"Don't feel pity for me, Incanto." I could scarcely make out the words. "I don't mind anymore."

Sfido asked me, "Can't you breathe new life into him?"

I shook my head yet again. "I've tried. I thought you wanted him dead."

"I do. But I want him standing before a wall to have his brains blown out."

The guard was taking off his military cloak. He gave it to Jahlee. "You put this on. Put it on now."

"Red's a good, dramatic color, isn't it?" She threw it over her shoulders and spread it wide, one foot on tiptoe, the knee bent. "Can you make a mirror for me, Rajan?"

"Perhaps I could," I told her. "I won't."

"You don't have to. I see myself reflected in his eyes." She told the guard, "You can look. Go ahead. You can touch, too, if you're nice."

* * *

For a moment I had feared that Hide might shoot him. His voice shook me from my reverie instead. "Father?"

"Yes. What is it?"

Fog was rising from the marsh like the fog that had risen from the river as that other-whorlly evening grew chill. I thought of Nettle's seeing the ghosts rise from Lake Limna on the last summer that she and her parents had vacationed there.

"What were you thinking about, Father?"

"Fogs and mists. They are almost as insubstantial as shadows, Hide. Yet they can unite our experiences in bonds of iron."

Following my eyes, he too looked out over the marsh. A solitary bird flew there, and for a moment I supposed that it was Oreb; but it flew on, intent like me upon returning to its nest.

"There was white sea fog," I told Hide, "a much thicker fog than this, when Krait and I put out in the sloop to look for Seawrack."

"Who's that?"

"The singer that Colonel Terzo and I hear at times."

Hide was silent once more and so was I, remembering the caresses of two lips and a single hand.

At length. "Father, can I ask you an important question?"

"Of course."

"It's going to seem pretty foolish to you. Probably it will. But it's important to me just the same."

"I understand, my son."

"When . . . Sometimes you act like my questions aren't very important."

I nodded. "Sometimes you question me out of mere curiosity, or when I'm deep in other thoughts. I have complaints to make of you, Hide, just as you have complaints to make of me. Perhaps we ought to be more tolerant of each other."

"I'll try. This is my question, Father. When you were my age, did you understand the whorl you lived in? The Long Sun Whorl?"

"When I was your age, Hide, I no longer lived there. Your

mother and I had been married, your brother Sinew had been born, and we were here on Blue." Recollections of struggle and despair displaced the golden days. "We weren't living on the Lizard yet, but we were here."

Hide began to speak; I raised my hand. "To answer your question, when I was your age I understood neither the Long Sun Whorl nor this one in which I was then living. I still don't. I understand more than you, perhaps. Perhaps. But I don't understand everything. You believe that I'm trying to withhold knowledge from you."

"I know you are, Father." His tone was firm and a little angry.

"I've already told you a great deal. A great deal that you've paid scant attention to, and a great deal that you've rejected because it has not fallen in with your preconceptions."

Grudgingly, "Sometimes."

"As you say. When I was younger than you are now, Hide, and lived in the *Whorl,* my father tried to teach me a great deal about his shop and its affairs. He sold paper, quills, ink, pencils, account books, and the like. I know I've told you about that."

"Yes, Father."

"I shut my ears to it. I have often wished since that I had heard him with the greatest attention. He wanted me to operate his shop, you see, when he grew old. I was determined not to. At times when I felt I had your entire attention, I have tried to tell you what I have, in ways that I believed you might recall after many years."

"I'm listening, now, Father. Really I am."

I, too, was listening, in the same way that I stopped to listen again a minute or two ago. Mostly I was listening for any sound that might herald Oreb's return; but I heard only the snort and stamp of one of our horses, and the slow beating of wings wider and softer than Oreb's.

"Aren't you going to tell me anything?"

"Perhaps. Hide, there is one matter, one very important matter, upon which I cannot speak. In the past I've tried to turn the subject when you came too near to it, and I suppose I will again."

"You understand about the Vanished People. I know you do."
"I do not."

He ignored it. "It seems to me like they're the key. If I could just understand them, I'd understand everything, even that place we went to when you thought we were going to Green. Only it wasn't Green, was it?"

I shook my head.

"What was it?"

"Duko Rigoglio said it was the Short Sun Whorl, the whorl from which he had been taken by force long ago to be put aboard the *Whorl*. To be put into the Long Sun Whorl, I ought to say, perhaps."

"But it was way too long, Father. You said that yourself. Thousands and thousands of years."

I nodded. "So I did, and so it was. That is why I will not call it the Short Sun Whorl."

His next question surprised me. "Do you think they buried him in that big cemetery?"

"Rigoglio? No."

"They said they would."

"So they did."

The guard had locked the gate, saying he was doing us a favor. "I could take you up the short way, there's a break in the wall up there, and I know how to find it."

I remarked that the long road was often the shortest in the long run.

"Only we'd have to go through the Old Yard, and come up on the barbican from in back. That's not regular." He paused. "Some that went in the Old Yard might not come out, too, if you take my meaning. Now get moving, all of you."

I walked beside him, Hide just ahead of us. "Are you bringing us to a physician?"

"To the lochage."

"Your officer?"

He nodded. "What's her name? The one with my cloak?"

"Jahlee."

"Jahlee! You get back here!"

She smiled at him. "Were you afraid I was going to run away?"

"You wouldn't get far, but you wouldn't be any use to me after, either."

Hide shot a glance at him that I hoped he did not see.

"That's mine you got on, and that means you're mine. Get me? You're not with the rest, you're separate."

"And yours." She had taken up a position on his left (I myself was on his right), and she linked her arm with his.

It had been a long and a weary walk, and we were all tired already. Duko Rigoglio had collapsed. His friends had carried him until they could carry him no longer; then the guard had stopped a wagon and compelled the driver to take all of us to the barbican, a low, frowning, thick-walled fortress built on arches over a dry ditch.

"We'll bury him there." The guard had jerked his thumb toward the cemetery. "Only not up here. Close to the river."

I shook my head. "He must live."

But the lochage was of the guard's opinion and told me that I was a master of the torturers' guild.

"I am not," I insisted. "We are poor travelers, visitors. We reached this city of yours only today, following the river north. I have never tortured anyone, and never will."

"He had a sword, too," the guard told the lochage, "only he did something with it when I wasn't looking. The rest say he's a witch."

The lochage nodded thoughtfully, dipped his pen, and scribbled on a scrap of parchment.

"He needs blood," Jahlee told him. "Understand, I don't care if he lives or dies. It's nothing to me. But he needs blood. He's bled nearly dry, anybody can see that."

The lochage looked up from his scrap of parchment. "Are you with them, strumpet?"

"I was, but I'm with him now." She pointed to the guard.

"Then get her out of here."

The guard obeyed.

The lochage motioned to me. "You're the leader?"

"I suppose so."

"Then I'm holding you responsible for the rest. Do you know where the Bear Tower is?"

I insisted quite truthfully that I had never been to this city before and had no idea where anything was.

"I'll send a boy with you." He handed me the parchment. "I've told them to doctor him, or try to, and put the rest of you up tonight. They get him." He pointed to the omophagist. "That's their pay. He'll die in the pit, which is better than he deserves."

I started to protest.

"He stabbed your friend, didn't he? You saw it?"

I nodded.

"All right then. Let him go fight a mastiff."

The omophagist spat at the lochage then, and the guard struck him methodically twice, forehand and back.

"Now, listen to me," the lochage said. "Your friend's likely to die. I've seen more wounds than I ever wanted to, and I think he'll die tonight. The bear keepers throw their dead beasts out with the refuse. I've told them they can't do that with him. It's all in that order I just gave you. They're to bury him like one of their own guild."

23

WHY ARE THE INHUMI LIKE US?

Father?"

I looked up at Hide, half expecting to see the stone walls and smoldering cressets of the guardroom. The desolate wastes of the marsh stretched behind him instead, eerily illuminated by starlight and Green's virescent glow.

"Why did the Vanished People die out here before they did there?"

"On Green you mean?"

"Uh huh. You were looking at it."

"So I was. Because of the depredations of the inhumi."

A breathless voice from the shadows beyond our fire said, "I see I'm just in time," and both horses neighed in fright.

I motioned to Hide. "See to our horses, my son. They'll bolt if they're not well tied."

Jahlee stepped into our circle of light, tossing back long, sorrel-colored hair that was not her own. "Never mind, Hide. I'll stay away from them."

"Go." I motioned to him again, and she snickered.

I said, "You've been close enough to frighten them twice. Why have you come?"

"You know."

I shook my head.

"To complete your son's education."

"I should kill you instead of inviting you to sit down." I listened again—this time to Hide, who was speaking to the horses to quiet them.

"Do you have a needler?"

"If I did, I wouldn't tell you."

"I suppose not. You're not going to kill me. Not really."

I shrugged. "Perhaps. Perhaps not."

"You care what your gods think, and you know I have a human spirit."

"Stolen."

"I was one of you when we went to that place, that old, rotten city."

Hide rejoined us. "Where the Duko died?"

Jahlee nodded. "They treated him with herbs and things when he needed blood. I told them."

I said, "You are an acknowledged expert, but they cannot have known that."

Hide asked her, "What are you doing here? Are you coming with us?"

She smiled, her heavy, crimson lips tight. "I may."

"All the way to New Viron?"

"Farther, I hope."

"I won't do what you want," I told her flatly, and Hide turned his puzzled expression from me to her and back.

"I'd like to show you Green," Jahlee explained to him. "It's the whorl on which I was born and on which I grew up, just as your father was born and grew up on that little white one he tries to point out to you sometimes."

"The Long Sun Whorl? I've seen it. Can I ask a question, Jahlee, while you're here?" He waited for her nod. "I'd like to ask you and Father both."

"Yes." Her intonation answered a question that Hide had not yet asked, and she favored him with the tight-lipped smile that hid her toothless gums.

"Why did the trooper who'd been watching the cemetery gate beat you? I don't know his name."

"It was Badour." For a moment her eyes watched something far away. "We had a falling-out, Hide. Men and women frequently do. Ask your father about that."

"I doubt that you will, Hide. But if you did, I would tell you that the fallings-out men have with women, and that women have with men, are in no essential way different from the fallings-out that men have with other men, and women with other women. Whenever a man and a woman come to words or blows, fools are quick to attribute it to the differences between the sexes. The sexes differ much less than they wish to believe, and such differences as are real tend less to promote strife than to prevent it."

He nodded slowly.

"The differences between an inhuma such as Jahlee and a human woman—Mora, for example—are far more profound than those between a man and a real woman. Have you ever seen an inhuma's fangs? Or an inhumu's?"

"No, Father." He paused. "I'd like to."

Jahlee told him, "Well, you won't see mine!"

"We human beings have fangs too, in some sense. We usually call them the eyeteeth, because they originate under the tear ducts." I drew back my lips and touched the small, somewhat pointed teeth that go by that name. "It doesn't trouble us when others see them, however. An inhuma's fangs are hollow, like a viper's; but instead of injecting poison as a viper does, an inhuma uses hers to inject her saliva, which keeps your blood from clotting, and then to withdraw the blood. You've been bitten by a leech at some time or other, I'm sure. They were only too common around Lake Limna when I was young; and they are equally common here, and a good deal larger."

Hide nodded again, and gestured toward the marsh. "I was bitten right here. I didn't have a horse then, so I got a man to take me across in his boat." He swallowed and drew a deep breath. "Silk was over here, they said. Over on this side. That was what I'd heard, and I knew you'd gone to look for him, Father. So I thought you might be with him."

I shook my head.

"Anyway, that's why I went across. I gave him some things I'd brought from home, and he poled us across. It took two days."

"And in the course of them, you were bitten by a leech."

"Yeah, a big blue one. It felt soft and slimy, but it was really tough."

I smiled, or at least I tried to. "That is a surprisingly good description of the inhumi. When you know them as well I do, you'll appreciate the justice of my remark."

Jahlee hissed, "Is this your thanks for my hospitality?"

"Fundamentally, yes. It is always a service to prevent someone from becoming worse than she is already."

"I pulled it off," Hide said, "and the place on my leg bled a lot. The inhumi are like that, isn't that what you're saying? They're like leeches?"

"Much more like them than may at first appear."

"Only they can fly, can't they? That's what everybody says."

I nodded.

"Leeches can't. People can't either, except in a lander or something. But we'd like to." He looked at Jahlee. "Could you show me?"

She shook her head.

"I understand about the teeth, but it must be wonderful to fly. It's not like I'd make fun of you or anything."

"No!"

He turned back to me. "I've seen it, but only when I was a long way away. They look kind of like bats?"

"Somewhat."

"Only their wings don't move real fast, I suppose because they're so much bigger. You saw them up close, I bet, on Green."

"Here too. I know I've mentioned Krait to you. He took wing once when he was close enough for me to touch him, because he was very frightened."

"Of you!" Jahlee spat.

"No. I gave him far too much reason to be afraid of me, but it was not of me that he was afraid at that moment."

Hide asked her, "Can you tell me what that trooper was fighting with you about?"

"I . . ." She fell silent, darting a glance at me. Her face, the face that she had molded and painted for herself, looked less beautiful than angry in the firelight.

"May I tell him?" I asked. "To help complete his education, as you say. It would be good for him to know."

"You don't know yourself!"

"Of course I do. I saw your trooper. Badour, isn't that what you said his name was? In the Bear Tower, as well as you and your bruises. I'm trying to be polite, you see. I haven't pledged myself to keep that secret."

"Then tell me, Father. It sounds like something I ought to know about. You said so yourself."

"I will, if Jahlee won't—or if she tries to deceive you."

She spat into the fire. "What a fool I was to come here!"

"Then go. No one will hold you here against your will."

"I can fly. I'm not your dog, and I won't do my little trick just because you tell me to, but I can."

"Surely you can. I've never denied it. Like Hide, I envy you that ability."

"I might be able to find a way across this swamp. It would be of service to you."

I shrugged. "Oreb's doing that now. Looking for a way across."

Hide said, "Sometime I want to ask you about him, too."

"Why he looked as he did in the Red Sun Whorl? Because he is more nearly human in spirit than he appears, I suppose, and larger, too."

Hide shook his head. "Why he's with us now. Why he was with you when I first met you. I mean, when they said you wanted to see me and gave me a horse and sent me back. I read some of that book you and Mother wrote. I know you didn't think we did, any of us. But we did."

"I'm flattered."

"He was Silk's bird. That's what you said in there. Silk's pet bird."

Jahlee laughed. She has a good laugh, but I found it unpleasant then. "Haven't you noticed that his bird calls him Silk?"

"I am his owner," I explained to Hide. "I feed him, play with him, and talk to him; therefore he calls me Silk, the name he is accustomed to give his owner. Haven't you noticed that he knows very few names? He calls you 'boy,' and Jahlee 'bad thing.' "

Hide nodded. "He doesn't know a lot of words, but he's really good with those he knows."

Jahlee rose. "Useless! Utterly useless! I flew thirty leagues to offer my friendship and my love. What a fool!"

When she had vanished in the darkness, Hide said, "I wonder where she'll go now? Back to the farm?"

I shook my head. "Its rightful owners will have reclaimed it by now, I would think." I sighed and tugged at my beard, my head overfilled with thoughts. "You've complained that I don't teach you enough. If I labor to teach you a little about the inhumi now, and perhaps a bit about the Vanished People—you seem very eager to learn about them—will you listen and store it up?"

He raised his hand solemnly. "I swear by all the gods that there are that I'll remember every word."

"Be careful of what you swear to," I told him. "The thought of your failures will haunt you as you grow older.

"About the inhumi first. They love abandoned buildings. You know what happened in the farmhouse in which we slept. The threat of war drove the family out, and Jahlee moved into it almost at once, perhaps that same day. Duko Sfido and I arrived with our troops and found her occupying it. We assumed that she had a right to be there. I identified her unconsciously one night when I heard her voice without seeing her face, which was then that of a toothless old woman and very different indeed from the starved, sensual face I had seen her wear in Gaon."

"They can just do that? Change the way they look?"

"Correct. They mold their features with their fingers, as a

sculptor does a piece of clay, and augment their artistry with cosmetics. What I began to say was that whenever you come upon what appears to be an abandoned house—or anything of that kind—and find that it is not really abandoned, that someone is in fact living in it, you should be very suspicious of that person."

"I will be."

"Fine."

Hide stared thoughtfully into the fire for a moment or two. "Couldn't Jahlee come back with a new face, pretending to be someone we didn't know?"

"Certainly, though I flatter myself that I would see through her imposture before long."

"Could I? I mean, isn't there some way I could tell she was a inhuma?"

"No certain way, unless you saw her feeding or flying." I considered the matter. "Be very suspicious of a man with powder on his face, or anything of that kind, and of a woman who wears more powder, more rouge, and more perfume than is customary." Recalling Fava, I added, "Also of a child who wears any at all. Be careful, too, of anyone who appears not to eat, or to eat very little."

"Somebody animals are afraid of," Hide offered. "Jahlee scared our horses, and Oreb doesn't like her."

"Very good. Most of all, be careful of anyone whose fingers seem clumsy, who has never learned to write or says he or she has not, and has difficulty effecting simple repairs, tying knots, or making common objects from wood. Hands are not natural to them, you see; because they are not, their minds never develop in that way as much as ours do. Imagine a baby who had no hands until he was old enough to make crude ones for himself."

"You said they were like leeches." Hide looked thoughtful.

"No doubt I did. Certainly there are marked similarities."

"When Hoof and I were real little we used to play in the pools up above your mill."

"I remember."

"One time we found a really pretty one, that had a lot of

pretty little fish in it, and spotted frogs. Green with blue spots, I think." He fell silent, and looked uncomfortable.

"Yes. What about it?"

"Well, while we were looking at them we saw this one leech, a red one. It was pretty big. It was swimming right at one of the frogs, and me and Hoof yelled for it to look out. You know how kids do?"

"Surely."

"Only the frog didn't pay any attention, and just about the time it opened its mouth I figured out that it thought the leech was a fish, and it was going to eat it."

To encourage him, I said, "They can't be eaten, not even by Oreb. I suppose it must be some chemical in their slime."

"Yeah. The frog got it in its mouth and spit it out, and it swam around in back where the frog couldn't get at it, and fastened onto the back of its head. When we came back there was a dead frog, only the leech was gone. What I was thinking of was they don't look enough like fish, not really, to fool us. But that one fooled the frog, he thought it was a little fish, and it probably fooled the fish, too. Jahlee fooled me the same way until you told me. I thought there was two women in the house, an old one and the young one, but they were both her."

I nodded.

"You said they made their hands. Could they make paws instead? Like dog or something?"

"I suppose they could. I've never seen it."

"And could they fool a real dog then?"

"I doubt it."

"You said you were going to tell me a lot about the Vanished People." His voice challenged me.

"I can't have said I'd tell you a great deal, because I don't know a great deal myself. But I will tell you something, and try to make it something that will bear upon the subjects we have been talking about tonight."

Oreb swooped to a landing on the handle of my staff, which lay across my legs. "Bird back! Bad thing!"

"Never mind. Did you find a way in which we can take our horses through the marsh? Or around it?"

"Bird find." He ruffled his feathers and spread his wings to make himself appear larger. "Come bird!"

"Not now. We must sleep. We will be very grateful, though, if you'll guide us in the morning."

Hide said, "Now I suppose you'll want to go to bed, and I'll never get to hear what you were going to tell me."

I shook my head, listening to the uneasy motions of the horses I had just mentioned to Oreb.

"Then tell me now." To give weight to his words, he added wood to our fire.

"I've told you that the depredations of the inhumi drove the Vanished People from Blue."

He nodded.

"Have you seen them? I mean the Vanished People; I know you've seen the inhumi only from a distance, save for Jahlee."

"No, never. People say you have. They say you talk to them and all that. I don't see how you could if they're really gone."

I sighed. "I grow tired of hearing what people say. Which people were these, and how did they know?"

"Colonel Sfido. I don't know how he knew. He was trying to find out things from me, anyway. He wanted to know how you did it, but I couldn't tell him."

"He had heard rumors from the mercenaries, I imagine, and from our troopers."

"Donna Mora said so, too. When we were all in the Bear Tower? She said, 'Your father talks to the Vanished People and calls them his neighbors, and whisks us off to other whorls in the blink of an eye. But you don't know a thing about all that, do you?' She was teasing me, sort of. I said I really didn't, and she laughed. I liked her, and she can't be a whole lot older than I am."

"She is younger. Two years younger at least."

Hide stared at me and shook his head.

"If you won't believe me about Mora, whom you've seen and

talked to and shared food with, why should you believe me about the Vanished People, whom you have never seen?"

Oreb championed him, croaking, "Good boy."

"Yes, he is. But he is skeptical and credulous by turns, as young men usually are, and very often skeptical of the truth and credulous of half truths and outright fabrications. Mora is substantially your junior, Hide, as I said; and if you could have seen her a month ago, you would have no doubt of it. May I burden you more? You may be as skeptical as you desire, yet it is the truth just the same."

"All right. What is it?"

"Adolescents are simply those people who haven't as yet chosen between childhood and adulthood. For as long as anyone tries to hold on to the advantages of childhood—the freedom from responsibility, principally—while seeking to lay claim to the best parts of adulthood, such as independence, he is an adolescent."

Hide stared at the flames and said nothing.

"Eventually most people choose to be adults, or are forced into it. A very few retreat into childhood and never leave it again. A larger number remain adolescents for life."

"I—" He paused and swallowed. "You mean Donna Mora grew up just by saying so?"

"Of course not. She couldn't, because no one can. She has married, and not to seek a new father—as so many young women do—but to become a full partner with Eco. She's become a new leader for the people of Blanko by the only possible means: that of offering her leadership when leadership was needed."

"You taught her all that?"

"No. I counseled her once or twice. So did Fava, I'm sure. So did her father. But what she's done, she's done herself, because she's the only person who could possibly do it."

"You don't think I'm grown up yet. An adult."

"I think that you are trying very hard to become one, and that you will soon succeed." I tried to make my voice, which I know is nearly as harsh as Oreb's, more gentle. "There must have been a time when Mora, too, was trying very hard to make herself an adult, though neither of us witnessed it. She was riding north then, or imprisoned by the Soldese."

"I've got to think about this, Father. I will tonight."

"Good."

"Can I ask about you? You don't have to tell me if you don't want to."

"Certainly. Adulthood was forced on me, in some sense, when I came to our quarter from the schola; but the change really occurred in the tunnels, when we were fighting the Trivigauntis and trying to reach the lander. My father had stayed behind in Viron—I'm sure I've told you this."

"Some of it. Go on."

"But your grandmother was there, and my younger brothers and sisters. So was your mother."

I, too, peered into the flames, remembering. I had not seen our quarter burn, having been aboard the Trivigaunti airship at that terrible time; but it seemed to me that I saw it then: old shiprock buildings that glowed with heat and crumbled, and troopers and soldiers clashing in the ruins.

"Go on," Hide repeated.

"When we reached Blue, my mother wanted to treat me as a child again, and my younger brothers and sisters wanted me to be one of them, as I had been in the *Whorl*. So Nettle and I left them, and got Patera Remora to marry us. You have aunts and uncles and cousins that you have scarcely seen, as you must know."

"Sure. And you and Mother moved out to the Lizard to get away from them."

"We went there, yes. Not for that purpose. I wanted to build the mill, which meant I had to have a good fall of water in a place to which the logs could be floated. I also had to have unclaimed land, since we couldn't afford to buy any. If I'd known how hard it was going to be . . ." I shrugged.

"Why'd you want to know if I'd seen the Vanished People? Are you going to show them to me?"

I had not thought of it and had to consider. "If I can, yes. But

I wondered how human they appeared to you, if you had seen them. When I have, their faces have always been in shadow. That may not be true for everyone."

"Aren't they people like us, only four arms and four legs?"

"I doubt very much that they looked exactly as we do, Hide. No doubt the Outsider made them from the dust of this whorl, just as he formed us from the dust of the Short Sun Whorl—that is what it says in the Chrasmologic Writings, and it's proven by the fact that the human body returns to dust in death—but there could be little point in creating us in one place and creating us again in another. Besides, the dust of that whorl can scarcely be identical to the dust of this one."

I was silent after that, thinking of our night in the Bear Tower, where Mora had mentioned the Neighbors and Rigoglio had died. Doubtless I was only staring into our fire as I had before; but I seemed to see the Old Court again, dark, cold, and sinister, so far below the little window of the little room the Bear Leaders had assigned to Hide and me. Across it stood the torturer's tower, against which even the Bear Leaders had warned me, a lander huge and sleek still although black with age and missing a few plates. To one side, the Witches' Keep (as it was called), yet more decayed. To the other, the Red Tower, ocher with rust. On Blue as on Green, we would have called all three landers. They were thought of as buildings on the Red Sun Whorl, and had accumulated accretions of masonry, dwarfish growths of brick and stone as hallowed by time now as the landers themselves.

I had died in a room not very different from the room I occupied there, in just such a lander, and the memory of death returned to me with a poignancy I have seldom felt. I looked up at the stars then, which were brighter then than they had been by day, and more numerous; but I could not find Green there, or Blue, or the *Whorl*, or even the constellations Nettle and I used to see when Sinew was small and we spread a blanket on the beach and sat side by side there long after sunset, her hand in mine as we stared up at the stars.

Hide spoke and I looked up, although I had not understood him.

"I wondered what you were thinking about, Father."

"About Duko Rigoglio's death in the lander."

Hide nodded. "You looked so sad."

"Good Silk!" Oreb declared.

"Aren't you going to tell me anything else about the Vanished People tonight?"

"Not until you consider what I've said about them already."

"I think I have."

I was weary, at that stage of weariness in which one tells oneself that one will lie down for a moment, but not to sleep. "As you wish."

"There was something I wanted to ask about. A lot of them, really. You said the Vanished People probably don't look much like us."

"I suppose I did."

"Only the inhumi look almost exactly like us. They do to us, I mean, just like that red leech I told about looked like a fish to the frogs."

I said nothing.

"Well, they can shape their faces to look right. You said that yourself. They paint them, too, like women do. Only they talk like us, too, and it seems to me sometimes like they even think like us. Jahlee did, I mean. She got mad at us exactly like a real woman would."

"Go on."

His eyes opened a trifle wider. "You mean you want me to ask you questions?"

"No. I mean that I want you to reason for yourself, Hide. It's good for you, and for the whorl."

"I've gone about as far as I can already. It seems to me like the Vanished People were a lot stronger and smarter than we are. That's what everybody says. So if they were different from us, and the inhumi are so much like us, they ought to have been able to tell the difference pretty easy. So how could the inhumi do so much harm to them? Do you know, Father?"

I asked, "Why are the inhumi like us?"

"Why do I think they are, you mean? Well, Jahlee is, and you said they were. Watching out for people in old buildings and all that. If they had tails or something, we could just watch out for those."

"Not why you think it—you think it because it is true. Why is it true?"

He looked baffled.

"In Gaon—forgive me if I have mentioned this before—men who hunt wallowers weave a wallower out of wicker, and cover it with a wallower's skin."

"You didn't. I don't think so, anyway."

"Then I mention it now."

"You mean they look like us so they can hunt us."

I shook my head. "I mean that they become like us so that they can hunt us. The leech you saw in the pool above our mill looked like a small fish to the frogs, you said."

"Yeah. I think so."

"Suppose it had been unable to swim."

He was silent; then, "They really do make themselves just like we are. That's what you're saying. Only they couldn't do it if they didn't have us to copy. You're smiling."

"I am. I'd scarcely hoped to take you this far without violating an oath, which I will not do. I commanded more than twenty inhumi in Gaon, Hide. We were at war with Han, and I found them extremely useful, both as spies and as assassins; the spells I'm supposed to have cast there were little more than their activities behind our enemy's line. But when I left the city by boat afterward, they tried to kill me."

"Why?"

"Because they were afraid I wouldn't keep the oath that I had sworn to your brother. He told me something in confidence that they believe might harm them greatly if it became widely known. I would probably violate my oath if I agreed; but I doubt that it—"

"Bad thing!"

"Yes. Certainly, Oreb."

"If they tried to kill you, I think you ought to tell everybody."

"For safety's sake, you mean."

Hide nodded.

"I won't secure my safety at the price of my honor. There have been times when I've longed for death, and even now I have no great fear of it. There's never been a time when I've longed for dishonor."

He nodded again, slowly. "I was going to say this isn't about the Vanished People. Only I have a feeling it is, that you'll tie it up someday."

"I'll tie it up, as you put it, right now. You said that the Vanished People were wiser and stronger than we are, which is certainly true. You also said that the inhumi become like us, not merely in appearance but in speech, thought, and action, in order to prey upon us. That is true, too. They cannot make themselves precisely like us in every regard, of course. Their legs are never as strong as ours, a weakness that they sometimes disguise as old age, as Patera Quetzal did. Nettle and I have mentioned Patera Quetzal often in your hearing, I believe."

"Sure."

"He made himself so much like an elderly augur that he became head of the Chapter in Viron. For thirty or forty years he deceived everyone, and if he had not been shot, he might be deceiving us yet. His counterfeit of a human being, though not perfect, was exceedingly good. Wouldn't you agree?"

"It sure sounds like it."

"Since we know that the inhumi preyed upon the Neighbors—the Vanished People, as we call them here—with great success, it seems reasonable that they could counterfeit them at least as well as they counterfeit us, and very plausibly better. Will you agree to that as well?"

Hide shook his head. "I don't see why it should be better."

"Think of the two whorls as they were thousand and thousands of years ago. The Vanished People were here on Blue, the inhumi on Green, where they preyed upon the great beasts in its jungles. They exterminated the Vanished People, Hide, or very nearly—that's why they vanished. Why didn't they exterminate the beasts on Green long before?"

"They wouldn't have had anything to eat."

"True. Did they have the intelligence to think of that? Without human beings to imitate?"

"I see. They were just animals, too. Big flying leeches. You're smiling again. You know, I like it."

"So do I. Eventually the Vanished People found some means of crossing the abyss to Green. Perhaps they built landers of their own—I believe that they must have. They went there, and the inhumi, too, became both powerful and wise, so powerful and so knowing that they hunted the Vanished People almost to extinction. The strengths of the Vanished People became their enemies' strengths, you see. They tried in their desperation to become stronger still, to know more and more and more, and succeeded, and were doomed by that success."

I thought then of the bestial men I had been shown in the Bear Tower, men who had surrendered their humanity, haunted by guilt or despair. Our omophagist had been caged with them; and when he had seen them, and understood what they were, he had striven to speak.

"Father?"

"Yes, my son?"

"Could they, the inhumi, wipe us out too?"

"Of course."

"Then we should have killed Jahlee."

I shook my head to clear it of the cages and the stench. "That would not prevent it."

"It would help!"

"It would not. If anything, it would do more harm. Never forget, Hide, that what we are the inhumi quickly become. Jahlee was an ally in Gaon, and a friend at the farmhouse. She had fought for me and slain my foes, and learned their secrets too, so that she might meet me with them in the garden or whisper them at the window of my bedroom. Suppose that I were to wait until her back was to me, draw the long sharp blade I have not got, and plunge it into her back."

"I wish you had!"

"You would not, if you had seen and heard it. Her terrible scream ringing over this silent, desolate marsh. The hideous, misshapen thing writhing and bleeding at your feet that just a moment before had appeared to be a lovely woman. Try to imagine all that. Can you?"

He said nothing.

"You would have battered her head with the butt of your slug gun then, trying to end her agony. Her wig would have fallen from her head, and her eyes—her eyes, Hide—would roll up to you while she begged for her life, saying please, oh, please, Hide. Mercy for your mother's sake. Mercy! We were friends, I would have lain with you in the Bear Tower if only you had come to me. You know it's true! Spare my life, Hide!"

"No talk!" Oreb commanded.

I spoke again anyway. "You would have struck all the harder, smashing her toothless, blood-drinking mouth with the butt of your slug gun; but you would never be able to forget those eyes, which would return to stare at you—and at me, as well—in the small hours of many nights. When you were as old as I am, you would still see her eyes."

Reluctantly, he nodded.

"And a hundred years from now, every inhumi in the whorl would be a little harder, a little more cruel and proud, because of what we did here tonight. Remember—what we are, they must become."

"All right."

"When the war in Gaon was just about over, I freed my inhumi from their service—Jahlee among them. Why do you think I did that?"

He shrugged uncomfortably. "You didn't need them anymore."

"I could have found a great many uses for them. Believe me, I thought of many. I could have conquered the towns downriver and founded an empire. I could have used them to consolidate my hold on Han, and to tighten my grip upon Gaon. Nettle sent you and your twin to look for me, not so long ago?"

Hide nodded.

"I could have sent my inhumi to fetch all three of you to Gaon, where we would have become the ruling family, the sort of thing that Inclito's family is clearly becoming in Blanko; and when I died, you and your brother would have fought to the death for my throne.

"I rejected those possibilities and surrendered the throne the people of Gaon had given me instead, in part because I know what happened to the Neighbors, or believe I do—because I know that their towers still stretch to the damp skies of Green, when their cities here have crumbled into nameless hills."

I waited for him to speak; he only stared at me, open mouthed but wordless.

"On Green, the Vanished People had done what I had done in Gaon, Hide. They had made the inhumi serve them; and as time passed they had become more and more dependent upon their servants, servants whom they permitted to come here to feed, and perhaps carried here to feed. I myself had allowed my own inhumi to feed upon the blood of the people of Han, you see. It was war, I told myself, and the Man of Han would surely have done the same to us; but I had set my foot upon that path, and I was determined to leave it."

"What happened when all the Vanished People here were dead?" Hide asked in a strangled voice.

"I'm not sure it ever occurred," I told him. "A very few may have survived; a very few may survive here still. But a time came—I doubt that it was more than a few hundred years in coming—when it was no longer worthwhile for the inhumi to come here."

"What happened then?"

"I think you know," I told him, and wished him a good night.

24

SINEW'S VILLAGE

So much has happened since I last wrote that I feel I should begin another book—or end this one. Perhaps I will do both tonight; that would be fitting.

For a long time I sat beside our little fire, writing and watching the stars rise above the scrub-covered hills through which Hide and I had ridden that day. Jahlee had never really gone, I knew. Oreb had testified to that, and testified to it still, although I cautioned him again and again to keep his voice down lest he wake Hide. Our horses had testified to it as well—the inhumi always frighten horses, I believe; perhaps they smell the blood.

I needed no more proof, but I soon had it. The cold winter wind seemed to carry with it a steaming, fetid wind from Green, as a frigid old man, penurious and hoary with age, might bear in his arms the rotten corpse of a beautiful young woman. My eyes were on my paper, squinting and straining to see each letter I shaped there, for it is no easy business to write by firelight. And it seemed to me that to my left, at or beyond the very edge of vision, a great man-killer of Green stalked, each slow and careful stride that crushed the too-thin ice devouring twenty cubits. When I looked beyond the fire, its light revealed wide, dripping leaves in silhouette; and once a moth with wings wider than the sheets on which I wrote, opalescent wings stamped by some god with a strange device of cross and circle, fluttered toward the flames—only to vanish when I blinked.

Jahlee was waiting for me the moment my eyes closed, more beautiful in her embroidered gown than she had ever been when she went naked in the Red Sun Whorl. "This steaming heat becomes you," I told her. "You were made for Green."

She pretended to pout. "I thought this was going to be a great surprise to you, if it happened at all. You expected it all along."

"My son should have joined you here some time ago. He fell asleep long before I finished writing."

She nodded, her face expressive of nothing.

"Did you seduce him? He would have had more than enough time to resume his clothing and go, I imagine."

"That's none of your business!"

"You did not, or you would boast of it."

"I said it's none of your affair. Hasn't it struck you that he may not have wanted to see you? I told him you'd be along."

"Of course. Particularly if you bit him on the neck at climax, as you bit the neck of the trooper who took us to the fort over the ditch."

"I didn't!"

"You didn't bite Hide because you were unable to seduce him. That's what you must mean, since—"

"Boy come!" Oreb sailed overhead, again three times his normal size, and absurdly resembling a feathered dwarf with overlong arms.

"If we continue this fight," I told Jahlee, "Hide and I will drive you away, just as we drove you away from our fire beside the frozen marsh. This is Green, and you are a human being here. Remember Rigoglio? The spittle running from his mouth? The empty eyes?"

She did. I saw her shudder.

"I won't pretend to value your life more highly than you do yourself, but I value it. Let us be friends—"

I had wanted to say, *Let us be friends again, as we were in Gaon, and in the farmhouse by the battlefield;* but she was weeping in my arms, and there seemed no point in continuing.

Hide found us like that, and was well-mannered enough to wait until we separated before speaking. "I found some people, Father. She and I didn't want to talk anymore, so I said I was going to have a look around, and told her to wait here for you."

"I'm not your servant, little boy." Jahlee wiped her nose on her sleeve. "I wanted no more of your company. Your father's twice the man you are."

"I know. Do you want to see them, Father?"

"Yes. Your brother will be among them, I think."

"You don't look very much like—like you used to," Hide blurted. "Not even as much as you did in that other place, with the big river."

I said nothing.

"Me and Oreb will show you, if you want us to."

Half a league brought us out of the jungle and into cleared land where a raised path let us walk with dry feet between wide, flooded fields of rice. The Short Sun glowed behind us like a disk of white-hot iron, sending our shadows, dark ambassadors inhumanly tall, before us. My staff had not come with me; so I made one like it for myself as we walked, watching with amusement as well as interest how its shadow, wan at first, grew thick and black as the staff acquired weight, solidity, and reality.

Blanko, as I have said, is the only walled city I have as yet seen here. Qarya was a walled village; I had seen such villages on Green before, but their walls had been no more than rough palisades of pointed stakes, scarcely more than fences. Qarya's palisade was surrounded by a wide, water-filled ditch; it surmounted a wall of earth faced with brick, and every lofty paling was thicker than a man's body.

"Impressive," I told Hide.

"I'd rather have stone walls like they do in Blanko."

"So would they, I'm sure—and they will have them soon."

Jahlee, clinging to my free arm, looked up quizzically. "What good is all this, when inhumi can fly?"

Half a dozen older men were sitting or lounging by the gate; thinking that they might have overheard her, I changed the subject as quickly as I could. "I have never seen you so beautiful, and I owe it to you to tell you that. The sun is very strong here, and I would have said that no woman's face could endure it without revealing some slight imperfections; but yours does."

She smiled at that, her beautiful, even teeth flashing in the brilliant light.

The oldest man there, a man as white-bearded as I, who sat his rough stool as if it were the throne of Gaon, spat. "She's no inhuma, miralaly, and the lad here's no inhumu. But what about you?"

"I am a man, exactly as you are."

"Push back those big sleeves and show your wrists."

I did, giving my staff to Hide and turning my hands this way and that, by no means certain what it was that he wanted to see.

One of the others, gray and lame, pointed to Jahlee. "This your wife?"

"Certainly not," I told him; she whispered in my ear, "You need only ask, Incanto darling."

"The boy's wife?"

"He's my son. His name is Hide, and he is not yet married. My own name is Horn. This woman is a friend, nothing more and nothing less. Her name is Jahlee."

The white-bearded man hawked portentously and spat, clearly a signal for the others to be quiet. "That's an evil name for any woman."

"Then I'll change it," she told him. "What would you like it to be?"

He ignored her. "What do you want here?"

"We've come to see another son of mine, Hide's older brother Sinew." There was a slight stir as I said this. "He lives here, I believe, and if someone will just tell us the way to his house, we'll trouble you no further."

"You're Sinew's father?"

I nodded.

The white-bearded man eyed the circle of onlookers and selected one. He made a gesture of command, and the man he had designated hurried away.

I started to follow him, but a fat man with an oily black beard blocked my path, saying, "Sinew's the rais-man here. You know that?"

I shook my head. "I didn't, but I'm delighted to hear it. Will he come when that man asks him to?"

"He's not going to. He's going to the maliki-woman by the well. That's the women's place. She'll talk to your woman."

Jahlee laughed as though she were at a party. "You had better be nice to me, Incanto, or I'll tell her all sorts of fascinating lies about you, beginning with the time you ate all those mice."

"Better you told the truth about him—" the black-bearded man began.

Hide drew me to one side, whispering, "He won't know you, or I don't think so."

"Then I'll have to prove that I'm who I say I am, as I did when you and I met."

Jahlee touched my arm. "I think this must be the whatever-they-said woman coming. Do you really want me to talk to her?"

"At first, at least."

She was taller than most women and stiffly erect, hatchet-faced and hawk-nosed. The white-bearded old man made her a seated bow, to which she replied with a frigid smile and an inclination of her head.

"We saw them coming, Maliki," he said. "They had something big flying right over them. Didn't seem like a inhumu, but big enough for a little one. It didn't like our looks in Qarya, and headed back to the jungle 'fore they come to our gate."

Jahlee curtsied. "That was Incanto's pet bird, Maliki. He lets it fly free and come and go as it wants. It's quite harmless, I promise you."

Maliki surveyed us; something about her iron-gray hair, straight and drawn back so tightly that it resembled a helmet, woke a spark of memory that flickered and died.

She turned to Jahlee. "Is Incanto the young one or the old one?"

"The old one, Maliki."

The lame man muttered, "He's Sinew's pa, he says."

She motioned for him to be silent. "What is the young one's name?"

"Cuoio, Maliki."

"It's Hide really," Hide told her, "and my father's name is really Horn."

Maliki did not so much as glance at him. "Are you lying to me, girl? What is your own name?"

"No, Maliki. Cuoio was the name he gave me when we met. I wouldn't lie to you, Maliki."

"You would lie to anyone." Coming nearer, Maliki stroked her hair. "You're very beautiful indeed, and a born troublemaker. I've seen a thousand like you, though most weren't half as good-looking. Where did you sleep last night?"

The question took Jahlee off guard. "Last night? Why, uh . . ."

"Tell me the truth. I'll know if you're lying."

"Bad thing!" Oreb croaked from the shingles of one of the blockhouses flanking the gate. "Bad thing! Thing fly."

Jahlee seized her opportunity. "That's Incanto's bird, Maliki. The one I told you about? It's a talking bird, but what it says doesn't make much sense."

She glanced up at Oreb. "I've never seen one like that. Where did you get him?"

"I didn't, Maliki. He doesn't even like me. He belongs to Incanto."

"Is he Sinew's father?"

"Incanto? I think so. He says he is, and he's, well, he's more truthful than I am."

"Most are." Maliki raised an eyebrow. "Do you love him?"

"Oh, yes!"

"What about his son Cuoio?"

"He's a hateful, ungrateful, vindictive little boy!" Jahlee seemed ready to spit like a cat.

"But a fair judge of women, I would say. Why are you here?"

"You—" Jahlee's eyes flashed. "I don't have to talk to you!"

"You're mistaken. Here we tie a long rope to a girl's feet and drop her in the well. When we pull her up, we generally find her cooperative. Or dead. If she is neither," Maliki smiled like a crocodile, "we throw her in again."

She turned to me. "You're Incanto? Why were you talking to these men?"

"They wouldn't allow us to proceed, and we hoped that they would show us where my son lives, or send someone to bring him here."

"Your son Sinew?" The eyebrow rose again.

"That's right."

"Your real name is . . . ?"

"Horn, as my son Hide told you."

"You were born in the Long Sun Whorl. Don't deny it. What city?"

"I don't. In Viron."

Maliki nodded, mostly to herself it seemed. "Sinew isn't here, though we expect him back shortly. His family affairs are his own, and it isn't my job to settle them. Come with me, all of you."

We followed her as meekly as three sheep down a narrow, dust-soft street lined with thatched log houses not greatly different from most of the houses in New Viron, until we came to a small square in which women sat talking in pairs or stood talking in groups.

"That's the well we'll throw your redhead down." Maliki pointed to the coping. "The water's high at this time of year, so it's not much of a drop. We'll probably have to throw her in several times."

Jahlee shook her head. "Incanto won't let you."

"Incanto—who says his name is Horn—has nothing to do with it. Out of common decency I should warn you that this water isn't safe. It's good enough for washing clothes and watering gardens, but we have to boil it before we can drink it, so try not to swallow any more than you can help."

As we started off again, I asked where she was taking us.

"To Sinew's house. Isn't that where you wanted to go?"

"Yes. Certainly."

"All right, that's where we're going. You can wait for him there. He should be back before dark, but if he isn't, his wife will put you up, probably, if you behave yourself. Do you know her?"

"Slightly. I doubt that she remembers me."

"She's a good swordswoman. When you see her, you'll say she's too fat for it, but she's a good swordswoman just the same. You used to be a good swordsman, or so we heard. I imagine your legs have gone?"

"I've used a sword," I admitted, "though with no great skill. Sinew magnifies my exploits, I'm sure."

"He never talks about you."

She stopped before a log house larger than its neighbors, drew the dagger hanging from her belt, and rapped the door with it.

It was opened by a smiling woman, broader than I recalled her, flanked by two small boys. Maliki said, "We need to come in and talk to you, Bala. Have you got a minute?" I was aware of a slight stench, which I attributed to the boys.

"Yes, yes! Come in! We have fruit. Would you like some wine?"

Maliki shook her head.

"You, sir?"

I thanked her and said I would be grateful for a glass. Hide and Jahlee nodded, and Oreb croaked "Bird drink?" and hopped after us.

"A little water for my bird, please? If you have some that's safe to drink?"

She looked curiously at Oreb, dropped heavily to her knees, and cocked her head as if she were a bird herself. "You're so big! Promise you won't peck Shauk and Karn?"

"Peck fruit!"

Bala looked up at me, her pink face pinker still. "Would he like grapes?"

"Like grape!"

"All right, they're in the bowl. Is he your bird, sir? Will you give him some? Sit down, please. Everybody please sit down."

She hurried away, and Oreb flew to the back of a big chair of smooth, waxed wood to escape the questing fingers of Shauk and Karn.

Maliki sat in a smaller one, leaving two considerable benches for us. "Two boys. They want a girl, naturally, but she never complains."

I had been studying them, recalling Hoof and Hide when they were much younger. "They're not twins."

"No. Shauk is three and Karn must be two now, if I remember Bala's confinements correctly." Maliki leveled her forefinger at Jahlee. "What is your name? I still have not learned it, and I will have to introduce you to Bala."

"You don't like my name here." She looked to me. "Can I give her another one?"

"Of course, Judastree."

"It's Judastree, Maliki."

"I see. And before you changed it?"

"Jahlee."

Maliki addressed me. "You name your woman after flowers in the Common Tongue. We use the high speech here for names and a few other things. Maliki is not really my name, for example. You probably thought it was."

I nodded.

"I am the maliki-woman, the village judge. Your son Sinew is the rais-man, our general if we had a proper horde, if he really is your son. He leads our war band in battle."

"He was always an excellent fighter. I'm sorry he's not here."

"So am I. I would turn this whole matter over to him if he were, but he is out hunting."

Bala, carrying in a tray with glasses and a carafe of wine, overheard this last and looked slightly startled.

"Sinew was always very fond of hunting," I said, "and very good at it. He kept us supplied with meat on Lizard."

Bala put down her tray and pushed a lock of pale hair away from her perspiring face. "You knew him there? He talks about it sometimes, mostly about his mother."

Jahlee said, "Incanto's his father," and Bala stared.

"More precisely, I am his father's ghost," I told her. "We're all three ghosts, in a way—ghosts or dreams. All four, including Oreb."

Maliki snapped her fingers. "That's it! Oreb. I have been going crazy trying to think of it. Have you got me yet, Caldé? I know you tried."

I shook my head. "I've no right to that title."

"No? I intend to call you that anyway, since I can't remember the other one." The corners of her lips lifted by the width of a hair. "Who am I?"

I shook my head.

"I have aged, I know. So have you. It has been nearly twenty-five years."

"Long time!" Oreb spoke to Bala, as well as I could judge.

Maliki did, too. "Sinew's father died here, I believe?"

"We think he must have."

Hide cleared his throat. "Can I talk? I'm Sinew's brother. I really am."

Maliki said, "If the Caldé's bird can, so can you."

"So I'm your brother-in-law." He rose and offered Bala his hand. "That makes you my sister-in-law, and these are my nephews." He laughed. "I've never been a uncle before."

She accepted it, and smiled warmly.

"We're not really here, we're really back on Blue. Only we wanted to see how Sinew was, Father and I did, so we came. And Jahlee came with us because she likes this better. And Oreb."

"Horn or Incanto or Silk or whatever his name really is, is your husband's father to the goddess, I suppose," Maliki told Bala. "His father in the sight of Mainframe, or some such claptrap. I just thought of his other title. Patera? Have I got that?" She looked at me quizzically.

"I've no right to that one either, but yes, you do."

"It means father in their own high speech, which they've practically forgotten. Patera, like papa."

Bala sat down. Her smaller son tried to climb into her lap at once, and she lifted him there. After a moment she said, "I wish Sinew were here."

"So do I," Maliki told her, "but I doubt that it would help much."

"And I'm sorry about the smell. Sinew doesn't want me to go down there and clean up, but I'm going to if he won't do it as soon as he comes back. I'll do it now if you'll stand by for me."

Maliki shook her head. "If I had the time I would, but men should do men's work."

"I'll do it," Hide told her. "You can stand by for me if you want to, I guess. What is it?"

"Prisoners." Maliki's face, always severe, was savage. "We got them in the last big fight, and they're chained in the cellar. Six, Bala?"

Bala shook her head. "Five. One died."

"The woman?"

"One of the men. He'd been shot." She put her hand to her own thick waist. "Sinew brought him upstairs, at the end. He was too weak to do anything, but I tried to keep the boys away from him just the same."

"He's dead 'cause he tried to burn our house," Shauk announced and vigorously nodded his own confirmation.

Oreb muttered, "Poor man."

I said, "I take it that the villages here are warring with one another? It isn't greatly different on Blue. Town fights town."

"Where is your lander?" Maliki inquired with studied carelessness.

"We have none. I was going to ask you—I do ask both of you now—if there isn't a lander near here."

Bala nodded. "The one Sinew's father tried to repair. It won't fly."

"I know."

Hide said, "I guess you need somebody to clean up after the prisoners? That's what the smell is? I could get started right now."

Oreb applauded him with flapping wings. "Good boy!"

"You had better leave that slug gun up here," Maliki told him. "Give it to me."

He looked from me to her. "I'll leave it with Father."

"This is my village!"

I took the slug gun Hide handed me and passed it to her. "So it is. You'll return this to Hide, I'm sure, when he has done a man's work."

She nodded, laying the slug gun across her thighs and eyeing Shauk and Karn warily.

Bala said, "I'll show you. Let me get my sword." She and Hide hurried away.

"You came in a lander," Maliki told Jahlee and me. "Most likely today. I knew it as soon as I saw the girl's hair. I want to know where it is."

"If we had, I'd tell you. We arrived today, you're quite correct about that; but not in a lander. We are not real—not really present in the way you are—exactly as my son told you."

She shook her head. "I would have thought that boy would tell the truth."

"I've heard him try to lie, and he's a very bad liar, just as I am. Jahlee's far better, as you divined at once."

"Bad thing! God say!"

A frosty smile crossed Maliki's face. "Your bird doesn't trust her."

"No," I said. "I do, but he doesn't."

Jahlee grinned at me, leaning back against the rough wall of logs, beautiful enough to rend a thousand hearts.

"I liked you, Caldé," Maliki said. "We all did. General Saba used to say you were the slickest character she ever met, man or woman, and it was a blessing from the goddess that you were so good, because you would have made a terrible enemy. There, I've given you a fine clue. It should help."

I shook my head. "By telling me you were a Trivigaunti? I knew it almost as soon as we met, and confirmation is of no value. As for my supposed cleverness, it doesn't exist, as you should be able to see for yourself. You no more know who I am than I know who you are. The only difference is that I'm aware of my ignorance. You think I'm Caldé Silk, which I find so flattering that I have difficulty denying it. You're quite wrong, nonetheless."

Jahlee asked, "If we sleep here, will we wake up in the morning? Wake up here, I mean?"

"I don't know. I doubt it."

"Then I'm not going to go to sleep. You and Hide will have to keep me awake. I'll keep you awake, too." There was mockery as well as sensuality in her eyes.

Maliki snorted.

I said, "I'd like to find out more about the situation here. Sinew's prisoners attacked this village, clearly. Where did they come from?"

She pointed. "The old city. It's full of them."

"I doubt it. It wasn't even full of inhumi when some mercenaries cleared it for me, though there were more than we liked. They will be far fewer now. Sinew's prisoners are or were their slaves?"

"Yes. We call them inhumans."

"Those men at the gate were afraid we were inhumans. Is that correct? They wanted to see my wrists; they were looking for the marks of shackles, I suppose."

"Right. I knew you were not as soon as I saw the girl's hair. No woman here has hair that well cared for. Did you notice Bala's?"

"I thought it clean and neatly arranged. So is your own."

"Thank you. But if I were to take it down, even you would see the difference."

Jahlee bowed, her long sorrel hair falling over her face.

I said, "I'm surprised the inhumi dare let their slaves have arms."

"I am, too," Jahlee told us, straightening up.

Maliki said, "They take precautions, I feel sure."

"No doubt. Jahlee, you've been here before. May I say that?"

"You just did."

"So I did. May I assume this wasn't done—I mean the arming of the slaves—when you were here?"

She nodded. "There weren't so many humans here then, I think."

"And how long ago was that?"

"I don't know."

"Years?"

She spoke to Maliki, "I was just a little girl when they put me on the lander."

"A lucky girl," Maliki replied.

"Oh, I don't know. I'd stay here if I could."

"But you are only a dream. I know. I hope you can manage without my sympathy."

"That's wrong, what the Rajan and Cuoio have been saying." Jahlee leaned forward, as sincere as I have ever seen her. "This is the real us. They talk like we're really back on Blue, but that's just the thing you bury. We're here."

"I believe the last part, girl."

I had been considering the village, Maliki's judgeship of it, and my son's part in it; and I asked, "Are most of you from Trivigaunte? You must be, since you employ its high speech for names and titles. *Shauk* and *Karn* must be Trivigaunti names—they're certainly not names I was familiar with in Viron. *Bala* is probably a Trivigaunti name as well."

Maliki nodded. "About two-thirds of us are, and the rest are from all over. Your son from Viron, for example."

"He's never seen the city; he was born on Blue. Still, I understand what you mean—he's of Vironese culture."

"Right. When I first got to Viron, I knew it was going to seem very foreign, but I was surprised at how foreign it was just the same. So many things we took for granted at home nobody had heard of there. Now Sinew seems familiar. I mean besides being a friend, which he is. I spent a few months in Viron once and got to know a few of you. The other foreigners here in Qarya are from cities I never heard of at home."

Jahlee sighed. "It must be a big whorl, the Long Sun Whorl, Do you think it's too far for us, Rajan?"

"I doubt that it's nearly as far as the place we visited with the Duko." I turned back to Maliki. "I want to ask you about your lander and the people who came with you from Trivigaunte; but first, I'd like to mention that Patera Quetzal was from this whorl. I know that now. Do you remember Patera Quetzal? He was our Prolocutor."

"Oh, yes."

"For years I've wondered how he reached the Long Sun Whorl. We were told that no landers had left before we got to Mainframe. Were you with us on the airship when we went to Mainframe?"

Smiling, Maliki shook her head.

"That eliminates one of my guesses. I thought you might have been the lieutenant who was in charge of us while we were prisoners."

Still smiling, she said, "I'm older than you think, Caldé."

"Old enough, and wise enough, to tell me how Patera Quetzal reached the Long Sun Whorl from Green?"

She pursed her lips. "Before anybody got here? You're saying he was an inhumu."

I nodded.

"That explains a great deal. I never thought of that back then. In fact, I had never heard of them."

"Neither had I, but I think the inhumi must have been one of the sources for our devil legends. If that's correct, he didn't come to the Long Sun Whorl alone."

"They can fly through the emptiness between Green and Blue. Did you know that, Caldé?"

I nodded again.

"Then they could have flown to the Long Sun Whorl the same way."

Jahlee said, "It's too far."

Maliki made a little sound of contempt. "You lived here as a child, so you're an expert."

"No, I'm not. But I know a few simple things and that's one. You asked about this once in Gaon, Rajan, and I told you I didn't know."

I said, "I remember."

"And I don't. But I do know this. He didn't fly like the

inhumi fly to Blue and back. It can't be done, because no inhumu can do without air for that long. Are you sure no landers left before the time you were talking about?"

I shook my head. "On the contrary. That information was surely incorrect, though I think it was given us then in good faith."

"Then that's the answer, and why ask us? The landers go down full and come back empty, if people let them."

Maliki's smile grew bitter. "That was my mistake, you see, Caldé."

"Call me Horn, please."

She ignored it. "We knew that. The men who went on board had no idea, but our goddess had told the Rani. So I went with them, and the generalissimo and I thought I could report back in a year or two. I went as her spy, if you want to put it like that. But I have done my level best for this colony, and the reason I came originally is no great secret anymore."

"I think I'm beginning to understand. You said Sinew was your general here, the rais-man. Trivigaunte would never have accepted a male general. Was Bala born there, by the way?"

"With all that yellow hair? Certainly not. Her father was, but her mother was one of the women our men picked up here."

"I see."

"What I am about to say is apt to sound conceited, and I hate to sound conceited." There was no hint of humor in Maliki's voice or face. "But a good many landers have landed here, and the colonists in most of them have not done anything like as well. Their men fight the inhumi and their inhumans, and die, and their women scatter. Most die, too, in the jungle. But a few get into other colonies, and that was how it was with Bala's mother. We accepted any women we could get in those days."

"Your lander couldn't return?"

"It could and it did, without me. I should have set a guard on it, but I didn't think it was necessary. Not that we had anyone to spare, anyhow."

"I have an idea," Jahlee said suddenly. "You'll both think it's silly—"

She was interrupted by Bala, who told me, "Your son did everything, Horn. He really is Sinew's brother. I knew it as soon as he started working and began talking to them. He's wonderful, just like my husband." Hide, coming in behind her, flushed and stared at his boots.

I thanked her, and Jahlee said, "He gets it from you, and that's what you ought to do, too. Talk to them. You want to find out how somebody got up to the Long Sun Whorl from here, and they might know. That was my idea, Rajan."

"A good one, I believe. May I go into your cellar to speak with them, Bala?"

"I must come with you," Maliki told me. "In the absence of Sinew, I must. Bala ought to come too."

Jahlee said, "And me. It was my idea."

Hide coughed, glanced at Bala, and muttered, "It's not very nice down there, Father. I mean we did everything we could, emptied their pots and washed them, but . . ."

"I understand. In Blanko I had some people chained to the wall in a dry sewer. They've been freed by this time, I hope."

"There's one I sort of think you ought to talk to."

"The leader?" I asked; and Bala, "The big one?"

Hide shook his head. "The woman."

Maliki smiled. "Ah!"

"And it might help if we brought her up here. Instead of everybody going down there. She's real weak, she couldn't do anything, and there's five of us. I don't think she can hardly walk."

"I'm sure you're right. She's more likely to talk freely when the others can't hear her. Would that be—I won't say agreeable. Permissible, Bala?" I sipped my wine, which was far from good.

"If it's all right with Maliki."

Hide began, "She . . ."

"She what? The prisoner? What were you about to say?"

"Can't we talk someplace else, Father? Just you and me?" He looked significantly at Jahlee and Maliki.

"You recognized her? Who is she?"

He shook his head, and Oreb croaked, "Poor boy!"

"Then she recognized you, or told you something else you don't want the others to hear, although Bala must have heard it already."

Reluctantly, he nodded.

Maliki said sharply, "Tell us, Bala. This is nonsense, and may be dangerous. Tell me!"

"It really wasn't anything." Bala sounded apologetic. "It was while he was taking off the bandage on her leg. She said he reminded her of somebody she used to know."

"Is that all?" Maliki snapped.

Bala nodded.

Hide muttered wretchedly, "Horn, Father. She said his name was Horn, and I looked kind of like him."

"Is that all?"

Oreb offered his advice: "No talk!"

"Yeah. I guess Bala didn't hear that last part, she wasn't paying much attention."

Maliki leveled her forefinger at me. "Your name is Horn. So you say."

"It is."

"Your son doesn't resemble you much."

Hide said, "He looks more like me here than back in camp."

"No talk!"

Maliki gave Oreb a hard look before turning back to Hide. "His appearance changes from place to place? Is that what you maintain, young man?"

The blood rose in Hide's cheeks, and he pointed to Jahlee. "So does she. Ask her!"

Maliki rose. "You people are crazy! Mad, absolutely mad, like Nadar."

"In that case there's no point in listening to us," I told her. "Let's listen to this woman prisoner instead. She is sane, presumably."

"Not from the way she fought," Maliki spoke with deep satisfaction. "It was one of the men who surrendered and made her surrender too, when they were cut off and Sinew had fifty all around them."

I started to say that we owed such a brave woman a hearing, but Maliki interrupted me. "Changing all the time, you claim, like dreams. Do you still maintain that all three of you are just dreams?"

"Where is my son's slug gun?" I asked her. "You took it—very sensibly, I thought—when he went into the cellar among the prisoners."

She looked around in some confusion.

"You were holding it on your lap, with both your hands on it, clearly afraid that my grandsons would want to play with it. Where is it now?"

"Gun gone!" Oreb announced.

I turned to Hide and Bala. "Bring her up here, please. I want to see her, and it may be important."

25

THE GOD OF BLUE

J ahlee was gone for two days. She came back tonight and sat
at our fire, looking so human that I had to remind myself
again and again that she was not. She said, "Aren't you going to
ask what I want?"

"No. I know what you want, and I can't give it to you."

"Temporarily, you can."

"You don't want it temporarily. You want it permanently—
something I can't provide."

"I can't provide what you want either, Caldé."

"I've asked you not to call me that," I reminded her.

"All right," she said.

"As for what I want, I want to go home. That is all I want, and
I'm doing it. I want to convene Marrow and the other leaders who
sent me out, confess that I failed, tell them how I failed, and give
them this to read. It's true, of course, that you can't help me with
it; but it's equally true that I—I should say we—don't need your
help. I only ask that you not hinder us. We have silver and a few
cards, and our horses. We—"

She interrupted me. "Horses I can't ride."

"You can't, but then you don't need to."

"I'd like to ride with you, like I did on Green when we went
to see the lander. I was a bad rider, I know."

"I'm a poor rider myself, even though I've had to ride so much of late. Certainly you were a better one than I expected."

"Your son, the big one, said we couldn't be ghosts." She giggled. "Because his horses weren't afraid of us. He thought he was making a joke, remember? And I said, oh, horses don't have to be afraid of me. He liked me, he really did. He liked me better than Bala fat."

I did not reply.

"So if I could ride with you here the way I did there, you could say I was your daughter-in-law, Hide's brother's wife."

"I could. I would not."

Jahlee seemed not to have heard me. "I've got enough money to buy a horse. Money is easy for us. For me anyway. Real cards. We like cards, because they're light."

"Taking them prevents the landers from returning to the Long Sun Whorl, also. That means fewer prey for you."

She gave me a tight-lipped smile. "Oh, there are plenty of you. More than enough for me."

I was busying myself with my pen case, sharpening the little quill I am using. "You don't care about your race."

"*You* are my race. You know that, why won't you admit it? Inside, I'm one of you. So was everybody who fought for you at Gaon."

"What about the inhumi who destroyed the Vanished People, Jahlee? Were they human too?"

"They were dead before I was born."

We sat in silence for a time, listening to the wind in the trees and Hide's slow breathing. From time to time he mumbled a word or two indistinctly; perhaps Jahlee could distinguish them or guess the content of his dreams from their tone, but I could not.

"Where's Oreb?" she said at last.

"Nearby, I imagine. He flew after warning me that you were coming."

"He doesn't like me."

I did not reply; or if I did, merely muttered something noncommittal.

"Do you?"

I had never thought about it. After a time I said, "Yes. I've been wishing you would go. But yes, I do."

"I drink blood. Human blood, mostly."

"I know it. So did Krait."

"We don't kill you, though. At least, not very often."

I nodded.

"When you were on the river with that little girl from Han, we all said we were going to kill you, that we had to. That was what we had decided. But none of us wanted to, not really. We kept hanging back, each of us hoping somebody else would do it."

"Were you one of them? Yes, I remember now. There were so many of you—almost all of you had to be there."

"But you thought I wasn't, because you like me. You hoped I wasn't, really."

"Also because you didn't try to kill me when we met again."

She looked pensive. "I kept thinking that you'd be killed in the fighting. That way I wouldn't have to. Rajan—?"

"Yes?"

"That woman. The big woman they were keeping chained up. I forget her name."

"Chenille."

"Yes, Chenille. They—we were going to kill her children, we inhumi. They tried for years to have children, she said, she and some man in the cellar."

"Auk."

"But they couldn't, so they had taken in children whose parents had been killed. Five of them, she said. It seems like an awful lot."

"There must be a great many children in need of parents on Green."

"Do you think we'll really do it? We inhumi? Kill those children? They were supposed to take your son's village, and they tried, but they couldn't do it."

"Abanja's village. That's Maliki's real name, as I realized when I had time to cast my mind back to the old days in Viron. Colonel

Abanja. Qarya is her village, not Sinew's. It may never be Sinew's."

"I'd argue with you about that, Rajan."

"Let's not argue."

She sat in silence for a while, and this time it was I who broke the silence, saying, "You can't cry, can you, Jahlee?"

"No. Not here."

She waited for me to speak, but I did not.

"Would you like me to go, Rajan? I mean, I'm coming with you. With you and Hide, no matter what you say. But if you'd like me to go away for now, I'll do it."

"Yes," I said. "Please go."

She rose, nodding to herself as she swept back the long sorrel hair of her wig. "You know where I would like to go, don't you? Where I'd like to be?"

I nodded.

"I can't go there without you. Where would you like to be, Rajan? Where would you like to be if you could be anywhere at all?" Her arms were growing wider and flatter already, her hands flattening, too, as they reached for her ankles.

"I'm not sure."

"In New Viron with Hide's mother? That's where you're going."

"Anywhere?" I asked her. "Possible or impossible?"

"Yes. Anywhere."

"Then I would wish to be back in our little sloop with Seawrack." I had not known it until the words left my mouth.

"Was that the girl from Han?"

I shook my head; and Jahlee gave me her tight-lipped smile, raised vast pinions, and flew.

From a branch overhead Oreb exclaimed, "Bad thing! Bad thing!"

★

★ ★

This morning Hide asked whether Jahlee had come back the night before.

"Bad thing," Oreb assured him.

"But did she, Father? Was she there with you while I was asleep?"

Puzzled and interested, I asked him what had made him think so.

"Because I dreamed I was back on Green. I know I wasn't really there. It was just a dream, but I thought she might have been here talking to you and it sort of spilled over on me, whatever it is the two of you do together that takes us to those other whorls. Father . . . ?"

"What is it?"

"Sinew and Bala and all the other people on Green? Are the inhumi going to kill them all the way they did the Vanished People that were there?"

"No," I said.

"Are you sure?"

"As sure as I can be without actually knowing the answer, Hide. I can't possibly know—I'm sure you must realize that. You were asking my opinion, and my opinion is that they won't."

I found his next question startling, as I still do. It was, "Because of something we did?"

I said, "Of course not. Do you think that we can save an entire whorl, my son? Just you and I?"

"It isn't just us. There's Sinew and Bala and their children, and Maliki, and a lot of others."

"Ah! But that's a very different question. In that case, yes. Green will be saved because of things we've done and things we'll do. So will Blue. The Vanished People know it already, and I should have known it too when they asked my permission to revisit Blue. If the inhumi were to enslave humanity here, the Vanished People wouldn't want to come back; and if they were to exterminate it, no such permission would be needed."

Hide nodded, mostly I think to himself.

"You are always bored when your mother and I talk about the

whorl that we left to come here—the Long Sun Whorl. So I'll try to make this as brief as I can. When we were on the lander, I thought as we all did that Pas had made a terrible mistake, that Green was a sort of death trap filled with inhumi."

"It is."

"No, it isn't. There are inhumi there, of course, and in large numbers. But not in overwhelming numbers. They prey upon the colonists—or try to—exactly as they prey upon us here."

"Sure."

"And they are killed in the attempt, not every time but quite often. Sinew and the colonists can kill them, you see, and frequently do. They lose nothing by it. The inhumi can kill them, too. I cleared a large sewer on Green once, Hide. It was choked with human bodies, several thousand I would say."

"That must have been horrible."

"It was. But, Hide, each of those bodies represented a slave or a potential slave, an inhuman who had bled to death instead of working and fighting for his masters. Sinew's victories leave him stronger, but the inhumi's leave them weaker."

Tonight Hide made the same argument to Jahlee, couching it in his own terms and presenting it much less concisely than I have given it here.

She shook her head. "We'll win. We're winning on both whorls already."

"Why?"

"Because you fight among yourselves far more than you fight us. Do you remember the question I asked your father when we came to the gate of Qarya?"

Hide shook his head.

"I asked what good the ditch and the wall of sticks were, when we inhumi can fly. He didn't answer me, because he knew the answer. Would you like to try?"

"I guess not."

"You sell your own kind to us for weapons and treasure," she told him almost apologetically, "and the more numerous you are, the crueler and more violent you are. Your cruelty and your violence strengthen us."

He stared at her, puzzled.

"Ask this man you call your father. He'll tell you."

I said, "He hasn't, and he won't."

She ignored it. "You took part in the war Soldo fought with Blanko. Who do you think won it?"

"Blanko," Hide said.

"You're wrong. We did."

When he had gone to sleep and Jahlee had flown, Oreb returned, saying, "Good things. Things come."

"Neighbors, you mean?" Although they had given me the chalice in Gaon and I had often sensed their presence at Inclito's, I had not spoken to one since they returned me to the Long Sun Whorl.

Oreb bobbed in agreement, his bright black eyes glowing like coals with reflected firelight. "Come quick!"

"Come already," a Neighbor said. I could not see his face, but his voice smiled.

Another joined him, and both sat with me at our fire, at my invitation. I said, "I know you won't eat our food or drink our wine, but I wish I had something to offer you."

"Wisdom," said the first, and the second, "Conversation."

"Wind and foolishness, I'm afraid. Will the inhumi really drive us away as they did you?"

The first shook his head. "You cannot go where we are."

The second asked, "Back to your ship, you mean?"

I had forgotten the word, and repeated it.

"To your starcrosser, to the hollow asteroid that you call the Long Sun Whorl."

"That isn't possible," I said. "There are very few landers in working order, and more of us every day."

The first said, "Then they cannot drive you away as they did us."

Oreb bobbed to that. "No go!"

"We must stay and fight." I felt my heart sink. "Is that what you're telling me?"

"We have nothing to tell you. We fought our inhumi a thou-

sand years ago, exactly as you are fighting yours. You know the
result. Why should you listen to us?"

"Good thing!" Oreb insisted. "Thing say."

I said, "Because you are wise, and have proven yourselves
friends. If I could ask only one question—"

"We will not answer."

"I would ask you what god it was that you worshipped at an
altar Oreb found for me in the hills between Blanko and Soldo."

"An unknown god," said the second Neighbor, but his voice
smiled.

"I have been thinking about all the gods we had in the Long
Sun Whorl, you see. Echidna, Tartaros, Quadrifons, and all the
others. I hadn't thought much about any of them for a year or
more."

The first Neighbor said, "We know very little about them.
Much less than you do."

"We had been talking about Pas—by *we,* I mean Hide and
Jahlee and I. Hide and I thought Pas had been correct to send the
Whorl to this short sun. Jahlee seems to feel quite certain that he
had miscalculated."

The second asked, "You do not agree?"

"No. But I may well be wrong. Years ago I concluded that Pas
was capable of error, because it seemed clear there should have
been female soldiers on the *Whorl* as well as male ones such as
Hammerstone."

"Good man!" Oreb declared firmly.

"Yes, he was a good man in his way. All the soldiers were,
perhaps."

The second Neighbor said, "If you do not wish to tell us about
the gods you had in your ship, you need not feel obliged to."

"They were many," I said, "and they often quarreled, which is
all you need to know. Echidna tried to kill Pas, and was killed by
him for that, and Sphigx's city of Trivigaunte tried to dominate
Scylla's city of Viron—which was my city, too."

He nodded.

"I was weighing the possibility that Pas had erred, as Jahlee contended; and it occurred to me that he had surely erred in permitting other gods in the *Whorl*. That had been a mistake, and in the end it nearly proved fatal to him."

The first Neighbor said, "Then this Pas may have erred in sending your ship here as well."

"Yes. But whether he erred or not, it is certain we did. We erred by accepting Echidna, Scylla, and all the rest as gods, and erred again by removing the Outsider from our prayer beads." I paused to clear my throat. "We took him out because we thought that he wasn't one of Pas's family, I dare say. We knew the names of Pas's seven children and he wasn't one of them. I doubt that it ever occurred to us that he might be Pas's father, or even that Pas had one."

"Pas is your god," the first Neighbor told me, "not ours."

"Exactly. But who were yours? That is the question."

"One we will not answer, for your sake."

"I don't see how I would be harmed by knowing who your gods were, unless you mean that it would be better for me to work it out for myself."

They rose to go.

"My son Sinew found an altar in the forest, the altar of an unknown god. Later I thought that Seawrack's mother must have been your sea goddess."

They backed away. "Farewell, friend!"

"Do you know about Seawrack and her mother? I told some of you."

They had vanished into the shadows before I pronounced the last word; but I heard one say, "Once, she was."

"Wet god? Wet god?" Oreb called plaintively after them. Did he mean the Mother? Or Scylla, who haunts my dreams? I have questioned him, but he refuses to answer or contradicts himself. Possibly he meant both.

★

★　★

It has been nearly a week since I wrote last, a week of constant rain and snow. Hide and I found a cave in the cliffside and spent many idle hours there, talking and playing draughts with stones. I did not write, having only this single sheet left.

This morning the snow stopped and the sun returned. We ventured out, determined to buy more grain for our horses, who are thin and hungry. It was clear and bright, but very cold. Every branch was covered with hard, bright ice, as they still are.

About midmorning we overtook a woman swathed in furs, riding sidesaddle upon a skittish white mule. Her face was hidden deep in a hood of white fur, but to me—and to Hide, too, I believe—she appeared regal. She asked to ride with us, saying that the road ahead was infested with bandits. Naturally, we consented.

Toward sunset we came to this inn, and the innkeeper ran into the road to speak to us. There were no more accommodations for ten leagues, he said, and dinner ready. "I'd stop, my lady, if I were you. You'll think I want your money, and I do, but it's good advice. We've food a-plenty here, and rooms for you and your servants."

She laughed at him. "These are not my servants, and everything I have is theirs if they want it."

I knew her by her laugh; and when I introduced her to the innkeeper's wife, I called her my daughter, Jahlee.